THAMES

◈ Oxford

◈ Abingdon

London ◈

KENNET

◈ Chieveley

◈ Newbury

◈ Andover

RIVER TEST

◈ Winchester

◈ Romsey

◈ Southampton

Isle of
Wight

The King's Spy

www.**transworldbooks**.co.uk

The King's Spy

Andrew Swanston

BANTAM PRESS

LONDON · TORONTO · SYDNEY · AUCKLAND · JOHANNESBURG

TRANSWORLD PUBLISHERS
61–63 Uxbridge Road, London W5 5SA
A Random House Group Company
www.transworldbooks.co.uk

First published in Great Britain as *The King's Codebreaker*
by Andrew Douglas in 2010 by Matador

Published in Great Britain
in 2012 by Bantam Press
an imprint of Transworld Publishers

Copyright © Andrew Swanston 2012
Map by John Taylor

Andrew Swanston has asserted his right under the Copyright,
Designs and Patents Act 1988 to be identified as the author of this work.

A CIP catalogue record for this book
is available from the British Library.

ISBNs 9780593068861 (hb)
9780593068878 (tpb)

Addresses for Random House Group Ltd companies outside the UK
can be found at: www.randomhouse.co.uk
The Random House Group Ltd Reg. No. 954009

The Random House Group Limited supports the Forest Stewardship Council (FSC®), the
leading international forest-certification organization. Our books carrying the FSC label are
printed on FSC®-certified paper. FSC is the only forest-certification scheme endorsed by
the leading environmental organizations, including Greenpeace. Our paper procurement
policy can be found at www.randomhouse.co.uk/environment.

Typeset in 12/16.5pt Caslon Classico by
Falcon Oast Graphic Art Ltd.
Printed and bound in Great Britain by
CPI Group (UK) Ltd, Croydon, CR0 4YY

2 4 6 8 10 9 7 5 3 1

For Susan

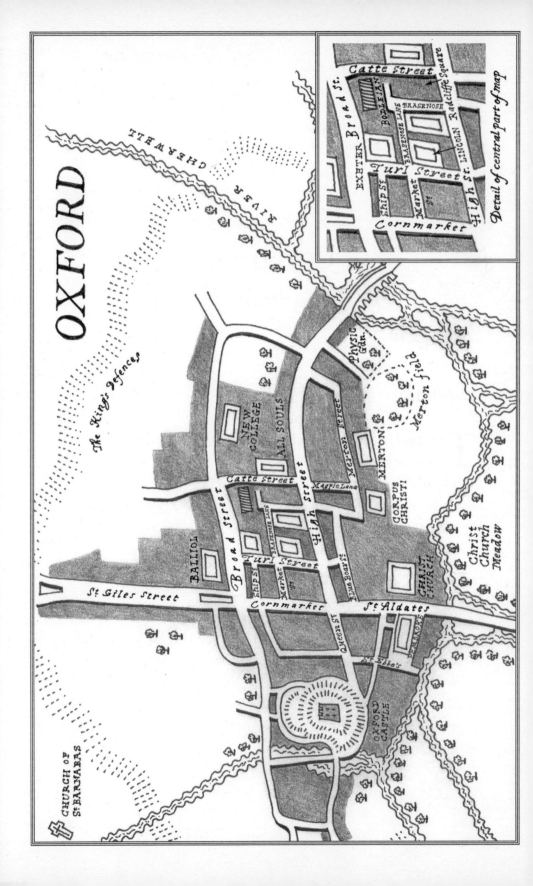

CHAPTER I

August 1643

Thomas Hill was not much of a drinking man — half a bottle of claret or a couple of pots of ale might last him an hour or more — but two or three times a week he would close his bookshop and stroll down to the Romsey Arms. The inn was only two hundred and ten paces from the shop and, if there was news of the war, that was where he would hear it. He knew it was two hundred and ten paces because he had counted them. It was the mathematician's curse — forever counting things.

The war. The wretched war. Bloody and brutal, and seemingly pointless. As far as Thomas could tell from the newsbooks that found their way to Romsey, neither side had yet shown evidence of real determination to win a decisive military victory, or even of a coherent strategy. While talks dragged on between the king and Parliament, the Parliamentarian William Waller and the Royalist Ralph Hopton, best of friends before the war, danced minuets around each other in the West Country, the Earl of Essex had settled comfortably into Windsor, and John Pym, reportedly dying from a cancer in his stomach, was busy building defences around London. Prince Rupert was thundering about the country at the head of his cavalry, attacking Lichfield, Brentford and anywhere else that took his fancy, and now there were rumours that his brother Maurice had joined him for an attack on Bristol. Thomas knew better than to believe all the reports, and in any case they were often contradictory. Sir Jacob Astley had been reported killed at Gloucester two days before arriving in excellent health at Oxford. And there were strange stories of ghostly battles at Edgehill, and witchcraft in East Anglia. In time of war, rational men very easily became irrational.

One thing, however, was clear. The talking had achieved nothing and there would be more bloodshed before England knew peace again. With King Charles gathering support in Oxford, and London in the hands of Parliament, something violent and bloody was inevitable, and probably soon. Either the king would advance on London, or Essex and Fairfax would try to surround Oxford. More bodies disembowelled by the sword and the pike, more eyes sliced from their sockets, more limbs left for the crows, more widows and orphans left destitute. Even in this little town, there were ten women widowed by the war, including his sister Margaret, and twice that number of fatherless children, his nieces among them. There was a one-legged tailor, a blind innkeeper and a farmer with half a face. The other half had been removed by a man with an axe. The farmer had lived but when he returned, his wife had taken one look at him and fled. The wags in the town said that even the man's sheep looked away when they saw him. Yet Romsey itself had seen no fighting — nothing like Stratton or

Hopton Heath, where there had been battles. Was there an able-bodied man left standing there? God forbid that the war should really come to Romsey.

It was August and the evening was warm, so Thomas wore no coat, just his white ruffled shirt with a high collar, white cotton hose, and a clean pair of linen breeches tied at the knee, a few shillings in one pocket. He seldom wore a hat, despite his lack of hair. Hats were hot and bothersome.

He reckoned he could tell how busy the Romsey Arms was by the time he reached the baker's shop on the junction of Love Lane and Market Street. If he could hear voices, it was busy; if he could see drinkers overflowing outside the inn, it was very busy; but if he could see or hear nothing, he might have only himself for company. That would be disappointing. He much preferred gossip and banter, and he liked being the source of news. An educated man, a writer and bookseller, he was expected to know everything before anyone else.

As he approached the bakery, he knew it would be gossip and banter. And on turning into Market Place, he guessed it might be rather more. At least a dozen men outside the inn had, by the sound of them, been there quite some time. Their coats were a hotchpotch of colours, but they all wore broad-brimmed, feathered hats and tall riding boots. Each man had a bandolier over one shoulder, a sword at his waist and a wooden tankard in his hand. A stack of short-barrelled calivers leaned against the inn wall. They were Royalist dragoons. Boisterous, celebrating dragoons. Thomas quickened his pace. This would be news. Terms for peace agreed perhaps, and an end to the war at last. He all but ran the last few yards.

'Well now, gentlemen,' called out a tall blue-coated dragoon when he saw Thomas, 'who have we here?'

Thomas had noted the black and white feathers and red band round the man's hat, and had immediately marked him as their leader.

'Doesn't look like the enemy, more's the pity. Not much taller than my wife, a bit on the skinny side and short of hair. Clean-shaven, clean shirt, clean boots. But you can never tell. Be on your guard, men. Who are you, sir, and have you the money to quench our thirst? If not, be on your way. We're hot and dry.'

He might have spoken in jest, or he might not. Thomas decided to risk it. 'My name is Thomas Hill, sir. I have a bookshop in this town. Alas, I don't have enough in my pocket to buy ale for all of you, unless you will settle for but a sip each. Perhaps if you pool your resources, however, you might have enough to buy me a glass of claret. The landlord here keeps a good cellar.'

The tall dragoon stared hard at Thomas, then laughed loudly. 'Good man, Master Hill. A glass of claret it shall be. A bookshop, eh? And what improving work would you recommend for a humble soldier of the king?'

'A difficult question, sir, as I know nothing of your tastes, and I would not want to cause offence,' replied Thomas, taking the measure of his man. 'I read that in London all manner of books are joining the king's *Book of Sports* on the fire, and it's much the same in Oxford. So nothing religious or political. Let me think. Not classical, I fancy, or poetic. *Henry the Fifth*, perhaps, or *Julius Caesar* — warriors both. Or philosophy. Or something more practical — a worthy volume on horsemanship or husbandry?' He paused, as if in thought. 'No. Philosophy it is. De Montaigne, my favourite philosopher of all.'

'Who? Doesn't sound English.'

'He was French, sir. Just as this claret is,' said Thomas, taking a glass from an outstretched hand, and raising it to the dragoon. 'Your excellent health.'

'And yours, Master Hill. We'll talk of philosophers later. Let me first introduce myself. I am Robert Brooke, captain of this troop of drunks, whom I'm instructed to take to join Lord Goring. It seems his lordship is in need of our assistance, though by all accounts he needs little assistance in the matter of refreshment.'

George Goring had changed his allegiance from Parliament to the Crown the previous year, and Thomas knew of his reputation as a drunkard. He offered a small bow. 'Captain Brooke. An honour. And what news do you bring? An end to the war, or is that too much to hope for?'

'Indeed it is. There can be no peace while Fairfax and Essex are at large, or any of their henchmen, and that's an end to it.'

'Alas,' replied Thomas, 'it seems so, though I wish it could be done without bloodshed. We hear there's been fighting in the north and the west. Adwalton Moor and Landsdowne, was it not?'

'It was. And splendid victories both. At Adwalton, the Earl of Newcastle sent Fairfax and his son running like hounds on the scent, and at Landsdowne our Cornish pikemen gave Waller's rabble bloody noses. The war goes well.'

'Happily, we have seen little of it in Romsey, though we thirst for news.'

'Then I shall have the honour of giving you some.'

'And what news is that, captain?'

'We come from Bristol, which, praise God, is now in Royalist hands. Three days ago the Princes Rupert and Maurice took the city. It was a glorious triumph, and I'm proud to say that my men and I were part of it.'

'Bristol. Noted for its ale, I believe. You didn't go thirsty then?'

Brooke let out a raucous bellow. 'We certainly did not, my friend. Nor hungry once we'd cleared the shitten scum out of their shops and houses and filled our stores with meat and bread.'

So much for an end to the war. Thomas said nothing. He could guess what was coming. Plunder, destruction, rape, murder. The usual litany of crime dressed up as a gallant victory. Another dragoon piped up. This one was short, with a face ravaged by drink, a big belly and the voice of a fishwife. 'Those traitorous, whoreson bastards got what they deserved. When Prince Rupert asked them politely to open the gates, they refused, the donkey-headed dung eaters. We had to breach the walls and storm the city. Good men died.'

'So they did,' agreed Brooke. 'We had to make an example of the place. They should have opened the gates. It was a bloody business getting in. Women and children were killed. I hate the sound of screaming women, it puts my teeth on edge. But it was their own fault. Later we hanged a few of the scroyles for good measure.' Thomas tried not to show his horror.

'They'll open the gates to the king next time,' said a dragoon, raising his tankard. 'The city's ours now, and everything in it.'

Thomas had heard enough. Another city destroyed, men hanged, women raped and murdered, children butchered. And these so-called soldiers boasting about it.

'Well, bookseller,' went on the fat dragoon, 'and what have you to say to that? A great victory, eh?'

Thomas did not want to say anything. He put down his glass. Before he could turn to go, however, he found himself flat on his back in the dust, struggling to breathe. The fat dragoon had punched him hard on his breastbone, knocking him backwards, and was now astride him, his backside planted on Thomas's chest. Thomas was quick on his feet and much stronger than he looked, but it had all been so fast that he barely knew what had happened. He gasped for air and opened his eyes. A bulbous nose, two watery eyes and a black-toothed mouth were inches from his face. He shut his eyes again and held his breath. The stench of the man was revolting, never mind his weight on Thomas's stomach. And he could feel something sharp pricking the skin under his left ear. The dragoon had pulled a knife from his belt. Blood trickled down Thomas's neck. The man hissed at him. 'So, Hill. You choose to ignore my question. Perhaps you didn't want to hear about our great victory. Perhaps you're a piss-licking Roundhead after all. Is that it? A piss-licking Roundhead is it, Hill?'

Thomas felt the point of the knife digging into his neck. Bile rose to his throat from the weight of the man, and he turned his head to the other side and vomited. It ran down his chin into the dust. He retched and coughed, his eyes clamped shut. Then, suddenly, the weight on his chest was lifted and he was being helped to his feet. He heard the voice of the captain.

'God's wounds, man, we're soldiers of the king, not highway-men. You've had too much ale again. Master Hill meant no offence, and even if he did there's no reason to kill him. Go and find a bucket of water and stick your ugly head in it until you're sober. Or as sober as you ever are.'

The fat dragoon, stunned by a heavy blow to his head with the hilt of the captain's sword, struggled unsteadily to his feet and, cheered on by his colleagues, stumbled off in the direction of the duck pond.

The captain turned back to Thomas. 'My apologies, Master Hill. The man's a drunken oaf. Are you recovered?'

From the winding, Thomas was recovered. From the shock, he was not. 'Thank you, yes, captain,' he replied quietly, wiping away the blood and vomit with a white handkerchief. 'I meant no offence, but I don't care for violence of any sort.'

'A soldier must do his duty and obey orders. War is violent.'

'Then let us pray that this war ends soon. Enough English blood has been spilled on the land.'

'I too pray that it ends soon, and with victory for our king. Now, will you take another glass of claret with me while that fat fool has his head in a bucket?'

'Thank you, captain, but I shall be on my way.'

'But what about your French philosopher? Mountain, was it? You were going to share his wisdom with me.'

'Montaigne, captain, Michel de Montaigne. He lived in the last century and said many wise things. Here's one with which to bid you farewell: *To learn that we have said or done a foolish thing is nothing; we must learn a more ample and important lesson: that we are all blockheads.* God be with you, captain.' Thomas bowed, and set off back up Market Street towards Love Lane.

Watching him go, the captain took off his hat and scratched his head. 'If any of you understood that, be sure to enlighten me. Now go and see if that gorbellied idiot is alive. We must be on our way.'

Still a little dazed, Thomas walked slowly. When he reached the bakery on the corner, he stopped to breathe in the aroma of tomorrow's loaves. His sensitive nose twitched in pleasure. The dragoon had smelt like a midden. It was a blessed relief to get the stench out of his nostrils. He breathed deeply and looked around.

From this point in the village, he had a good view of the countryside. To the west, he could see the great oaks of the New Forest, and to the south, fields of wheat and barley yellowing in the summer sun, copses of oak and elm, and the Test winding down towards Southampton. Every time he stood here, he offered a silent thank you to the Benedictine nuns who had chosen this lovely place for their abbey more than seven hundred years earlier. It was an abbess who had been granted a charter to hold fairs and markets, from which the town had grown and prospered. The nuns might have left, but the good people of Romsey had managed to save the abbey from destruction by buying it from the king for a hundred pounds, and now it was their parish church. Even with the country at war, Romsey was a thriving market town of over a thousand souls and a centre for the trading of wool and leather, with busy watermills all around. Now it stood precariously between the Royalists in Winchester and the Parliamentarians in Southampton, and at the risk of being ravaged as so much of England had been ravaged.

Margaret was sitting outside the shop on her wicker chair, reading a book and enjoying the last of the evening sunshine. When she saw Thomas coming up the street, she put down her book and watched him. 'There you are, brother,' she greeted him, 'and walking steadily, I'm pleased to see.' She had never seen him less than sober, but teasing ran in the family.

'Certainly, my dear, though I was sorely tempted. A troop of dragoons on their way through were washing the dust out of their throats. I'm surprised you didn't hear them from here.'

'Royalists, Thomas?'

'Yes, Royalists. I'll tell you their news later. Are the girls in bed?'

'I've just put them down. They'll be asleep.'

Pity, thought Thomas. He liked telling them a story before they fell asleep. It was usually something from the Bible or the classics. Hercules was popular, so was David, though Polly was already expressing doubts about a giant as big as Goliath being felled by a little pebble. 'There's chicken from yesterday, if you're hungry,' said Margaret, 'and plenty of cheese.' So far, the privations suffered by so many towns and villages had not come to Romsey, and no one was starving. 'You can tell me what the dragoons had to say while you're eating.'

In between mouthfuls, Thomas told her the news of Bristol. He left out the worst bits, and Margaret knew that he had. She had heard it all before, and she too was sickened by it. 'God forbid that Polly and Lucy should grow up in such a country. They've lost their father and, if it goes on much longer, they'll lose their childhood. Polly asked me today what happened to the farmer's face. We saw him in the market. What am I to tell her? That he tripped over a plough, or that it was hacked off by a man with an axe? One's a lie, the other would give her nightmares. She's only five, for the love of God.'

Thomas sighed. 'I have no answers, my dear. A war that was supposed to be about the principles of government is nothing of the kind. Men change sides as it suits them, and mercenaries fight for whoever offers them most. It's a war driven by fear. Fear of a king with a Catholic queen, fear of Puritanism, fear of the Irish, fear of losing. Perhaps all wars are the same. We all fear something.'

Margaret smiled. 'Philosophical as ever, Thomas. Does your great Montaigne have anything helpful to say on the matter?'

'Probably. I offered the captain of dragoons a little something to send him on his way.'

'Something from Montaigne, Thomas? You're lucky he didn't run you through on the spot.'

'Am I?' he asked thoughtfully, but told her nothing of his brush with the fat one.

When Margaret was five, Thomas's mother had died giving birth to him. Their father, a Romsey schoolteacher, had brought them both up to love learning for its own sake, and, from an early age, to think for themselves. 'It is the duty of a father to teach his children how to think, not what to think,' the old man had been fond of saying. 'If only more fathers understood that, there would be fewer wars and less poverty.' Thus encouraged, Thomas had learned to read and write by the age of five, and to read Latin and French by eight. Much as he loved words, however, he loved numbers better. Numbers fascinated him, especially the ways in which a simple symbol could reveal the truth about something. Pythagoras and Euclid had led him to Plato and Aristotle. While Margaret had stayed at home to run the household, at fifteen Thomas had gone to Oxford. A scholar of Pembroke College, he had studied mathematics and natural philosophy, had excelled at tennis on the court at Merton, had been much in demand as a dance partner for his boyish good looks, nimbleness of foot and grace of movement, had first bedded a girl, and had learned to make up for his lack of height and weight with speed of hand and quickness of eye. More than one fellow student had come to regret a drunken insult or unwise challenge to Thomas Hill.

Yet for all this, Thomas had always found it difficult to conform. He avoided societies and associations, attended chapel only because he had to, moved in small circles, and preferred the company of teachers to that of students. He had intended to stay in Oxford to continue his studies but after three years, when his father became ill, he had returned to Romsey to help care for him. After the old man died ten years ago, Thomas had stayed in the town, bought the house and shop in Love Lane, and settled down to the quiet life of a writer, bookseller and occasional publisher of pamphlets on matters philosophical and mathematical. And when Margaret had married Andrew Taylor and moved to Winchester, he had been content with his books and his writing for company. But the war had changed that. Andrew had left Margaret and their two daughters to join the king's army and within six months had been killed in a skirmish near Marlborough. Margaret had sold their house and returned with the girls to Romsey. Now they all lived together. Thomas had many friends in Romsey and Winchester, including the unmarried sister of an old Oxford colleague whom he visited every month, and had never seriously considered marriage. At twenty-eight, an age when some men were still searching for their path through life, Thomas was settled and content.

His was only a small shop, made smaller still by crowded shelves and tables overflowing with books and pamphlets. As well as Thomas's writing table and chair, there were two more chairs for the use of customers and visitors. The latter being more frequent than the former, the shop barely provided them with a living, but Thomas's inheritance and Margaret's money from the sale of her house kept them comfortable. While in Oxford and London both sides in this war burned books they found offensive — how an inanimate object could give offence was a mystery to Thomas — he lived his life happily surrounded by them, appreciated the scholarship even of the self-regarding John Milton, with whose opinions he largely disagreed, and waited for peace to return. He knew it might be a long wait.

Ten days after his brush with the fat dragoon, Thomas and Margaret made their regular trip to the market with the girls. Ever since the charter had been granted three hundred years earlier, market day had been by far the most important day in Romsey. Farmers sold eggs, poultry, meat, vegetables and fruit; clothiers and haberdashers set up stalls to show off their finery, and everyone from the mayor and aldermen down came to meet friends and exchange news. The town population seemed to double on market days. Polly and Lucy wore their best bonnets, Margaret her shawl and her string of pearls. She insisted on them when out with Thomas, wanting him to be proud of her.

'You're a respected man in this town, Thomas,' she had said more than once. 'You're educated, you write important pamphlets, and you're looked up to by everyone. It wouldn't do to let you down.'

'Thank you, sister,' he would reply, thinking privately that Margaret could never let him down, and that she always exaggerated a little for the girls' benefit.

She was a very good-looking woman. Few in Romsey could match her long brown hair, brown eyes and flawless skin, and Thomas reckoned it was only a matter of time before one of the town worthies asked for her hand. He would allow whatever she wished, although he dreaded the day. Margaret and her daughters were his family. He adored them and they him.

Since the visit by the dragoons the town had been quiet, and little news had arrived with the merchants who came from all over the county to buy the wool finished and dyed there. Hoping that market day would prove more informative, Thomas and Margaret shut the bookshop and walked hand in hand with the girls down Love Lane and Market Street to the square between the Romsey Arms and the old abbey.

While Margaret took the girls to buy flour and eggs, Thomas wandered through the market. Stopping briefly to talk with the Court Recorder and a town burgess, he made his way through the crowd to the inn, where six women were paid two shillings each to keep every mug topped up from the big jugs they carried in and out. Chosen by the innkeeper for their speed with the jug, the size of their bosom and their ability to keep his customers coming back for more, not one of the women would go home that evening without having made at least one visit to the little copse behind the inn. The innkeeper allowed them to keep whatever rewards they received for these absences, as long as they were no more than ten minutes each. He reckoned ten minutes was good for business.

'Morning, Master 'ill. Pot of ale, or a little walk by the river first?' One of the girls had seen him coming. She was a large, blonde girl with a notable bosom, and she knew what his answer would be.

'Neither, thank you, Sarah. Next time, perhaps. Have you heard any news today?'

'Not much. Unless you count Rose. 'er belly's full again, silly bitch.' Unlike Sarah, Rose was small, dark and often pregnant.

'Does she know whose it is?'

'Ha. Course not.'

'Ah well. Perhaps he'll grow up to be a bishop.'

'Bishop, my arse,' roared Sarah, chest heaving and ale slopping out of her jug. 'Thief more like, same as 'er eldest. 'anged he was, and only ten. Good riddance, I say.'

'Let's hope not. If there's no other news, I must go and find the girls.'

Having filled one basket with eggs and another with a small sack of flour, Polly and Lucy were to be found with their mother admiring ribbons at a haberdasher's stall.

'Ribbons, ladies? I thought we needed eggs.'

'We've bought the eggs, Uncle Thomas,' said Polly sternly, 'and the flour. And now we need ribbons. Pink ones.'

'Good morning, Master Hill,' said the haberdasher, tipping his hat. 'Pink certainly suits both the young ladies.'

'Oh, very well. Pink ones it is. Shall I help you choose?' But before Polly could decline her uncle's offer, a thundering of hooves brought the market to an abrupt standstill. Twenty horsemen wearing the round helmets and leather jerkins of Parliamentary cavalry galloped into the square. Their mounts, teeth bared and flanks glistening, were reined sharply to a halt outside the Romsey Arms. Every head in the marketplace turned towards them, and every eye searched for a hint of menace in their demeanour. These were the first soldiers of Parliament the town had seen. Margaret instinctively gathered the girls to her, and Thomas put himself between them and the troopers.

All but one dismounted and faced the crowd, reins in one hand, the other on the hilts of their swords. The captain of the troop remained mounted. He addressed the crowd, his voice carrying easily around the square. 'Hear this, people of Romsey. We are soldiers of Parliament, on our way to Southampton. We need food and drink, and our horses need rest. If you cooperate, there will be no trouble. This evening we shall depart. Until then, we will take our ease here.'

Thomas turned to Margaret and whispered, 'Take the girls home. Keep an eye on the street. If you see soldiers coming, hide in the usual place. Here's the key. I'll be back soon.' Leading the girls by the hand, Margaret slipped unnoticed out of the square and up the street towards the bookshop. When they had left, Thomas sat on the abbey steps and waited. He did not trust soldiers. Having refreshed themselves in the Romsey Arms, they might well start foraging for food, and plundering whatever else caught their eye. That was what soldiers did.

He was right not to trust them. Before long, two troopers, each holding a bottle of claret by the neck, stumbled out of the inn. They were followed by two more, these two holding Sarah and Rose by the hair. The men were laughing and the women cursing. Rose struggled to free herself and yelled at the man holding her to leave her and her baby alone and go and stick his prick in a sheep. He slapped her hard, shook her like a rat, and told her he had humped prettier ewes than her. Sarah was trying to reach her man's eyes with her fingers. 'Put that scabby thing in me and you'll never see it again,' she screeched. So, thought Thomas, this is how God-fearing soldiers of Parliament behave with drink inside them. This was to be no shilling tumble by the river. Sarah and Rose, hard-bitten whores though they were, were frightened. Thomas looked around. The twenty or so townsfolk watching were unarmed and unwilling to interfere. There was nothing he could do. He should go home.

Not all the troopers had gone into the inn. Some had taken the horses off to find stabling; others, the most avaricious, had set about hammering on doors and demanding to be let in, threatening to burn down any houses where they were not swiftly admitted. On Love Lane, Thomas could see a two-handled cart standing outside a large house owned by a wealthy wool merchant. Inside, he heard voices raised and a woman wailing. When he reached the cart, he saw that it was loaded with cloth, plate, bottles and an enormous pair of silver candlesticks. Two troopers came out of the house, carrying a heavy gilt mirror. They dropped the mirror clumsily into the cart, shattering its glass. One of them pointed at Thomas. 'You there, who are you, and what are you looking at?' It was a rough London voice, more at home in Spitalfields than Romsey.

'My name is Hill. I'm looking at nothing and I'm going home.'

The trooper eyed him suspiciously. 'And where is that?'

'A little further up the lane.'

'Well, Hill, you look a generous fellow. I think we'll come with you,' said the other one.

Thomas shrugged. 'As you wish, but I'm only a bookseller. You'll find little of value, unless you're fond of books.'

'We'll see about that, master bookseller. Lead on, and you may show us your wares.'

Thomas had no choice. Walking as slowly as he dared, he led the two men with the cart towards the bookshop. He could only hope that Margaret was watching out, as he had told her to. He spoke loudly. 'It's only a small shop. I have little money there.' Perhaps Margaret would hear him in time to hide with the girls. From these two thieves she would certainly be in danger.

When they reached the shop, the door was locked. Thomas put his hand in his pocket for the key, and swore silently. He had given it to Margaret. Without a key, the soldiers would know that the door had been locked from the inside, and that there must be someone there. He almost panicked. 'Fire and damnation. My key's gone. It's been stolen, or I dropped it in the market.'

'No matter, bookseller. I have a key,' replied Spitalfields, and with two hefty kicks he broke the lock. The door swung open. 'There. Now let's see what you have for us.'

As Thomas had warned them, in the shop he had little but books and pamphlets. The narrow door in the rear wall was closed. Thank God, Margaret must have seen or heard them, and taken the girls to the hiding place. All was quiet. The troopers looked around. 'Where's your money, bookseller?' demanded Spitalfields.

'I have very little, as I told you.' Thomas went to his writing table, took a small bag of coins from a drawer and tossed it to the trooper. The trooper opened the bag, looked inside and scoffed.

'Is this all? I don't believe you, you lying turd-sucker. Where's the rest?'

'That's all there is.' The trooper took two steps forward and aimed a blow at the side of Thomas's head. Thomas ducked it, only to catch another one from the other side. He stumbled and fell.

'Then we'll look for ourselves, shit-eater.' While Thomas sat on the floor, the two men attacked the shop. The drawers of the desk were pulled out and the contents — more paper, quills and ink — strewn about the shop, books were dragged off the shelves, and the front window smashed with a chair. Thomas said nothing. Wanton destruction he could cope with. God forbid there would be anything worse.

When the whole floor was covered with damaged books, paper and ink, and the desk and chair reduced to firewood, the two troopers stopped for breath. 'So. No money in here,' said one, then pointed at the narrow door. 'Where does that lead?'

'To my rooms. A kitchen and bedrooms, nothing more.'

'Come on, Jethro. We'll take a look.' The door was unlocked. They went through, and up the short staircase immediately behind it. Thomas sat on the floor and held his breath. If the girls were going to be found, it would be now. He listened as the men climbed the stairs and entered the bedrooms above, their boots clattering on the floorboards. He heard beds being tipped over and a mirror being smashed. He shut his eyes and waited.

Eventually, the men stomped back down the stairs and into the shop. They carried a few plates and a silver cup. 'Is this all you've got, bookseller?'

'I fear so.' A sword was unsheathed and pointed at his throat.

'No hiding places, bookseller? You look prosperous enough.'

'No. All my money is in the books. Or it was.'

'And whose are the women's clothes? Women's and children's.'

'My sister and her daughters are away in Winchester.'

'A pity. Though if she looks like you, we'd have to put a sack over her, eh Jethro?' Luckily she doesn't, thought Thomas, but said nothing. 'Come on, we've wasted enough time in this shithole.'

Thomas got up and, from the door, watched them swagger back down the lane. They had taken a little money, some plates and a silver cup. They had wrecked his bookshop and destroyed many of his books. They had smashed furniture. But they had not harmed Margaret or the girls. When he was sure it was safe to do so, Thomas went back into the shop and through the narrow door at the back. He stopped at the bottom of the staircase, knocked three times on the first stair and said 'Montaigne' loudly. Then he stood back as the first three stairs detached themselves, and put out a hand to help Polly and Lucy crawl out from the tiny space behind. Terrified, they had both wet themselves and were sobbing miserably. Thomas hugged them. 'All's well now. The soldiers have gone. We're quite safe.' Margaret emerged behind them, stretching her back and legs. Her face was ashen.

'Did they hit you, Thomas?' she asked, peering at him. 'Your face is bruised.'

Thomas put his hand to his cheek. 'It wasn't much. The books suffered more.'

In the shop, they stared aghast at the devastation. Polly held on to her mother and Lucy started wailing. Margaret picked up some pages from a small volume from which the cover had been ripped. 'I fear that the Prince of Denmark has suffered somewhat,' she observed, looking at a page and picking up another. 'And so has Romeo. How wanton and stupid and cruel. What did they think they would gain by this?'

'God alone knows. I told them I had no money except for the purse, and they took your silver cup.'

'And broke the door and the window, I see.' Margaret stood with hands on hips. 'Well, Thomas, we must mend both at once and start to clear up this mess. Go upstairs, girls, please, change your dresses, and do what you can to sort out our clothes. I'll be up soon.' The girls, drying their eyes, did as they were told. 'They're shocked, Thomas, as well they might be. Polly asked if they were the men who killed her father.'

'What did you tell her?'

'I said they weren't. She might have screamed otherwise.'

'Thank God they stayed quiet while those animals were here.'

'Thank God, indeed. Royalist drunkards one day,

Parliamentary thieves another. What next, do you think? A Spanish Armada?'

Thomas laughed. Humour in times of trouble. Montaigne would surely have approved. 'Probably. Now we'd better set to. I'll mend the door and board up the window. You salvage whatever books you can. I may be able to put some together again as long as they're complete.'

It took all afternoon to clear up the shop and the bedrooms. Ruined books went on the kitchen fire with the desk and chair, and Thomas had a pile to rebind. Upstairs, the beds were righted and clothes sorted out. The door and window were secured. By evening, they were exhausted. Margaret put the girls to bed and sat with Thomas in the kitchen. In his hand he clutched a copy of Montaigne's *Essais*. Miraculously, it had escaped unharmed. He opened a bottle of his very best hock.

'Just the time for it,' said Margaret, taking a sip. They sat quietly and shared the wine.

Thomas had just lit a beeswax candle when they heard a knock on the door. Margaret started. 'Please God, not again. I couldn't bear it,' she whispered.

'Hush now, Margaret, it was a gentle knock. Probably just a neighbour. I'll go and see who it is.' More nervous than he pretended, Thomas went cautiously to the door. 'Who is it?' he called.

'A friend. I seek Master Thomas Hill.'

'I am Thomas Hill.'

'Kindly open the door, sir, and you will see that I mean you no harm.'

'My home and shop were destroyed this very day by soldiers of Parliament. How do I know I can trust you?'

'Abraham Fletcher.'

Thomas wondered if he had heard correctly. Abraham Fletcher? His old tutor at Oxford? Surely not. 'What of Abraham Fletcher?'

'He sends greetings.'

Thomas hesitated, saw the kindly face of his old friend in his mind's eye and made a decision. He unbolted the patched-up door and opened it. Outside stood a man in the grey, hooded habit of a Franciscan friar. When he pushed back his hood, Thomas saw a bald head and cheerful blue-eyed face with a long nose and a strong jaw. It was not a face he knew. 'Thomas Hill?' enquired the friar. Thomas nodded. 'I am Simon de Pointz. I carry a message from the king.'

CHAPTER 2

The friar dropped his bag on the kitchen floor, and stood with his back to the stone oven. Thomas and Margaret waited for him to speak. Even with a slight stoop to his shoulders, he was a head taller than either of them. Entwining his fingers, he stretched his arms and sighed with relief. 'God knows but that bag was heavy. It's far enough from Oxford without having to carry a load.' Neither Thomas nor Margaret spoke. 'Well,' he went on, 'I must give you an explanation. May I sit?' Without waiting for an answer, he hoisted his habit above his ankles and pulled up a chair. 'First of all, Abraham Fletcher is well, and hopes you are the same.'

'Thank you,' replied Thomas stiffly, 'and what does Abraham have to do with your being here?'

'It was Abraham who suggested you to the king.'

'And why would he do that?'

'That is a question which I can answer only in part.'

Thomas spoke sharply. 'In that case, Father de Pointz, I may be able only to listen in part.'

The friar laughed. 'Abraham said you might be difficult. I'll explain as best I can. The king, as you doubtless know, is in Oxford. Queen Henrietta Maria joined his majesty there a month ago. Her majesty recommended me to carry this message.'

'Why you?'

'The queen is a devout lady. I've been with her for three years, and travelled with her from Holland.' He grinned broadly, showing two rows of unusually large white teeth. Devotion must be good for the teeth as well as the soul, thought Thomas. 'Now that was a voyage. Nine days at sea, the weather so bad that the ladies had to be strapped to their beds. Eventually we turned around and went back. We waited ten more days before trying again. By the grace of God it was calmer the second time. We stayed a while in York, before meeting the king at Edgehill and travelling with him to Oxford. I am a devoted servant of her majesty and, happily, she trusts me.'

'And what is the message you carry?'

'The king is aware that at Oxford you distinguished yourself as a mathematician, and became an expert in the matter of ciphers.' Thomas nodded. It was true that he had won prizes for mathematics, and had much enjoyed studying the science of codes and ciphers. So much so that he and Abraham had amused themselves by sending each other coded and encrypted messages – scurrilous poems, invitations to dinner, barbed criticisms of colleagues – and challenging the other to decipher them. As a new code or cipher had to be devised for each message, they had both become adept at inventing and breaking all manner of alphabetic ciphers, and numeric and homophonic codes. 'For reasons that I cannot disclose,' continued de Pointz, 'his majesty has need of your skills, and has instructed me to escort you to Oxford.'

The looks that Thomas and Margaret exchanged were part astonishment, part alarm. Margaret recovered first. 'Reasons that you cannot disclose? My brother abhors violence, as do I. Why should he leave his sister and nieces unprotected to help prosecute a war which should never have started, and in which innocent women and children are dying every day? This is not a war against a cruel invader. It's a war between Englishmen on English soil. How can it possibly be condoned?'

'Are there not important principles at stake?'

'What principles can justify innocent blood being spilled?'

'Principles of justice and liberty?'

'You speak as if such principles were espoused by one side alone. They are not. The king would rule without reference to his subjects, Parliament would restrict our civil and religious freedoms,' replied Margaret with unaccustomed force.

'And what principle are the king's mercenaries fighting for? The right to kill for money, I suppose?' demanded Thomas. 'And what of the turncoats? A sudden epiphany? I doubt it. This war, like all wars, is about fear and self-interest. Claims of justice and liberty are no more than fancy covers on a miserable book.'

The friar held up his hands. 'Master Hill, I cannot persuade you against your will.' He smiled. 'Nor can I take you to Oxford by force. I can tell you that Erasmus Pole, the king's cryptographer, has died, and that Abraham Fletcher has particularly recommended you to replace him. That is all I can tell you. The king has sent for you, and you must decide whether to obey his summons. If I return without you, he will be disappointed, but I don't think he will send Prince Rupert with a troop of cavalry to do what I had failed to do. Either way, I must leave tomorrow. Not even time to visit your lovely abbey.'

'So, Father de Pointz, you arrive unannounced at our door, you claim to bring a summons from the king for my brother to join him in Oxford, and you expect him to make a decision immediately. Is that it?'

'I fear, madam, that it is. Wholly unreasonable, quite indefensible, insupportable and unjust. That's exactly how it is.'

Again Thomas and Margaret exchanged looks. The friar's frankness at least deserved the courtesy of a considered reply, thought Thomas. 'Then so be it. You shall have your decision in the morning. Do not expect it to be the one you would like. I cannot say that you're welcome, but you may sleep here.'

'We'll give you a blanket,' said Margaret.

'Thank you. Your floor will be much more comfortable than the places I've slept these past three days. I shared a barn in Newbury with a blind beggar, two sows and a family of rats as big as hounds.'

With the blanket, and his bag for a pillow, they left him to sleep on the kitchen floor and went upstairs. Margaret looked in on the girls, then came into Thomas's room. They sat side by side on his bed. 'Well, brother. Plundering soldiers, the queen's priest, a royal summons. Surely this day can bring us nothing more.'

'Other than a visit from Banquo's ghost, I think we're safe. But there'll be no sleep, I fear, until we've come to a decision.'

'The decision must be yours, Thomas.'

'No, Margaret. It must be ours.'

An hour later, they had debated the conflict of loyalties to country and to family, the threat to the safety of Margaret and the girls, Thomas's own safety on the journey, how Margaret would cope with the shop, what they had heard of Oxford now that the king had made it his capital, and their impressions of Simon de Pointz. Thomas had spoken of his friendship with Abraham Fletcher; Margaret had reminded him of his hatred of the war. They had wondered aloud whether Thomas's skills would be used as a force for good or evil. And they had reached no conclusion. At last, quite exhausted, Margaret said, 'Thomas, I have nothing left to say. You have my support whatever you decide, but, if you choose to go, please do so before the girls are awake. It will be bad enough for them without seeing you leave.' With that, she returned to her room, lay down and immediately fell asleep.

Thomas, however, tossed and turned until dawn, when, while the house was still quiet, he went down to the kitchen to speak to the priest. De Pointz, too, was awake, and had stoked the oven fire to a good flame. He sat at the table with a cup of water. 'Good morning, Master Hill. How did you sleep?' He was horribly cheerful for such an hour.

'Not at all, thank you, father. And you?'

'The sleep of the just and pious. Have you come to a decision?'

'We have. Although there are two things I hate about this war — the Parliamentarians and the Royalists — it may be that, by being of service to the king, I can contribute to its early end. Or, if not, at least to the saving of lives. And I trust Abraham Fletcher. He knows my views and would not ask me to come unless he thinks I can help. Be sure of one thing, however. I will never take up arms against Englishmen.'

'That is understood. The king knows it.'

'Good. Then, on that understanding, and for Abraham's sake, I will accompany you to Oxford.'

The friar picked up his bag and emptied its contents on to the floor. 'I am much relieved. To have carried these all the way here and then all the way back would have been most tiresome.' On the floor lay a hooded habit with a black rope for a belt, the same as the friar himself was wearing, a heavy silver cross on a silver chain, a pair of sandals and two small bags. He passed the habit and the sandals to Thomas. 'As a Franciscan, even in these perilous times, I choose to dress as St Francis did. I find the habit comfortable and convenient. For the journey, you'd best be a Franciscan too. God will forgive the deception. If asked, we are returning from Canterbury to Worcester. Wear this cross, and these,' he said, handing over the bags, 'are for you and for your family while you are away. Please take them.'

When Thomas opened the bags, he saw that they contained a number of gold sovereigns, certainly enough to keep Margaret and the girls fed and clothed for a year or more. He put one bag on the table and the other in his pocket. 'Thank you. Although I hope I shall not be away for as long as this suggests.'

'I pray not. When will you be ready to leave?'

'We should be away before my nieces are awake. They would be upset to see me go, and that might weaken my resolve. We will breakfast and leave.'

Within the hour, they had left Romsey and were on the road to Andover. It had been a hot summer and the early-morning sun was already warm, the baked earth made for hard walking, and Thomas took frequent sips from a leather flask of water filled from the rain barrel behind the shop. The flask, his razor, a set of clean linen, a translation of Michel de Montaigne's *Essais* and half the sovereigns were all he carried. The other half of the money he had left for Margaret. His habit itched like the devil. When he asked Simon where it had come from, the priest grinned. 'The owner was a saintly man, if a little reluctant to wash. I did my best to clean his habit when we'd buried him.'

They walked steadily, between hedgerows adorned with wild flowers — candytuft and cranesbill, mallows and periwinkles — and the oaks and elms that grew so tall all over Hampshire. Although he knew the names of almost none of the local flora, it was a countryside that Thomas loved. At the hamlet of Timsbury, they picked up a horse Simon had left there, and a second for Thomas. Simon produced another bag of sovereigns from which to pay for them. Riding one behind the other, there was little opportunity to talk — a blessing for Thomas, who wanted to be left alone with his thoughts. He tried to rationalize his decision to leave Margaret and the girls unprotected, and to make a dangerous journey to carry out an unknown task for a king who limped and stammered, and who had led his country into a bloody civil war. Would he, he wondered, have done the same for John Pym and Parliament? No, he would not. Pym did not have an Abraham Fletcher at his disposal, and had not been born to the throne. Did that make Thomas a Royalist? Probably, although he would rather be neutral. Did he really hope to shorten the war? That would depend upon what he was asked to do. Codes and ciphers were commonly used in the diplomatic world as well as in the military, and there were others perfectly capable of devising and deciphering them, yet Abraham had recommended him. Why?

Deciding finally that he would find out soon enough, Thomas allowed his thoughts to wander. To the bookshop and the repair work that awaited him on his return, to Polly and Lucy, whom he had left to sleep, and to his student days at Oxford. He wondered how much the town had changed. Soldiers and courtiers and their trappings no doubt, but surely still the ancient buildings, the castle, the meadows by the river, the Bodleian Library, the Physic Garden, the tennis court, the tranquillity of the colleges and, in every inn and tavern, the clamour of opinionated scholars wanting to be heard. At Pembroke, newly built in the middle of the town, Abraham Fletcher had become a dear friend. Now well into his seventies, he remained one of the few with whom Thomas still exchanged letters. It would be good to see him again.

By the time they neared Andover that evening, Thomas knew that he could not have made a worse decision. His chest and back were covered in livid sores, which incessant scratching only made worse, and he was hot, tired, thirsty and hungry. Unlike Simon, he needed food to sustain him. Simon appeared to go comfortably from dawn till dusk on a cup of water and a piece of bread. Thomas offered a silent prayer that some form of dinner would be available in the town. As for the scratching, the previous owner of the habit must either have had cow's-hide skin or have actually enjoyed the torture of biting fleas. He would burn the loathsome thing that evening and find something cleaner to wear. Either that or go naked. Was there a Lord Godiva? he wondered.

No more than half a mile from the town, they heard horses approaching. Simon signalled Thomas to stop, and then to make quickly for a stand of elms fifty yards to their right. They had barely reached cover when the first horsemen appeared. They were Parliamentary cavalry. Thomas held his breath. They were not in-visible from the road, but dared not move for fear of being noticed. They sat quite still until the cavalrymen had cantered past. 'I dare-say they'd have ignored us,' said Simon, 'but better not to be seen. We'll avoid the town and stay here for the night.'

'Here? Here I see neither food nor bedding. Are you not tired and hungry?'

'A little, perhaps. I'll find us something to eat, and we'll sleep under God's heaven.'

'Excellent, Simon. Poisonous berries and damp leaves. Not to mention this revolting garment, home to families of voracious insects with a particular taste for the flesh of peaceful booksellers.'

'You'd have made a poor friar, Thomas. We're expected to rise above such trivial matters.'

'An empty belly and festering sores may be trivial to you, friar, but not to me. Go and find food. I'll find grass for the horses, and then try to dislodge some of the inhabitants of this infernal thing.'

When Simon returned with their dinner in a fold of his habit, Thomas, naked but for his sandals, was thrashing his habit against the trunk of an elm. 'Take that, you devils. And that. And that. Be gone, and don't come back.'

'English-speaking fleas are they, Thomas? How fortunate. Here's dinner.'

Thomas dropped the habit and inspected his next meal. It looked as if it might kill him.

'God's wounds, what in the name of all that's holy are those?'

'*Coprinus comatus*, Thomas. Country people call them shaggy inkcaps. Just the thing for a man of letters. Delicious when roasted like chestnuts over a fire.'

Simon produced a knife and a flint with which he started a small fire, and set about cooking the inkcaps on the end of a stick. Thomas watched miserably. He took a tiny bite of the first one Simon offered him. It was good. He ate four more, washed down with sips of water from his flask. 'Better?' asked Simon.

'A little,' replied Thomas, 'but I still have to put this instrument of torture back on.'

'Get some sticks about a yard long. We'll hang it over the fire and smoke them out.'

An hour later Thomas risked getting back into the habit. It was warm, the smoky smell was not unpleasant, and he was not immediately devoured. Somewhat cheered, he scraped out two places to sleep among the leaves, while Simon, having moved a little away, knelt to pray.

'I have prayed for a dry night,' he said later, 'and a flealess one.'

Next morning, they skirted Andover before dawn, and continued towards Newbury. The road here was wider, enabling them to ride side by side. Simon was in a talkative mood. 'You haven't asked me much about myself, Thomas. Nothing, in fact. Why's that?'

'You're a Franciscan friar. What is there to ask?'

'Not all friars are the same.'

'Yes they are. They wear flea-ridden habits, eat little, drink less and pray a lot.'

'Ah, but what if you scratch the surface? Will we all be the same then?'

'Scratch is the very word. Very well, Simon, do tell me about yourself. I suppose you can't always have been a priest.'

'I was born in Norwich. Ours was a God-fearing family. My father was a tailor, prosperous and respected. My mother died when I was twelve. I have two sisters, both older than me. One is a sister in the Dominican convent in Prouille, the other is married to a farmer.'

'Nothing all that odd, so far. Why did you become a Franciscan?'

'After my mother's death, I turned away from God, left home and lived on the streets. I begged and stole and learned how to survive. I got into a fight over a girl, was badly beaten and left in a ditch. I managed to struggle to the old abbey, which like your abbey in Romsey survived, where they took me in. There I recovered my health and my faith, and eventually became a man of God. Mind you, I still don't much like dogma and rituals. They lack humour.'

'Yet our devout queen surely insists on all the Catholic rituals.'

'She does, and I'm happy to advise and support her in the way she practises her faith.'

'And you are equally happy to lure a peaceful man to Oxford without confiding in him the truth of the matter.'

'As long as the ends justify the means, and her majesty wishes it, I am. A pragmatic approach, I think. Pragmatism and humour. Both essential to a happy and fulfilled life on earth.'

'I do hope that my happy life on earth is not about to be curtailed. Romsey has its faults but it's a good deal safer than Oxford, by the sound of it.'

'Have no worries, Thomas. You will be under the protection of the king, and quite safe.'

They avoided Newbury, where Simon had seen Parliamentary infantry on his way to Romsey, and arrived that evening at the village of Chieveley. To Thomas's relief after forty miles in the saddle, they found there a simple inn with a room available for travellers, and a landlord who thought nothing of a pair of friars arriving at his door. He had no other customers, and fed and watered his visitors and their horses without enquiring as to their business. While they ate the landlord's eel and oyster pie with purslane, Thomas tried to draw Simon out. 'Why would Abraham recommend me when there must be others in Oxford quite capable of encoding and decoding messages?' he ventured.

For a moment, Simon looked thoughtful. Then, 'Now that we're on our way, I think I can tell you that Erasmus Pole was murdered.'

'Good God, Simon. So I'm to replace a man who was murdered? Very pragmatic of you not to tell me that before we left. You'd have returned alone.'

'It was a little deceitful, I admit. I have prayed for forgiveness.'

'Anything else you'd like to tell me? Why he was murdered, for instance?'

'That is a question to which we do not yet have an answer. Abraham knows that you can be trusted, and he thinks you might find out the truth.'

'Does he? Abraham was ever the optimist.'

Thomas slept little that night. Again and again his thoughts returned to what had persuaded him to leave Romsey, his family, his business. Vanity? To be sure, it was flattering to be summoned by the king, but what was really behind his decision to go to Oxford? Curiosity? What was he curious about? Could he really hope to bring the war to an end? It seemed far-fetched. And what was he going to find there? He had heard stories about the royal household. Only stories, mind you, nothing more. And now he had been told that he was to step into the shoes of a man who had been murdered. For the love of God, why had he not stayed at home?

They set off again at an early hour, intending to cover the twenty or so miles to Abingdon, a small town some ten miles from

Oxford. Twice they left the road when they heard horses — both times horses of the king's cavalry — but otherwise saw almost no one. Even the fields were deserted. 'England has never been so quiet,' remarked Simon, 'at least away from the fighting. People are too frightened to venture out.'

In Abingdon, after a day of late-summer showers, they found another inn with a room, this one busy and noisy. They sat quietly in front of the fire drying themselves, eating onion soup and rough bread and listening to the talk around them. It was about little other than the war. Once their tongues were loosened, the drinkers spoke freely, ignoring the two friars in the corner. 'King or Parliament — do I have to choose?' asked one. 'How can I? Which one will put food on my table and clothes on my back? I don't know.'

'Better stay out of it then,' replied another. 'Keep mending shoes. It's safer.'

'I'd rather support the king,' offered a third, 'only not this king. A lame Scot who cares nothing for us. It's Queen Bess's fault. No heirs. We should find a better king.'

'Hush, William,' hissed the first man, 'you could lose your head for saying such things. And anyway, where do we find another king? We don't want a Frenchman or a Dutchman, do we?'

For the first time, a large man, black-bearded and deep-voiced, spoke. 'We should do what they're doing in Cornwall. Organize ourselves to defend our homes and families from both sides. Arm ourselves with whatever we can find and frighten off any who approach the town. Kill them if we have to.'

'Jeb, do we really need another army? Aren't two enough?' asked the first man.

'Maybe that's just what we need. Show them what we really

care about. Our wives, children, land, homes. Food to eat and ale to drink. Not who sits on his arse in Parliament, nor who wipes the king's. That makes no difference to us. Fight fire with fire, I say.'

'And I say we should keep quiet and wait for peace,' said the one called William.

'And what good will peace be if our women have been raped and our homes torched?' demanded Jeb. 'Tell me that.'

Thomas and Simon sat and listened until the drinkers had left. Then Thomas said, 'This is a strange war, don't you think? Who wins or loses seems less important than how long it goes on and what happens afterwards.'

'Strange indeed, Thomas.' Simon poured his companion a glass of wine, and went on, 'Now this seems an excellent opportunity for you to enlighten me on the matter of codes, a subject about which I know next to nothing.'

Thomas feigned surprise. 'Oh, come now, a man who can tell a shaggy inkcap from a poisonous fungus has surely studied cryptography. And you are a Catholic friar.'

'How is my faith relevant to codes, Thomas?'

'Hmm. If you really want to understand the subject, I shall have to start with a history lesson.'

'I am listening, Thomas. Please begin the lesson.'

'Very well. The use of codes and ciphers is almost as old as warfare itself. The Persians and Greeks used them, and a very well-known cipher is named after Julius Caesar, who used it frequently when he was on campaign. Would you like me to show you how it works? It's very simple.'

'I would.'

'Then find paper and ink, and a quill.'

Simon disappeared and came back within a few minutes clutching them. 'The landlord was surprisingly obliging once I'd put a sovereign in his hand.' He put the things on the table.

Thomas took the quill and wrote two lines on the paper.

A B C D E F G H I J K L M N O P Q R S T U V W X Y Z

S I M O N A B C D E F G H J K L P Q R T U V W X Y Z

He turned the paper around for Simon to see. 'This is a cipher encrypted with a Caesar shift, using SIMON as the keyword. The cipher begins with the letters of your name, which do not then appear where they should in the alphabet. In a message encrypted using this keyword, for example, the letter C would appear as M. As I said, simple. But also simple to decrypt, using routine techniques.'

'Why is it a cipher, not a code?'

'When an individual letter is replaced by something else, it is a cipher. When a word or phrase is replaced, it is a code. You will have already realized that any number of variations on this cipher are possible.'

'Will I?'

'I imagine so. The alphabet could continue where the keyword leaves off. In that case, the sequence would be S I M O N P Q R T U V W X Y Z A B C, and so on.'

'And what, pray, is the relevance of Catholicism?'

'The Vatican has used ciphers for centuries, and has produced some of the most important cryptographers. About two hundred years ago, a certain Leon Alberti thought up the idea of using two cipher alphabets at once, and alternating between them.' Again

Thomas took the quill and wrote on the paper, adding a third line of letters.

A B C D E F G H I J K L M N O P Q R S T U V W X Y Z

S I M O N A B C D E F G H J K L P Q R T U V W X Y Z

R O M S E Y A B C D F G H I J K L N P Q T U V W X Z

'Using this cipher, the word THE would be encrypted as TBN.'

'Looks devilish, even if he was a Christian.'

'Not so devilish. An experienced cryptanalyst will recognize a double or even a triple substitution without much difficulty. But Alberti's work also led to the development of the Vigenère cipher, which is so devilish that it has never been broken.'

'How does the Vigenère cipher work?'

'You're not ready for that, Simon. Next time, perhaps.'

'As you wish. What else should I know?'

'You should know that messages are often encrypted using what are known as homophonic substitutions.'

'Homophonic. Something that sounds the same as something else,' said Simon with a grin.

'Exactly. A number or a symbol which represents a letter. Numerical ciphers are common – each number representing a different letter. Encrypted texts may also include nulls, which are no more than meaningless symbols or letters designed to confuse. Deliberate variations in spelling are used for the same reason.'

'Wouldn't the recipient of the message also have to know about these?'

'Well done, Simon, he would. If, for example, each letter in a text is replaced by a single number, no more than twenty-six numbers are needed. So if all the numbers between 0 and 49 appear, twenty-three of them will be nulls. However, those that are nulls must be memorized or written down, and that is also the weakness of codes, as opposed to ciphers. Codes are almost always written down somewhere. If they are easy enough to remember, they are also easy enough to decode, and therefore vulnerable.'

'Keywords, double and triple alphabetic ciphers, homophonic ciphers, numerical substitutions, nulls, spelling mistakes, what else?'

'Much else, Simon, including Monsieur Vigenère. Oh, and nomenclators, of course.'

'What are they?'

'A nomenclator is a mixture of code and cipher. The messages smuggled to and from the Queen of Scots when she was held prisoner were nomenclators. It was a priest who smuggled them in. His name was Gifford. Cunning fellows, priests. I can remember the numbers used.' Again Thomas wrote on the paper.

$$2 = AND, 3 = FOR, 4 = WITH, 7 = X, 8 = Y, 9 = Z$$

'And there were shapes and Greek letters for individual letters and words. It took an odd and very clever little man named Thomas Phelippes to decrypt it. If he hadn't, who knows who would be on the throne now?'

'How did he do it?'

'It took him some time and much effort, but eventually he did it in the way most ciphers are decrypted. The Queen of Scots and her supporters did not know that their messages were being read, and with enough texts he was able to analyse how many times each symbol or number appeared and its position in relation to all the other symbols and numbers. In English, the most common letter, E, is about twice as common as S and six times as common as F. Each letter can be ranked according to the frequency of its usage. Despite the nulls and misspellings, Phelippes worked the cipher out, and proved that the Queen of Scots was plotting to murder Queen Elizabeth. It's the way we cryptographers work. Much hard work, a little imagination and the occasional guess.'

Simon stood up and sighed. 'Thank you, Thomas. An excellent first lesson. Tomorrow I shall reciprocate by teaching you about the life of St Francis.'

'Thank you, Simon, that won't be necessary.'

Again they left at dawn, riding side by side on a road that widened as they approached Oxford. Thankfully, the showers had cleared and the August sky was blue. 'When were you last here, Thomas?' asked Simon, when the city defences came into sight.

'It must be eight years ago now. I went to visit Abraham and to attend a college feast.'

'You'll see much changed. The king is in Christ Church, the queen in Merton, and their households are billeted everywhere.' He hesitated. 'Their presence has sharpened the divide between university and town.'

'In what way?'

'Both the king and the queen have large households. And there are the soldiers. They all have to be housed and fed. The king urges restraint, but is not always heeded. And his nephews are not easily controlled when they're here. If they weren't royal princes, Rupert and Maurice would be highwaymen. They exert much influence over the young. The townspeople can be resentful.'

'With good reason, no doubt. The town must be overflowing. And not just with bodies.'

'It is. Humans and animals create waste. Much waste. The drains can't cope.'

Two miles from the town, Thomas's sensitive nose had already detected the stench of excrement and decay. He shuddered at the thought of what lay ahead. 'And the town itself? Is there much damage to buildings or to the colleges?'

'You'll see for yourself. I thought it best to warn you.'

'How pragmatic of you.'

Soon Thomas did begin to see for himself. They passed through the remains of three deserted villages burned to the ground as a precaution against siege, and rode around huge earthworks thrown up as defences. Long poles, sharpened to a wicked point, had been stuck into the earthworks to deter oncoming cavalry, and gangs of bare-chested labourers with shovels and picks worked frantically to build more. It was as if Fairfax, Waller, Ireton and their entire armies were all expected within the hour.

As they approached the ancient city wall, also strengthened by earthworks in the gaps where the stone had crumbled away, the stench of death hit Thomas in a wave so thick he could almost touch it. He put a hand to his face and tried to take shallow breaths. Just outside the wall, they came upon a heap of decaying corpses and a gang of women digging a large pit. 'Plague, Simon?' asked Thomas.

'*Morbus campestris*. Too many people and too much foul water.'

Inside and outside the wall, the streets overflowed with people, and the open sewers with their waste. Damn my nose, thought

Thomas, too sharp for its own good. They made their way slowly up St Aldate's towards Pembroke. Soldiers and their horses blocked the way, beggars pleading for alms pulled at their habits, and pigs foraged among mounds of stinking refuse. There were even dung heaps on the street corners. It took them more than an hour to reach the entrance to Pembroke. There they dismounted and led their horses through a side gate and into a small paved courtyard, where a college servant took charge of them.

They walked through an arch into the main courtyard, and Thomas looked around at his old college. It was unrecognizable. What had once been a neat cobbled yard, surrounded by high stone walls and the arched entrances to staircases leading to the scholars' rooms, was a mess of wrecked furniture, broken bottles, old clothes and rotting food. Most of the doors around the yard had been pulled off their hinges, windows had been shattered, and a chimney had fallen off a roof, scattering bricks below. Thomas saw no scholars. Three officers in dashing blue uniforms stood talking in one corner, while their swords were sharpened by a grinder with a whetstone. A woman with two small girls, all three wearing ribbons in their hair and fine lace aprons over their dresses, emerged from a doorway and picked their way across the yard to the main entrance. The officers swept off their feathered hats and bowed low. Courtly manners and high fashion amid squalor and decay. Soldiers for scholars, guns for gowns. Thomas stood and stared.

There was a tap on his shoulder. 'Master Hill?' Thomas turned and saw a familiar face, more lined now but as open and kindly as it had always been. 'I thought it was you, sir. Master Fletcher told me to look out for you. He said you might be a monk.' The man tipped his cap and held out a hand, which Thomas shook warmly.

'A friar, Silas, and only pretending. Father de Pointz is the real priest. Simon, this is Silas Merkin, head servant of the college.'

'Welcome, sirs. I'll show you to your room, Master Hill. It's a little small but it's the best I can do. I had to get rid of a young captain to get it for you. Nasty beggar, he is. Made a great fuss. I couldn't have shifted him without Master Fletcher's help. We've over a hundred in college, including women and children. They've been throwing out the furniture and making beds on the floor.' Silas had never been short of a word or two.

'Now you're safely here, Thomas, I'll say farewell,' said Simon. 'I'll be at Merton with the queen. I'll call on you soon.'

Silas showed Thomas to a room under a low arch at the opposite end of the courtyard to the one through which they had entered. It was indeed small — nothing like the comfortable room near the main entrance in which he remembered reading and rereading Plato and Aristotle, poring all night over Euclid's geometry, and occasionally entertaining a young lady. He would have but a narrow bed, a low chest, a washstand with a jug of water, a small table and a hard chair for company. On the bed, two linen shirts, two pairs of breeches, three pairs of stockings, a plain brown coat and a pair of boots had been laid out. 'Master Fletcher asked me to find these for you, sir. There's clean water in the well by the chapel, and a new privy beside it. We dug the drain ourselves. It runs into the sewers, but now they're blocked it won't be long before it's overflowing. Soldiers do seem to shit a lot. And here's your key. Be sure to keep the door locked. I'll tell Master Fletcher you're here. He's still in his old rooms, thank the Lord. It wouldn't do to move him now, not with his eyes as they are.'

'His eyes, Silas?'

'Yes, sir. Didn't you know? Master Fletcher sees very little now.'

'I didn't know. Thank you for telling me.'

When Silas had gone, Thomas got out of his habit, washed his face and hands, trimmed his new beard with the razor, and put on a clean shirt and breeches. He would call on Abraham immediately.

CHAPTER 3

Abraham's rooms were directly across the courtyard. Thomas climbed a narrow spiral staircase, knocked on the door, and entered at the familiar sound of his old friend's voice. God's wounds, he thought, I could be sixteen again. Abraham was sitting by the window in a high-backed oak chair. In profile against the light, he looked just as he had a dozen years ago. Hair swept back from a high forehead, Roman nose, back straight. But when he turned his face to the room, Thomas could see that his old friend had aged. His hair and beard were white, and he wore a shawl over his coat. His blue eyes were watery, his skin pale, and two deep lines ran from nose to mouth. The remains of a meal were on a table beside him. 'Is that you, Thomas?' Abraham asked, when he heard his visitor come in. His voice, too, had aged. The muscular baritone had lost much of its power.

'It is, Abraham,' he replied, taking the outstretched hand in both of his. 'Do I find you well?'

'Quite well, thank you, except for these.' Abraham pointed

to his eyes. 'They see only shadows and shapes these days.'

'I'm truly sorry to hear it. Can you read?'

'Alas, no. It's a curse. How are your sister and nieces? I was sad to hear of Andrew's death.'

'They thrive, thank you. The girls are as bright as buttons. Polly will make someone a very demanding wife one day.'

'Ha. And your writing? Still persevering, I trust.'

'Still persevering. And still reading Montaigne.'

'That old cynic. I don't know what you see in him.' He paused. 'Thomas, my eyes are one reason why you're here.'

'But not the only reason, I gather.'

When Abraham laughed, his eyes still sparkled. 'What has that priest been telling you? He never could keep his holy mouth shut.'

'Very little, in truth. I hope you will tell me rather more.' Thomas looked around the room. It was little changed since he had last seen it. Simple wooden furniture, oak panelling, a door leading to a small bedchamber, and books. Piles of books on the table and on bookshelves. A scholar's room. A scholar who could no longer read. It was a cruel thing.

'Come and sit near me, so I can see your shape against the light. There's wine in the corner if you're thirsty. At least Silas has managed to keep some of our cellar intact. Brasenose and New are reduced to ale and sack. Their lodgers have had every bottle of wine, along with every piece of plate.'

Thomas found a dusty bottle of claret, poured them both a glass and sat by the window. 'How's that, Abraham? Can you see me here?'

'Well enough. Now, as time is our enemy, I shall tell you what I can. My old friend Erasmus Pole, with whom I shared lodgings fifty years ago, was the king's chief cryptographer. His position was known to very few. He dealt with all the messages and reports coming in and out of Oxford, and decrypted the intercepted ones. They never amounted to much, but they did keep us informed about our enemy's ciphers — inferior to our own, I'm pleased to say. Until my eyes betrayed me, I helped him whenever he asked me to. It wasn't often. Erasmus was a fine scholar.' Abraham paused for a sip of wine. 'He was also a creature of habit. On Wednesday evenings, he always dined at Exeter. Exeter serve venison on Wednesdays. Alas, Erasmus's taste for it may have been his undoing. It was a Thursday morning when his body was found in Brasenose Lane on the south side of the college. His throat had been cut, and he'd been robbed.' Abraham took another sip from his glass.

'Such deaths are not uncommon, Abraham,' remarked Thomas quietly, thinking again that this was not the Oxford he remembered, or should have returned to. His place was with his family, not here among murderers.

'Indeed they're not, especially now. I daresay he'd enjoyed the hospitality of the evening, but Erasmus was a cautious man. He would not have walked in the dark down that foul lane. And remember that Erasmus was the king's cryptographer. He had access to almost every order and report to and from the king's commanders. He knew a great deal.'

'As do you, my friend. Yet, happily, I find you alive and well.'

'Happily, you do. But there's another thing. I knew Erasmus as well as any man. In the weeks before his death, something was troubling him. He didn't speak of it and I didn't ask, yet I'm sure of it. I wish I had asked. Erasmus might be with us now. As my sight has deteriorated, so my hearing has become more acute.

Interesting how the body works, don't you think? I could hear fear in his voice. Fear, and something else. I think it was guilt.'

'Guilt? But why?'

'I believe his role was discovered by an enemy, and he was being threatened. There are many spies in the town. One of them may have got to him, and frightened him into betraying secrets.'

'And killed him when he refused?'

'It's more likely he was killed because the enemy thought he was about to be exposed as a traitor to the king. If so, he would have suffered greatly, and would eventually have revealed the identity of the spy.'

'Had they grounds for thinking that he was under suspicion?'

'Possibly. When a message arrived from Lord Digby inform-ing the king that he planned to attack Alton, the town garrison was immediately strengthened. The attack never took place. It looked suspicious.'

'If you're right, there is a vicious traitor in the town.'

'And not just one, Thomas. Oxford seethes with unrest and deception. There are two worlds here now — one you can see going about its daily business, and another which lurks in the shadows and listens at keyholes. I doubt we shall ever know who killed Erasmus.'

'Already you make me wish I had stayed at home, Abraham.'

'But you are here now.' Abraham's voice was suddenly brusque. 'Thomas, the king, with reason, trusts almost no one. I've persuaded him that you're the best cryptographer in the land, and that I would gladly put my life in your hands. We need you. We want you to take Erasmus's place.'

'Abraham, you know my views on this war,' replied Thomas evenly, 'and on any war. On the journey here, I asked myself again and again why I was coming to take part in something I am so opposed to. And, when I saw what has become of the city, I very nearly turned round and went straight back to Romsey. Beggars, soldiers, whores, poverty, destruction, filth. Barely a scholar to be seen.'

'So why did you come?'

'I'm still not sure. The pleasure of seeing you, of course. The vain hope that I might hasten the end of the war. Perhaps even loyalty to the king. He is the king, after all, for all his faults. I would not have done the same if the summons had been from Pym.'

'Of that I am sure, Thomas. But will you do as I ask?'

Thomas took a deep breath and spoke slowly. 'For your sake, my old friend, I will. I would not see you embarrassed before the king, and, in any case, I have no wish to climb straight back on a horse for four days. But it's some time since I worked on ciphers. I shall need help.'

Abraham found Thomas's arm, and laid his hand upon it. 'And you shall have it. Tomorrow morning I'll take you to meet the king, or rather you'll take me as I shall need your arm for guidance, and then we'll talk. It'll be just like it used to be.'

'Only a little more serious.'

'Yes. A little more serious.'

Outside they heard the clatter of boots on cobbles, the clash of sword and armour, voices raised, orders being given. Thomas rose and gazed out of the window. 'Who would have imagined it?' he asked, as much to himself as to Abraham. 'Pembroke College a soldiers' billet. Our beautiful place of learning turned into this.'

'I still awake some mornings having forgotten what has

happened. Then I hear the war outside my window and it all comes flooding back. Is it as bad out there as it sounds?'

'Worse. The college is in ruins. I haven't seen a scholar since I arrived, and there are soldiers everywhere.'

'So Silas tells me. He found you a room, I trust?'

'He did, and thank you for your help. I gather the previous occupant was less than happy at being asked to leave. A nasty beggar, Silas called him.'

'So I believe. I had to enlist the help of Tobias Rush to have him removed, but he was one of the few with a passable room to himself, so he had to go. We couldn't have the king's cryptographer sleeping on a bench.'

'Who is Tobias Rush?'

'He's an adviser to the king, perhaps his most trusted adviser. Not a man I would invite to dinner, but useful to know if you want something done. You'll meet him tomorrow, I expect. Call for me at ten.'

'I will, Abraham, and it's a joy to see you again.' Thomas rose to leave. As he did so, he saw the old man's eyelids droop. He was asleep before Thomas had closed the door.

Thomas, too, was tired. Four days in the saddle and three nights away from his own bed were taking their toll. His shoulders ached and his backside was sore. But his legs needed stretching, he wanted to see the old sights again, and he was famished. In his room he splashed his face with water from the ewer, adjusted his dress, carefully locked the door behind him, and then went to find Silas Merkin.

Silas was in his little room by the college entrance. His guard-room, he called it. From there, he could see the courtyard and all its comings and goings. Thomas smiled at the memory of trying to slip past him unnoticed with a willing girl from the town. It had not worked. Silas had pounced, the girl had been sent on her way and Thomas had slept alone.

'Ah, Master Hill. How did you find Master Fletcher?'

'His mind is still sharp, Silas. Would that his eyes were too. Old age can be a terrible thing.'

'I do take care of him, sir. Make sure his food is how he likes it, help him with washing and dressing, that sort of thing.'

'I know you do, Silas, and I thank you for it. He's a good friend and a fine scholar. Now, I'm hungry. Where shall I go for my dinner?'

'I can easily have the kitchen prepare something for you, sir. No need to go foraging.'

'Thank you, Silas. But I need to walk off the stiffness in my back, and I'd like to see something of the town.'

Silas was a little put out. The kitchens came under his control, and he liked his scholars and visitors to use them. 'As you wish, sir, but do take care. The town is much changed, as you may have noticed. The Crown in Market Street still serves well. You could try there.'

'I will, Silas. And I'll take care.'

Leaving the college, Thomas made his way down the lane and up St Aldate's towards Cornmarket. In the streets, soldiers jostled with townspeople, and at Golden Cross a noisy crowd had gathered to watch a woman in the pillory being pelted with muck. It must have been stony muck because blood dripped from her mouth and cheek. 'What did she do?' Thomas asked a young soldier.

'The old hag tried to steal a trooper's breakfast. She's lucky not to be on a gibbet,' the man replied.

Thomas moved swiftly on into Market Street, making for the Crown. Market Street was even busier. Uniformed men and women in rags bargained noisily with the tradesmen hawking their wares from stalls on either side of the street. At least the town's bakers, brewers and tailors were doing well. The crush of bodies around the stalls forced him to the middle of the street, down which ran a reeking open drain, half blocked in places with shit and refuse. He took care to avoid being jostled into it, as some had been. On a whim, he continued past the Crown and into Brasenose Lane — the lane Erasmus Pole had walked down after dinner at Exeter. It was a stinking, rough, narrow passage, uncobbled and with high walls on both sides, dark even at that time of day. Avoiding the worst of the muck, he kept to the middle of the lane, skirting the drain that ran down it. He had taken barely ten steps when a foul whore, what was left of her face pitted by pox, emerged from the shadows on his left and grabbed his arm.

'Looking for company, sir? Meg'll make you stand to attention.'

Yellow spit oozed out of her toothless mouth like pus from a boil. Thomas recoiled in horror and pulled his sleeve away. Resisting the urge to turn back to Market Street, he swallowed hard, squared his shoulders and carried on up the lane. Beggars lined the walls, some crippled, others diseased. Hands were held out as he passed, and pleading voices raised. He ignored them all. Abraham was right. A cautious old man would not have walked this lane in daylight, never mind at night. At the east end of the lane, where it met Radcliffe Square, a whore was being humped against the wall by a grunting soldier. When the woman saw Thomas, she called out to him.

'Won't be long, sir. Be your turn soon.'

He quickened his pace, turned right into the square and made his way back to the Crown, where he found a corner seat and ordered a bottle of port wine.

On a table at the back of the inn, a noisy game of hazard was in progress. Four well-refreshed soldiers were laying down their money and cheering or cursing loudly at each throw of the dice. Knowing from experience that it was a game which required a clear head and a quick brain, Thomas wondered that they could play with such speed despite being full of ale. The loudest of the men was the caster, a fair-haired captain who stood out like a peacock in a chicken run. Flowing locks over his shoulders, a short cape over a fine linen shirt and tight blue knee-breeches marked him as a man who did not wish to be mistaken for a supporter of Parliament. And his manner was as brash as his dress. He thumped the dice on to the table, roared lustily if they behaved as he wished, and cursed his foul luck if they did not. Now and again he hurled them so hard that they rolled off the table and on to the floor. When that happened, he yelled at one of his companions to pick them up and be quick about it. The peacock evidently saw himself as the leader of this flock. The others, more soberly attired in the leather jerkins and loose breeches of fighting men, merely grinned and raked their coins off the table. Thomas could not help noticing that the stakes in the game were a good deal higher than those he had once played for on the same table. A scholar's penny had become a soldier's shilling.

As Silas had said, the Crown did serve well. After a plate of good roast mutton with oysters and radishes, and a sweet apple cream flavoured with ginger and lemon, Thomas felt more himself. Taking his purse from his pocket, he asked the landlord how much he owed. 'How will you be paying, sir?' asked the man suspiciously.

Taken aback at the question, Thomas held up his purse. 'The usual way, landlord. Coins of the realm.'

The landlord grinned. 'In that case, sir, two shillings'll do nicely.' Thomas handed over the coins.

'What other case is there?'

'Ah. You must be new in Oxford, sir. We have to take tickets from the king's men. Tickets instead of coins. Worthless, if you ask me. We'll never see the money.' He glanced pointedly at the dice-players. A woman stoned for stealing a soldier's breakfast. An innkeeper robbed by gambling soldiers who did not pay for theirs. Not the Oxford he remembered.

His belly full and his spirits a little restored, Thomas decided to risk another stroll before returning to his room. He walked down High Street and into Magpie Lane. The crowds had thinned and it was a route he knew well. It would take him past Merton and over Merton Field, from where he would turn towards Christ Church and into St Aldate's. Ignoring the beggars and whores and the black smoke of coal fires, he reached Merton Street. He was about to cross the street to join the path leading to the field, when a sudden scream from his right stopped him. Turning sharply, he saw a woman in a yellow gown and a short black cape beating fiercely at an attacker with her hand. With the other hand she was trying to wrest her purse from him. Despite the scream, she looked unhurt. Indeed, her assailant, who could not have been more than twelve years old, seemed to be losing the battle. His shoulders hunched, he was trying vainly to cover his head with his arms.

'You there,' shouted Thomas, hastening to help. 'Thief!'

The thief let go of the purse and ran.

Thomas shouted after him, 'Stop, thief. Thief! Stop that boy.'

But the few people in the street ignored him, and the thief disappeared around a corner.

'So much for Oxford,' said a soft voice behind him. 'Home to king, queen, army, exchequer and mint, but apparently not to gentlemen.'

Turning, Thomas saw a lady of about his own age, black curls to her shoulders, cheeks flushed and a little smile playing on her lips. Slim of face and figure, and dressed in a cream silk gown embroidered with tiny red and white flowers, she was not a lady whom one might have expected to find unaccompanied in the town, especially this town. Thomas tried not to stare, and failed miserably.

'Except for you, sir, naturally. I thank you for your assistance, although the wretch would soon have surrendered.'

'I don't doubt it, madam. Are you hurt?'

'Quite unhurt, thank you. It was my own fault. I seldom venture out alone, but I needed air. The college can be so restricting.'

'Why did no one stop the boy?' asked Thomas.

'Alas, sir, the people of Oxford do not all welcome us here. They look out for their own.'

'Then it's fortunate that I too am a visitor. Thomas Hill, madam, newly arrived from Romsey, and visiting my old tutor at Pembroke College.' The deception had been agreed with Abraham.

'A dangerous time to be visiting Oxford, Master Hill.'

'Indeed, madam. He's an old man, and nearly blind. Another year and I might have been too late.'

'I'm sorry. My name is Jane Romilly. I attend Queen Henrietta Maria at Merton.'

'Allow me to escort you there, madam.'

Jane Romilly smiled. It was an inviting smile, hard not to respond to. 'Thank you, Master Hill. It's very close, but I should be glad of company.'

At the entrance to Merton, she held out a hand. 'My thanks again, sir. Perhaps we shall meet another time.' Thomas took the hand, bowed and brushed his lips against it.

'I hope so, madam.' He watched her safely into the college before making his way back to Pembroke. Jane Romilly. An unusual lady, he thought, and an elegant one. Striking looks and an easy manner. Certain to be married. I wonder in what way she attends the queen? And there was something arresting about her face. He tried to picture it, but could not.

Later, he lay on his bed and thought of the day. Pembroke a soldiers' quarters, blind Abraham, that filthy lane, the poxed whore, Jane Romilly. It came to him just before he fell asleep. Jane Romilly's eyes were different colours. The right was brown, the left blue. Extraordinary.

The prospect of meeting the man to whom Parliament had presented a list of two hundred and four grievances and demands did not fill Thomas with joy. Charles's supporters claimed that he had done much to rid the court of the debauchery of his father's day, and to cleanse the administration of corruption and in-competence. His critics, however, and there were many of them, trusted neither his honesty nor his judgement. Either way, he was a king who had divided his country and brought it to this parlous state. That was something that Thomas could not condone. War could and should have been avoided. Still, Charles was the king, and must be treated accordingly. And Thomas, after all, had come to Oxford at his request, and to work in his service. He would behave himself and carry out his duties as best he could. Then he would go home. He washed and shaved, dressed carefully and set off to collect Abraham.

On the other side of the courtyard, a tall soldier was lounging against the wall, with a woman hanging on to his arm. As Thomas approached, he could see that she was the sort of woman who might spend a good deal of time hanging on to men's arms. Her cheeks were powdered and her lips painted the colour of a radish. The soldier was the loud dice-player Thomas had seen in the Crown the previous evening. Still dressed in clothes more suited to a ball than a battlefield, he was not difficult to recognize. When he noticed Thomas, he pushed the woman away and pointed a finger at him. 'You there, who are you and what are you doing here?' It was the same haughty voice, loud and demanding. Thomas stopped and looked at the man. He was perhaps six feet tall, his fair hair long and curled and his dark eyes hooded. A handsome man, despite his manners.

'My name is Thomas Hill and I am here on private business. And who, may I ask, are you?'

'I thought as much. Not that it's any concern of yours, Hill, but I am Captain Francis Fayne of Colonel Thomas Pinchbeck's Regiment of Foot. The officer whose room you have stolen. And I wish to have it back. Immediately.'

'I fear that will not be possible.'

Fayne stepped forward and stood in Thomas's path. 'Do you now? Is that what you fear? Well, you've got something else to fear now, Hill. Me. I do not take kindly to being thrown out of my room on the orders of Tobias Rush, and I intend to have it back.'

Thomas took a deep breath and tried to stay calm. 'I daresay you shall have it back, captain, as soon as my business in Oxford is completed.'

'And what business is that? You don't look much like a fighting man.'

'I am not. I'm a bookseller.'

Fayne guffawed. 'A bookseller? Since when did the king's army need booksellers?' He peered at Thomas. 'Or are you one of her majesty's household? She likes puppies.'

Thomas ignored the question and made to continue on his way. The captain, however, had not finished. 'I don't like having to share a room with a snoring oaf, Hill. It's inconvenient.' He put his arm round the woman and squeezed her backside hard enough to make her squeal. 'Isn't it, my lovely? So get out, man, or I'll put you out.'

Thomas stepped to the side, bowed politely and walked on. 'Good day, Captain Fayne. Good day, madam.'

Good God, Thomas, he thought to himself as he climbed the stairs to Abraham's room, why do you persist in discomposing these men? Captain Brooke and his dragoons, Pym's thieves and now Francis Fayne? Do try and take more care. By nature or by training, soldiers are soldiers. Keep away from them. He had never held a high opinion of tall, good-looking, fair-haired men, and Fayne had done nothing to change his mind.

Abraham was dressed and ready when Thomas knocked on the door. To attend the king, he wore a long black jacket and carried a broad black hat in his hand. 'Take this,' he said, holding out another hat, 'I'm quite sure you don't have one.'

Thomas put it on and took the old man's arm. 'It's no distance to Christ Church. We'll walk slowly. I want to ask you something.' Thomas led Abraham through a side gate to avoid the risk of another confrontation with Captain Fayne, and, once outside the college, told him about the attempted robbery of Jane Romilly. 'No one even tried to arrest the boy, never mind help the lady. I couldn't believe it.'

'Thomas,' replied Abraham quietly, 'you and I serve the king, but we must accept that feelings in the town are running high. Oxford has always favoured Parliament, and the townspeople have good reason to resent the presence of the court and the army. They say there are ten thousand men and women in the colleges and the town. Some are even billeted in almshouses. Jesus is full of soldiers, All Souls is an arsenal and Brasenose a food store. We can't walk in the meadows for artillery pieces. Every day there's pillaging and theft. And not just by the men. The women are worse, especially the Irish and the Welsh, whom no one understands when they speak that impossible language of theirs. Do you know who your lady was?'

'Jane Romilly, lady-in-waiting to the queen.'

'I have met Lady Romilly. Sir Edward died at Edgehill.'

'Her husband?'

Abraham nodded.

'A widow, then.'

'Yes, and by her dress she would have been marked as a member of the royal household. That's why she went unhelped. Except by you.'

At Christ Church, they were admitted by the guards, escorted around the Great Quadrangle where lines of soldiers were at their drills, and shown to a chamber near the Great Hall, where the king had established his parliament. In defiance of the elected parliament in London, the king called it his 'parliament', although, in truth, it was more of a royal court, with advisers and courtiers ready to do the royal bidding. Abraham sat. Thomas stood nervously, trying to remember what Montaigne would have advised. After a couple of false starts, he had it. *Au plus eslevé throne du monde, si ne sommes assis que sus nostre cul*; upon the high-est throne in the world, we are seated, still, upon our arse. The chamber door opened and a tall man, dressed, like Abraham, entirely in black, entered. He looked about forty and carried a silver-topped cane.

'Good morning, gentlemen,' he said affably. 'Master Fletcher, the king is expecting you. And,' turning to Thomas, 'you must be Master Hill. Welcome. I am Tobias Rush, adviser to his majesty.'

'Master Rush.' Thomas offered a small bow. So this was Rush. Abraham said nothing.

'If you would follow me, gentlemen. His majesty is suffering a little this morning. His legs often trouble him. Your audience will perforce be brief.'

They followed Tobias Rush into the hall, where the king was seated at the far end. Oddly, Thomas had never before been inside the Great Hall of Christ Church, despite its reputation. He glanced up at the high oak beams and around at the magnificent panelling and tall windows. It was foolish of him not to have visited the hall while he had the chance. It was a room very much fit for a king. Abraham held Thomas's arm. At Rush's signal, they bowed low and walked slowly up the length of the room. The king, surrounded by courtiers, watched impassively. Thomas could see that he was a small man, slight of build, with a narrow face and a short pointed beard. His dark eyes showed nothing. He did not rise as they approached.

'Your majesty,' said their escort, 'may I present Master Thomas Hill, with Master Fletcher, whom you know?'

The king held out a limp hand. Not knowing quite what to do with it, Thomas took it very lightly in his fingers, and bowed again. Abraham followed suit.

'Master Hill,' said the king in a gentle Scottish voice, 'we are pleased that you have arrived safely. Your skills come highly recommended, and we have grave need of them. Once Master Fletcher has acquainted you with our methods, we shall depend upon you to render our orders and reports entirely secure, and to reveal the enemy's secrets when you have the opportunity to do so. Have you anything to ask me?' Thomas had not. 'Master Rush will see to your needs. Ask him for whatever you require to carry out your loyal duties.'

'I shall, your majesty.'

'Good. Then lose no time. England's enemies must be defeated.'

Tobias Rush nodded to Thomas, signalling the end of the audience. The three men took two steps backwards, Abraham holding on tightly, bowed, then turned and left the hall.

Outside, Rush escorted them to the college entrance. 'His majesty has instructed me to provide you with whatever you need, Master Hill. Is your room adequate? Food, wine, company, you have but to ask.'

'Thank you, sir. I shall be sure to do so.' Thomas wondered if he should mention Captain Fayne.

'Excellent. We're much relieved that you're here. I never trusted Erasmus Pole,' said Rush, 'and told the king so more than once. I wasn't surprised that his body was found in that vile lane. He was a man of odd habits.'

Thomas glanced at Abraham, who was silent. At the gate, Rush shook their hands and watched them turn towards

Pembroke. As they did so, two riders, yelling at them to get out of the way, swept past and into the college. Both wore pale blue hats with long feathers, and dark blue coats festooned with ribbons and lace.

'Sounds like the royal princes,' said Abraham, drily. 'Rupert and Maurice. Probably boasting about their exploits in Bristol. If they aren't drunk, they soon will be. The king should send them back where they came from.'

'Who were all those people around the king, Abraham?' asked Thomas.

'I couldn't see them, but the king has a full court. The Master of the Revels was probably there, and William Dobson, the court painter. He's much in demand, I hear. Unspeakably vain, some young men these days. Care to have your portrait painted, Thomas? Rush could arrange it.'

'I think not, thank you. Although it sounds as if Tobias Rush could arrange anything. What do you know of him?'

'Rush is not to my taste, but the king relies on him,' replied Abraham as they entered Pembroke. 'He organizes the king's affairs and runs his household. He's skilled at playing on the king's insecurity. He's a clever man, and an ambitious one. Treat him with caution, Thomas.'

'I certainly shall. Now, when shall we start work?'

'This morning. I'll have food and wine sent to my rooms. Silas will escort me there. Come in an hour.'

An hour later they were seated at Abraham's table, a pile of papers before them. 'Since the king came to Oxford,' the old man began, 'we've been using substitution ciphers devised and developed by Erasmus. The ciphers are based on an eight-letter keyword, changed on the first day of each month. In the final week of the month, Erasmus sent out the first four letters of the new keyword, encoded according to the current keyword and hidden in the text of the message. Each recipient then sent back four more letters, also encoded and hidden, to make up the full keyword.'

'So each recipient has a unique keyword, which lasts for a month?'

'That is right. It means that we have to know from whom each message has come, but that is easily dealt with. Each message carries the encrypted name of the sender, again hidden in the text. Each name has its own codeword. If one forgets to include his name, we simply use all the current keywords until we find the right one for the text.'

'There are weaknesses in this, Abraham, as you know. The messages carrying either half of the new keyword might not arrive, and a list of all current keywords and codewords must have been kept somewhere.'

'Indeed they were. Inside Erasmus's head. He never wrote them down. As to the other point, we've had no serious difficulties. Process of elimination and a bit of guesswork have sufficed.'

'How many keywords are there?'

'Currently, twenty.'

Thomas looked thoughtful. Twenty names with fixed codes, and twenty different keywords each month. Not difficult. Abraham passed Thomas the top sheet of paper.

'This is an encrypted message, received three months ago. If you were the enemy, how long would it take you to decrypt it?'

Thomas looked at it. It was six lines long, each line consisting of about fifty seemingly random letters. 'This is about the right length for a military report, rather than a battlefield order. It looks like a substitution cipher, probably with a keyword. A simple shift would be too easy, and a cipher alphabet would be written down somewhere, which would make it vulnerable to capture. So I'd assume a keyword. With only one encrypted text to work with, perhaps a morning.'

'That's what I thought. Not secure from the attentions of a good cryptographer.' Abraham passed over another sheet. 'What about this one?'

Again, Thomas studied the sheet for several minutes. 'This message is shorter. It could be a military order. I guess that there are some coded words. Not knowing the context, I'd go about it as with the first message — frequencies and letter relationships — but if there are codes it would take longer.'

Abraham smiled. 'Your instincts are as good as ever, Thomas. Now what about this one?'

Immediately Thomas said, 'This is alpha-numeric.' He imagined lines running through each number. 'I think some of the numbers are nulls because there's a pattern to them, but the others could be codes.'

'Excellent. Now take these and practise your skills on them. Note that they may not all be what they seem.' Abraham passed over the remaining papers. 'Some of these are ours, others were intercepted. All incoming and outgoing messages will now be passed through me to you, for encryption and decryption. Next week you will need to send out the first half of a new keyword. Here is a list of all recipients. Please commit them to memory and destroy the list.'

'And if I don't, sir? Will I be confined to college?'

Abraham could hear the raised eyebrows and the mocking smile, even though he could not see them.

CHAPTER 4

Armed with a handful of good duck-feather quills, a sharpening knife and a large pot of oak-apple ink supplied by Silas, Thomas set to work, starting with the simple task of memorizing the names of the twenty recipients of messages. He used a memory trick based on the vowels in each name which Abraham had taught him years ago, and most names surrendered without much of a fight. Within half an hour, he had them all.

Next he counted the papers. There were twenty of them. Deciding to tackle them in the order in which Abraham had put them, he took the first one from the top of the pile. Twenty lines of ten letters each, written in a neat hand in brown ink and with spaces between every four or six letters, covered one side of the paper. Thomas held it up to the light, looking for unusual marks or letter formations. There were none. He smiled. Kindly old Abraham had given him a simple substitution cipher to start with. On a blank sheet, he prepared a table with each letter of the alphabet across the top. Then he counted the number of times each letter occurred in the message, and wrote the number below it. He found that the letters C, F, and P appeared most often. They would probably represent E, A, and T, although not necessarily in that order. They were the three most commonly used letters in the alphabet, and if he could identify those he would be on the way to breaking the cipher. As C and P were preceded and followed by fifteen different letters, but F by only eight, F would represent T, which would appear between fewer letters than either E or A. Ignoring the spaces, which were merely intended to confuse, there were six instances of double Cs, but none of double Ps. C would represent E, leaving P as A.

Continuing with this strategy, Thomas quickly identified ten letters, which revealed the common words AND, A and THE, and parts of other words. With a little intuition and guesswork, he had found the keyword, ADVANCE, and decrypted the message within an hour. It revealed that Sir John Berkeley, with modest help from Sir Bevil Grenville and Sir Ralph Hopton, had defeated a strong Parliamentary force at Braddock Down in Cornwall, capturing cannon and muskets. Reading the plain text, Thomas wondered why Sir John had troubled to have the message encrypted. The gallant knight clearly wanted the king, his court and all his subjects to know of his valour and the great victory it had brought. No doubt there had been similar messages from the other two gentlemen.

Thomas moved on to the second paper on the pile. Roughly the same length as the first, this one was also a mixture of letters and spaces. As before, he checked it for hidden signs, found none, wrote out each letter of the alphabet across the top of a blank page, and put under each one the number of times it appeared. When this produced a more even distribution than he expected, Thomas suspected he was facing a more complex cipher. Twenty minutes later, he knew he was right. Two substitutions had been used alternately, and he had to find both, just as he had shown Simon in the inn. After another hour, Thomas had identified fifteen letters, which was enough for him to fill in the gaps and write out both substitution alphabets. The substitutions were random sequences of letters, which made them more difficult to decrypt, but both sender and recipient would have had copies, making them vulnerable to discovery.

A B C D E F G H I J K L M N O P Q R S T U V W X Y Z

P L O M K I N J U B H Y V G T C F R X D E Z S W A Q

L A M Z P Q K S N X B C V J D F H G W I O R Y T E U

It was an intercepted message, revealing that in March Sir Thomas Fairfax had been concerned about his troops' morale and had asked for them to be paid without further delay. As the message had failed to reach its intended destination, Thomas assumed that Sir Thomas's troops had remained unpaid.

By the end of the first day, Thomas had decrypted seven complete documents. They were all alphabetic ciphers, using mixtures of single and double substitutions, and keywords. His eyes and back ached, his legs were stiff and he needed refreshment. He was about to go off in search of food and drink when there was a loud knock on the door. He opened it to find Tobias Rush outside, silver-topped cane in hand and, as at court, dressed all in black.

'Master Hill, I find you hard at work no doubt. I trust I'm not disturbing you. I merely wondered if I could be of any assistance.'

Caught off balance, Thomas was less than articulate. 'Master

Rush. Good evening. No, no disturbance. I've just finished for the day, and was about to take some air and stretch my legs.'

'In that case,' replied Rush, smiling his thin smile, 'perhaps I may accompany you. You can tell me how you're progressing.' Without waiting for an answer, he turned and strode out into the courtyard. Thomas locked his door and followed. 'I do admire Pembroke,' said Rush, as they picked their way through the debris towards the college gate. 'A lovely building, and attractively small, although I see the officers here have paid scant regard to its care. Alas, it's the same everywhere. Military mess and careless destruction.'

'Yes,' agreed Thomas, 'there is something blinkered about the military mind. It seems able to ignore almost anything other than itself.'

Rush laughed. 'Nicely put, Master Hill. Let us pray that this war is soon over, so that the university can resume its former life.' They left the college and turned north up St Aldate's. 'And how does your work progress?'

'It has not been arduous. So far, Abraham has given me quite simple tasks, although I expect them to get harder.'

'Good. On Master Fletcher's advice, the king has put his absolute trust in you. If we can anticipate the enemy's movements while leaving him ignorant of ours, we shall gain a great advantage. You have a vital duty to perform.'

Thomas hesitated. 'Erasmus Pole was an able man. Has the king not enjoyed such an advantage since the war began?'

Rush stopped and looked hard at Thomas. 'We were never sure about Pole. There were incidents. His loyalty to the king was beginning to be questioned. The affair at Alton was an odd thing — most suspicious. No sooner had we received word that Lord

Digby was planning to attack the town than the enemy reinforced its defences. Most suspicious. And the judgement of an elderly man who walked down that foul lane at night must also be questioned.'

'Do you think he was killed there?'

'That's where he was found.' Rush's eyes narrowed. 'Or do you suggest that he was murdered elsewhere and his body taken there?'

'No, sir, I know only that I have walked down that lane in daylight and shall not do so again, never mind at night.'

'Very wise of you. It's a noisome place.'

'Noisome and evil.'

'Indeed. Master Hill, if I may proffer some advice, take great care to whom you speak in Oxford. The town is full of men who are not what they seem.'

'Abraham Fletcher said much the same thing.'

'I daresay he did. And, Master Hill, you will report anything at all suspicious to me, won't you?'

'I shall.' Approaching Queen Street, Thomas changed the subject. 'Master Rush, you kindly asked if there is anything you can do for me. I do have one favour to ask.'

'Of course. What is the favour?'

'I should like to let my sister know that I have arrived in Oxford safely, and am quite well. Would you be able to have a letter delivered for me?'

'That will present no difficulty. Messengers are in and out of the town every day. I will find one heading for Winchester or Salisbury and have him deliver the letter. Romsey, is it not?'

'It is. My thanks, Master Rush. I am in your debt.'

'Say no more about it. Let me have the letter, and I shall deal with the matter at once. Now, allow me to propose a happy diversion from your labours. The queen is presenting a masque in honour of the king on Wednesday next. She is fond of masques. Her court, and much of the king's, will be there. You are invited to attend.'

Thomas hesitated. A masque was not his idea of a happy diversion. It would be formal, lavish and extravagant. He had no suitable clothes, and little to say to members of either court. He tried to think of an excuse. Then he remembered the lovely Jane Romilly, lady-in-waiting to the queen. An acquaintance he would much like to renew. 'Thank you, Master Rush. I should be delighted.'

'Excellent. Two o'clock in the afternoon on Wednesday, at Merton. The masque will be followed by a reception. I will arrange for a suit of clothes to be sent round to you. Their majesties are most particular as to dress. I shall look forward to seeing you there. Now I shall leave you and return to Christ Church. Good day, Master Hill.'

'Good day, Master Rush.' Alone, Thomas turned into Broad Street, intending to follow Catte Street to the High Street, and thence to St Aldate's and Pembroke. It did not take him long to change his mind. Broad Street was more Bedlam than street. Realizing that he would have to run a gauntlet of beggars, whores and pickpockets, he turned back towards Cornmarket. He was not quite quick enough. He smelt the woman before he saw her. Out of a dark doorway she came, another stinking, poxed, toothless crone, this one with a humped back. She grabbed his shirt, and pressed herself against him. 'Good evening, sir. You're a fine gentleman and no mistake. For a sovereign, I'll make you a happy one.' Bile rising in his throat, Thomas wrenched his shirt free and ran. He kept running almost as far as Pembroke. Outside the gates, he stopped, took deep breaths until he was calm, and walked slowly into the college.

'Good evening, sir. You look a trifle flushed. Are you well?' Silas, keeping watch from his room, had seen him come in. Silas missed nothing. Thomas's face was red and his shirt askew.

'Quite well, thank you, Silas. I should be grateful for a bottle of hock and some dinner. Would you have them sent over?'

Silas looked him up and down. 'As you wish, sir. Nothing the matter, I hope.'

'Nothing, Silas, thank you. The evening is warm. Walking too fast, I daresay.'

Silas looked doubtful. 'Indeed, sir. I'll have the bottle and a plate sent over directly.'

In his room, Thomas took off his shirt and breeches and lay on his bed. They would have to be washed. Waiting for his dinner, he wondered what he had agreed to. Queen Henrietta Maria was known to be fond of masques, and even sometimes appeared in them herself. It was said that in London the most extravagant of her entertainments had cost over twenty thousand guineas. Twenty thousand guineas. Enough to build two hundred cottages or a hundred schools, feed an entire town for a year, provide for every beggar and orphan . . .

Before he could add to the list, his dinner arrived, brought by one of Silas's boys. Intending to give the boy a few pence, Thomas reached for his purse on the table. Then he remembered that it was in his pocket. He picked up the discarded breeches and felt for the purse. The pockets were empty. He looked around the room in case he had been mistaken. No purse. Then he realized. The hump-backed hag must have picked his pocket. Silas's boy was not going to get a whole sovereign from the bag hidden under the bed, so he would have to go unrewarded. 'Thank you, young fellow,' said Thomas graciously, 'you shall have a shilling next time.' Unsure whether to be pleased or not, the boy departed.

Thomas's last waking thought that evening was whether there was anyone in Oxford who was what he seemed. Abraham, of course, and Silas. But what about Simon? What about Rush? What about Fayne? He acted like an arrogant oaf, but could he be a traitor? Or even a mild-mannered scholar in disguise?

For two more days, Thomas saw little of the sun. He was determined to decrypt every one of the documents perfectly. When working, he found that he could blot out the clash and clamour outside. Only when he left his room for trips to the privy, to fetch water from the well or to find food did he have to face the awful squalor and destruction that had been brought on his old college.

As he always had, Thomas found himself giving each encoder a personality. He could look at a sheet of paper covered in random letters, numbers and symbols, and, after identifying just a few letters, could often divine its soul. And, even before starting the decrypting process, he sometimes recognized the hand of the sender. By visualizing the man – fat, thin, tall, short – and his traits – tidy, careless, quick, slow – he could anticipate the methods he was likely to use. It was a marriage of science and art that Abraham used to call Hill's magic.

He expected to find the remaining documents encrypted much as those he had already decrypted, but it did not take him long to discover that Abraham was up to his tricks. The old fox had mixed up the documents to conceal their context and chronology. The tenth document surprised him with an unusually high proportion of the letters A and I, until he realized that it had been written in Latin. In the other documents, there were deliberate misspellings, and some parts of the texts — the most difficult to decrypt — were nomenclators — combinations of letters, symbols and numbers. The symbols and numbers were either homophonic substitutions for single words or meaningless nulls, sometimes both in the same message. Much like the cipher Phelippes had decrypted, although simpler. Thomas started with the assumption that the most common letter combinations, such as THE, AND and TION, would appear most often, and proceeded from there. The approach was laborious but effective.

By the evening of the third day, Thomas had a pile of twenty plain texts to match the twenty coded ones, and his skills had become as sharp as they had ever been. Although Abraham had said that their own codes were superior to those of the enemy, Thomas disagreed. He found little difference between them, and the messages were just as tedious. Demands for men and supplies, complaints about the lack of pay, boasts and excuses. The most interesting text turned out to be a description, written backwards, of Abraham's favourite wines. How typical of his old friend to lighten the day with a joke.

Thomas decided to wait until the morning to deliver the decrypted texts to Abraham. After a walk to the Cherwell and back, and an excellent plate of black pudding with capers and pickled cucumbers, he was undressing for bed when there was a knock on the door. He quickly pulled up his breeches. 'Who is it?'

'It's your favourite friar, Thomas. Simon de Pointz.' Thomas opened the door. 'And I come bearing gifts,' said Simon, handing over the clothes he was carrying. 'These are from Tobias Rush. I do hope they fit.'

'Good evening, Simon. I had thought you might have called earlier, although I have been busy.'

Simon looked at the pile of papers on the table. 'So I see. Have your efforts met with success?'

'Happily, yes. But it was only practice. The real tests will come later. Should I try these on?' He held up the clothes.

'I would recommend it. Queen Henrietta Maria can't help but notice an ill-fitting shirt or coat. She has an eye for such matters.'

Thomas took off his plain breeches again, and tried on the new ones. They were dark blue, loose-fitting, tied at the knee with yellow ribbons, and with bows and rosettes attached to the sides. A pair of white silk stockings were embroidered in blue and red. Over a fine lace shirt, he donned a short pale-blue coat with a red lining and red ribbons on the sleeves, then, finally, pulled on a pair of soft leather boots with silver buckles. Simon, who had watched the process intently, was delighted. 'Master Hill, who would have thought a Romsey bachelor could be turned into such an elegant and courtly gentleman? Their majesties will share my admiration. And it all fits perfectly. How clever of Master Rush.'

Thomas was doubtful. 'Are you sure, Simon? I feel like a popinjay.'

'Nonsense. You look splendid. Now take them off and put them away somewhere safe. It would be a pity to spill your soup on such finery.'

As Thomas was undressing, he asked Simon if he knew Lady Romilly. 'Of course I do,' replied the priest. 'She is a lady-in-waiting to the queen. A lovely lady, sadly widowed. Why do you ask?'

'I chanced to meet her in the town. Will she be at the masque?'

Simon raised an eyebrow. 'I imagine so. The queen is seldom seen in public without her ladies.' He paused. 'Now I must be away. Wednesday, at two in the afternoon. I shall not be present, as Franciscans and masques do not go well together, but I hope you enjoy the spectacle. The queen is much looking forward to it.'

Soon after Simon had left, Thomas fell asleep wondering whether or not he too was looking forward to it.

Before visiting Abraham the next morning, Thomas wrote his letter to Margaret. He told her that, except for the shaggy inkcaps for dinner, their journey had been uneventful, that he was well and comfortable, and that he had met the king. He said nothing about squalor and poverty, nor about the masque, of which he knew his sister would disapprove. He enquired after her health and that of the girls, expressed the fond wish that he would see them all again soon, and entreated her to write back. Lacking a seal, he tied the rolled letter with a red ribbon stolen from his new outfit. He would give it to Tobias Rush at the masque.

The courtyard, to Thomas's relief, was deserted when he crossed it, and Abraham was sitting in his chair by the window when he entered. 'I thought you would come this morning, Thomas,' he said. 'Three days for twenty simple documents seemed about right. Or have any of them defeated you?'

'Happily not, although homophonic substitutions and nomenclators do take time. Here they are.' He put the twenty plain texts on the old man's table.

'I'll have to take your word for it. Did you learn anything from them?'

'Three things. The science of cryptography has progressed very little in the last ten years, military despatches are invariably as dull as a Scottish sermon, and your choice of the Portuguese wine was surprising. Isn't it a little too sweet?'

Abraham beamed. 'A little sweet, perhaps. Well done, Thomas. Whatever tiny doubts I had have been banished. You would have been a match for the great Phelippes himself. In fact, if the Queen of Scots had had the benefit of your services, she might have kept her head. Now we can put you to proper work. Take the papers on the table for encoding, please. The first half of this month's keyword is ROSE. The other halves are on this list, with the owner's name and codeword. Please memorize them.' He reached into a pocket, extracted a small sheet of paper and held it out to Thomas. 'Next week you'll need to send out your new key-word, and remind them to send theirs. All despatches will go through me. There's no reason for any of our people to know who you are. It's safer that way.'

'Are there any intercepted messages?' Encrypting was easy work; decrypting was what Thomas had regained his taste for.

'No. But be assured that you will see the next one as soon as it arrives. It'll come to me. I'll send word. Now you'd better get back to work.'

'Before I do, Abraham, Tobias Rush has invited me to attend the queen's masque on Wednesday. He's even provided a new suit of clothes.'

Abraham groaned. 'I don't envy you. The last one I attended went on for two hours, and was quite unintelligible. Something to do with Venus and Neptune. And Cupid, I think. It was hard to know. And the extravagance is unspeakable. Thousands of guineas. No wonder her majesty is less than popular in the country. However, Thomas, remember what I said. Tobias Rush is a powerful man, with the ear of the king. You had better go.'

*

Thomas set off for Merton half an hour before the masque was due to start. With some difficulty, he had put on his fine new shirt, breeches, stockings and coat, tied ribbons around his knees, set Abraham's hat on his head, wiped the silver buckles on his boots with a cloth and made his way through the courtyard to the college entrance. Silas, as always, was at his post. 'Master Hill. I hardly knew you. The queen's masque, would it be?'

'It would, Silas. How do I look?'

'Magnificent, sir. Almost like royalty. Enjoy the masque.'

'Thank you, Silas. I'll try.'

The quickest route to Merton took Thomas up St Aldate's, along Blue Boar Street and into Merton Street. They were as busy as ever. Remembering the hump-backed hag, he carried no money. He walked slowly, taking care not to be jostled, and picking his way around the heaps of butchers' offal and human excrement that blocked sewers and overflowed into the streets. The soft boots did not help. They were a little too big, and flopped about his ankles. Despite concentrating on not tripping over something revolting, he could not help noticing the sullen stares that followed his progress. Blue Boar Street was the beggars' favourite. Limbless, sightless, diseased men and women lined both sides of it, those with arms holding out their hands and pleading for a farthing or a penny, those without standing guard over tin plates on the ground. A tradesman casually dropped a penny on to a plate in front of a blind man. The blind man heard the coin on the plate, bent to pick it up, and immediately let out a stream of blasphemous curses. The coin had gone in seconds — taken by the one-armed man beside him.

Halfway down the street, the abuse started. 'Bit too tall for a queen's dwarf.'

'Must be one of the king's bed boys.'

'Have a care, sir. Be a shame to spoil those pretty rags.'

Thomas affected not to hear, and managed not to quicken his pace. It was broad daylight, there were people about and, for all they knew, he might be armed. He should be safe.

At Merton, he was met by a college servant bedecked in powdered wig in the French style, cream stockings, wide crimson breeches and an embroidered coat. The man wore a pearl and ruby brooch. Two lines of guards armed with muskets and swords stood on either side of the gatehouse. Thomas gave his name, and was shown to a seat at the far side of the courtyard. It was bigger than the Pembroke courtyard, but much smaller than Christ Church's. The queen must have wanted the king to be untroubled by the preparations for the performance. Thomas nodded politely to the two portly gentlemen on either side of him, noting that, compared to theirs, his outfit was only just up to standard. The masque was not due to start for another ten minutes, but almost all the seats were already occupied. No one wanted to risk the embarrassment of arriving after their majesties. Thomas looked around, hoping to see Jane Romilly. She was not there. Perhaps she was taking part in the masque.

At exactly two o'clock, the king and queen entered the court-yard from the royal apartments. The audience rose and applauded loudly as the royal couple walked slowly to their seats on a raised dais to Thomas's right. The seats were covered in gold cloth, with gold cushions and gold footrests. The king, limping slightly, walked with a stick. The queen, resplendent in satins and pearls, auburn hair curling around her neck, smiled and waved to the crowd. At her heels were four fat spaniels and a dwarf. Thomas guessed he was Jeffrey Hudson, known to be her favourite.

When the king and queen were seated, a herald called the audience to attention with a blast on his horn, and announced that the masque they were about to see was *The Triumph of Peace*, written by James Shirley, and first performed for her majesty in London nine years earlier. With due regard to cost and the sacrifices of her loyal subjects, her gracious majesty had command-ed that this production be made suitable to the present time and place. The entertainment would therefore be modest, and would last but an hour. At this there was more applause, although whether this was in appreciation of her majesty's concern for her subjects or the reduced length of the performance, Thomas was uncertain. He took another look around the courtyard. Still no Jane. The masque began.

From the Fellows' Quadrangle behind Thomas, a procession of courtiers entered through a high arch, to joyous acclaim. There were perhaps twenty of them — Thomas guessed at a fifth of the number employed in the London production — fantastically dressed and bejewelled in costumes of crimson, blue and gold. Having proceeded in stately fashion around the courtyard, they took up station near the gatehouse. These magnificent courtiers were followed by a coach transformed into a golden chariot, and drawn by four matched white stallions in gold and crimson cloths. The chariot carried two lutenists, and four singers dressed as celestial bodies. Thomas recognized the sun and the moon, but the other two defeated him. The celestial bodies sang a fulsome eulogy to the king and queen, as their chariot cautiously circled the narrow courtyard.

Two more chariots, similarly decorated, followed, this time

from the direction of the chapel. These, the herald told them, carried the spirits of Peace, Law and Justice, who descended from the chariots to honour the king and queen in speech and song. While they were doing so, a second troupe of courtiers entered the now rather crowded courtyard. These too wore a variety of dazzling costumes and headdresses. The herald helpfully informed the audience that these performers represented Opinion, Fancy, Jollity, Novelty, Confidence and assorted other qualities, as well as the customary tradespeople. One of them, who Thomas thought might be Jollity, was dressed as a morris dancer.

Poems and songs, all declaiming the many virtues of their majesties, and expressing the loyal wish that they be swiftly restored to their thrones in London, occupied most of the allocated hour. The finale, against the backdrop of a windmill, featured an elderly Don Quixote, his plump steward Sancho Panza and an unnamed knight. Between them, they staged a brief mock battle, much appreciated by the audience. As they left the courtyard, followed by the chariots and horses, the procession of musicians, singers and courtiers bowed low to the king and queen, and waved gaily to the delighted audience. It was hard to be sure, but Lady Romilly did not appear to be among them.

Despite the queen's avowed sensitivity to the needs of her citizens, Thomas thought, the masque must have cost a tidy sum to stage. Taking his lead from his large neighbours, he rose and wandered into the middle of the courtyard. While their majesties, beaming and waving, remained seated, an army of servants arrived to clear away the seats of the audience, and to bring out from the college kitchens trays laden with claret and hock, pastries, fruits, sweetmeats and cakes. Thomas took a glass of hock and edged round the crowd towards the gatehouse. Not wanting to be drawn into discussion of the entertainment, or indeed of anything else, he planned to slip away unnoticed. He was about to make his escape when he glimpsed Jane Romilly. She was on the far side of the courtyard, deep in conversation with a tall man in a dazzling blue coat and crimson breeches. Thomas peered through the crowd. It was Francis Fayne. Jane Romilly and Francis Fayne, and giving every appearance of being well acquainted. How unexpected – and how disappointing. He turned to go. Then, from behind him, a voice he knew at once said quietly, 'Master Hill. I had not thought to meet you in such a place.' She had seen him and walked over.

Thomas turned back, and took the outstretched hand. 'Lady Romilly. An unexpected pleasure.' Today she wore a pale blue skirt, embroidered, as before, with tiny flowers, and with a low neckline and narrow sleeves decorated with royal blue ribbons. Her black curls tumbled about her bare shoulders. The lady Thomas had chanced to meet in the street was a very beautiful lady indeed.

'And how do you come to be at the masque, Master Hill?'

'I was invited by Master Tobias Rush. No doubt you know him.'

Jane's eyes narrowed. 'Indeed I do, sir. You are well connected.'

'Not really, madam. Master Rush is acquainted with my old tutor, Abraham Fletcher.'

'I recall that you are visiting him at Pembroke. How is he?'

'Blind, madam, and a little infirm, but his mind is as sharp as ever.'

'And how long shall you be staying?'

'That I am unsure of, madam. There are affairs that may detain me.'

'I see. And what did you make of the masque?' asked Jane, changing the subject.

'I found it, ah, extraordinary.'

Jane laughed lightly. 'Nicely put, sir. I am devoted to Queen Henrietta Maria, a gentle and pious lady, but her masques are indeed extraordinary. She was a dear friend to Master Rubens, you know, and to Inigo Jones, who designed the original set for *The Triumph of Peace*. Her majesty takes a great interest in the arts of painting and drama.'

'Your devotion does you credit, madam.' Thomas hesitated. 'And I see you know Captain Fayne.'

'Slightly. Oxford is not a large town and we all move in small circles. Captain Fayne and I have met before.'

'Quite so. May I ask you a question?'

'Certainly, sir, as long as it is a respectable one.'

'I think it is. What exactly does a lady-in-waiting do?'

Again Jane laughed. 'She waits, mostly. Waits for her majesty to call upon her services. Then she attends to her majesty's needs, and sees that she is comfortable and content. Sometimes she is also required to attend to the queen's spaniels.'

'And her dwarf?'

'Mr Hudson, thankfully, looks after himself.'

'Thank you, madam. Was the question respectable?'

'It was. I thought you might ask about my eyes. They are frequently asked about.'

'I had noticed them. Most unusual, if I may say so.'

'I'm fortunate to have been born the daughter of a squire. My father says that, had I been born to a carpenter, I would have been burned as a witch long ago. No one in Yorkshire had ever before seen eyes of different colours on the same face.' Jane put out a hand to pick a stray thread from Thomas's coat. As she did so, she noticed Tobias Rush looking at them with interest. 'I see Master Rush is observing us closely, Master Hill. He is a loyal friend to the king, yet he always reminds me of a raven. Black feathers, black eyes, long beak. He stands out in a crowd of peacocks.'

Thomas turned and bowed to Rush, who acknowledged him with a tip of his black hat. 'Master Rush has been most solicitous to me. But I know what you mean. There is something unsettling about him. Do you know anything of his history?'

'Very little, except that he's highly regarded by the king. The queen, on the other hand, does not care for him. I did hear that he is of humble origins, and that his father was a turnkey in London. If that's true, he's come far.' Jane looked over his shoulder. 'Here is Captain Fayne. Allow me to introduce you. He too is staying in Pembroke.' Thomas turned to see Fayne striding towards them. 'Francis,' she said, 'allow me to present Master Thomas Hill, in Oxford to visit an old friend. Master Hill, this is Captain Fayne.'

'Captain Fayne and I are acquainted, Lady Romilly,' replied Thomas with a smile. 'We happened to meet in the college.'

Fayne's hooded eyes narrowed. 'Indeed we did. A bookseller, was it not?'

'Indeed, sir.'

'A bookseller with a comfortable room to himself.'

'I am fortunate in that respect.'

'You are a bookseller, Master Hill?' asked Jane.

'I am, madam. I have a small shop in Romsey.'

'I recall your mentioning Romsey.'

'I cannot imagine what a little bookseller is doing in Oxford at such a time, Hill. Can you enlighten us?' asked Fayne.

'I am on the king's business. I can say no more.'

Fayne bent his head to put his face in front of Thomas's, and hissed, 'Well, make haste and do the king's business, Hill, because I want my room back.'

Thomas retreated a step, and looked enquiringly at Jane. How did she come to know this creature? Fayne sounded as if he would like nothing better than to tear Thomas into small pieces and, if they had been anywhere other than at a royal masque, he would have done so. Jane glanced to her left. 'Master Hill, the queen is signalling. She requires my presence, and, if I'm not mistaken, yours too.'

'Mine? Surely not.'

'Her majesty takes a close interest in her staff and their friends. She probably wants to know who you are. Come. I shall present you.' Together they left Fayne standing on his own. Thomas sensed dark eyes boring into the back of his neck. Just as well the king and queen were present or he might by now have been disembowelled.

Before the queen, Jane curtseyed and Thomas bowed.

'And who is this, Lady Romilly?'

'Your majesty, this is Master Thomas Hill, in Oxford visiting his old tutor. We met by chance in the town.' Thomas bowed again. The queen peered at him. She looked a formidable lady. No wonder some called her the 'Generalissima'.

'Master Hill. We welcome you to Oxford, now capital of England, and the seat of its lawful parliament.'

'Thank you, your majesty.'

'Lady Romilly is a loyal servant and a dear friend. He who harms her harms me. If she is also your friend, be sure to protect her from danger at all times. With your life, if needs must.'

'That I certainly shall, your majesty.'

'Good. We are pleased to have met you, Master Hill.'

A third bow, and a cautious retreat.

'With my life? A little dramatic on so short an acquaintance, don't you think?' said Thomas.

'The queen is not given to understatement. Do not take her too literally.'

'I shall try not to. Now, if you will excuse me, Lady Romilly,' he said, when they had moved into the crowd, 'I have a letter to give to Master Rush. Then I will slip away. Perhaps we shall meet again.'

'I would like that, Master Hill. You have told me little about yourself. Or about what really brought you to Oxford.' Thomas took his leave with a polite smile.

Rush watched him approach. 'Master Hill, I see you are acquainted with Lady Romilly. A charming lady. How do you come to know her?'

'We met by chance in the street. I was able to render a small service to the lady.'

'How fortunate. A lady to whom many would like to render a small service.'

Thomas ignored the unexpected vulgarity. 'You kindly agreed to have a letter delivered to my sister, sir. Here it is.'

'By all means. It shall go with the next messenger.'

'I'm grateful, sir.' Thomas retreated towards the gate. Tobias Rush was indeed an unusual man. Forbidding in manner, kindly in deed. Scrupulously polite one day, coarse the next. Not an easy book to read.

Having successfully navigated Blue Boar Street, he arrived back at Pembroke to be greeted just inside the gate by an indignant

Fayne. 'And what, may I ask, was a miserable bookseller doing at the queen's masque?' he demanded.

'I was invited, sir, as, I imagine, were you.'

'Naturally I was invited. I have been presented more than once to her majesty. She is aware of my loyalty to her and my interest in the dramatic arts. What I want to know is why you were invited, and by whom?'

'I was invited by Master Rush.'

'Rush. I might have guessed it.'

'Now, sir, if you will excuse me,' said Thomas politely, 'I have work to do.'

'And what work would that be? Selling books? Or something more sinister? If I thought for a second that you were disloyal to the Crown, Hill, I'd have you interrogated. And don't forget it.'

'I shan't. Good day, sir.'

'And another thing, Hill. Keep away from Jane Romilly.'

Thomas did not reply. Would he have to endure this every time he set foot outside his room? The man was obsessed. A tiny room and now Jane Romilly. Why could Fayne not find somewhere else to take his pleasures? Down by the river, perhaps, where Thomas had taken them himself all those years ago. Should he tell Rush about the man? No, let it be. Perhaps the oaf would go away.

CHAPTER 5

He stared at yet another pile of papers. The only thing at all interesting about decoding military reports, thought Thomas, was finding the mistakes made by their incompetent encrypters. Very few of them remembered to use the right code-word and they all sent messages full of careless errors. The only source of comfort was that, judging by the few intercepted messages that had landed on his table, the enemy's efforts were every bit as feeble.

The subject matter was irredeemably tedious. When lacking anything better to occupy them, the king's commanders relieved their boredom by firing off despatches on matters of excruciating banality. Why Sir Marmaduke Rawdon on the south coast thought that his majesty should be apprised of his recent attack of gout, or Sir John Owen in North Wales felt it necessary to remind him that, to be effective, wagons need horses and horses need hay, defeated Thomas. Neither, however, were as regular in their correspondence as the gallant Earl of Northampton. By now, Thomas knew everything he could possibly wish about his lordship's household, hopes and health. But each message had to be decrypted, rendered into plain text and passed to Abraham, and thence to the king. Whether his majesty bothered to read them, Thomas doubted. He longed to find a message of extreme urgency and vital importance. Sighing, he picked up the pile and went to see Abraham.

Thankfully there was no sign of Fayne, although the courtyard was busy. He made his way past a dozen soldiers noisily complaining to a baker's boy about the price of his bread and around a pile of calivers waiting to be cleaned by an armourer. At Abraham's door he knocked and entered without waiting for a response, knowing that the old man might be dozing in his chair. 'Good morning, Abraham,' he said loudly, just in case.

'Ah, Thomas, I thought I heard your footsteps on the stairs. What have you brought me today?' Abraham rubbed sleep from his eyes and smiled. 'These days, I never quite know if I'm asleep or not. Somewhere between awake and dreaming, I think. One of the curses of old age.'

'I fear that this lot will do little to waken you,' replied Thomas, putting the pile of papers on Abraham's table. 'They're as dull as ever.'

'How dreary for you. I had hoped you would find the work more stimulating. What about the intercepted messages?'

'Just as tedious. Rheumatism and rations, pikes and pay, fodder and flintlocks. Why can't we intercept a message telling us that Essex is about to surrender or the London-trained bands have turned on Pym?'

Abraham laughed. 'Ever the way with words, Thomas. Alas, military despatches are like poems. You might read a hundred before you come across a good one.'

'I wonder then why you thought to send for me. Anyone could do this work. And I have no more inkling of who murdered Erasmus Pole than I had when I arrived. There hasn't been a hint of it. Please may I go home?'

'I fear not, my friend, not until the king says so.'

'What if I just leave?'

'Then you would be in danger, and so would I. The king would take it as a personal insult.' Abraham turned his face to the window. 'I shall have to think of something to amuse you.'

'I do wish you would. At the moment I'm thoroughly unamused. Bored to my bones, in fact.'

Abraham changed the subject. 'How are you getting on with Tobias Rush?'

'I haven't seen much of him. He's a little unsettling perhaps, but I've no complaints.'

'Do take care, Thomas. He's a dangerous man and a powerful one.'

'So you've told me. A certain Captain Fayne, however, strikes me as more dangerous.'

'Fayne?'

'The man you and Rush had removed to make way for me. A most unpleasant specimen.'

'Is he? Oh dear. Do let me know if he becomes a serious problem. I'll have a word with Rush. Now, I shall have one of my half-sleeps and hope that inspiration pays a visit. We must keep you fully occupied, mustn't we?'

'Please. Goodbye, Abraham. I'll call again when I've dealt with the next batch.'

There was still no sign of Fayne outside, and Thomas reached his room unmolested. There another pile of paper awaited him, and, with a deep sigh, he took up the first sheet. More of the same, Thomas, more of the same.

After three hours of reading, writing and rewriting, Thomas threw down his quill and stood up. He stretched his back and yawned. He was tired and hungry, and he needed fresh air. The rest of the pile would have to wait.

Having visited the kitchen, which was as obliging as ever, he left the college, turned south into St Aldate's, made his way to Christ Church Meadow, threading a path between long lines of mortars and cannon, and thence towards Merton. The food and the warm afternoon sun did much to lift his spirits and, by the time he reached the Merton gate, he was feeling brave enough to call on Lady Romilly.

In the college courtyard, golden chariots, white horses, singers and lutenists had been replaced by a large troop of the queen's Lifeguards, ready to challenge and, if necessary, dispose of un-welcome intruders. Each trooper carried not only a pike or an arquebus and ammunition, but also a sword and a knife. When their captain asked Thomas his business, he gave his name, mentioned Simon de Pointz, and asked for Lady Romilly. He was escorted to the Warden's lodgings, which the queen and her court had taken over, and told to wait outside. Merton showed signs of the war — soldiers and their paraphernalia, guns and powder, arms and armour — but it was nothing like Pembroke. The queen and her ladies would not have allowed it.

When Jane appeared, black curls framing her face, and dressed today in pink and blue, she was distinctly flushed. 'Master Hill. A surprise. I was quite unprepared. Had we made an appointment?'

'No, madam, and my apologies for surprising you. I was walking in the meadow, the day is warm and it occurred to me to call.
Would you care for a stroll through the Physic Garden? I hear it is
lovely at this time of year.'

Jane hesitated. 'I'm not sure. Her majesty is at her toilette.
She may need me afterwards.'

'If the question is not treasonable, how long does her majesty's
toilette take?'

'Perhaps an hour more.'

'Then let us enjoy the sunshine for exactly fifty-five minutes.'

Jane smiled. 'That would be delightful,' she said, taking his
arm. 'Not a minute more, though.'

On the path towards the garden, they passed a young woman
pulling a handcart. On it was a body wrapped in a dirty sheet. She
was heading for the south wall and, beyond it, the communal grave
Thomas and Simon had seen when they arrived. Thomas put his
hand to his face. The body was not a new one. Jane crossed herself
and looked away. 'Another widow,' she whispered. 'The disease is
everywhere.'

'Too many people in too small a space,' replied Thomas. 'It
seldom occurs in the countryside.'

They followed the path by the river towards the garden. It
was lined by willows, and bulrushes and sedges grew along the
banks. Jane bent to pick fleabane. 'The queen loves gardens. She
hates to see the gardens in the colleges destroyed. Do you know
what this is, Master Hill?'

Thomas examined the fleabane. 'A white and yellow flower of
no particular distinction?'

'Tush. Daisy fleabane is its common name. More properly,
Erigeron strigosus.'

'Madam, you're as learned as Simon de Pointz. Are all the queen's staff instructed in botany?'

Jane laughed. 'It's as well to know a little. The queen herself is very knowledgeable. Thomas, can you not call me Jane?'

'If you wish it, Jane, I can. You're very fond of the queen, are you not?'

'I am. She's a gracious lady with a deep love of nature and art. The more extravagant masques I put down to her rare artistic temperament. The king is devoted to her, as I believe the country would be if they knew her better. Her faith tells against her. In that, she is uncompromising.'

'The country is suffering, Jane,' said Thomas delicately.

'Indeed. The queen knows it.' She paused. 'Thomas, can I entrust you with a secret?'

'Of course.'

'The queen is expecting a child in the spring. Her physician has just confirmed it.'

'Why is it a secret?'

'She fears the reaction of the people.'

'The people will know soon enough.'

'She will go to France for her confinement, and return with the child.'

'Let us hope they both return to peace.'

When they reached the Physic Garden, Jane asked about Thomas's family, and he about hers. She told him that when Sir Edward had died at Edgehill she had returned to York, and joined the queen's court when it arrived there from Holland. In July, she had left the safety of her family home and travelled with the queen to Oxford. She had hated leaving her elderly parents, but had believed it her duty to do so. They had been accompanied by three thousand men and a hundred wagons. The Generalissima had proved herself a most persuasive recruiter. She spoke of the queen's hardiness on the journey, and her kindness to a young woman recently widowed. She spoke also of her husband, whom she had known since they were children, and of her fear that she would now never have children of her own. Thomas told her about Margaret and his nieces, his time as a student in Oxford and his interest in books and philosophy, just managing not to mention Michel de Montaigne.

The garden was tended by a dozen gardeners in leather jerkins and straw hats. It, at least, had so far survived the ravages of war, although at the end of a hot summer it was showing signs of fatigue. Jane and Thomas walked between tidy beds of lavender and violets, and around a patch of mallows. Jane picked a stem of St John's wort. 'And how do you occupy yourself in Oxford, Thomas, when you are not with Master Fletcher?' she asked.

'Abraham has given me work to do. It keeps me busy.'

'You told Francis Fayne that you are on the king's business. May I enquire what business it is?'

Thomas sighed. 'Jane, this is awkward. My work is known to very few – the king, Abraham, Simon de Pointz, Master Rush. I should not tell you.'

'I have entrusted you with a secret, Thomas. Can you not entrust me with one?'

He hesitated. Abraham's censure or Jane's approval. He chose the middle ground. 'I studied mathematics here, as well as philosophy, and have been asked to devise a new group of codes and ciphers.'

'Somehow I knew you would be doing that kind of work. Scholarly and solitary. Is it difficult?'

'Not really. Not too difficult, even a bit dull.'

'No vital secrets?'

'No, no, nothing like that. My role is very minor.'

'I'm sure you underestimate the value of your work. You must be very good at it, or the king would not have given you the responsibility. You will take care, Thomas, won't you? The queen says that Oxford is full of spies, and the king trusts almost no one. I imagine you would be in danger if your work were known.'

'I shall certainly take care, Jane. As should you. I might not be at hand next time you start an unseemly brawl in the street.'

Arm in arm, they strolled around the garden, stopping occasionally to examine one plant or another. Jane told Thomas the Latin name for each one, which he repeated and then immediately forgot. He could not be expected to concentrate on herbs and flowers with this ravishing lady on his arm. He racked his brains for something suitable to contribute to the discussion, and, as usual, it was Montaigne who came to the rescue. 'Gardens and philosophers are often friends,' he said. 'Michel de Montaigne said that he wanted to meet death when he was tending his cabbages.'

'Did he? What did he mean by that?'

'That he was happiest with his cabbages, I suppose, and hoped that was where he would be when he died.'

'What a wise gentleman.'

'Yes. I find him a great support in life. Would you care to borrow a book of his essays?'

'Thank you, Thomas. If you find him a support, I'm sure I shall too.'

Back at Merton, Thomas took his leave outside the Warden's lodgings. 'Do call again soon, Thomas,' said Jane, before disappearing inside. Thomas turned to go. As he did so, he caught a glimpse of a black-clad figure ducking into a doorway on the other side of the courtyard. He was sure it was Tobias Rush. But why would Rush not want to be seen? There must be times when he had reason to visit the queen. Had he seen Thomas with Jane? What if he had? Why hide? Thinking that he must have been mistaken, Thomas was about to return to Pembroke when Jane came running out. 'Thomas, Thomas,' she called, 'the queen wishes to meet you again. Come. I will take you in.' And before he could say anything, she took his hand and led him into the Warden's house.

In the Warden's receiving room, the queen was sitting on a crimson cushion set upon a large oak chair. Around her sat her spaniels and behind her stood two ladies-in-waiting. There was no sign of dwarves. Thomas bowed and stood before her. In a long gown of cream silk, her auburn hair teased into ringlets around her face, and wearing pearls in her ears and at her throat, she looked every inch the Queen of England. When she spoke, however, it was with a hint of a French accent, which he had not noticed at the masque. 'Master Hill. A pleasure to meet you again. Lady Jane tells me you are interested in gardens.' Thomas glanced at Jane and saw the twinkle. Wicked woman.

'Indeed, your majesty. And I have found her to be an excellent tutor. On matters philosophical as well as botanical.'

The queen looked at Jane in surprise. 'Really, Jane? I was not aware that you took an interest in such matters.'

'Oh yes, your majesty,' replied Jane with a grin at Thomas. 'I am particularly fond of Michel de Montaigne. I find him a great support in life.'

'How sensible of you to rely upon a Frenchman, my dear. We are a most practical race.' The queen turned to Thomas. 'And what do you do in Oxford, Master Hill, when you are not walking with Lady Jane?'

'I am his majesty's cryptographer. I deal with messages and despatches coming in and going out.'

'Indeed. I recall his majesty mentioning the matter. Was it your predecessor who was found in an alleyway?'

'I fear so, your majesty. Erasmus Pole.'

'I trust such a fate will not befall you, Master Hill.'

'As do I.'

'Alas, there are many in Oxford who do not share my faith or understand the king's resolve to carry out his duty. The king is a most honourable man and a courageous one. He would rather die than surrender his throne and his right to rule the country. On this, he will not compromise.'

'I believe the country understands this, your majesty.'

'Does it?' The queen sat for a moment in silence; then a broad smile lit up her face. 'I brought three thousand men to Oxford, you know. They called me the Generalissima for it. I rather like the name, don't you?'

'I am sure it is meant as a compliment.'

'So am I. Do take care in Oxford, Master Hill, and take care of Jane Romilly. She is very dear to me. Now, I must be about my affairs. Good day, Master Hill.'

'Good day, your majesty.' Thomas bowed again, took two steps backwards, then turned and left, hoping this was roughly what he was supposed to do. Jane escorted him to the door. Outside, he said, 'A little more warning next time, if you please, madam. Unlike you, I am unaccustomed to being in the royal presence.'

'Your conduct did you credit, Thomas. What did you make of the Generalissima?'

'I would not care to cross her. Formidable, I believe, is the word for her in both English and French.'

'She has a kind heart. And she is quite devoted to the king, as he is to her.'

'Is she always accompanied by waiting ladies and plump spaniels?'

'Always.' Jane reached up and lightly kissed Thomas's cheek. '*Au revoir*, Thomas.' And she was gone before Thomas thought to mention Rush.

At Pembroke, any hope of reaching his room unimpeded was swiftly dashed by the sight of Fayne lounging in the courtyard with what looked like a group of fawning admirers. He stood half a head taller than any of them and was evidently holding court. His voice carried easily around the yard, bouncing off the wall of the chapel at the northern end. 'She's a pretty wench, and most accommodating. Knows a trick or two, I can tell you. I find it's the high-born ones who do. The tavern girls could learn a lot from them.' Fayne looked up and saw Thomas. If his audience were hoping to hear more about the high-born lady, they were disappointed. Fayne pushed past them and strode up to Thomas, blocking the route to his room. Unless Thomas's nose betrayed him, the man had taken strong drink, and a good deal of it. He smelt like a brewery.

'Well, well. The bookseller has returned to us. Just what we need in time of war, gentlemen, eh? A bookseller. Bound to strike fear into the hearts of the enemy. Perhaps we should have a regiment of them.' Fayne and his companions laughed loudly.

For a moment, Thomas was tempted to land a punch on the grinning face. What he lacked in height, he more than made up for in speed and skill, and he knew he could put Fayne on his back without undue difficulty. That, of course, was what the vile creature wanted — a reason to have him thrown out of the college — and his companions would swear to a man that the blow was unprovoked. Thomas stepped aside and carried on towards his room, ignoring the vulgar jeers that followed him.

He locked the door behind him and poured himself a glass from the bottle of good claret Silas had thoughtfully provided. Then he sat down at the table to tackle the rest of the pile. After two dreary messages, however, his mind wandered. Not long ago, he was a respectable and unremarkable bookseller and writer of minor papers on mathematics and philosophy. Now he had conversed with the king and the queen, been abused by a drunken oaf of a soldier, seen for himself what war could do to a town as lovely as Oxford, met a beautiful lady with eyes of different colours, and been warned by almost everyone to beware of everyone else. Why in the name of God had he allowed himself to be caught up in this bloody war? Why had he not stayed in Romsey and taken care of Margaret and the girls? That was his proper place, not here among soldiers, beggars and spies. The harvest would be in, there would be the first touch of autumn in the air, and the stream would be alive with jumping trout. He loved early autumn in the countryside. In this benighted town there were no seasons, just noise, stench and death. With a sigh, he forced himself from his reverie and went back to work.

After three more days and nights, dozens of dreary reports and an almost total lack of contact with the world outside his room, Thomas could face no more. Despite his labours, the number of incoming reports had at least matched the number he had decrypted, and the pile on his table was no lower. After breakfast supplied by the kitchen, he locked his door, strode through the courtyard and left the college. It was time to pay a call he should already have paid.

The shop stood on the corner of Broad Street and Turl Street, not far from Balliol College. Braving the morning crowds in Market Street and the beggars and whores in Turl Street, he walked briskly to it. The outside was as he remembered it — a narrow two-storey building with glazed windows and timber framing, the upper storey jutting out over the street. It was typical of the buildings that had sprung up all over Oxford sixty or seventy years earlier, and had probably been built for a local merchant. Now it was home to John Porter's bookshop.

Thomas pushed open the door and stepped inside. Despite the windows, it was dark enough for candles to have been lit and placed on a table in the middle of the room. There were bookshelves around the walls and two uncomfortable-looking chairs by the table. Unlike Thomas's shop, however, there were few books. No untidy piles on the table or the floor and not very many on the shelves. As Thomas looked around, an old man came bustling in from a back room. He was exactly as Thomas remembered him and exactly as a bookseller should be. Unkempt, shabby, down-at-heel, for as long as Thomas had known him John Porter had put him in mind of Chaucer's clerk in his *Canterbury Tales* — spectacles perched on the end of his nose, unruly white hair which might not have been trimmed for a year, and hands stained with dirt and ink.

'Good morning, sir,' he croaked at Thomas. 'Everything you can see is for sale, and I will make you a good price. Are you in search of a particular book?'

Thomas stepped a little closer. 'John, do you not recognize an old customer?'

The old man peered over his spectacles at Thomas, looked puzzled, and then smiled a toothless smile. 'Good Lord, if it isn't Thomas Hill. And what brings you to this benighted town at such a time?'

Thomas held out his hand and took the old man's. His skin was as thin and dry as parchment. 'Good morning, John. A pleasure to see you again. I have come to visit Abraham.'

John Porter nodded. 'Of course. Your old tutor, as I recall. It must be more than a year since I last saw him. No more books for him, I fear. His eyes were getting very bad.'

'He sees almost nothing now. Shapes and shadows only, he says, although his mind is still clear. And how do you fare, John?'

The old man spread his arms in a gesture of resignation. 'As you can tell, Thomas, it is not the shop it used to be. The University Press has closed, it's impossible to get books from London and I'm reduced to what you see. Not that it matters much. There are no scholars, and few soldiers care to spend their pay on books. I should have an inn or a bakery. Then I'd be a wealthy man.'

'You'd be a hopeless innkeeper or baker, John. You'd drink the ale and eat the cakes. Much better to stick to your books.'

John Porter laughed. 'Perhaps you're right. Is it any better in Romsey? It is Romsey, isn't it?'

'It is. I don't sell many books either, and we have had trouble with soldiers, so I suppose it's much the same. Let's hope the war ends soon and we can get back to normal.'

'Normal. I've forgotten what that is. I hardly dare go out after dark for fear of being robbed or worse, I go for days without seeing a customer, and the army takes everything there is. I couldn't even buy an egg last week.'

'Do their majesties' households not read?'

'They do not. I daresay the king's lot are too busy having their portraits painted, and the queen's being lectured on her faith. When she's not throwing money away on her masques, that is. I heard the last one was her most extravagant yet.'

'So I heard.' Thomas thought it prudent not to mention that he had actually attended the masque. 'This war is a terrible thing, is it not, John? What would Queen Elizabeth have said if she'd known what was going to happen to the country less than fifty years after she'd gone?'

'I shudder to think. And what will men say fifty years from now? That we destroyed England or that we set her on a new road to peace and prosperity?'

'I suppose that will depend upon the outcome. It's hard to imagine an England without a king or without a parliament, yet one of them may not survive.'

'If they can't find a way to work together, one of them indeed may not. I'm a Royalist at heart, if only because, like every other man alive, I've never known an England without a monarch. Yet, in Oxford, for all the university's traditional support for the king, most of the townspeople are against him. And the longer his court and his army are here, the more they're against him. It doesn't take much to understand why.'

Thinking of the Pembroke courtyard, Thomas could only agree. Filth and squalor among the beauty of the colleges, Francis Fayne and his like in place of books and scholars. The University's support would soon be wavering, too. He was about to say so, when the door opened and in came two familiar figures. One was a tall, bald Franciscan friar, the other a slim, elegant lady in a long yellow coat and a wide-brimmed yellow bonnet.

'Your luck has changed, John,' cried Thomas. 'Here are two enthusiastic customers, thirsting to spend their money. No need to offer them special prices. They'll happily pay as much as you ask.'

'Thomas,' said Simon sternly, 'you know perfectly well that Franciscans eschew worldly possessions. I have no money, even for books. I am merely escorting Lady Romilly, who wishes to purchase a present for a friend.'

'He is not a close friend,' added Jane, pointedly ignoring Thomas, 'so a small present will suffice. Can you suggest anything, Master Porter?'

'Do you know anything of his tastes, madam?' enquired Porter.

'His knowledge of plants and flowers is pitifully slight. Have you anything of that sort?'

'I fear not, madam. Is he perhaps of an artistic turn of mind?'

'Literary, I think, rather than artistic.'

'Then may I suggest a volume of poetry?'

'You may. If you have concluded your business with this gentleman, of course.'

Porter glanced at Thomas, who was thoroughly confused. 'While Master Hill is considering the matter, madam, allow me to show you what I have,' he replied, leading Jane to a corner of the shop where a few dusty volumes sat on a shelf.

'Take no notice, Thomas,' whispered Simon. 'You are the last person she wanted to find here. Better disappear.'

Taking the hint, Thomas waved a farewell to his friend and slipped out of the shop. A book of poetry for a literary friend who knew nothing about flowers was grounds for hope. But no more

Milton, please. If John Porter had them, Shakespeare's sonnets would be excellent. He would commit the best of them to memory when he was back in Romsey and time permitted. In Oxford, alas, time did not permit.

He could not dwell on the matter. He felt guilty enough at having missed most of a morning's work, and he should get back to it without delay. The pile of paper would soon be growing again. Putting the lure of the meadows out of his mind, he went straight back to Pembroke.

The remainder of the day and part of the night were spent with quill and ink, encryptions and decryptions. Erasmus Pole must either have been a genius or, more probably, inclined to overlook some of the paper that came his way. It was hard to believe that one man could have coped adequately with the volume. When at last Thomas could do no more, his eyes and head ached and his hand was shaking from holding the quill.

Early the next morning he struggled awake to answer a knock on his door. It was Silas. 'Good morning, sir. Master Fletcher asks that you join him at the gatehouse. I've just taken him there.'

'Do you know why, Silas?'

'He said something about seeing the town.'

'But he can't see.'

'I know, sir. That's why he wants you.'

Torn between duty and pleasure, Thomas had no difficulty in choosing pleasure. Another diversion, and Abraham's company was always good. He pulled on a thick shirt and followed Silas to the gatehouse, where Abraham was waiting for him. There was an early-autumn chill in the air and the old man wore a heavy cloak and a hat. 'Good morning, Abraham,' called Thomas as he approached. 'I gather you want a walk around the town.'

'I do. And I need you to accompany me to make sure I don't fall into any drains. I have enough problems without being covered in shit.'

'I should be delighted, although I have had no breakfast and my pile of papers is a foot tall.' Thomas took Abraham's elbow and guided him out of the college. 'Is there anywhere in particular you would like to go?'

'Around the meadow and by the river, along High Street and into a college. I want to find out if I can tell which one it is by the sounds and smells.'

'Very well. Let us be off.'

They made their way cautiously down St Aldate's as far as the entrance to Christ Church Meadow, where they turned in and walked towards the river on the other side. Here the sounds were of the comings and goings of soldiers and townsfolk about their business. Men and women were cleaning and polishing the long lines of artillery pieces. I suppose a clean cannon must be more deadly than a dirty one, thought Thomas. More impressive, anyway. Some thirty yards from the river bank, they stopped.

'I can hear the river and I can smell it,' said Abraham. 'How is it looking today?'

'It's running slowly. The level is low.'

'I thought so. The sound is gentle. Last winter it was running very fast down to the Thames.'

They walked along the bank, neither man saying much, until Abraham stopped again. 'Last night, I had a premonition of impending death. It rather frightened me, Thomas. That's why I asked you to accompany me this morning. I feel it might be the last time I leave the college.'

Thomas was taken aback. This was most unlike his old friend, the most rational of men. 'Oh come now, Abraham. It's not like you to pay heed to such a thing. I daresay you'll live to be a hundred.'

Abraham laughed. 'Good God, I do hope not. I'd be deaf and crippled, as well as blind. Still, it did shake me. Foolish, of course. I'm an old man and we all have to die some time.'

'We do, but not yet, if you please. I'd have to carry you back to Pembroke.'

Another laugh. 'I'd best hang on, then.' They entered High Street at the eastern end and passed University College on their left. 'Not University, then?' enquired Abraham, who had sensed where they were. Thinking that he might make Abraham's task more difficult, Thomas led him up Catte Street, along Broad Street and down Turl Street as far as Lincoln College. Inside the college gate, he stopped. Abraham sniffed the air and listened. 'Trust you to try a deception, Thomas. It didn't work, though. I smelled the coal smoke and heard the beggars. This is Lincoln.'

'How do you know? It could be Exeter.'

'It feels small and I can hear the kitchen. The Lincoln kitchen is just inside the gate.' He sniffed again. 'Fish for dinner, I think.'

'Fish, certainly.' Thomas's nose seldom let him down.

'There. One sense replaced by another. Although a nose is a poor substitute for a good pair of eyes.'

'I sometimes wish my nose was rather less good. Especially in this town. Are you ready to return?'

'I am. Thank you, Thomas. I have enjoyed the walk.' They left Lincoln and walked along Market Street and down Cornmarket towards Pembroke. Both, as ever, were heaving with market stalls and traders, and Thomas had some difficulty in guiding Abraham through them without tumbling into a drain. On the corner of Queen Street, Thomas noticed a tall soldier and his lady walking away from them along High Street, and having what sounded like an animated conversation. With a shock, Thomas realized that the man was Fayne and the lady Jane Romilly. He stared after them. He saw Jane put a hand on the captain's arm. He went cold. Abraham sensed his change of mood. 'What is it, Thomas?'

'Oh, nothing. I may have just had a premonition, that's all.'

'Foolish things, premonitions, I've been told. Put it out of your mind.'

'Good advice. I shall try.'

With Abraham safely back in his room, Thomas left Pembroke again and returned to the meadow. He did not feel like being cooped up in his room and he wanted to think. He retraced their steps past the rows of artillery and towards the river, where he found a quiet place to sit. Jane had said that she was no more than acquainted with Fayne. Yet they were walking together, and she had put her hand on his arm. Then he remembered Fayne's vulgar boasts about a high-born lady. God's wounds, surely not Jane Romilly? It was beyond belief. What on earth would she see in a loud-mouthed, ill-mannered oaf like Fayne? And why had she lied? Or had he misunderstood? No, he had not misunderstood. At the masque, she had been quite clear. Clear but untruthful, it appeared.

For nearly an hour Thomas sat and pondered. He was angry and jealous. Angry with her for deceiving him, jealous of him for having Jane. Suddenly he got up. Enough of this, Thomas. You're a fool. Her business is no business of yours. Forget it. You've work to do.

*

For two days, Thomas attacked the pile of papers with renewed vigour. The despatches were still as interesting as one of Knox's sermons, but he set himself the task of getting through them twice as quickly as before. It helped to keep his mind off other matters. He left his room only for food and drink and brief bouts of exercise. He did not want to run into Fayne.

After one such excursion, however, he found that Fayne had run into him. Returning to his room, he found the lock broken and his clothes and papers thrown around the floor. He went at once to fetch Silas, who tut-tutted at the mess, arranged to have it cleared up and replaced the broken lock with a new one. While he was working on this, Thomas asked him about Fayne.

'I don't like him,' said Silas. 'He's rude to the college servants and finds fault whenever he can. Do you think Captain Fayne did this?'

'It is possible. Who else has a reason? His nose must still be out of joint at being turfed out of the room. A man like him would take offence easily and harbour grudges. He seems to have time on his hands.'

'That he does. I couldn't rightly say how he spends his days other than entertaining women in his room. Common whores, all of them. I haven't seen him doing any soldiering.'

'No ladies, Silas? Decent ladies, I mean.'

'Not that I've seen.'

'Do you know anything else about him, Silas?'

'Only that he comes from a wealthy and respected family.'

'So he told me.'

'You don't think this has anything to do with your work, sir? Not that I know what that is, of course,' Silas added hurriedly.

'Possibly, although, as far as I can tell, nothing has been taken. It looks more like an act of malicious spite to me.'

Silas finished the lock and handed Thomas a key. 'There, sir, good as new. I'll keep both spares.'

'Thank you, Silas, I'm obliged.'

'You will take care, Master Hill, won't you?' said Silas before he left. 'Oxford is not the place it was when you were a scholar.'

'You're the fifth person to tell me to take care, Silas. Anyone would think I'm a child.'

'My apologies, sir.'

'No apologies necessary, Silas. Thank you for your concern and be sure that I shall take care, just as everyone wishes me to.'

Thomas sat at his table and gazed once more at the pile of recovered papers. A pity Fayne did not take them away, he thought. Then he wouldn't have to read the wretched things. He was sure it was Fayne. He certainly hoped so. If not, it was serious. Someone knew who he was and what he did. Someone distinctly unfriendly.

Another day of drudgery, then another, and Thomas was beginning to wonder if he might be on his way to the House of Bedlam. Pages and pages of badly encrypted reports from under-occupied military commanders, the occasional equally tedious despatch found on an enemy messenger, and orders from the king, largely consisting of demands for absolute loyalty and stead-fastness at a time of grave danger to the country. The madhouse looked a more likely destination than a bookshop in Romsey.

He had just about banished Jane from his mind when she arrived. She carried a small parcel and had a livid bruise on her cheek. 'Good morning, Thomas,' she said cheerily. 'I trust that I find you well. May I come in?'

Thomas did not reply, but stepped aside to allow her into the room. She looked about.

'Not large but almost dry, and adequate to your needs, I hope.' Still Thomas said nothing. 'Thomas, what on earth is the matter? Have you lost your tongue?'

'I had not expected to see you.'

'And I had not expected you to be struck dumb. I have come to borrow Montaigne's *Essais*, as you suggested I should, and in return I have brought you this.' She handed him the parcel. 'Are you not going to see what it is?' Thomas unwrapped it. It was a slim volume entitled *The Sonnets of William Shakespeare*. On the title page, Jane had written *To Thomas from his friend Jane, with affection*. He should have been pleased. He put it down on the table.

'Thank you. Here are the *Essais*.'

She took them and looked at him quizzically.

'Thomas, you are out of sorts. Please tell me what is troubling you.' Without invitation, she sat on the edge of the bed and waited for a reply. It came eventually.

'My apologies, madam. I have had much work to do.'

'Is that all? I sense there is more.'

'I would not wish to come between you and another man.'

'What other man, Thomas? What are you talking about?'

'I daresay I misunderstood. I thought you told me that you and Captain Fayne were merely acquaintances.'

Jane's hand went to the bruise on her cheek. 'Captain Fayne. So that's it. And what exactly has discomfited you, if I may ask?' Her voice was suddenly sharp.

'It is not my affair.'

'Indeed it is not. For your information, however, I have known Captain Fayne since we were children. Our families were neighbours.'

'You were more than neighbourly when I saw you together in the town.'

Jane jumped off the bed and looked furious. 'Have you been spying on me? How dare you!'

'Certainly not. I happened to see you in High Street.'

'Did you now? Well, you won't be seeing me again.' She threw the *Essais* on to the bed and stormed out.

Thomas stood and stared at the door. You handled that well, Thomas, he thought. You clod. Although I'd wager it was Fayne who gave her that bruise.

Not many minutes later, there was another knock on the door. Not daring to hope that she had returned, Thomas opened it. She had not returned. Captain Fayne had, and he was smirking.

'I saw your visitor leaving, Hill. Seemed upset. Take the advice of a man who knows, and take her for a run while you may.'

'Go away, Fayne. You are offensive.' He made to close the door, but Fayne held it open.

'Why don't you go and sleep in the stable, Hill? The mare might join you there. She enjoys a morning gallop. Then I can have my room back.'

With a shove, Thomas closed the door and locked it. God in his heaven, what next?

What next came as a surprise: Silas's boy with an urgent message from Abraham. Thomas was to come at once.

In his rooms, Abraham was waiting impatiently. When

Thomas knocked, he was summoned brusquely in. 'Thomas? You've work to do.'

'Good day, Abraham. Why so urgent?'

'This is why,' said the old man, holding up a rolled document. 'It arrived this morning from London. It was found on a man known to be one of Pym's most trusted messengers, leaving the city at night on the Cambridge road. Quite by chance, the man was apprehended by a troop of our dragoons, and thoroughly searched. They found this hidden inside the lining of his hat.'

'What is it?' asked Thomas.

'That is what I want you to find out. It's quite long, and it was hidden. A double precaution. A very fortunate interception, which might be important. Hidden messages often are, more so the longer ones. The messenger was no help. They got nothing out of him before he died. Here it is.' Abraham handed Thomas the roll. 'Can you start at once?'

'I can. I'll give you the plain text as soon as I can.'

'Good. I have another young man who can do all the routine work. I want you to concentrate solely on this. And, Thomas, be particularly careful. Say nothing to anyone but me. And do not make any copies. We don't want this falling into the wrong hands. I sense that it is valuable.'

CHAPTER 6

Thank God for the dragoons who found this. Something promising at last. Thomas laid the document on his table, smoothed it out and studied it. Good rag paper, an unremarkable hand.

URF UBD HE XQB TF KGA OEMD RRFUO TLC WMG LRB WHT R XHGORKZ IO KPW769

WA MQFV BVMF HPL ZFTD RVV57 4SEWMFREJ VGL SVKMGE 852 GTSC WZTD QE

TIJG IVL GJT RA KDOE IK EOJAAQLV GGJR MQU IOIGSI GRQF HBFZG JGY

ALG EE OLWEEA GJR YIFS1 82AEL2 64SGE SC AAD ZVY JP KP WXR JB JTN XBZ77

5XNW WJBS LA LWAK371 EAIH TPA AD RVV BAP TWPVV AGDN WWJ URR VUT

IW EW HTI QCT WY QDT37 1IE852 769UMHT RKC CONT WSGV WMG IEN DJEE KW

IHV ZW PNU EAIH371 ZV GJR YIFSS NQ DA BV NGGCVL LD SVMC IRLKW DN

KMJ BS WINDU IITAE KW42177 5OX LCIVK IJM LXMV IFS PCI UT FFZ

SEPI MZTNJQGCOW3 71E ZDWZTD QE SZGJ GYB LD 574SKIFS RVIV N GFL

OX LC QFV WV AZPLCJJX NX IF TNU BG IHZA OP RJWGC

He started counting. On a single sheet there were ten lines of text, made up of four hundred and fifty-six letters, forty-five numbers and one hundred and thirty eight spaces. This intercepted message was not just longer than any other he had seen: the combinations of letters, spaces and numbers had a different feel to them. Ignoring all spaces, which would almost certainly have been inserted at random, the numbers appeared in sequences of three or six. That suggested that they were probably codewords, perhaps for names. If so, the text was a nomenclator — a mix of code and cipher — which would make it more difficult to break than a plain cipher, but still breakable. There would be clues somewhere.

Despite the length of the text, the sender did not reveal himself at all. Thomas studied the writer's hand and tried to visualize him. He tried fat and thin, short and tall, old and young. He tried divining the man's nature — mean, generous, kind, cruel. Nothing. After he had stared at the text for an hour, the man who had encrypted it remained hidden. Thomas's magic, for once, was not working.

'So much for art,' he said aloud, 'time to try science.' Once again, he wrote out the letters of the alphabet across the top of a sheet of paper. Then he counted the number of times each letter appeared in the message. He wrote this number below each letter, and E, A and T under the highest numbers; then he examined the juxtaposition of each to other letters, found three instances of double letters, and concluded which encrypted letter represented each of them. He repeated the process to find the letters I, O, S and R, and tentatively applied this to the first few lines. For this exercise, all numbers were ignored. The result was nonsense. As he had expected, this was not a straightforward alphabetic cipher, either shifted by a keyword or mixed by a system of substitution. At least two substitutions had been used, perhaps more, and there was still the matter of the numbers. A double or even triple alphabetic substitution would eventually yield to close analysis and a little intuition, but it would take time. And Thomas's instincts were shouting at him that this decryption was going to require all his skills. Hoping that sustenance would bring more success, he put down his quill and went to find food.

Fortified by an excellent mutton stew from Silas's kitchen and half a bottle of claret from his cellar, Thomas lit a cheap tallow candle and started again. This time he attacked the forty-five numbers. He still suspected that they were codes for names, but needed to be certain. Assuming that the numbers were actually in sequences of three digits, the sixes being two names together, he found eight separate numbers, of which 769, 574, 852 and 775 were repeated once, and 371 occurred four times. That made a nomenclator almost certain, and decoding 371 would be a huge step forward. After two more hours, however, and four more candles, he had made no further progress. He had identified not a single word from the letters or numbers, and had no more idea what secrets they held than when Abraham had handed the paper to him. Beyond the facts that a complex system of encryption and encoding had been used, and that the message must be important, he still knew nothing about it. Without bothering to undress, he lay down and slept.

Next morning, Thomas went first to visit Abraham, hoping his old friend would provide an insight into the problem. He described the text in detail – forty-five numbers, 456 letters and 138 spaces. He told Abraham how he had approached the task, the old man nodding encouragingly as he did so, and finally he told him that he had learned nothing. They discussed poly-alphabetic substitutions, nomenclators, variable Caesar shifts, homophonic substitutions, keywords and codewords. At the end of the morning, they had agreed only that this was not a message intended to be decrypted quickly, even by someone with the key. It was too complex. So it was not a standard military despatch, and, although important, would not be battlefield-urgent. That made it of strategic rather than tactical value. There was no context, and there were no other clues. They still had no idea what it was about, who had written it or for whom it was intended. Abraham could tell from Thomas's voice that he was tired and frustrated.

'My best advice is that you put it away for today. Go for a walk. Hill's magic might return with the dawn.'

Taking heed, Thomas spent the afternoon by the river, and the evening with his friend Montaigne. He fell asleep thinking of Polly and Lucy, and of Jane Romilly, who had stormed out of his room in a fierce temper.

The next three days were spent on the intercepted message. The marks on the paper had become his enemies. He tried a variety of double and triple alphabetic substitutions, he tried assuming that all the numbers were meaningless, that they hid keywords, that the message was in Latin, that it had been written backwards, and he even guessed at a few possible keywords to create alphabetic shifts, such as PARLIAMENT, OXFORD and PROTESTANT. The guesswork was futile without at least some facts, and he knew it. He gave it up when Montaigne tapped gently on his shoulder, and whispered in his ear, 'Thomas Hill, have I taught you nothing? Rational thought is greatly superior to intuition. Think, don't guess.'

On the fourth morning, he went again to see Abraham, and again reported his lack of progress. Abraham tried to be encouraging. 'Thomas, you *have* made progress,' he said. 'You know a good many things that this cipher is not.'

'Indeed. But if I have to eliminate all the things it is not before discovering what it is, I shall be even older than you when I finally do so.'

Abraham laughed, and then voiced the thought that both had so far left unspoken. 'Could we be facing Vigenère, Thomas?'

'It's possible, of course, although the numbers must also be serving some purpose. Have you heard of a square used with numerical codes?'

'I haven't, but that doesn't mean they don't exist. If the numbers are codes, the cipher will work just as well if they are ignored.'

'Abraham, a Vigenère cipher has never been broken, with or without word codes.'

'I know. Trust a Frenchman to come up with such a diabolical thing. Tedious to encrypt, tedious to decrypt, and proof against even you, Thomas, unless you can divine the keyword.'

'I can try, Abraham, but you know it'll take a miracle.'

Abraham was thoughtful. 'Perhaps not. Look again at the numbers. Could they be telling us which rows on the square to use? If so, the cipher would still be secure against anyone unfamiliar with Monsieur Vigenère.' He picked up a thin strip of wood with a straight edge and passed it to Thomas. 'If it's Vigenère, you'll need this.'

Thomas took the strip of wood. 'Thank you. I'll assume it's Vigenère and try the numbers again. Prayers thrice daily, Abraham, please. I shall need them.'

*

That evening, Tobias Rush visited again. All in black, silver-topped cane in hand, he called to tell Thomas that his letter had been safely delivered to Margaret. 'Was there a reply?' asked Thomas hopefully.

'Unfortunately, no. The courier had to reach Southampton by dusk and could not afford to wait,' said Rush with a shrug. 'No doubt your sister will find a way of writing back, however. Do let me know when she does.' He paused. 'And how did you enjoy the masque?'

'Masque? Oh, the masque. Remarkable. A remarkable entertainment.'

'Indeed. Their majesties have unerring eyes for beauty. And speaking of beauty, how did you find Lady Romilly? Well, I trust?'

'Quite well. An unusual lady.'

'You refer to her eyes, I imagine?'

'In part, yes. They are striking. But not just her eyes. She's a lady of spirit.' As I am only too well aware, thought Thomas.

Rush smiled his thin smile, and changed the subject. 'How goes your work, Master Hill?' he asked, looking casually around the room. His working papers were underneath others on the table. Just as well, thought Thomas, although I must be more careful in future. Abraham had insisted on absolute secrecy, even from Master Rush. He dissembled. 'Routine matters only. Not much has changed since I last worked with codes. I would prefer something more interesting.'

'Oh? Have the enemy not offered you anything at all appropriate to your skills?'

'Not as yet, sir.'

'Be sure to let me know if they do. The king has impressed

upon me my duty to assist you in any way that I can. I would not wish either of us to disappoint him. Now, I shall bid you good day.' And he was gone.

Odd how he's here one minute and gone the next, thought Thomas, and how he changes the course of a discussion. A hard book to read and a hard bird to cage.

Work on the numbers began before dawn. If this was a Vigenère square, the king's enemies would assume that its secrets were safe and would see no need to change their plans. The square itself had remained unbroken for over seventy years. Using the strip of wood as a guide, Thomas began by writing out the square.

If the message had been encrypted using the square, each letter would have twenty-six possible encryptions. The letters in the top row represented the letters used in the message, and the letters of the keyword were contained in the first column. So if the keyword began with the letter T, the letter O would have been encrypted as H.

Then he wrote out the forty-five digits at the top of the message. For some time, he sat and stared at them. Apart from the duplications, he saw no patterns. If the numbers were indicating the rows of the square to be used for decrypting, any number above twenty-six must be either a null or have some other function. Proceeding on this basis, he divided the digits into arbitrary one- and two-digit numbers and tried decrypting the first line according to the rows indicated by his selection. When the word DOG appeared, he thought he was on to something. But when the following words turned out as KTLO, BQICMS and XPD, he knew that the dog's appearance was no more than chance.

	A	B	C	D	E	F	G	H	I	J	K	L	M	N	O	P	Q	R	S	T	U	V	W	X	Y	Z
A	A	B	C	D	E	F	G	H	I	J	K	L	M	N	O	P	Q	R	S	T	U	V	W	X	Y	Z
B	B	C	D	E	F	G	H	I	J	K	L	M	N	O	P	Q	R	S	T	U	V	W	X	Y	Z	A
C	C	D	E	F	G	H	I	J	K	L	M	N	O	P	Q	R	S	T	U	V	W	X	Y	Z	A	B
D	D	E	F	G	H	I	J	K	L	M	N	O	P	Q	R	S	T	U	V	W	X	Y	Z	A	B	C
E	E	F	G	H	I	J	K	L	M	N	O	P	Q	R	S	T	U	V	W	X	Y	Z	A	B	C	D
F	F	G	H	I	J	K	L	M	N	O	P	Q	R	S	T	U	V	W	X	Y	Z	A	B	C	D	E
G	G	H	I	J	K	L	M	N	O	P	Q	R	S	T	U	V	W	X	Y	Z	A	B	C	D	E	F
H	H	I	J	K	L	M	N	O	P	Q	R	S	T	U	V	W	X	Y	Z	A	B	C	D	E	F	G
I	I	J	K	L	M	N	O	P	Q	R	S	T	U	V	W	X	Y	Z	A	B	C	D	E	F	G	H
J	J	K	L	M	N	O	P	Q	R	S	T	U	V	W	X	Y	Z	A	B	C	D	E	F	G	H	I
K	K	L	M	N	O	P	Q	R	S	T	U	V	W	X	Y	Z	A	B	C	D	E	F	G	H	I	J
L	L	M	N	O	P	Q	R	S	T	U	V	W	X	Y	Z	A	B	C	D	E	F	G	H	I	J	K
M	M	N	O	P	Q	R	S	T	U	V	W	X	Y	Z	A	B	C	D	E	F	G	H	I	J	K	L
N	N	O	P	Q	R	S	T	U	V	W	X	Y	Z	A	B	C	D	E	F	G	H	I	J	K	L	M
O	O	P	Q	R	S	T	U	V	W	X	Y	Z	A	B	C	D	E	F	G	H	I	J	K	L	M	N
P	P	Q	R	S	T	U	V	W	X	Y	Z	A	B	C	D	E	F	G	H	I	J	K	L	M	N	O
Q	Q	R	S	T	U	V	W	X	Y	Z	A	B	C	D	E	F	G	H	I	J	K	L	M	N	O	P
R	R	S	T	U	V	W	X	Y	Z	A	B	C	D	E	F	G	H	I	J	K	L	M	N	O	P	Q
S	S	T	U	V	W	X	Y	Z	A	B	C	D	E	F	G	H	I	J	K	L	M	N	O	P	Q	R
T	T	U	V	W	X	Y	Z	A	B	C	D	E	F	G	H	I	J	K	L	M	N	O	P	Q	R	S
U	U	V	W	X	Y	Z	A	B	C	D	E	F	G	H	I	J	K	L	M	N	O	P	Q	R	S	T
V	V	W	X	Y	Z	A	B	C	D	E	F	G	H	I	J	K	L	M	N	O	P	Q	R	S	T	U
W	W	X	Y	Z	A	B	C	D	E	F	G	H	I	J	K	L	M	N	O	P	Q	R	S	T	U	V
X	X	Y	Z	A	B	C	D	E	F	G	H	I	J	K	L	M	N	O	P	Q	R	S	T	U	V	W
Y	Y	Z	A	B	C	D	E	F	G	H	I	J	K	L	M	N	O	P	Q	R	S	T	U	V	W	X
Z	Z	A	B	C	D	E	F	G	H	I	J	K	L	M	N	O	P	Q	R	S	T	U	V	W	X	Y

All morning Thomas sat at his table, the encrypted page, sharpened quills, inkpot and a pile of blank papers before him. The pile diminished as the floor became covered in used and discarded ones. Just as well Abraham had laid his hands on a good supply. By the time his stomach started complaining, however, he had achieved very little. Nothing, in fact, except the growing certainty that these numbers did not hold the key to the rows. He had tried adding and subtracting, transposing the digits of the higher numbers, multiplying and dividing — all to no effect. Apart from dog, not a single plain word had appeared from the text. It was a bad start. He did not need the unwelcome complication of codewords, tricks or traps. What he did need was a clue to guide him to the keyword. And he needed fresh air.

Emerging into the daylight, Thomas was greeted by a beautiful late-summer day — dry and windless. The Pembroke courtyard was still a military dump, young officers and their women still lounged about doing very little, and the stench of human waste was still sickening, but the sky was cloudless and the sun warm. Thank God one was permanent and the other, God willing, merely temporary. Perhaps very temporary if he could break the encryption.

Thinking that he had been so preoccupied with the message that he had again lost touch with what was happening beyond his room, he wandered down to the meadow. As always, it was a mass of soldiers and their weaponry, and, unless he was mistaken, there was even more hustle and bustle than before. No one made any objection as he walked among the lines of artillery pieces and the knots of men gathered around them, for the first time paying the armoury more than passing attention. He stopped to examine a huge cannon loaded on to a long flat cart with wheels of different sizes. Two shafts protruded from the back, into which a horse would be harnessed. Wondering how far a ball would travel when fired from such a monster, he stooped to peer down the barrel. There was a tap on his shoulder and he turned to see a grinning artilleryman. In a thick shirt, leather trousers to the knee, woollen stockings and wooden clogs, the poor man must have been slowly cooking.

'Take care, sir,' he said cheerfully. 'If you fall in, I'll have to fire you out.' He spoke with a strong accent – German perhaps, or Dutch.

Thomas returned the smile. 'I fancy that would damage me more than the enemy.' To make conversation, he asked, 'How many horses does it take to pull this?'

'One in the shafts, sir, and six pairs in the traces,' adding helpfully, 'It can fire a two-pound ball as far as a mile.'

And knock over a line of men like so many skittles, thought Thomas. Lifeless skittles if they're hit by a ball from this beast. 'There's much going on today. Do you know what's happening?'

The man laughed. 'God bless you sir, I'm just a poor soldier from Amsterdam. No one tells me anything.'

'Nothing at all?'

'Not much anyway. We've been told to make ready to march. Where to and for what, we'll find out when we get there.'

'No rumours at all?'

'Gloucester's most people's choice as Prince Rupert is still laying siege to the town, but I've had a wager on Reading. They say the Earl of Essex is heading that way. If he is, we'll be sent to stop him reaching London, and I'll be five guineas richer.'

'I hope you are, and that you're able to collect it.'

'If I'm not, sir, it'll go to my wife. I mean widow. That's the agreement.'

Thomas nodded. 'Good luck then.' A Dutch mercenary, fighting for a living. Hardly a matter of principle for him. Not all the cannon were as enormous as his. As he walked down the line,

Thomas counted four other types, right down to a little fellow with its own wheels. He stepped around heaps of rope, piles of cannon-balls of different sizes, blankets, sacking and barrels of powder. What an immense undertaking war was. Immense and costly — and not only in money. How many men would die when these merciless destroyers started dealing out death? A thousand? Five thousand? Ten thousand?

At the end of the line, he came to the river and looked across. In the fields on the far bank, infantry were gathering. Among their tents he could see pikemen in their helmets and breastplates practising their drills, and musketeers with their long-barrelled matchlocks, ammunition, cleaning prickers, gun rests and swords. The word 'apostle' came to him — it was what the small flasks of powder on their bandoliers were called. An odd choice of word. The wise musketeer measured out each charge very carefully before going into battle. Too little and his musket would not fire, too much and he might go up in flames. Who would be a soldier? Having to carry pounds of equipment all over the countryside, sleeping in the open or, at best, in a leaky tent, surviving on scraps, and if the enemy do not kill you, you'll probably kill yourself. Infantry drilling, artillery making ready — there was something afoot, to be sure.

From the meadow Thomas made his way to the Crown. He was in need of refreshment before going back into battle with that wretched message. As before, the inn was busy — soldiers enjoying a final drink or two before marching off to war, perhaps. Thomas had to shoulder his way in and shout to be heard over the hubbub. Having ordered a bottle of claret and a rabbit pie, he looked about for somewhere to sit. Seeing no spare chairs, he made his way towards the back of the inn, hoping to find one there. Right at the back, at the same table as when he had first seen the man, was Fayne, unmistakable in a short crimson coat and tight crimson breeches. There were three others with him, and a game of hazard was in progress. Despite himself, Thomas moved quietly up behind Fayne, the better to observe the game. As a student, he had prided himself on being rather good at it, and had paid for many a meal out of his winnings. It was a game of chance, but a mathematician's knowledge of the odds and a quick way with numbers were a decided advantage. It would be interesting to see how well these soldiers played.

The man on Fayne's right was the caster, the man opposite him the setter, who acted as banker for the three players opposed to the caster. As Thomas watched, he picked up the two dice, shook them in his hand and rolled them out. They showed a five and a six. The caster cheered and the setter pushed a pile of coins towards him. It was the setter's job to make sure the right amounts were paid out on each hand. As different combinations of main and chance points were played at different odds, he had to have a quick head for figures. Sensible fellow, thought Thomas. He must have set a main point of seven, thus winning with a throw of eleven. Seven was very slightly the best number to set as a main in hazard, and the wise caster never chose anything else. His opponents groaned and fished in their pockets for more coins. 'The devil's balls,' cursed Fayne, 'do you never choose anything but seven? Where's your spirit, man?'

Undeterred, the man again set a main of seven, pushed a crown into the middle of the table and watched as each player did the same. There were no scholars' pennies or farthings in this game. This time, however, both dice showed six, and the caster had to find two more crowns to cover his loss. Thinking his luck had changed, he chose nine as the main for the next round and tossed more crowns on the table when he threw eleven. Foolish fellow, thought Thomas, another main of seven and he would have won. The caster tried nine again, and this time threw four followed by nine. Unlucky, but it happened. Having lost three consecutive hands, the caster passed the dice to Fayne, the man on his left.

'Now, gentlemen,' barked Fayne, 'time to make things more interesting. The main point will be five.' He put down four crowns and waited to see who would wager against him. All three did. Fayne rattled the dice and threw them down. They showed a four and a one. With a roar of delight, he scooped up the coins and put them in his pocket. 'There you are, that's how a sporting man does it.'

One of the players stood up. 'I'm finished,' he grumbled. 'No luck today.' And he sloped off towards the door.

'No spirit, young William,' sneered Fayne. 'Still, perhaps there's someone else who'll join us, eh, gentlemen?' He turned in his chair and looked around. He saw Thomas immediately. 'Well, well, if it isn't the little bookseller. Care for a hand of hazard, bookseller, or haven't you the head for it?'

If you're going to choose mains of five, thought Thomas, I have the head and the heart. 'Captain Fayne, you look a most accomplished player. I am little more than a novice, and I could not play for crowns. A shilling or two would be my limit.'

Again Fayne sneered. 'Hardly worth the effort, bookseller. What do you think, Philip?'

'If this gentleman cares for a hand, I say we should oblige him,' replied Philip, clearly seeing in Thomas the price of a good meal or two. 'I am Philip Smithson.'

The third player, who offered his name as Hugh Tomkins, agreed.

'Very well,' said Fayne. 'Take a seat, bookseller, and get out your shillings.'

Claret and pie forgotten, Thomas took the empty seat. In his pocket he had six shillings. If he lost those, that would be it.

Fayne, having won the previous hand, was still the caster. He put a shilling on the table and announced that the main would be seven. Damn, thought Thomas, who was hoping he would stick with five. He put down his shilling and hoped for the best. Fayne shook the dice and rolled them out. Two fives. That set ten as the chance point. Now, if he threw ten before he threw seven, Fayne would win, and if he threw seven before he threw ten, he would lose — a reversal of the first throw in each hand, and a reversal of the odds. Thomas knew that it was the moment to lay a side wager and ordinarily, he would have. But he had only six shillings, so he kept the other five in his pocket.

Fayne threw again. This time, the dice showed six. He threw for a third time. A six and a four. He raked in the shillings. 'Never mind, bookseller, you'll do better on the next hand,' he gloated. 'The main will be seven again.' Three shillings were wagered against him, and he threw the dice with a flourish. When they showed a four and a three, he had won again. Thomas was down to four shillings, and needed a change of luck.

Fayne had won six shillings in the last two hands, and could afford to raise the stakes. 'Two shillings it is, gentlemen,' he announced, putting the coins down, 'and a main of eight.' That's better, thought Thomas. A man who thinks his luck is in, and is willing to lengthen the odds against himself in order to tempt the gamblers. He took two of the remaining four shillings from his pocket and placed them on the table. The other two players did the same.

Fayne gave the dice an extra shake and rolled them out. Seven. A good number for the caster, and a bad one for his opponents. Fayne put another two shillings on the table, indicating that he was betting on throwing a seven before an eight. The odds favoured him. Thomas had no choice but to put down his last two shillings. With sixteen shillings on the table, Fayne picked up the dice and shook them. Thomas closed his eyes. It was not the money — he would survive the loss of six shillings — it was the thought of losing to Fayne. If he lost this hand, he would just have to put on his bravest face. There would be gloating and taunting and accusations of being feeble. It would not be pleasant.

When he heard Fayne curse, he opened his eyes. Two fours make eight, and Fayne had thrown two fours. Thomas had recovered his four shillings and was back in the game.

Fayne also lost the next two hands and passed the dice to Philip. Philip won a hand, then lost three in a row. Thomas took the dice. For five consecutive hands he chose a main of seven, winning each one. He had twenty-five shillings in his pocket. Fayne had gone very quiet and looked as if he might strike someone.

'Damn your luck, bookseller,' he muttered. 'Put down a guinea, and we'll see who's the winner.'

It was strictly against the etiquette of the game for a player other than the caster to suggest a stake, but Fayne did not look in the mood for etiquette. A guinea. Much more than Thomas had ever played for, and if he lost he would be unable to pay all three opponents. That would be dangerous. He really should walk away.

'As you wish, Captain Fayne. But on condition that the hand is played by the two of us only. I should be embarrassed to relieve you gentlemen of your guineas.' He looked enquiringly at the other two.

'I am content to watch,' said Tomkins.

'And I,' agreed Smithson.

'Very well, bookseller,' hissed Fayne. 'Just you and I.'

Two guineas went on the table and Thomas nominated seven as the main. He shook the dice and rolled them out. A one and a three. He would have to throw again, and now the odds were against him. If he threw a seven, Fayne would win. He picked up the dice and threw them down. Two fives. He must throw again, and still the odds favoured Fayne. He shook the dice hard and let them roll along the table. Both dice showed two. Fayne stood up and cursed.

'Damn your eyes, you lucky little runt.'

For a moment Thomas thought Fayne was about to hit him. Then the captain turned on his heel and stormed out. Smithson and Tomkins shrugged apologetically and got up. Tomkins put a hand on Thomas's shoulder and said quietly, 'Well played, sir. Francis is an ill-mannered beggar when he loses. Take care, won't you. He's a vindictive beggar, too.'

Another man telling him to take care, and Thomas could well believe it about Fayne. For now, however, with forty-six shillings in his pocket, he could afford to order another rabbit pie and a bottle of the Crown's best claret. An hour later, his stomach full, he walked back to Pembroke trying not to look smug. If only the message would be as obliging as the dice, all would be well.

CHAPTER 7

The message, however, was thoroughly disobliging. For two more fruitless days Thomas wrestled with it, his frustration growing with the knowledge that the army would soon be on the move. If there was to be a battle, this message might have something to do with it. If he could only do his job, lives might yet be spared. Other than being sure that Monsieur Vigenère was behind the encryption, however, he had learned almost nothing about it. Sheets and sheets of paper, each one covered in combinations of numbers and letters making no sense whatever, littered the floor. He had got through gallons of ink and dozens of quills, and went to bed each night with a throbbing ache behind his eyes. Damnable Frenchman, damnable cipher. Damnable war, damnable Oxford. He longed to go home and forget about all of them. But he could not. He might be hanged for his trouble, and so might Abraham.

On the third morning, he awoke thinking of Jane Romilly. While he had been engrossed in the cipher, she had barely entered his mind. Today, however, she was there. The beautiful lady-in-waiting with eyes of different colours, who had walked with him in the gardens, asked about his family and lied to him about Francis Fayne. And had stomped out of his room, leaving him speechless. What was he to make of her?

Before he could begin to make anything of her, there was a loud knock on the door. Thomas struggled out of bed and opened it. It was Tobias Rush, who this time did not bother with pleasantries. 'Master Hill,' he said, 'kindly make ready to travel. The king has returned from Gloucester and wishes you to accompany him to Newbury, where he will join forces with Prince Rupert.'

Not Gloucester or Reading then. No five guineas for the Dutch artilleryman. 'Is the king expecting to fight?'

'It is likely. We have information that the Earl of Essex, with at least fourteen thousand men, is also marching there. Prince Rupert is racing there with his cavalry and we will march to join him. We must reach the town before Essex does, to prevent his returning to London with his army intact. You are to be responsible for the security of the king's despatches.'

'When do we leave?'

'By noon. Three infantry regiments with artillery are assembling on Christ Church Meadow. Present yourself there within the hour. I shall be accompanying you to Newbury.' And with that, Rush hurried off.

Newbury, which Simon and he had avoided on the way to Oxford. About halfway home. Strategically important, Thomas supposed, either for an attempt by Essex and Fairfax to take Oxford or for a Royalist attack on London. Otherwise, a modest town of no great merit or distinction, which he had visited several times to buy books. Fourteen thousand of the enemy against how many of us? he wondered. Would he be obliged to carry arms? God forbid that he might have to use them. Simon had said that the king knew he would never take up arms against Englishmen, but in the heat of battle would the king care? Would he care himself? A sword in the stomach for Thomas, or a musket ball in the eye of the other fellow? He might be about to find out.

It took Thomas very little time to be ready. He packed his few spare clothes, quills, his sharpening knife and papers into his bag, and hid the encrypted message under his shirt. It felt safer there. He did not want to leave it behind, and he might have time to study it some more. His box of quills he wrapped in a shirt for safety. When he arrived at the meadow, a light rain was falling and the ground was a muddy mass of soldiers, tradesmen, women, horses, wagons, supplies, ammunition, carts and cannon. The camp followers and baggage train had joined the fighting men. He could discern no semblance of military order, nor of anyone attempting to impose any, and he could make little out of the incessant clash and clamour of an army preparing to march. Soldiers stood in small groups, apparently waiting to be told what to do, and grooms tried in vain to keep their horses calm, while lines of townsmen and women, supervised by young officers, loaded every transport with as many crates and boxes as it would take. As long as they had insisted on payment in advance, the butchers and bakers of Oxford were in for another quick and substantial profit. Thomas stood under an elm on the north side of the meadow and watched.

By the time the king and his entourage arrived, some form of order had miraculously appeared, and his majesty, enthusiastically greeted by his guards, rode a grey stallion to the front of the lines.

He wore a gleaming breastplate, carried a heavy cavalry sword, and acknowledged the loyal cheers with a regal wave of his gauntleted hand. On horseback, his lack of height was less obvious, and he looked cheerful and confident. The queen, also mounted, approached the king and bade him a fond, very public farewell. The Generalissima and her unborn child would not be marching to battle.

Beside the queen's horse walked her personal bodyguard and ladies-in-waiting. No spaniels or dwarves today. One of the ladies turned her head and stared straight at Thomas. He returned the stare. He was too far away to see them, but he knew her eyes were different colours. Neither of them smiled or gave a hint of recognition. Then she turned and walked on.

Thomas, unsettled at seeing Jane, and unsure where to go or what to do, stayed where he was and waited for instructions. They came from Tobias Rush, who appeared quietly beside him. 'Master Hill, if you would make your way to the main gate of Christ Church, you will find a carriage waiting for us. I will join you as soon as the king has departed.'

Wondering how Rush had found him, Thomas edged his way around the meadow and up the path between Christ Church and Corpus Christi to the Christ Church gate. The carriage that awaited him was painted in royal blue, emblazoned with the gold monogram TR, drawn by four matched black geldings and driven by a magnificently uniformed coachman, whose assistant, equally magnificent, sat beside him. Inside, the seats were padded and covered in soft red leather. While the army trudged over mud, splashed through ankle-deep puddles, twisted its knees in ruts and holes and took its rest in dripping hedgerows, Master Rush and Master Hill would travel to battle in style. Thomas wondered whether the king intended to ride bravely at the head of his men, or to abandon his stallion for the comfort of a royal carriage.

It was not long before two college servants appeared carrying between them a large chest, which, with the help of the coachmen, they manhandled on to the coach. The chest was closely followed by its owner. Tobias Rush, angrily shouting at them to make haste and allow him room to board the carriage, swept them aside with his silver-topped cane and sat down opposite Thomas. 'I do so dislike travelling,' he said with a sigh, 'and, with this rain, the journey will not be pleasant. Luckily, I know a tolerable inn in the village of Drayton, where we'll spend the night. It's about ten miles from here. Tomorrow we'll continue to Newbury, another eighteen miles or so. The king, I believe, plans to stop at Wantage.' Rush eyed Thomas's small bag. 'Is that all you've brought, Master Hill? We may be away for some days.'

'Master Rush, it's all I have,' Thomas replied sharply. 'I was not permitted to bring anything more to Oxford, and have not been inclined to make purchases here, with the prices three times those in Romsey.'

'In that case, feel free to ask for anything you need. I will arrange for it.' Rush smiled his thin smile, then called to the coachman, 'Let us make haste. We must be away before the army sets off, or we'll be trapped among them.' Thomas heard the coachman snap his long whip and they were off, bumping and lurching over the cobbles. They left Oxford by the south gate, passed through the town's defences and round three huge burial pits, and were soon on the road to Newbury. Somewhere behind them, the king and his Lifeguards marched to battle.

Conversation in the carriage was difficult, and little was said until they approached Drayton, when Thomas asked about his duties.

'If we face Essex,' replied Rush, 'despatches will be coming in and out all the time. Orders to our commanders, their reports, and intelligence from our observers as to Essex's movements. Some will be encrypted. And there is always the chance of interceptions. If they are to be of any use, you will have to decrypt them immediately. Otherwise the moment will pass and any advantage will be lost.'

'Do we know what ciphers they will use?'

'We don't, but, like ours, they will perforce be simple. In battle, there is no time for complexity. Please give some thought to the cipher you will use, and advise me of it. I will communicate it to our commanders in the field.'

'As you wish, Master Rush,' replied Thomas, thinking that a simple alphabetical shift might be best suited to a simple military mind. Certainly not Vigenère squares.

At Drayton, the carriage pulled up outside Rush's inn. The carriage driver's assistant jumped down and opened the door for them. Thomas picked up his bag and was about to step out of the carriage, but Rush would not hear of it. 'The men will take your bag, Master Hill. Leave it for them.'

'It's only light,' protested Thomas. 'I can easily manage it.'

'Nonsense, that's what servants are for. They'll bring it with mine.' Reluctantly, not wishing to make a scene, Thomas put down the bag and alighted. The innkeeper emerged, all smiles and hand-wringing, to greet them.

'Gentlemen, welcome to the White Hart. Your rooms are ready and your dinner is being prepared. The stables are at the back.' Rush nodded and strode into the inn. Thomas followed him. A fire had been laid in the hearth, the floor had been swept and the tables wiped clean. There were no other customers. The innkeeper had been warned. Tobias Rush did not like unwelcome company or unnecessary discomfort. While Rush supervised the unloading of his chest, Thomas was shown upstairs to a small room. There he found a straw mattress on the bed, a woollen blanket, a bowl for washing and a jug of water. It was clean enough, smelt only slightly of mice, and was superior to either of the inns he and Simon had sampled on their journey from Romsey.

The coachman's assistant soon arrived with his bag. 'Here you are, sir,' said the young man with a grin. 'Not too heavy. We can't get the chest up the stairs, so it'll have to spend the night downstairs by the fire, same as us. Master Rush isn't too happy about that.'

Thomas thanked the young man, and opened the bag. He knew at once that it had been tampered with. His box of quills was no longer wrapped in the shirt, and a corner of one sheet of paper was slightly torn. Either the coachmen had been looking for coins, or Master Rush had seen fit to conduct a search. For what? wondered Thomas. Doesn't he trust me? No, it was probably the coachmen. Too bad they had found no coins. He decided to say nothing, but to keep the encrypted message with him at all times. That, if nothing else, must not fall into the wrong hands.

The innkeeper had certainly made an effort with their dinner. After bowls of hot vegetable soup, they were served a good pigeon pie with pickled cucumbers, and a sweet apple tart with cream. While Thomas tucked in happily, washing the meal down with half a bottle of claret, Rush ate and drank little. And he would not be drawn in by Thomas's questions about himself. He admitted to having been born and brought up in London, but that was about it. Nothing about his family, his education or his home. By the end of the meal, Thomas had given up and turned the conversation, instead, to the battle that lay ahead. 'If Essex has fourteen thousand men,' he asked, 'will he outnumber us, or we him?'

'I believe the king will have the advantage in cavalry numbers, and his enemies in infantry. As to artillery, about the same. Much like Edgehill.'

'Were you at Edgehill?' asked Thomas, surprised. He had not thought of Rush in battle.

'I was, as a member of his majesty's household. But for Prince Rupert's cavalry who preferred to chase a broken and fleeing rabble rather than wheel and charge at the rear of the enemy centre, we should have enjoyed a great victory. As it was, we could only claim one.'

'It was certainly reported as a victory in the newsbooks.'

Rush smiled. 'Yes. For that, I must take some responsibility. The king insisted upon as glowing a report as I could write. The truth, however, is that the battle was inconclusive. Many are.'

'On that we agree,' said Thomas. 'Inconclusive and pointless. Much suffering, little progress. Will we never learn?'

'Who knows? For now, our task is to win. When the king is back in London, we will turn our attention to the future. There is much to do to secure England against our enemies, and to expand our influence and interests overseas. Sugar, cotton and tobacco from the Caribbean islands and Virginia, spices from the East Indies, slaves from Africa. The opportunities for wealth and prosperity are limitless, as long as we have the courage to take them. If we don't, the French and the Dutch will.'

'How will we do it?'

'The navy. A strong navy is the key. If we control the trade routes we control the trade, and if we control the trade we control its sources. The Americas, Africa, India. We must build a navy that cannot be challenged by our enemies.'

Thomas did not respond. He had never thought much about such matters. Rush clearly had. Abraham had called him an ambitious man. Ambitious and clever. Looking to the future, and ready to take whatever opportunities came his way. Not a man to be trifled with. He changed the subject. 'Do you know Lady Romilly well?' he asked.

Rush looked surprised. 'Not well. I have little reason to speak to her, or, indeed, to the queen. My time is taken up with serving his majesty. Why do you ask?'

'Mere curiosity. I understand that she is a widow with family in York. I wondered why she had left there to accompany the queen to Oxford. It seems an odd thing to do at such a time.'

Rush shrugged. 'Loyalty, like beauty, is a matter of taste. Lady Romilly must have put her devotion to the queen before her duty to her family.' He grinned unpleasantly. 'Either that or she's looking for another husband.' Rush raised his eyebrows and looked hard at Thomas. 'A courtier, I imagine, Master Hill, rather than a bookseller.'

As he had at the masque, Thomas let the insult pass. He did not want to get on the wrong side of this man. 'Possibly, Master Rush, although she gave me the impression that her service to the queen would take precedence over marriage, as it has over her family.'

'So you have spent some time with the lady, have you?'

'A little. She seemed interested in why I was in Oxford.'

Again the eyebrows were raised. 'Did she now? And what did you tell her?'

'That I am visiting my elderly tutor. It was what Abraham and I agreed.'

'You didn't tell her anything of your work, I trust?'

'No indeed. That would have been quite improper.'

'Improper and foolish. Oxford is a dangerous place, and it is best to trust no one.'

Thomas was sick of being told that Oxford was a dangerous place, and having started it he now wanted to end this conversation before it got any more awkward. 'Quite so. I shall take every precaution. Now, if you will forgive me, I shall retire. The journey has tired me.'

'As you wish. Good night, Master Hill. And remember what I have said.'

Lying on his bed, Thomas replayed the dinner conversation in his mind. Was Rush suspicious of Jane Romilly? Or was he just suspicious of everyone? Thomas had not asked about seeing Rush in Merton. Best not to ruffle his feathers. And 'The king will have the advantage in cavalry,' Rush had said, 'and his enemies in infantry.' No 'we' or 'they'. An oddly dispassionate manner of speaking. Intellect rather than emotion. A clever man. And his bag had been searched — he was sure of it. A thief or a traitor?

They set off again at dawn and covered the eighteen miles to Newbury in a little over three hours. Outside the town they encountered a troop of dragoons who had been sent to meet them. From the dragoons' captain, they learned that Prince Rupert and his cavalry had arrived from Gloucester two days earlier to find the town already occupied by Essex's quartermasters, busy arranging provisions for the Parliamentary army. The prince had wasted no time in taking them prisoner, and had assumed control of the town. The bulk of Essex's army was still twenty miles from the town, having been overtaken by the prince's cavalry.

Their carriage passed through the cavalry's encampments, proceeded into the town, which, like Oxford, was heaving with soldiers and their equipment, and was led to a large house by the market square. There the carriage stopped and they were shown inside by the captain. 'This house has been requisitioned for you, Master Rush. Sir Henry was happy to oblige.'

Rush looked around. 'It will do well enough, captain. Master Hill and I will base ourselves here. Have the men bring in my chest and Master Hill's bag.'

It will do well enough to be sure, thought Thomas, admiring the high ceiling and tall windows. The walls of the entrance hall were decorated with tapestries and paintings, including a sumptuous Rubens nude and two portraits by Van Dyck, which he took to be of the owner of the house and his wife. An enormous red and gold Persian carpet covered the floor. This Sir Henry was a man of wealth, a man who would have much to lose in the event of a Parliamentary victory in this war. No wonder he had been ready to offer his house to the king.

Having taken his bag from the coachman, Thomas climbed a magnificent curving staircase, more family portraits covering the stair wall, and found a bedroom with an elegant window looking out over the square. He threw his bag on the four-poster bed and deposited himself into a large padded library chair. As he admired the room, also adorned with tapestries and paintings, the thought occurred that even war might have its good side. It was nothing short of luxurious. Velvet curtains, an embroidered silk cover on the bed, a collection of miniatures, a handsome fireplace, the padded chair and a fine rosewood writing table. Then he caught himself. It was a disgraceful notion. Nothing could excuse war and there was nothing good about it. And he had work to do.

He laid the intercepted message out on a writing table and concentrated on it once more. To Thomas, it had become the 'Vigenère message'.

URF UBD HE XQB TF KGA OEMD RRFUO TLC WMG LRB WHT R XHGORKZ IO KPW769

WA MQFV BVMF HPL ZFTD RVV57 4SEWMFREJ VGL SVKMGE 852 GTSC WZTD QE

TIJG IVL GJT RA KDOE IK EOJAAQLV GGJR MQU IOIGSI GRQF HBFZG JGY

ALG EE OLWEEA GJR YIFS1 82AEL2 64SGE SC AAD ZVY JP KP WXR JB JTN XBZ77

5XNW WJBS LA LWAK371 EAIH TPA AD RVV BAP TWPVV AGDN WWJ URR VUT

IW EW HTI QCT WY QDT37 1IE852 769UMHT RKC CONT WSGV WMG IEN DJEE KW

IHV ZW PNU EAIH371 ZV GJR YIFSS NQ DA BV NGGCVL LD SVMC IRLKW DN

KMJ BS WINDU IITAE KW42177 5OX LCIVK IJM LXMV IFS PCI UT FFZ

SEPI MZTNJQGCOW3 71E ZDWZTD QE SZGJ GYB LD 574SKIFS RVIV N GFL

OX LC QFV WV AZPLCJJX NX IF TNU BG IHZA OP RJWGC

Twenty-six possible encryptions for each of the four hundred and fifty-six letters, plus forty-five numbers and one hundred and thirty eight spaces. A cipher that had never been broken. Where to begin? He made another effort to envisage its encrypter, this time with more success. He saw a small man, precise in dress and manner, a pair of spectacles perched on his sharp nose and a cap on his head. He sat in a dark room, working by the light of a single candle. This man would work carefully and make no mistakes. He might well use the square, he might use codes, but he would not use nulls or misspellings, which would offend his sense of order. What sort of keyword would he use? Nothing random, nothing too complex. A Latin word perhaps, or a religious one, or something historical. Or a million other things. Use your head, Thomas. There's no future in playing guessing games. Concentrate on the cipher. There must be a way.

He gazed idly out of the window at the toings and froings in the square below. It was a square full of noise and bustle, and the hubbub of a town preparing to defend itself. Officers about their duties, soldiers about theirs, tradesmen about their businesses, fascinated children standing in huddles around the square, noise and movement and excitement. The king and his army were coming to Newbury, and there was to be a great battle. A great battle in which Thomas would have a part to play. That reminded him that he needed a keyword. Not too long for the sake of speed, not too short for the sake of security. Five or six letters, with no repeats. It came to him. MASQUE. Perfect. He would tell Rush the keyword for all incoming and outgoing despatches would be MASQUE.

He decided that nothing of the cipher would reveal itself for the moment and ventured back downstairs, intending to take a stroll around the town. He was met by Rush hurrying in through the door, cane in hand. 'Master Hill, there you are. I have word that the king will arrive this evening, and the bulk of the infantry tonight. We believe that Essex's vanguard will not arrive until tomorrow, so we shall have the advantage of him. Kindly remain here until I give you further instructions.'

'I was about to take a walk around the town.'

'That will not be possible. You are safer here, and you might at any time be needed. Is your room comfortable?'

'Very comfortable, thank you.'

'Is there anything you need?'

'Some ink, if you please. Nothing more.'

'It will be arranged. Have you decided upon a cipher?'

'I have. A simple alphabetical shift, using the keyword MASQUE.'

Rush's smile was as humourless as ever. 'Very appropriate. I will inform the king and our commanders.' And with that, he was off. Here one minute, gone the next, thought Thomas again. A busy bird, with a nest to build and food to gather. An odd man, but I'd rather be with him than against him.

Unfortunately, Sir Henry, for all his interest in art, was not a literary man, and there was not a book to be found in the house. Thomas had little to do but make himself comfortable and await events. Having been admirably fed and watered by Sir Henry's cook, he sat by the window in his bedroom, staring at the encrypted text and thinking about Jane Romilly. Those eyes had looked straight through him. Would they always?

News of the king's arrival came from Tobias Rush that evening. 'His majesty is housed safely in the town, and the army, as expected, will be in position by tomorrow morning. There is every chance that Essex will also arrive during the night, and, if so, the king intends to join battle tomorrow.'

'Have I any instructions?'

'Remain here for now. I will escort you to your station in the morning. You and I will be with the king and his personal guard at the rear of the lines. From there, you will deal with all despatches, taking instructions only from the king or from me.'

'Very well, Master Rush. I shall be ready.'

Thomas slept badly, tossing about on the four-poster bed until dawn. On the eve of battle, he was nervous. He could only guess at what it would be like actually to witness a battle, but he knew he would see blood and carnage, and a good deal of it. He wondered how he would react, and how his brain would work in the heat of the moment. Would he have much to do? Would he make mistakes? If he did, would they matter? Would they win? If they did not, what would happen? A hasty escape, capture, death? He thought of Hannibal, who was reputed to be able to go without food and sleep for as long as was necessary, and of King Henry, moving freely, according to Shakespeare, among his soldiers' camp fires on the eve of Agincourt. If all soldiers lay awake on the night before a battle, there would be two very tired armies facing each other in the morning. The Earl of Essex and Prince Rupert had both marched from Gloucester, and the king from Oxford. Every man on both sides must already be weary and footsore, not to mention cold and wet. A sleepless night, and they would scarcely have the energy to draw their swords or lift their muskets. Although that might not be such a bad thing. Everyone too exhausted to fight and anxious to get home as soon as they could. Take up your weapons, men, and follow me to London, or back to Oxford. Wives, sweethearts, warm beds and strong ale await us. Could it happen?

It could not. Thomas was up, dressed and breakfasted when Rush arrived to fetch him before dawn. 'It is as we expected,' he reported. 'Essex's army arrived during the night and has taken up position outside the town. He cannot reach London without engaging us. The king is determined on a victory which will greatly set back the cause of Parliament, and open the way for his own advance on London. Follow me, Master Hill, and we will join his majesty on Wash Common.'

Wash Common lay less than a mile to the south-west of the town. They rode through dozens of tents and carts belonging to the camp followers and wives upon whom the army depended for

its food, drink and necessities of life, to the king's station. It was on
a low rise behind the centre of the Royalist infantry, from where
they had an excellent view of the surrounding country. Two tents
had been pitched on the mound, both flying the royal standard.
The king sat in full armour on his grey stallion, his heavy cavalry
sword resting across its back. His Lifeguards and servants
surrounded him. A heroic figure with a righteous cause, or so he
made it look. Staring fixedly into the middle distance, his majesty
acknowledged neither Thomas nor Rush. Thomas could not even
guess what was going through the royal mind, but he hoped it was
more than the fixed smile on the royal face suggested.

From their vantage point, Thomas saw four ranks of infantry
and artillery — pikemen, musketeers and cannon — in the centre of
the line, with massed cavalry on either wing, the whole army
stretching across perhaps as much as a mile. Facing them, drawn
up in similar fashion, was Essex's army. Rush had been right. The
king's cavalry was the stronger, his infantry weaker.

At his first battle, and wanting to be properly informed,
Thomas asked a young captain of the king's guard to point out the
salient features of the terrain and the armies' dispositions. The
captain was most obliging and seemed pleased to be asked to
explain how matters stood.

'We are formed up on Wash Common,' he replied, 'and our
enemy opposite on land known as Crockham Heath. The area
between us is open but marshy. Our position is essentially a
defensive one, as our first task is to prevent Essex reaching
London. Thus, Sir John Byron's Lifeguards rest on the river
Kennet.' He pointed to their right. 'And the prince's cavalry
near the river Enborne.' His arm traversed the battlefield
and settled on a point to their left. 'Essex cannot reach the

road to London without engaging us. It is as we would wish.'

'I notice the enemy hold some higher ground, captain,' remarked Thomas quietly. 'Is that as we would wish?' He pointed to two low hills upon which Parliamentary infantry had been drawn up.

'I confess that it is not. They presently occupy Round Hill and Biggs Hill, and I daresay we shall have to clear both.' The captain glanced at Thomas and smiled. 'Worry not, sir. We shall make short work of them.'

Thomas thanked the young man for his help, and asked him if he had much experience of battle. 'Very little, sir,' he replied. 'I was at Gloucester, but that was more of a siege than a battle.'

'What made you become a soldier of the king?' asked Thomas.

'I was a schoolteacher, sir, and hope to be one again. I joined his majesty's Lifeguards because I believe his cause to be just.'

A schoolteacher. That explained why he was pleased to answer Thomas's questions. 'You have been most civil, captain. I wish you a safe day and an early return to the classroom.'

Wondering how the enemy came to occupy the high ground when Prince Rupert's cavalry had been first on the scene, Thomas steeled himself not to worry. He dismounted, handed his reins to a groom and followed Rush into one of the tents. There a table and chairs had been placed ready for them. On the table were papers, ink, sand and quills. Thomas took a seat. The king had still not favoured them with so much as a glance.

There was no time to dwell on the matter. Shots were being fired and the battle had started. Thomas heard the sound of Flemish pipes in the distance and wondered where his friend from Amsterdam had been stationed. Rush left the tent, returning within a minute to hand Thomas a despatch to be encrypted and delivered to all commanders. As there were five of them, five copies would be needed. The despatch was from the king and informed them that the infantry must hold firm against the expected enemy advance, while both wings charged forward to outflank them. With these tactics, the day would surely be theirs. Thinking that this was not entirely consistent with holding a defensive line, Thomas dutifully wrote the date – 20 September 1643 – at the top of the page, encrypted the order, using the keyword MASQUE, made four more copies and handed them to Rush. Five messengers on five horses galloped off to deliver them. Each commander had an aide to make the decryption, and they too would have to work fast.

It began slowly. Essex's infantry, firing as they went, advanced steadily towards the king's musketeers. As ordered, the musketeers returned fire, but did not advance to meet them. The lines on both sides thinned as the Parliamentary infantry approached. It had not occurred to Thomas before that, in battle, it was the screams of the wounded which were most terrible. The dead simply fell and lay still. Although from his table in the tent he could see very little, he could hear everything.

For ten minutes or so, Thomas could do no more than sit, listen and wait. By that time, the sounds of battle were deafening. Cannon and muskets fired, swords clashed, and men shouted and screamed. Deciding that not seeing was even worse than seeing, he stood up and went outside. Immediately, he regretted it. To his right, a cannon fired, and he saw three heads detached from three bodies by the shot. He turned away and vomited. More cannon fired, and more men fell, headless, armless, disembowelled. One file of infantrymen, struck by a cannon shot, fell like ninepins. Thomas wanted desperately to look away, but found that he could not.

He might have stood there until nightfall had Rush not appeared beside him and handed him a second order. It was for Sir John Byron on the right wing, and instructed him immediately to take Round Hill, which lay before him. Wondering how Sir John was going to manage this, given that his cavalry would have to find a way over a muddy mess of fields and ditches before they could even think of attacking the hill, Thomas returned to his table, encrypted the order and sent it off. Having seen the carnage already being wreaked on the cavalry by Essex's men hidden among the trees and hedges below the hill, he thanked God that he was not with Sir John.

Thomas could not sit still. Again he left his post and went outside. The king sat unmoved on his grey stallion, his Lifeguards and entourage still surrounding him. Thomas hoped they had more idea of what was happening than he did. As the air grew blacker with smoke and thicker with the smell of gunpowder, a curtain fell across the field. Muskets and cannon went on firing, soldiers went on bellowing and shrieking, and horses screamed, but only occasionally did the clash of swords and the thrust of pikes appear briefly through the smoke. It was ghostly and unreal. Yet these were real men, real weapons, real wounds, real deaths, real war. Noise, pain, fear, confusion.

From somewhere on the left, news arrived that Prince Rupert, in typical fashion, had charged the enemy, and might have broken through to attack from their rear. On the right, Sir John Byron's cavalry was probably being destroyed as it struggled towards the hill. With the battlefield all but invisible, there was no way of telling how they were faring, or even if they were still alive.

Thomas half expected a troop of Parliamentary infantry suddenly to emerge out of the smoke and shoot him. By this time, he could barely see the king.

Two messages from Sir John Byron arrived in quick succession. The first, speedily decrypted by Thomas, reported that, despite strong resistance, he had captured Round Hill, and the second, in clear text, that he had lost it again. Thomas was glad that he did not have to decrypt the second one and hand it to the king himself. Rush could do that.

All morning, and for most of the afternoon, the fighting continued. The king was forced to deploy troops to plug a gap in the lines caused by a successful advance by Essex himself, Rupert led his cavalry in charge after murderous charge at the Parliamentary pikemen, Sir John Byron battled in vain to recapture Round Hill, and Thomas sat in his tent, decrypting incoming reports, encrypting outgoing orders, trying to assess the state of the battle by the reports and wondering if he would still be breathing that evening. There were no captured despatches to deal with, which was just as well as they would inevitably take longer. Rush came and went, saying little and asking nothing. He seemed quite unruffled. Thomas reckoned that if anyone knew the state of affairs, Rush did. He probably had his own army of messengers, galloping backwards and forwards with news. He was not a man to tolerate being in the dark; he would have to feel in control.

In mid-afternoon, a report came in that Colonel Thomas Pinchbeck's Regiment had taken heavy losses, and the colonel had been killed. Thomas wondered fleetingly if a certain Captain Fayne had been among the casualties.

Then another report came from Sir John Byron. It too was in clear text and respectfully begged to inform his majesty that his friend Lord Falkland had been killed. Falkland's death would be a cruel blow to the king, who was known to be fond of him. A second despatch came from an aide of Prince Rupert, and was encrypted. The cavalry had at last broken through the enemy lines, and was engaged in attacking their infantry from the rear. They had been temporarily stalled, however, by renewed resistance on the part of the Parliamentary pikemen and musketeers.

Then the Earl of Carnarvon was reported killed, as was the Earl of Sunderland. Two more cruel blows. On it went all afternoon and into the evening. Thomas imagined cannonballs crashing into ranks of infantry, cavalry horses shying away from raised pikes, wheeling, trying again and shying again, and musketeers picking off targets from the safety of hedgerows and ditches. Through all of it, he carefully carried out his duties. In one hour several reports might arrive; in the next, none at all. As far as he could tell, by five o'clock neither side had achieved much, other than a severe reduction in their numbers.

As the autumn dusk fell, the cannon at last began to grow silent, and the air to clear. On the far left, Thomas could then see that Prince Rupert had failed to break through the enemy infantry from the rear, and had withdrawn to his original position. Both infantry centres had done the same, and only the remains of Sir John Byron's cavalry, now well short of Round Hill, were fighting in the fields below it. Everywhere, bodies and bits of bodies lay mangled on the field, spent muskets and broken swords among them. The walking wounded were being helped to safety by their colleagues, those without hope being left to die where they had fallen. Thomas, horrified, could only stand and stare, until Rush hurried up and handed him another order. Thomas forced himself to encrypt it and sent it off. He barely noticed that it instructed Sir

John Byron to withdraw immediately and to return to the king's headquarters.

Sporadic fighting went on even after darkness had fallen, but by about nine o'clock it was over. The king had departed the field, and Tobias Rush had accompanied him. Thomas watched bodies being stripped and carted away for burial, exhausted soldiers, their hands and faces blackened by powder, staggering off in search of water, and bewildered horses, many fearfully wounded, wandering forlornly among the dead. Some soldiers found a stream from which riderless horses were drinking, and, desperate for water, lay down on their bellies in it. In one day thousands had died, hundreds more would die, and many more had lost arms, legs and eyes. After a day of hacking each other to pieces, would either side, he wondered, claim victory? Unable any longer to think clearly, he drifted off in the direction of the town.

By the time he reached the market square, lit up by a fire set in the middle to provide warmth and light, Thomas too was exhausted. He had wielded neither musket nor sword, he had suffered no wound, he had never been in real danger, and he had had enough water to drink. Yet his back and neck were knotted with tension, he was filthy, his head ached from the powder, he could barely speak and his hands were shaking. God alone knew what state the fighting men were in. Barely registering a troop of infantry led by a tall, fair-haired captain march into the square from the direction of Wash Common and towards an inn on the far side, he entered the house, clambered up the staircase, fell on to his bed and passed out.

When he awoke twelve hours later, his head still ached, his throat was still sore and he was still filthy. He held out his hands; they at least were steady. Rising with difficulty from the bed, he stripped off his clothes, retrieved the Vigenère message which fell from under his shirt on to the floor, and did his best to wash off the worst of the dirt and powder. In his bag he had the change of clothes provided by Silas. He put them on. Then he went to see what news there was.

Downstairs, Tobias Rush was in the entrance hall, busily supervising the two coachmen who were carrying his chest outside. 'Master Rush,' said Thomas hoarsely, 'what news is there?'

Rush looked up sharply. 'Master Hill, good morning. The king leaves within the hour for Oxford, and I am to travel with him. You may have my coach. Prince Rupert will stay in Newbury until Essex leaves. If he marches towards London, the prince will pursue him. Our troops will follow us to Oxford.' Rush's voice seemed unaffected by the gunpowder.

'What of the battle?'

'There is little to report, other than heavy casualties on both sides.'

'Can we claim victory?'

The thin smile. 'Alas, no. Even I would be hard put to write an account of a victory, even Pyrrhic. If Essex does reach London, however, he might very well claim one.'

'Master Rush, may I ask another question?'

'You may, of course.'

'How did we allow the enemy to occupy the high ground on both wings? Shouldn't we have taken it before they arrived?'

For a moment, Rush was silent. 'I too have pondered that. One does not care to comment on military matters, but one does wonder about some form of deception.'

'What sort of deception?'

'False intelligence, perhaps, or an intercepted message. Either might have led the prince to believe that we held the ridges, until it was too late to act.'

'Surely that would be unlikely.'

'Who knows? But enough, Master Hill. I must join the king. My carriage is at your disposal. We will expect you in Oxford within a day or two.'

Well, I suppose it's possible the prince was misled, thought Thomas when Rush had gone, although drunk and incapable seemed more likely.

CHAPTER 8

Thomas intended to cover the thirty-odd miles to Oxford in a single day. He did not care to stop overnight, and urged the coachmen to make all speed. After the horror of Newbury, he wanted solitude and he wanted to get back to work on the message. If he could break the cipher, he might shorten the war. A shorter war would mean fewer Newburys, fewer widows and orphans, fewer lives pointlessly wrecked. The battle had given him new purpose.

Having settled as best he could into the cushioned seats of Rush's carriage, he shut his eyes and tried again to concentrate on the problem. Was there a way to break the Vigenère square? Twenty-six possible encryptions for each of twenty-six letters, and, in this message, numerical codes added for good measure. Instinctively, his hand went to the paper hidden under his shirt, and a thought struck him. Was it safe there? What if the carriage broke a wheel and he was tossed out on to the road? Might a helping hand not happen upon it while he was unconscious, and, with the best intentions, remove it? Feeling only a little foolish, he took the paper out, rolled down his left stocking, carefully folded the paper up as tightly as he could, slipped it under his foot and adjusted the stocking. There. Surely even the most helpful hand would not want to examine his left foot.

They made good time to the hamlet of Chilton, rattling along even over the roughest stretches of road. At Chilton they stopped at a coaching inn to give the horses a rest and to refresh themselves. Thomas had made not a jot of progress on the cipher but he had been reasonably comfortable, Rush's cushions having absorbed the worst of the bumps and lurches. In a wooded area two miles beyond Chilton, however, just as Thomas was becoming drowsy, there were two loud cracks, and the carriage shot forward so violently that he was thrown from his seat. Unsure what had happened and unable to get to his feet to look out of the window, Thomas lay on the floor, rolling from side to side with the swaying of the carriage. If the noise had frightened the horses, the coachmen should have reined them in. A carriage pulled by four bolting horses would not stay upright on a road such as this for very long. He offered a silent prayer to the God he chose to believe in on such occasions, and hung on to a seat as best he could.

It seemed that his prayer had been answered. The horses slowed and the carriage soon came to rest. He got shakily to his feet, stumbled out and went to speak to the coachmen. At once it was clear why they had not reined the horses in. Both were sprawled across their seat, one on top of the other, blood pouring from their heads. He did not need to look more closely to know that they were dead. And the two men who had shot them were holding the leading horses' bridles. They must have galloped after the carriage and caught it. Each man was hooded and masked, and had a pistol in his belt and another in his hand, pointing at a spot between Thomas's eyes. Thomas stood motionless and stared at them.

'Lie down with your face to the ground,' ordered one of them. Thomas obeyed. 'Keep the pistol on him, and I'll search inside.'

He heard the man dismount and climb into the carriage, thinking that a couple of murderous highwaymen would not be best pleased to find nothing but his bag containing paper, quills and a few clothes, and a handful of coins in his pocket. He heard the seats being ripped up, and his bag being emptied on the ground.

'Nothing,' said the leader. 'Just paper and rags. Empty your pockets, little man.' Thomas sat up, fished out three shillings and threw them on the ground. 'Is that all? Three shillings from a man in a carriage like this? There must be more.' He walked towards Thomas, his pistol held unwaveringly in front of him.

'There's no more,' said Thomas. 'The carriage is borrowed from Tobias Rush, adviser to his majesty the king. I advise you to do it no more damage and to be off while you can. Master Rush is not far behind, and he is not a man who will take kindly to his coachmen being murdered and his carriage destroyed.'

The man laughed. 'That's a risk we'll have to take. Stand up and take off your shirt, boots and breeches and roll down your stockings.'

When Thomas stood in just his drawers and rolled-down stockings, the highwayman walked around him, patted his backside and groin to make sure nothing was hidden there, and then swore loudly. 'The devil's balls. You really are a pauper, aren't you? I haven't even the heart to shoot you.' He walked to his horse and took from a leather bag hanging from the saddle a short-handled axe, with which he split the spokes of one wheel. While he did so, his companion kept his pistol aimed at Thomas. 'You're a lucky man, my friend,' said the man with the axe, 'and you can tell your Master Rush so from us.' And with that, they wheeled their horses and galloped off towards Chilton, leaving Thomas staring after them. They had not even taken the three shillings.

This was not the time to wonder why he was still alive. He must get away from there at once, and back to Oxford. He pulled up his stockings, thanking providence that he had changed the hiding place of the message, and put his shirt and breeches back on. The carriage was unusable, the horses unsaddled and possibly unused to being ridden. Still, he was a good rider and there was nothing else for it. Not even stopping to heave the dead men off the carriage, he unhitched the leading horses, holding grimly on to one of them by the long reins. Before the horse could bolt, he grabbed it by the mane and sprang on to its back. It was a trick he had used to impress young ladies – an advantage of being light and agile. He pulled hard on the bit to gauge the horse's reaction, and was relieved when it stood still. This one had certainly been ridden before.

Thomas started at a trot and went to a canter as soon as he felt the horse was used to him. Without a saddle, a canter was smoother and easier for a rider than a trot. He did not care to risk a full gallop, so a canter home it would have to be. And, in any case, with only three shillings to his name, he would not be able to buy another horse if this one became lame or exhausted. Horse and rider would pace themselves over the distance.

North of Abingdon, the road ran over a narrow stream, where they stopped to drink. Until then, Thomas had concentrated entirely on not falling off. Now, sitting on a grassy bank, the horse tethered to a tree and quietly nibbling grass, he thought about the incident. Both coachmen shot dead by men who knew how to use pistols, the carriage searched, his three shillings ignored and his life spared. Damned odd. More to the point, what would Tobias Rush make of it all? He had not been joking when he said that Rush would not take kindly to the deaths of his men and the damage to his carriage, and he might very well want to know why Thomas had allowed it to happen, and how he had escaped being shot. All manner of reasons might occur to Rush's suspicious mind, and he did not look forward to making his report.

The image from the night before of the troop of infantry led by the fair-haired captain also came back to him. It was Fayne, no doubt about it, and looking for all the world as if he had spent a peaceful day fishing. No signs of blood or battle on him or his men, despite their regiment having reportedly been in the thick of the fighting. Thomas stored the unspoken thought away. One day it might be needed.

Now, he had to reach the safety of Oxford. After a short break he remounted, and, still at a canter, made steady progress along the road, trying to ignore the stares of the few travellers he passed, and untroubled by the lack of a saddle or the state of the road. In an odd way, he found himself rather enjoying it. When his father was alive, they had often ridden together over the downs and through the woods, sometimes bareback, and the old sense of elation came creeping back. It was certainly less grim than his last journey to Oxford in that flea-ridden habit. He grinned at the memory.

When the late-September light began to fade, however, he was still six or seven miles from the town, and the Oxfordshire countryside was no place to be after dark. Deserters from both sides, none too particular about whom they robbed and killed, and bands of clubmen, armed with axes, scythes, cudgels and whatever else they could find, were known to hide out in the woods all over the county. The clubmen were becoming a serious problem for both sides, ferociously attacking anyone who strayed into their locality and might be a threat to their villages and families. And there were highwaymen, of whom Thomas had had quite enough that day. A solitary rider would make an easy target for any of them, especially one going at no more than a canter.

As it grew dark, Thomas found himself looking nervously over his shoulder and peering into the shadows at the side of the road. He started when a dog barked, then laughed at himself in embarrassment. God's wounds, Thomas, he thought, you are a feeble creature. There are only a few miles to go, so make haste and stop being spineless.

He knew from the stench when he was nearing the town. It came from the burial pits outside the walls, drains overflowing with human excrement, rotting middens and animal carcasses left to fester in the streets. When a breeze from the north blew the mixture straight into his face, Thomas gagged, and only just kept his seat. Not daring to risk holding the reins in one hand, he left his handkerchief in his pocket and tried not to breathe.

With relief, he entered the town through the south gate, and, just as he had with Simon a month earlier, made his way up St Aldate's towards Pembroke. By this time, the streets were quieter, and he was soon able to hand the horse to one of Silas's boys, with an instruction to look after it well. He walked stiffly across the courtyard to his room. There he rubbed his backside, stretched his back and took off his clothes. He retrieved the message from its hiding place and unfolded it carefully. It seemed none the worse for the journey, and its secrets were as safe as ever. Thomas laid it on the table and sluiced himself with water from the jug; trust Silas to keep it full for his return. Much as he wanted to eat and sleep, he tucked the message under his shirt and set off for Christ Church. Master Rush would have to be faced sooner or later and it might as well be sooner.

When Thomas arrived at Christ Church and asked for Tobias Rush, he was instructed to wait in a small room just off the gatehouse. 'Master Rush does not care for visitors to call at his rooms. Wait here, if you please, sir, and I will send for him,' said the guard.

Thomas stood waiting and tried to rehearse what he was going to say. When Rush swept in, he looked anything but pleased to have a visitor. 'Master Hill, after a long and unhappy journey from Newbury with the king, I was at my dinner. What brings you here? Have the coachmen not taken my carriage to the stables?'

'My apologies for disturbing you, sir. I did not think this matter should wait. On the way from Newbury, we were attacked by highwaymen who killed your coachmen and ransacked your carriage.'

Rush peered at him. 'Were you harmed?'

'Strangely, I was not.'

'Both coachmen killed, yet you were allowed to escape? That is strange indeed.'

'I cannot account for it.'

'I imagine not. And what of my carriage?'

'I left it with the dead men and three of the horses two miles north of Chilton. I rode the fourth horse back. The carriage is damaged but not, I think, beyond repair.'

'Did the criminals take anything?'

'Nothing. Not even my three shillings.'

'Yet they let you live to tell the tale.'

'Master Rush, I have no more idea than you why that is so. I am not familiar with the ways of such men.'

'One would hope not.' Rush's black eyes were boring into Thomas's head, as if trying to see into his mind.

He does not believe me, thought Thomas. 'There is one other thing.'

'Yes?'

'Before we departed for Newbury, my room in Pembroke was broken into and turned upside down.'

Rush looked surprised. 'Why did you not tell me this earlier?'

'I did not wish to trouble you. I think it was the work of the man who occupied the room before me, Captain Fayne. He resents my having taken his room, and he is a gambler. He might have been looking for money. Both the intruder and the highwaymen were certainly looking for something.'

'And what would that be?'

Absolute discretion, Abraham had said. Not a word. 'Again, Master Rush, I have no idea. All the despatches I have dealt with so far have been trivial in the extreme. Not a hint of a military secret from either side.'

'So nothing was taken from your room either?'

'As far as I could tell, nothing.'

For a few moments, Rush was silent. Then, abruptly, his mood changed and he smiled. 'It seems to me unlikely that the two events are connected. How would the men who attacked you know you were alone in my carriage on the Newbury road? And I daresay you are right about your room. Fayne was most reluctant to hand it over to you. The important thing is that you are unharmed. The deaths of the coachmen are of course regrettable, but in war there are casualties. I will send men to bring their bodies back to Oxford, and to arrange for my carriage to be repaired.'

It was the longest speech Thomas had ever heard Rush make. Almost effusive. 'Thank you, sir. Now, if you will excuse me, it has been a tiring day for me too.'

'Quite so. Put the whole thing out of your mind and leave me to deal with matters. The king will wish you to be at your best for the work that lies ahead.'

Somewhat confused, Thomas made a swift exit and walked quickly back to Pembroke. What a strange man indeed. His mood could shift in a trice, and for no apparent reason. Still, better a friend than an enemy.

The college kitchen was as obliging as ever, and, with a full stomach, and exhausted in mind and body, Thomas was asleep within the hour. The message was safely hidden beneath a floor-board under the bed, with a pisspot on top of it, and there it would stay when he was not working on it.

Ten hours later, his first thoughts on waking were of Margaret and the girls. Conscious that there had been other matters to occupy him, and that he had given them less thought than he should have, he allowed himself the indulgence of lying on his bed and watching them in his mind's eye. He saw them in the kitchen, Margaret reading, Polly and Lucy playing one of their games or struggling with the sewing stitches they were trying to master. He saw them at the market, with baskets of eggs and vegetables. And he saw them asleep in their beds. God forbid that any harm should come to them, and God forbid that he should be apart from them for much longer. If it had occurred to him, he might have ridden that horse straight to Romsey, not Oxford, and damn the consequences. He missed them terribly.

Then he thought of Jane Romilly. What exactly was her relationship with Fayne? 'Just an acquaintance', as she had claimed, or something more? It had certainly appeared more when he had seen them in the street. Yet Jane had called on him in this very room and brought him the book of sonnets she had bought in John Porter's shop. There was only one thing for it. He would call on her in Merton. First, however, he must visit Abraham.

The old man was in his usual place by the window, his unseeing eyes looking out on to the courtyard. He heard Thomas knock and enter unbidden. 'Is that you, Thomas?' he asked.

'It is, Abraham. How are you?'

'Much as before, thank you. More importantly, how are you? I hear you've been to war.'

'Reluctantly, and, thank God, I did no fighting.'

'Was it as bad as they say?'

'Whatever you've heard, it was worse. Thousands dead and maimed, families destroyed, and for nothing. Nothing whatsoever. Prince Rupert and the king have now returned to Oxford, and Essex will march on to London. If it goes on like this, the war will end only when there are no men left to fight.'

'Yes. I sometimes think we'd do better if we left it all to

the women. We men make such a bloody mess of everything.'

'I don't know, Abraham. Queen Elizabeth claimed to have the heart and stomach of a king and threatened to take up arms herself. And she cut off more than a few heads.'

'Had them cut off, I think you mean, Thomas. Now, what else have you to report?'

'Rush lent me his carriage for the journey home. He travelled with the king. We were attacked by two highwaymen, who shot both coachmen and searched the carriage.'

'Good God. Did they shoot at you?'

'Oddly, no. They wrecked the carriage, found nothing of value and made off. I rode home on one of the carriage horses.'

'And what did Master Rush have to say about that?'

'At first, I don't think he believed me. Then he seemed convinced and was quite solicitous.'

'Did they take nothing at all?'

'Nothing. Nor, thank the Lord, did they find Monsieur Vigenère, who was hiding in my stocking.'

'Do you think they were looking for him?'

'I did wonder, but how could anyone have known I was in that carriage, or that I even have the message?'

'You haven't told anyone, have you, Thomas?'

'On my life, Abraham, I have not. Not a soul.'

'Good. Then Rush is probably right. Just two robbers who went home disappointed. Although why they did not shoot you, too, or take the horses, is a mystery.'

'It is. I can only suppose they took pity on a poor fellow with but a few coins and a small bag of clothes to his name.'

Abraham closed his eyes. 'Have you made any progress with the message?'

'I fear not. The square has been unbroken for over seventy years and it may well stay that way for another seventy. I have come up with nothing.'

'Then back to work with you, Thomas. The more I've thought about it, the more I'm sure this is something of grave importance. Vigenère, numerical codes, hidden in a hat on the London to Cambridge road. It all points the same way.'

'Any advice, Abraham?'

'Encouragement rather than advice. You were a brilliant scholar, you have a rare talent for cryptography, and if anyone can break the code you can. Assume it can be broken. There's a key there somewhere and you will find it.'

'I wish I shared your confidence, but thank you for yours. If I fail, it will not be for want of trying.'

'Off you go then, and leave an old man to his rest.'

Back at his table, Thomas took his copy of the square out. It was time for a fresh start. Taking a new quill and a clean sheet of paper, he wrote out the square again.

Twenty-six possible encryptions for each letter. Using Abraham's straight edge to guide his eye, Thomas imagined the keyword to be LOVE, and the encrypted word to be JANE. Using the letters in the square where each letter of JANE met its counterpart in LOVE, the encryption would be UOII. Proof against any known method of analysing the frequency with which each letter appeared in a text. And proof, so far, against the attentions of Thomas Hill. For an hour Thomas sat and stared at the square, hoping for inspiration. None came. Then he retrieved the message itself from under the floorboard and stared at that. Still nothing. Not a glimmer.

By that evening, after another day of boiling frustration,

Thomas had given up hope. He was not going to be the man who broke the Vigenère square. Whatever this message contained would remain a secret until too late and there was nothing he could do about it. He had failed. He put it back under the floorboard, poured himself a glass of Silas's claret and tried to think about something else. Anything but the infernal square.

It took most of the bottle to do it, but eventually his brain surrendered.

As soon as he had breakfasted the next morning, he washed, shaved, dressed carefully and set off for Merton. He was resolved. Monsieur Vigenère might have defeated him, but Jane Romilly would not.

At Merton he was escorted to the Warden's lodgings by a member of the queen's guard, and asked to wait while the guard informed Lady Romilly of his arrival. Nearby he could see the tennis court, where he had learned the game and become proficient enough to defeat all but the best of his fellow scholars. He wondered how he would fare now, ten years on. He was fit enough, and strong, but would some of his old speed have deserted him? Idly, he practised a few strokes, imagining the corners into which he was aiming to hit the ball. It would be good to try his hand again.

The guard returned, shaking his head. 'Lady Romilly is not present, sir. Another of the queen's ladies suggests you return tomorrow.'

Thomas did not believe the man. All the queen's ladies would be present at that time of the morning to ensure that her majesty was suitably attired for the day and wanted for nothing. 'Kindly try again,' he said, 'and if, by some chance, Lady Romilly has unexpectedly returned, tell her that I am here on a matter of great importance and will wait until she consents to see me.' With a shrug, the guard did as he was asked. He was back within a minute.

'It seems that Lady Romilly does not wish to see you, sir. I am to escort you to the gate.'

Damn the woman. Stubborn and obstinate. Now there was nothing for it but to swallow his disappointment and find something else with which to occupy himself. A game of tennis, perhaps. The accursed message could stay under the pisspot.

He wandered disconsolately back to Pembroke, where he found the courtyard filled again with soldiers and their ladies. He stood quietly in a corner and listened to the men exchanging stories of Newbury. What he heard reflected well upon each story-teller, but made no mention of the horrors of the day. He heard of fearless advances, enemies slain and ground captured, but of dead and screaming men, horses crippled and dying, smoke, gunpowder and, above all, the futility of it, he heard nothing. Wondering if he had been at a different battle altogether, he carried on towards his room. He had taken no more than a few steps when a loud voice, loud enough to be heard by every man and woman there, came from the far corner of the yard.

'Well I'm damned, if it isn't the lucky little bookseller. Back from the bookshop, are we?' Thomas had not noticed Francis Fayne in the crowd. Fayne, however, had noticed Thomas. He turned and glared at the man, then continued on his way. 'Nothing to say, bookseller? Nothing to report while we've been fighting for the king at Newbury?' It was too much.

'I too was at Newbury,' he said quietly. 'And where were you?'

'Is that so?' laughed Fayne, ignoring the question and looking around for support. The men near him also laughed and one or two of the ladies put their hands to their mouths. 'I didn't see a book-shop at the battle.'

'I was with the king all day.'

'Were you now? Advising his majesty on his reading or skulking behind the lines? And what about the mare with the eyes? Was she with you or did you leave her here? Don't tell me you left her here, bookseller. She must have had to take her pleasures with ancient scholars and pimply stable boys. I doubt they were up to the task.'

It had happened only once before. In this very courtyard twelve years earlier, when a loud-mouthed braggart had taunted Thomas to breaking point and lived to regret it. Afterwards, Thomas had called it the 'Ice' — the absolute calm that had come over him that day. Unshakeable calm, and icy clarity of purpose. He had been aware of nothing — neither sound nor sight — other than his cold anger and the man on whom it was focused.

Now it happened again.

He strode up to Fayne and shot a fist into his face. Blood ran from Fayne's nose and he staggered backwards in astonishment. Thomas stood quite still and waited for the attack to come. He knew how to cope with an opponent taller and stronger than him-self, and felt not a twinge of fear. Every ounce of him was concentrated on the task.

Fayne wiped away the blood with the back of his sleeve, snarled and, arms outstretched, launched himself at Thomas. 'I'll break your scrawny neck, you shitten little worm.' He spat out the words like poison. Thomas danced to one side, stuck out a leg and helped Fayne on his way with a shove in the back. He stood over Fayne, who was sprawled face down on the ground, and allowed him to haul himself to his feet. By this time, the courtyard was silent. Every voice was hushed and every eye watching.

Before Fayne knew it, Thomas had landed two more punches, and stepped nimbly out of his reach. The first blackened an eye, the second split a lip. The handsome face was twisted and bloody. Fayne, though, was strong. He shook off the blows and swung a fist at Thomas. It was slow and cumbersome, but brushed Thomas's shoulder, knocking him slightly off balance. Fayne saw his chance and grabbed Thomas's throat. Thomas found himself pushed back against the wall, struggling to take a breath. Fayne hissed at him through the blood, 'Now, bookseller, now I'll break your neck.'

Thomas knew he had to move fast. He grabbed Fayne's hair with his left hand and got his right hand under Fayne's nose. He pulled the hair backwards and pushed as hard as he could with the ball of his thumb. No attacker's nose could resist that, and Fayne's head was forced back and away until he had to release his grip on Thomas's throat. The moment he did so, Thomas kicked him hard on the knee and landed two more blows to his nose, drawing more blood. Fayne subsided to the ground with a grunt of pain, his hands covering his face. It was over. Thomas could see no point in waiting for the mewling oaf to recover, and, with a bow to the ladies, adjusted his dress and left them to offer their friend whatever assistance they could.

Just as it had the first time, the icy calm departed as quickly as it had come. And when it did, it left a void. Thomas was drained of strength and emotion. He lay on his bed and closed his eyes. He had always regarded violence as a form of weakness, and he knew he had been weak. He should have ignored Fayne. He should not have allowed himself to be provoked. Perhaps it had been Jane's refusal to see him, perhaps a reaction to the battle and his journey from Newbury, perhaps neither. 'You are a feeble fellow, Thomas Hill,' he said to himself, 'and I trust you will not allow such a thing to happen again.'

CHAPTER 9

Abraham was blunt to the point of rudeness. 'You will not give up, Thomas, until I say you can. And I am unlikely ever to do so. I have told the king that you are the most accomplished cryptographer in England, and you are not to embarrass me by quitting.'

'Abraham, I've tried everything. The cipher is unbreakable. I cannot do it.'

'You can, Thomas, and you will. There will be a way. Find it.'

Thomas sighed in resignation. 'Oh very well, Abraham, for you I'll keep trying. I wouldn't do it for anyone else.'

'Good. Go now and begin again. I wish to be informed the moment you have made progress.'

'Rest assured that you will be the first to know if there is even a hint of it.'

For two days, he laboured on the message and his square, trying all manner of approaches — some logical, others absurd, all futile.

None worked. On the third morning, he sat at his table and tried again.

Can there really be such a thing as an unbreakable cipher? he asked himself for the hundredth time. Monsieur Vigenère thought so, and so far he was right. Twenty-six possible substitutions for each letter, determined by an agreed keyword, from whose own letters the encryption row was taken. If the keyword were THOMAS, a single letter in the text might have been encrypted according to any of the rows starting with T, H, O, M, A or S. It would not respond to analysis of frequencies. Yet the more he thought about it, the more Thomas's logical mind could not accept the concept of an unbreakable cipher. That the square had not yet been broken did not mean it never would be. Abraham was right. There would be a way.

Putting himself in the shoes of an encrypter, he wrote down five repetitions of his keyword THOMAS, and, underneath them, his 'message' in plain text.

THOMASTHOMASTHOMASTHOMASTHOMAS

ONEEYEISBROWNYETTHEOTHERISBLUE

Then, using the square he had already constructed, he encoded each letter of his message according to the letter above it, which indicated which row of the square to use. This gave him a third, enciphered line:

HUSQYWBZPDOOGFSFTZXVHTEJBZPXUW

The recipient of this message would decrypt it by reversing the process, as long as he knew the keyword, or the sequence of rows to be used, which could, less securely, be communicated by numbers. But as the numbers had proved time-consuming and unhelpful, Thomas had decided that they were codes and that he would return to the letters. Two things stuck out from his encryption. Double letters were coincidental, and would be no help in decryption, and any letter encrypted according to the letter A would appear as itself. Without his knowing if there were any As in the keyword, this too was unhelpful. He also noticed, however, that the sequence of letters BZP appeared twice, because they happened to coincide twice with the plain text letters ISB. A thought struck him. He knew why BZP appeared twice because he knew what the keyword was. In a Vigenère square, single-letter repetitions were meaningless, but repetitions of sequences might not be.

For an hour he pondered the question. The answer did not leap at him as it did to Archimedes in his bath, it crept up slowly. If he just knew the length of the keyword it would be a start. Common letter sequences, such as THE, AND and TION, would have been repeated in the text, and would sometimes have coincided with repeats of the letters of the keyword, thus leading to repetitions in the encrypted text. If he measured the distances in letters between each repeated sequence, he should be able to calculate the length of the keyword. In his 'message' BZP were letters seven to nine, and twenty-five to twenty-seven. So the start of the second sequence fell eighteen letters after the start of the first. His keyword, THOMAS, had six letters. Eighteen was divisible by six. The letters of the keyword had been repeated exactly three times before meeting the same plain-text sequence of letters again. It was a matter of simple arithmetic. Then an awkward thought occurred. Eighteen was also divisible by one, two, three, nine and itself. Not so simple, after all. Time for another stroll. He locked his door and set off.

Outside Pembroke, Thomas turned left towards the ancient castle. Head down and lost in thought, he barely noticed the beggars and whores who infested this part of the town. Jumbles of letters and numbers tumbled about in his mind, as if trying to make some sort of sense but never quite managing it. He walked round the castle and back towards St Ebbe's. Could he find the length of the keyword from repeating sequences of letters, and, if so, how could he use it? He felt the vague stirring of an idea.

He did not see the boys until it was too late. Three of them came hurtling towards him, and, before he could move aside, knocked him off his feet into a drain. At least they had the grace to stop and help him up, dusting him down and enquiring if he was hurt. Although he knew that his shoulder was bruised, he assured them that he was only shaken, and advised them to take more care in future. They promised to do so and offered to help him home. Not wishing to be helped, he declined the offer and walked alone back to Pembroke, conscious that he looked and smelt exactly as if he had fallen into a drain.

For once, Silas was not on sentry duty, so he did not have to undergo an inquisition. At the door to his room, he reached into his pocket for the key. It was not there. He tried the other pocket. Not there either. 'Damnation,' he said out loud, 'it's in that shit-filled drain. And it'll have to stay there.'

He returned to find Silas back at his post. Having offered a feeble lie for his condition and for the loss of the key, he was grudgingly given a replacement. 'I keep three keys for each lock, sir. One for the gentleman, one for me and one spare. Now you've lost yours, I've got no spare until I can get another made, and only the good Lord knows when that will be. The forges are all busy sharpening swords and shoeing horses.'

Inside his room at last, Thomas stripped off his foul clothes, washed himself down with water from the jug and tried to examine his shoulder. It hurt, but he could see no signs of a wound. Tomorrow he would be fine.

At dawn, the vague idea stirred again. In a longer text, there would be more than one letter sequence repeated. If he took the letter measurements between all repeated sequences of the same letters, he should find a common factor, suggesting the length of the keyword. To test this theory, he started by counting the number of different repeated sequences in the text, ignoring those of less than three letters. He found ten of them, including three repetitions of IFS. He could not be entirely sure that he had not missed any, but ten should be enough for a test. He drew a line under the repeated sequences and counted the letters separating each repetition of each sequence.

URF UBD HE XQB TF KGA OEMD RRFUO TLC WMG LRB WHT R XHGORKZ IO KPW769

WA MQFV BVMF HPL ZFTD RVV57 4SEWMFREJ VGL SVKMGE 852 GTSC WZTD QE

TIJG IVL GJT RA KDOE IK EOJAAQLV GGJR MQU IOIGSI GRQF HBFZG JGY

ALG EE OLWEEA GJR YIFS1 82AEL2 64SGE SC AAD ZVY JP KP WXR JB JTN XBZ77

5XNW WJBS LA LWAK371 EAIH TPA AD RVV BAP TWPVV AGDN WWJ URR VUT

IW EW HTI QCT WY QDT37 1IE852 769UMHT RKC CONT WSGV WMG IEN DJEE KW

IHV ZW PNU EAIH371 ZV GJR YIFSS NQ DA BV NGGCVL LD SVMC IRLKW DN

KMJ BS WINDU IITAE KW42177 5OX LCIVK IJM LXMV IFS PCI UT FFZ

SEPI MZTNJQGCOW3 71E ZDWZTD QE SZGJ GYB LD 574SKIFS RVIV N GFL

OX LC QFV WV AZPLCJJX NX IF TNU BG IHZA OP RJWGC

The results he wrote on a table, with the sequences in the left

column, the letter distances he found for each in the second
column, and the numbers three to ten across the top row, working
on the assumption that the keyword would be more than two and
less than eleven letters long.

		3	4	5	6	7	8	9	10
RFU	20		X	X					X
WHT	210	X		X	X	X			X
QFV	370			X					X
RVV	150	X		X	X				X
IFS	60	X	X	X	X				X
IFS	45	X		X		X		X	
IFS	105	X		X		X			
WWJ	35			X		X			
AAD	40		X	X			X		X
WZTD	300	X	X	X	X				X

Only the number five divided into all ten separations. The
keyword must have five letters.

So delighted was he at the first hint of progress that Thomas
almost forgot to hide his papers before hurrying to tell Abraham.
He prised up the floorboard, put the papers in the space below it
and replaced the pisspot on top. Then he picked up the pot and
filled it up. Oddly, it reminded him of the king's musketeers piss-
ing down the barrels of their muskets to cool them down. That
should keep prying eyes at bay. He locked his door and went to
give Abraham the good news.

Expecting to be summoned straight in, he knocked loudly on
Abraham's door. When there was no response, he knocked again.
Still no response. He tried the door, which was locked. Odd.

Perhaps Silas would know where he was. He found Silas at his post. 'Silas, Master Fletcher's door is locked and he appears to be out. Do you know where he is?'

'No, sir. Master Fletcher never goes out unaccompanied, and I haven't seen him today. Perhaps he's asleep.'

'Have you a spare key to his rooms?'

'I have, sir,' replied Silas suspiciously, 'but I'd prefer not to lose it. If you don't mind, I'll come with you and unlock the door myself.' He took a large bunch of keys from a drawer and followed Thomas to the room. They knocked again, but there was still no response. Silas found the right key and unlocked the door. Thomas entered first, and gasped. The room had been ransacked. Every one of Abraham's books had been torn from its spine and thrown on the floor. His chair and table were in pieces, and his few clothes and other possessions were strewn about everywhere. Thomas went cold. What in the name of God had happened here?

He called out. 'Abraham? Where are you?' There was no reply. They went cautiously in, and tried the door to the small chamber where Abraham slept. It was unlocked. Thomas entered. On his blood-soaked bed lay the naked body of the old man. His face and chest bore the signs of torture, his eyes had been gouged out and his throat cut. Thomas's stomach heaved. He put his hand to his mouth and closed his eyes. Silas looked past him into the chamber, and vomited. For several minutes, neither man could speak. Both stood with hands on knees, trying to breathe. Thomas was the first to recover. 'What manner of human filth could have done this? And why?'

Silas, too, was recovering. 'I'll fetch the coroner, sir. You'd best stay here.'

'Be quick, Silas. The coroner must see this at once.'

When Silas had gone, Thomas sat on the floor by the door. His old friend, a gentle man who had never harmed a soul and had helped many, foully murdered in this monstrous, sickening, obscene way. His tears flowed and he howled in anguish. God in heaven, how could any man commit such an act? What could drive a man to inflict such suffering on another? Why take the eyes of a man who could not see?

For an hour, Thomas barely moved. The strength had gone from his legs and his mind was numb. He sat staring at the room and thought of nothing but Abraham's premonition. Somehow the old man had known. God forbid that he had known it would be like this.

He was still on the floor when Silas returned with the coroner, a fussy-looking little man with a red-veined face and a pair of pince-nez perched on his nose. Thomas took a deep breath and rose to meet him. 'Henry Pearson, sir, coroner. It is my duty to investigate all unnatural deaths in the city and in cases of murder to identify and bring to trial the murderer.'

'Thomas Hill, sir. An old student of Master Fletcher, and an old friend.'

'Did you find the body?'

'I did. Master Merkin was behind me.'

'Have you left everything as you found it?' The coroner was brusque.

'I've touched nothing. The body is in the bedchamber.' Pearson bustled past him and into the chamber. When he emerged, he was ashen.

'Master Fletcher suffered greatly before he died. Judging by the state of rigor mortis, I would say he has been dead for a good seven hours.'

'So he was murdered in the night?'

'That is my opinion. Have you any idea why anyone would do this?'

Thomas had no intention of disclosing Abraham's position, or his own, to Henry Pearson, coroner or not. 'None, sir. Abraham was a quiet, scholarly man. I can conceive of no reason for this barbarity.'

'Have you seen anything suspicious?' he asked Silas.

'No, sir,' replied Silas firmly. 'Both college gates are locked from midnight to six in the morning. Anyone wishing to enter must ring the bell. I only let them in if I know who they are.'

'Then the murderer was already in the college before you locked the gates. Either he's still here or he must have slipped out again this morning. Have you been at your post all the time?'

'Yes, sir, except when I came to unlock the door for Master Hill.'

'Then if he left, that was when. He would have been watching, knowing that sooner or later the door would be found locked. Alternatively, he is living here.' Pearson changed direction. 'You say the door was locked. Could the murderer have had a key?'

'No, sir,' replied Silas firmly. 'Master Fletcher had his key. I have the other two.'

'Could one have been stolen, and later returned?'

'No, sir. I'd have noticed. I check all the keys every morning.'

'Then either Master Fletcher opened the door to his murderer, or the door was unlocked. The murderer took his key and locked the door when he left. Master Fletcher probably knew the man.'

'Not necessarily, Master Pearson,' pointed out Thomas. 'Abraham Fletcher was blind. He could have opened the door to a stranger without knowing it.'

'In that case, he would have been an easy victim and the murderer's motive will be more difficult to establish. Had he any relatives in Oxford?'

'Not as far as I know, sir,' replied Silas. 'He never mentioned any.'

'A pity. You'd be surprised how many murderers turn out to be wives, husbands and sons. Did he have any enemies?'

'I can think of none.'

'Alas, Master Hill, it seems he had at least one. One who was searching for something. What could that have been?'

'I doubt it was money. Abraham was not a wealthy man.'

'It looks more like a document or information of some kind. The murderer must have hoped to find it in a book. What subjects did Master Fletcher teach?'

'Mathematics, philosophy and a little divinity.'

'What might be secret about those?'

'Very little. He was just an elderly scholar who loved books and learning.' Thomas was getting angry. He was feeling the strain of answering the coroner's questions, and of having to lie. He did not know who the murderer was, but he was quite sure about the motive. It was about ciphers, and, most probably, the one under Thomas's floorboards. But he could not risk telling the coroner that.

'And why would he have been tortured?' The little man was persistent, as coroners usually were.

'Master Pearson, I really have no idea,' said Thomas. 'Abraham Fletcher was my friend. This has been a terrible shock, and I would like to go now.'

'Before you do, sir, someone will have to come to my house formally to identify the deceased. I will have the body taken there as soon as I have inspected the room.'

'I will come tomorrow,' said Thomas. 'May I go now?'

'You may, sir. I know where you are if I need you.'

In the courtyard outside, Thomas was horrified to find a curious crowd of soldiers. The coroner must have been recognized, and word spread around the college. Soon it would be around Oxford. He wondered if that was the murderer's intention. Ignoring the stares and whispers, he hurried past the soldiers and across the yard, hoping not to be accosted again by Fayne.

He opened the door to his room, and stood staring. In the time he had been in Abraham's room, someone, and it was not hard to guess who, had been there. The bed had been stripped of blankets, papers were strewn across the floor and his clothes had been dumped in a corner. Fayne. The cowardly oaf had taken his revenge in this petty way. Then Thomas looked around. It was subtly different to the last time. Not only had the lock been opened with a key, rather than broken, but this time he had the impression that the room had been searched. The papers on the floor had been placed rather than thrown there, as if the intruder had gone through them. Thomas pushed aside the bed, moved the pot and pulled up the loose floorboard. The message and his workings were still there. He replaced the board and sat on his chair. He wrinkled his nose — there was the faintest trace of a sweet smell he did not recognize. He put the notion aside and looked about. The room reminded him of the bookshop after the soldiers had wrecked it. For some time he sat and thought. Erasmus Pole and Abraham Fletcher cruelly murdered, a message encrypted with the Vigenère cipher, an unseemly fight and his room ransacked. What in God's name had induced him to come to Oxford? He went to fetch Silas.

Silas too was horrified. 'Master Fletcher and now you, sir,' he said. 'As well you weren't here, or . . .' He stopped himself just in time.

'Did you have a spare key made, Silas?'

'No, sir. It was only yesterday you lost it.'

'And you've had yours on your ring at all times?'

'I have, sir.'

Had his key not disappeared down that stinking drain after all? And if it had not, who now had it? Certainly not three small boys, who had no idea which door it opened. He thought about it, and about all the other things that had happened, and it hit him. Surely not. 'Silas, please send a boy for Father de Pointz at Merton. Ask him to come at once.'

'At once, sir.'

'And, Silas, tell no one about this. It would only complicate matters.'

If Silas was surprised, he did not show it. 'As you wish, Master Hill.'

When Silas had left, Thomas made no effort to put the room back together. He wanted Simon to see it.

Simon arrived within the hour. 'What's been happening, Thomas?' he asked. 'We hear there has been a murder. Is this connected to it?'

'It is. And it's Abraham who's been murdered. Murdered and tortured. Simon, his eyes were cut out. How could any man do such a thing?'

Simon crossed himself. 'Someone who wanted something badly enough, and thought Abraham had it. Poor Abraham. He was a good man. I grieve that he suffered. I shall pray for his soul.' He paused and crossed himself again. 'When did it happen?'

'The coroner thinks it was during the night. The door wasn't forced. Abraham let his own murderer in.'

'And this?' He indicated the ruined room.

'When I was at Abraham's room.'

'Then the murderer did not find what he wanted in Abraham's room and came here to look for it. Did he find it here, Thomas?'

'Thankfully, he did not. I have it safe.'

'And can you tell me what it is?'

No more pretence. Thomas retrieved the message from its hiding place and handed it to Simon. 'This is what he was looking for. A text encrypted with a Vigenère square, a cipher thought to be unbreakable.'

'A Vigenère square? I recall your mentioning Vigenère in the inn at Abingdon. Is this the same man?'

'It is. And you must have your second lesson. If anything should happen to me, it would be as well if someone else knew about it.' Thomas patiently described Blaise de Vigenère's square with its twenty-six possible encryptions of each letter of a text, rendering analysis of individual letter frequencies useless. Only a possessor of the keyword could decrypt a Vigenère text. He told Simon how the message had come to him, and that Abraham was sure it contained information vital to the outcome of the war. 'Texts which use the square are laborious to encrypt and decrypt,' he explained, 'so it's seldom used for military purposes. This message is hiding something the king needs to know, and his enemies will do anything to prevent him knowing. That's why Abraham died.'

'If you're right, Thomas, you're in grave danger. You certainly can't stay here.'

'Simon, what do you know of Tobias Rush?'

'Rush? Come now, Thomas, surely you don't think he's behind Abraham's murder? Rush is one of the king's closest advisers. That would make him a traitor as well as a murderer. An unpleasant fellow he may be, but a traitor? Surely not.'

Thomas told him about Rush's visit and the questions about his work. He described the journey from Newbury and the deaths of the coachmen, and he pointed out how easy it would have been for Rush to gain entry to Abraham's room by pretending to be on the king's business. And he told him about the 'accident' in the street and the loss of his key. He guessed that the boys who had knocked him down had been paid by Rush to steal his key. Simon listened carefully. When Thomas had finished his account, he said, 'Thomas, even if Rush did murder Abraham, he could not have searched your room.'

'Why not? He could have hidden in the college and watched me cross the courtyard.'

'No. The king is away from Oxford and sent for him last night. He left around midnight and has not yet returned. I know because two of the queen's men went with him as guards. If he were back in Oxford, so would they be.'

If the coroner was right about the time of death, Rush could have murdered Abraham and been back in Christ Church before the summons from the king arrived. But he could not have ransacked Thomas's room. 'Then he had an accomplice. Before departing to join the king, Rush sent someone to watch for a chance to enter the room, using my key, and to find the message. And I believe I know who it was.'

'Who?'

'Captain Francis Fayne, the man whose room this used to be.

And there's another thing. I've walked down the lane where Erasmus Pole was found, and I don't believe he would have gone there at night. He was murdered elsewhere and his body left in the lane. The coroner wouldn't have bothered with just another dead body there. What's more, both Pole and Abraham had their throats cut. The same method of killing. The same killer.'

'Thomas,' said Simon when Thomas had finished, 'even if Tobias Rush is a traitor and a murderer, all you have is supposition. Supposition, not proof. If the king is to be persuaded of the guilt of one of his closest advisers, absolute proof will be needed. He trusts Rush implicitly.'

'And how are we to get proof? The man's cunning and devious. Proof will not be easy to come by.'

'We'll have to think of a plan. Meanwhile, we must find you a safe haven.'

'I didn't know the king had left Oxford again. Where is he now?'

'I don't know. A secret rendezvous somewhere. He must have needed Rush urgently. Her majesty is despondent. She always fears the worst when the king is away. It's her nature.'

'So what do you propose?'

'When it's dark, we'll slip out of Pembroke and go to Merton. You can stay in my rooms tonight. Even Rush wouldn't dare enter the rooms of the queen's priest without permission. Until then we'll stay here.'

'I have to visit the coroner tomorrow morning to identify Abraham's body.'

'In that case, I shall accompany you there. Then we'll think of a way to get you home.'

'Simon,' said Thomas, 'there's one more thing. I've made

some progress on the cipher. Given time, I think I may be able to decrypt it. I must stay here until I have. And, in any case, Rush's long arm will certainly reach Romsey. I'm safer here.'

'What about your family?'

'I worry for them day and night. I've had no word from them. Rush offered to have my letter delivered to them, but I doubt it ever got there. Yet they're probably safer without me. If Rush's men came calling for me, they would all be in danger. I want to go home, but Abraham's death has changed things. He thought this message was important and he was right. I must decrypt it.'

'If that's what you want, Thomas. Now, Rush or not, there is a vicious murderer in Oxford, so we'll stay here until dark. Would you care to show me the cipher and what you've been able to do?'

Better to keep the mind occupied, thought Thomas, as Simon well knows. 'Very well, I'll explain.'

It was a long afternoon. When darkness eventually fell they left the room together, taking only the message and Thomas's papers. The courtyard was empty and Simon diverted Silas's attention while Thomas slipped out, then joined him outside the gate. Even Silas must not know where Thomas was going. They walked quickly to Merton, taking care to keep their distance from anyone passing in the street. At Merton, Simon took Thomas to his room in the little quadrangle behind the chapel, and left him there while he went to arrange for food and drink, and to find a pallet for Thomas's bed.

Thomas slept little. The image of sightless, eyeless Abraham, his chest and face bloody, his hands tied and his throat cut, had imprinted itself on his mind. It was a different sort of horror, and even more terrible than what he had seen at Newbury. Abraham had been his friend. He might have admitted to knowing about the message or he might not. It was of no account. The old man had suffered beyond imagining, and Thomas could do nothing about it. He could only grieve.

Simon, too, slept little. He asked Thomas to repeat the account of his being knocked down in the street, and he asked about Rush's questions relating to Thomas's work. He gave Thomas the impression that he knew something more, something not even Abraham had known. He did not say what, and Thomas lacked the will to ask. Simon would tell him if he wanted to.

Next morning, having hidden the papers in Simon's Bible, they left Merton for the coroner's house. In order not to attract attention, Simon walked well behind Thomas, and kept an eye out for danger. At the corner of Cornmarket and Ship Street, where the coroner's house stood, Thomas suddenly stopped and ducked into a doorway. Not knowing why, Simon did the same, and waited until Thomas emerged before going on. Thomas waited for him to catch up.

'It was Rush, Simon. He's back. I saw him leaving the coroner's house.'

'Did he see you?'

'I don't think so. He was hurrying.'

'Good. Well, you'll have to visit the coroner or he'll be suspicious. I'll wait outside for you.'

When Thomas knocked on the coroner's door, it was opened immediately. Henry Pearson was waiting for him. Without saying a word, he led Thomas to a back room, empty but for a low table on which lay Abraham's body, covered by a grey cloth. Pearson raised the cloth. 'Do you recognize this man?' he asked briskly.

'I do. It's Abraham Fletcher.'

Pearson replaced the cloth and ushered Thomas out of the

room. Indicating for Thomas to follow him, he opened the door to another room and went in. This too was bare of furniture but for a small desk and two chairs.

'While you are here, Master Hill,' said Pearson, 'I have some questions to ask you.' He remained standing and did not offer Thomas a chair.

'Very well,' replied Thomas, 'although I believe I have told you everything I know.'

'That we shall soon ascertain. I have examined the body and established the cause of death as the severing of the deceased's windpipe with a very sharp blade. The cut was clean. Before he died, his face and chest were cut with the same weapon, and his eyes removed, probably also with the same blade. The eyes were not at the scene of the murder. There are marks on his wrists consistent with their being tied with rope, no doubt in order to restrain him. There are also signs that a rag or cloth was stuffed into his mouth to prevent his crying out.'

Thomas felt his knees give, and reached for a chair to steady himself. The coroner ignored his distress.

'Can you confirm that you were the first to find the body?'

'I can. Silas Merkin and I.'

'Quite. You used Merkin's key to enter the room?'

'We did. When there was no answer to my knock, I fetched him.'

'Were you surprised that there was no answer?'

'I was. Abraham was blind, but his hearing was good. And he seldom left his rooms.'

'Why were you calling on him?'

'Abraham taught me mathematics and philosophy. He was a good friend and a fine scholar. I came to Oxford to visit him before he died. We spent the mornings together discussing philosophy and books.' It was the story they had agreed.

'I see. And how long have you been in Oxford?'

'I arrived some four weeks ago.'

'Indeed? A long visit.'

'I enjoy Oxford, even in time of war, and I enjoyed Abraham's company. I am unmarried. I saw no need to hurry home.'

'Where is your home, Master Hill?'

'I live in the town of Romsey, in Hampshire.'

'A long journey, not to be lightly undertaken.'

'Long enough. The more reason not to make it again too soon.'

'I believe Master Fletcher was killed during the night before he was found. Perhaps six hours earlier. Where were you at that time?'

'Asleep in my room, naturally.' Thomas was fast losing patience. 'Master Pearson, do you suspect me of this unspeakable crime? For heaven's sake, Abraham Fletcher was my friend.'

'So you say. I am of the opinion that the murderer resided in the college. A stranger would have been noticed.'

'The college is full of soldiers and their families. Which of them would want to kill an elderly scholar, and why?'

'Why, indeed? The motive is as yet unclear, but I have received information that Master Fletcher performed certain services for the king. Services important to the conduct of the war. If this became known to a traitor, he might have been in danger.'

And I know who you received it from, thought Thomas. Tobias Rush, a murderer and a traitor. 'I know nothing of such matters.'

'I have also been informed that you were recently found drunk in the street.'

'Drunk in the street? Nonsense. I was knocked into a shit-filled drain by three boys. I was quite sober.'

'Were there any witnesses to this?'

'I expect so. There were people in the street. Someone must have seen it happen.'

'I shall make inquiries. Meanwhile, Thomas Hill, a coroner's jury will be summoned to examine the death of Abraham Fletcher. I have no doubt that the jury will reach a verdict of murder. I also have no doubt that you had the means, and probably the motive, to commit this awful crime, and that the jury will send you to the Court of Assizes to stand trial for murder. While I conduct further investigations, you will be held at Oxford Castle. Guard!'

Before Thomas could protest, two guards who must have been waiting outside threw open the door.

'Bind the prisoner and take him immediately to the castle. He is to be held there until I order his release or transfer elsewhere.'

When his hands were tied and he was marched out of the house, the terrible truth hit Thomas. Rush had bribed the coroner, and he really was being taken to one of the most notorious gaols in England. He shouted for help, and was struck in the face for his trouble. Outside, he searched frantically for Simon. At first he could not see him, and was almost panicked into calling out again. Then Simon appeared briefly from behind a wall, signalled that he had seen Thomas and disappeared again. He must have feared that they were being watched.

At the castle, the coroner's guards told the gatekeeper their business, and they were escorted through the castle yard to a thick oak door on the other side. The gatekeeper unlocked it, and

Thomas was manhandled into a dingy guardroom, where a pox-scarred man with a huge belly sat eating a chicken leg. His guards handed their charge over to the fat gaoler. 'Room for a small one? Shouldn't be here long. He'll be off to the Assizes for murder.'

'We'll fit 'im in somewhere,' replied the gaoler, through a mouthful of chicken. 'If 'e's a murderer, we'd better chain 'im.' He took an iron ring attached to a short chain from a row hanging on the wall, and locked it round Thomas's neck. 'That'll keep 'im out of trouble.'

The guards left, and Thomas was led by the chain to a flight of stone steps which spiralled up the ancient tower of the castle. The steps were so narrow that the gaoler could only just squeeze himself up them. The iron ring was rusty and cut into Thomas's neck, and his hands were still bound. His legs were shaking and his eyes refused to focus. From inside low doors leading off the steps at intervals came the sounds of human beings in pain. In this tower, prisoners-of-war, convicted criminals and men awaiting trial were all thrown in together. The prison made no distinctions. The stench of filth and misery was overpowering. At the fourth door, the gaoler stopped. He unlocked the door with a key from a bunch tied to his waist, pulled Thomas inside, kicked something out of the way and forced Thomas to his knees. He fastened the chain with a lock to another chain hanging from the wall, unbound Thomas's hands and left. The door clanged shut, and Thomas was in darkness.

CHAPTER 10

Even the blackest darkness could not hide the pool of shit and vomit in which Thomas was sitting, or the noxious slime that ran down the wall behind his back. His stomach heaved, and he added his own contribution to the pool. As his eyes adjusted to the meagre light from a tiny window high up on one wall, he began to make out the shapes around him. They sat, chained as he was, around all four walls of the cell and, unchained, back to back in the middle. In a space no more than twenty feet by fifteen, he counted forty bodies, including three that were so small they could only be children, not one of which could move a muscle without sloshing about in a sea of muck. No one spoke, or even raised a head to look at the new arrival. Some were moaning, a few weeping. Most were silent. Chained or unchained, every prisoner sat, knees up and head down, in whatever space he could get. There was scant room to stretch a leg, never mind lie down. Not that lying in six inches of piss and shit held much attraction. Thomas looked to his right, and, with a shock, saw that the thing the gaoler had kicked out of the way was a body. A dead one. And as the cell became clearer, he realized that it was not the only dead body. There were certainly four others, and might be more. It was hard to be sure. He rested his head on his knees and closed his eyes. Smell, sound and touch, he could not avoid. Taste and sight, he would try to. It was at least something to concentrate on.

After a while, the door was unlocked and the fat gaoler waddled in. He grabbed a boy by the hair and dragged him outside. The boy went without a sound. Again, no one showed the slightest interest. For all they cared, the boy might be going to the gallows or on his way home.

They cared when he was brought back, however. They heard his screams coming up the steps, and they saw him tossed like a doll into the cell. Holding his hands out in front of him, the boy sat and howled. For the first time, someone spoke.

'Shut up, boy, or I'll snap your neck.'

'They burned my hands,' wailed the child. 'They tied leaves and twigs between my fingers and burned them.'

'Piss on them. That'll cool them down.'

Thomas had heard of this. The governor's fire, it was called. Torture for pleasure, and on a boy of no more than ten. Gradually, the boy's howls became sobs, then stopped altogether. He slumped to the floor and lay still. The first voice spoke again.

'If I 'ad a knife, I'd eat the little bugger.'

'Me, too.'

''e's only a runt. Wouldn't be enough on 'im to go round.'

God in heaven, thought Thomas, how in the name of everything holy did I get here? He knew, of course. It was the very unholy Rush. With the king away, he thought he could get away with anything. First Pole, then Abraham, now him. Whatever was in it, Rush wanted that message. It was more than a routine despatch, much more. Somewhere hidden in it was information of critical importance to the outcome of the war. A peace proposal, perhaps, or news of help from the Dutch? Or something more devious? Simon must keep it hidden until he got out of here and could work on it again.

Some time later the door to the cell was unlocked and the fat gaoler came in again, this time carrying a heavy-looking cudgel. A younger man, who might have been his son, followed with two loaves of bread, which he threw on the floor.

'Dinner time,' croaked the gaoler. 'Eat up. Too skinny and you'll go slow on the rope. And be grateful. Remember I 'ad to pay for it from me own pocket.'

Even before the gaolers had left, an unchained boy leapt on a loaf and sank his teeth into it. He had barely done so when he was knocked aside by a large, black-bearded man, whose arms were just long enough to reach the bread. No one else got a bite, and Thomas did not see where the other loaf went. It hardly mattered. He was not yet hungry enough to take a mouthful of stale, shit-covered bread.

He sat against the slimy wall, and tried to think of Margaret and the girls. But he could not. The walls of the gaol would not let him. He could see only gangs of men, serfs and slaves, digging out the foundations of this place, lowering down stone and bricks and timbers on ropes, clambering down rickety ladders to dig and build foundations, and watching a great castle slowly emerge. They had built well. The castle and its tower had stood for five hundred years. How many men had died in it? How many had died in this very cell? If it stood for another five hundred years, how many more would die here? He wondered who had designed the castle, where the stone had come from, where the iron had been forged. He wondered how long it had taken to build and how many men had toiled on it. Gazing at the stone walls, he wondered about the mason who had built it. Was he tall, short, fat, thin? How did he speak? Did he have a family? How old was he when he worked here? What tools had he used?

Realizing that he was doing just as he did when faced with a new cipher, Thomas smiled and tried something else. Starting from the top left corner, he began counting the stones in the wall. He counted along the rows, noting that the odd-numbered rows began with a small stone and the even-numbered ended with one. The same occurred where a row met the door. He counted two hundred and sixteen stones in the wall. Building a wall must be like decrypting a cipher. It had to be done stone by stone. One stone out of place and the wall would be weak, and would fall. One mistake in a decryption, and the system would fail. Lay a strong foundation, take careful measurements and lay one stone squarely on top of another. Check your work regularly. Wall building and decryption. Much the same.

By the following evening, Thomas was ravenous. No more bread had been brought by the gaolers, and no bodies removed. His stomach was racked with cramps, and he longed to stand or stretch his legs. But whenever he tried to, his legs were grabbed and twisted until he moved them back. He tried to think about the cipher. He saw letters and stones, shapes and patterns. He saw Vigenère's square as a rippling wave and as a wall of stones. He knew that something important was eluding him, but lacked the strength to search for it. He fell into a sleep which was not a sleep. He saw shapes and heard noises, but he could not tell whether they were real or imagined. He no longer noticed the stench, or the sounds of men retching and defecating. His world began at the wall behind his back and ended at his toes.

Some time that night, the door was opened and the fat gaoler came in again. He unlocked Thomas's chain and pulled him roughly to his feet. Thomas immediately fell, and was hoisted up by his arm. He struggled to stand.

'You've a visitor, 'ill. Downstairs.'

Thank God. Simon, or even Jane. The gaoler tied his hands behind his back with a short length of rope, and led him by the chain around his neck through the door and down the stone steps to the guardroom.

''ere 'e is, sir. I'll be outside.'

Thomas went in and heard the gaoler lock the gate behind him. In the room were a small table and two chairs. On one of them sat Tobias Rush.

'Master Hill,' said Rush, not bothering to stand. 'I'm greatly distressed to find you here. Do sit down.' As always, Rush was all in black, hands resting on the silver-topped cane. Thomas sat. 'News of your arrest reached me only yesterday. I came as soon as I could.'

It was a lie. Thomas stared at him and said nothing.

Rush continued. 'Master Pearson, the coroner, tells me that there is evidence against you for the murder of Abraham Fletcher. I could scarcely believe it, and told him so. Absurd, I said. Why would Thomas Hill murder Abraham Fletcher?' He paused. 'Did you murder Master Fletcher, Thomas?'

You know I did not, Rush, because you did, thought Thomas, saying nothing. Rush's voice turned menacing.

'Nothing to say? Then let me assist you. The coroner believes that the murderer resided in the college. An intruder would have had difficulty hiding and would have been noticed. His inquiries have turned up nothing to suggest this. On the contrary, he is certain that the murderer was well known to Master Fletcher. As to motive, the culprit was obviously looking for something, and was prepared to kill to get it. I wonder what that could have been. Have you any idea, Thomas?'

Still Thomas remained silent.

'No? Let me remind you that you are suspected of a murder for which you have no alibi. Whatever secret Abraham Fletcher was guarding, it would have been dangerous to someone, and who is to say that that someone isn't you? And I warned you to guard your tongue. Oxford is full of spies and traitors to the Crown. No one is above suspicion, even a lady-in-waiting to the queen.' He sneered. 'Now the coroner suspects you of being one of them. If you do not confide in me, there is little I can do to help you. At the very least, you will hang.'

Thomas stared across the table at the black eyes, and saw the evil in them. 'Thomas, this is foolishness.' Again Rush's voice had changed. 'If you tell me everything, I can help you. I have influence with the king. If you know why Master Fletcher was killed, I urge you to tell me. Otherwise . . .'

Thomas rose and went to the door. Rush leapt off the chair and exploded in fury.

'You stupid little man. Tell me what you know, and you may live. Stay silent and you will die. You have my word on it.'

Thomas ignored him, and rattled the door. It was opened by the gaoler.

'Take him up,' yelled Rush, 'and make him suffer. I want the truth out of him.'

Hands still tied and neck in the iron ring, Thomas was

dragged up the steps to the cell. The gaoler locked him back in his place, untied his hands and left without a word.

Thomas tried again to concentrate on the wall. He could not do it. His mind was not working. He needed food and water. Without them, the vague idea would stay vague.

'On yer feet, 'ill,' ordered the gaoler the next morning. 'You're a popular little bugger. You've got another visitor.' After the same procedure with the chain, Thomas was led roughly through the door. He could barely stand and the light outside the cell hurt his eyes. He stumbled down the steps to the guardroom, expecting to see Rush. A figure was standing by the gaoler's table. He squinted at it. It was Jane.

'Bring two chairs, man, and be quick about it,' she snapped at the gaoler. 'You've been well enough paid.' He lumbered off to find chairs. Jane came to Thomas and held him by the shoulders. 'Thomas, I weep to see you like this. Have you been harmed?' Thomas shook his head. The gaoler brought the chairs. 'I wish to speak privately to Master Hill,' Jane told him. 'Return in half an hour.' As soon as the gaoler had disappeared up the steps, Jane produced from under her shawl a bottle, half a chicken and a small loaf. 'I thought you might need these.' Thomas smiled as she untied his hands. 'Eat first, then we'll talk.' She watched silently as he drank ale from the bottle and ate a chicken leg.

'Jane . . .' began Thomas, when he had finished.

She put a finger to his lips. 'Let me speak first, please.' He nodded. 'There are things you should know. After Edward was killed at Edgehill, I was lonely and vulnerable. My family had been friends with the Faynes for years, and I had known Francis since we were children. At first, I thought he cared. He can be charming if he wants to be, and he's always attracted the ladies. He comforted me, but I broke it off as soon as I realized his true character — jealous, vindictive, violent. He was furious. He wasn't used to being rejected. It was an unpleasant time — threatening letters, unwelcome meetings in the street, insults. He made up stories about me, malicious and untrue. That's what he's like. I thought it was over when he left with his regiment. Then I came to Oxford with the queen and found he was here. When I refused him, the insults started up again.' Jane's words had come tumbling out, as if they could wait not a second longer to be spoken. Now she stared into Thomas's eyes. 'I'm sorry I lost my temper in your room. I have missed you.'

'And I you,' he croaked. 'I'm sorry you see me like this. I do not recommend gaol for an invigorating change of scene.'

Jane smiled. 'Your old wit, Thomas. That's good, and much needed. This is a fearsome place. Until we have you released, you will need all your courage and humour.'

'Jane, I did see you walking with Fayne.'

'I know. I decided to try to placate him. I reminded him that our families were close, and said that I hoped we could be friends. He wanted to sleep with me. When I refused, he accused me of being a bookseller's whore, and hit me. I left him in the street, ranting and raging like a lunatic.' She smiled. 'I heard that you exacted retribution for me. I must say I was surprised, Thomas. You had given no hint of your fighting skills.'

'I am not proud of what I did. I abhor violence. I can scarcely believe what I saw at Newbury.'

'We hear that six thousand men died there. The king grieves greatly for the loss of his friends, especially Lord Falkland. His mood is sombre.'

'It was pointless, Jane. Thousands more widows and orphans, and for nothing.'

'I know. For nothing. As Edward's death was for nothing.' She paused. 'Thomas, Simon has told me about Erasmus Pole, about Abraham Fletcher's murder, about your room being searched and about your lost key. You are in grave danger.'

'Rush came here yesterday, hoping to find out what I know. I am sure it was he who had me sent here. He offered help and he made threats. Why would he do that unless he is serving another master?' Thomas paused. 'And he has tried to divert attention from himself by warning me about you.' The colour drained from Jane's face. Thomas looked down at his feet. 'Tell me you had no part in this, Jane, please.' It was no more than a whisper.

'Thomas,' she replied softly, 'I swear that I had no part in the murder of Abraham Fletcher. I heard of it only from Simon.'

Thomas nodded. 'Thank God. In this hellhole, the mind plays tricks. We know Rush had an accomplice who searched my room. He could not have done it himself. I believe it was Fayne.'

Jane shut her eyes and breathed deeply. Then she took his hands in hers. 'Rush is a monster. But he has the ear of the king, and it would be foolish to move against him without proof. Have you any proof?'

'No. We have evidence of opportunity and we have our instincts, but we do not have proof. Not yet.'

'Not yet?'

'Jane, has Simon told you about the message?'

'Not a particular message. I know about your work because you told me. That's all.'

'Then, for your own safety, I shall not tell you either.

However, there is a slight chance that, if I can escape from here, I will be able to furnish proof.'

'Thomas, the coroner's jury will assemble in three days. In the absence of the king, Simon is trying to persuade the queen to sign an order for your release. The queen is always reluctant to act without the king's agreement, and would prefer to wait until he is in a more receptive mood. That might be too late. If the coroner's jury send you for trial at the Assizes, even the king would hesitate to intervene.'

Jane reached for Thomas's hands. They were trembling. 'Then we must hope for the queen's assistance,' he whispered. 'Rush is a vile murderer, a torturer and a traitor. He must be exposed.' His voice was trembling too.

The half-hour was almost up. Jane retied Thomas's hands. As they heard the gaoler's footsteps on the stones, she leaned forward and brushed her lips against his. 'Simon will bring news as soon as there is any. Be brave. I shall be thinking of you.'

'And I you, Jane. Thank you for coming.'

Back in the cell, fortified by the food and water, Thomas tried again to trap the elusive thought that somehow linked the wall and the cipher. He counted the stones again, and pictured the mason. Neither helped. He stared at the wall, willing it to speak to him. For a long time, it remained silent. Then, without warning, it spoke.

The patterns made by the rows of stones jumped out of the wall. He could see them clearly. There were four distinct vertical columns of stones, each one with a pattern of its own. Half-stones and whole stones in the first column, and whole stones attached to one or the other in the second column. He saw four columns making the whole. All day, he studied the rows of bricks and thought about how he would use the insight he had at last captured to break the cipher. The Vigenère square could be broken. He was sure of it.

The cramping pains began that night. They started in his stomach and spread rapidly to his chest and legs. His joints ached and his head was on fire. He sat shivering and trembling until morning, unable to prevent his stomach convulsing and his bowels voiding themselves, until, too weak to sit any longer, he slid down the wall and lay on his side, his head resting on his dead neighbour and his legs pushed up into his stomach by the man in front.

At first he was conscious. He saw the gaoler come in and the big bearded man seizing a loaf. He heard the whimpering of men dying and in pain. And, as clearly as if he were looking into a mirror, he saw himself. His mind, cruelly separated from his body, hovered in the foul air of that hellish place and watched death take him.

Later, slipping in and out of consciousness, he lacked the strength to move and knew that the will to survive was draining out of him. Courage and humour, Jane had said. Thank God she could not see him like this. When the gaoler next came in with bread, he was kicked in the back, and heard a distant voice say 'finished'. He knew then that it was over.

An hour later, he did not hear the commotion outside the cell door, and he did not see the door open and the iron collar removed from his neck. When strong arms lifted him from the floor, he opened his eyes and tried to focus. He vaguely saw a face he recognized and heard a voice he knew, but could not place them. The effort was too much. His eyes closed and he passed out.

CHAPTER 11

*O*n a glorious June day Margaret and he had taken the girls for a
walk in the water meadows outside Stockbridge. They were
bright children, especially interested in nature and words. Both were
blonde, with their mother's brown eyes and dimpled chin. They set out
a meal under an oak tree near a narrow stream, normally clear and
shallow, but on that day running faster and deeper than usual from the
recent rains, and brownish from mud that had slipped from the bank.
Sometimes they saw trout in the stream, but not that day. It was too
muddy. Margaret and he put out a cold chicken, small loaves she had
baked herself, cheese, butter, apples stored since the autumn and a dish
of early raspberries. There was apple juice for the girls and bottles of
sweet elderberry wine for them.

After they had eaten, Thomas entertained the girls with a game he
had invented for them. He spelt out a new word, and they had to find
its meaning. They could ask him ten questions and then had to make a
guess. That day, the first word had been arboreal. It was a difficult one,
they did not guess it, and he had to explain it to them. The afternoon

was warm and they dozed under the oak tree. The girls were old enough to play by themselves for a while, and he and Margaret would be woken if they were needed.

It was cooler when Thomas managed to open his eyes. He could not see the girls, so he called for them. There was no reply. Margaret immediately awoke. They called again and again, and walked up and down the bank of the stream. Surely it was too shallow for either of the girls to have been in danger, even if they had somehow slipped in? They walked back and forth calling the girls' names. Still there was no reply. Margaret began to panic.

'Thomas, where are they? They wouldn't run off. Someone must have taken them. Please God, no. Who would have taken them? Thomas, who would have taken them?'

'Hush now, Margaret. They haven't been taken. They've wandered off and will be back soon. We'll wait here a while.' But he too was worried. This had never happened before.

They stood together under the oak tree, taking it in turns to call out, and scanning the meadow and hedgerows for a glimpse of the girls. There was neither sight nor sound of them. Suddenly, a shower of twigs landed on their heads. They looked up expecting to see red squirrels in the tree. There were indeed squirrels – two of them – but they were blonde, not red, with brown eyes, dimpled chins and big grins. Margaret was furious.

'Come down at once, you two. What are you doing up there? We were worried. Didn't you hear us calling?'

The girls climbed out of the tree. 'Of course we heard,' said Lucy. 'You were asleep, so we climbed the tree.'

'Yes,' said Polly, 'we wanted to be arboreal.'

Margaret did her best to be cross. 'Arboreal, indeed. That's the last time you play your uncle's games, if they give you ideas like that.'

He winked at them. 'I'll think of a better word next time. Something safer. Terrestrial, perhaps.'

'That's enough, Thomas. Gather up the things, girls, and we'll go home.'

Thomas woke and called for Margaret. His room had been changed. His bed was against the wrong wall, and the window had been covered. Why had she covered his window? He struggled off the bed and stumbled to the window. It was not there. He looked about. Where was the window? He saw a door. It was locked. He rattled the handle and called again for Margaret. There was no answer. He fell to the cold stone floor and passed out.

When he woke again he was on the bed, a thin blanket over him. He was hot. He threw off the blanket and immediately started shivering. He retrieved the blanket and lay on his side with his eyes open. The shivering stopped, and he was hot again. His mind registered a fever. Images of the castle and the cell came back to him. Gaol fever. Where was he now, and how did he get here? Why was he alone? He reached out a hand to a small table beside the bed and lifted a cup to his mouth. Cold water dribbled between his cracked lips and down his chin. He held on to the cup and managed a few more sips. Then his eyes closed.

While Thomas slept, Simon de Pointz came quietly into the room, carrying a wooden chair. He felt Thomas's forehead, wiped it with a damp cloth and sat down on the chair. He smiled and said a short prayer of thanks. Boyish but for his lack of hair, Thomas Hill, at no more than five and a half feet tall, philosopher, cryptographer and pacifist, was not a man to be taken lightly. By the grace of God, he was going to survive.

Simon was still sitting by his bedside when Thomas awoke

again. He handed Thomas the cup of water and helped him to drink. 'There you are, Thomas,' he said quietly, 'and looking a little better. Best stay on the bed, though. I found you on the floor yesterday.'

Thomas had no recollection of the floor, or of anything much else. 'Simon? Where am I?'

'You're in a safe place. A Benedictine abbey near Botley. Another of the few that survived. The abbot is an old friend. The monks know they have a visitor, but none of them knows who you are. They won't trouble you.'

'How long have I been here?'

'This is your third day. Are you hungry?'

Thomas realized that he was. 'Ravenous.'

'Then I'll fetch something for you. Stay on the bed unless you need the bucket. It's in the corner. I don't want to have to scrape layers of shit off you again.'

Simon was back in a few minutes with soup and bread. With a little help, Thomas managed to swallow some of each, and immediately felt stronger. His arrest and the castle gaol came back to him. 'When did I last eat?' he asked.

'I can't be sure,' replied Simon, 'but at least four days ago.'

'What was it? Gaol fever?'

'Probably. We got you out just in time.'

'How?'

'Jane Romilly persuaded the queen to sign a paper ordering your release. It might or might not have been lawful but it impressed the gaoler, and he had little choice but to obey.'

'Is Jane safe?'

'Quite safe. Rush won't risk the queen's anger.'

'And Rush?'

'Furious. He's got half of Oxford looking for you, but he won't find you. Even the queen doesn't know where you are.'

Thomas hoped that Simon was not just saying that for his sake. Rush would indeed be furious that Thomas had been released and was not likely to give up the search easily. 'And what now?'

'Now you stay here until you're fully recovered. The message is safely hidden, as are your papers. Tell me when you're ready to resume work on them.'

The message. The Vigenère cipher. Abraham. The cell. Stones in the wall. An idea. What was it? Thomas could not remember. It would come to him later. 'Simon, is there any way I can send a message to my sister? The letter I entrusted to Rush will have got no further than his fire. After he'd read it, of course.'

Simon looked doubtful. 'It won't be easy. Since Newbury, it's hard to know which side is where. And bands of clubmen are attacking them both. The roads are much more dangerous than when we came here. Still, I'll try to think of something. Now rest again, Thomas. I'll come back this afternoon.'

The pattern of Simon's visits continued for two days. Morning and afternoon, he came bearing food and news, and to observe the patient's progress. He brought a copy of a new Oxford newsbook, *Mercurius Rusticus*. 'There you are, Thomas,' he laughed, 'you'll enjoy that. Full of careful scholarship and excellent writing.' Of course, it was nothing of the kind, being little more than satirical attacks on high-minded Puritans and their ill-disciplined soldiers. It could just as well have been written by high-minded Puritans about ill-disciplined Royalists, as most of the London newsbooks were. *Verborum bellum*. A war of words. John Hampden and 'King' Pym were vilified for their treachery, and there was an article on the so-called 'Rules of War', an expression that had always struck Thomas as absurd. There were no rules, or, if there were, neither side took any notice of them unless it suited them to do so. A town was sacked and burned. One man killed another. A woman was raped and her child slaughtered. At Bristol, Captain Brooke and his men had acknowledged no rules. War was not a game of tennis. The loser could not protest that the winner had broken a rule, nor did the winner have to play a point again. His opponent was dead. *C'était tout.*

And so was dear Abraham. His old tutor and friend, nearly blind, scholarly, gracious — tortured and murdered, and almost certainly by a man whom the king trusted unquestioningly. Rush. A monster capable of inflicting indescribable pain on an old man. And worse, there had been something about that awful scene in Abraham's chamber that suggested the torturer had enjoyed it. Otherwise why take his eyes? Thomas screwed up his own eyes and tried to make the picture of that room go away. He knew Rush was the murderer. All he lacked was proof.

He was desperate for news of Margaret and the girls. With Simon's money, they should want for nothing as long as the farmers and merchants could still bring their wares to market. But he had been away for six weeks. Had the war come to Romsey, had there been fighting in the streets and the fields, or was there still peace? Had there been more unwelcome visits by men of either side? Perhaps Margaret had closed up the shop and gone to stay with her sister-in-law in Winchester. If she had, no letter would reach her. He could only hope Simon would come up with something.

When he was not thinking about home, Thomas thought about the senseless war which had brought him here. A war started by a stubborn king, who was distrusted by his people and had proved himself capable of serious lapses of judgement, and an equally stubborn Parliament which craved power and demanded the reform of government. A war which should never have happened, but which had now taken on a momentum of its own. Politics, religion, greed, fear — all were now contributing to the bloodshed. God alone knew how long it would go on and what would remain of England when at last it ended. Would brother still fight brother? Would Catholic still hate Puritan? And who would rule the country — king or Parliament, both or neither? Might the Dutch or the French grasp the opportunity to overpower a weakened foe and send their ships across the Channel? Would we have to face another Armada, and if we did, where was Drake to lead the way?

It was a war, too, which found Thomas Hill, peaceful bookseller of Romsey, alone in an abbey room outside Oxford, having witnessed a brutal battle, having himself resorted to the violence he so hated, and having been thrown into the foulest imaginable gaol, in which he had nearly died. And having seen the body of his old friend mutilated by a vicious traitor. It was a war which affected every man, woman and child in England, and which might yet make brutes of all of them.

On each visit, Simon also brought a cup of water into which he had mixed equal amounts of chamomile, sage and garlic, claiming that this was an ancient cure for all manner of diseases, including *Morbus Campestris*. Complaining that the brew tasted revolting and would do him no good at all, Thomas dutifully forced it down, and by the morning of the third day was strong enough to accompany Simon around the abbey garden. Dressed once again in a plain brown Franciscan habit and leather sandals, he carried an elm branch as a walking stick. Hooded monks worked away in the garden, carefully tending beds of herbs and flowers. They took no notice of Simon and Thomas.

'Is this where that noxious brew of yours comes from, Simon?' asked Thomas as they walked.

'It is. And, noxious or not, it has got you back on your feet. We friars may seem unworldly but we know a thing or two. Which reminds me, I have found a way to get a letter to your sister. Write it today and it will go tomorrow with a troop of the queen's guard, who are riding to Exeter. Her majesty will be travelling there to embark for France. The guard are preparing the route for her, so that she will be inconvenienced as little as possible on her journey. One of them will make a short detour to Romsey to deliver the letter. If there's a reply, he will bring it back to Oxford. But be careful what you say. Confine yourself to telling her about your excellent health and the splendid company you keep. Messages can always be intercepted.'

Intercepted messages, thought Thomas. Yes. 'Thank you, Simon. If you can provide paper and ink, I'll write a letter this evening.' They walked slowly around the garden, which was enclosed by a high wall. The wall was old, its bricks and mortar brown and moss-covered. Near the gate, however, a short section had recently been repaired. It stood out against the rest of the wall, and caught Thomas's eye. The bricks were new, and had been correctly laid so that the vertical lines of mortar between them did not meet. One row began with a whole brick, the next with a half, so that after two bricks in each row one could make out four vertical patterns. Thomas's memory stirred.

'You'd better bring plenty of paper and ink, Simon,' he said. 'And please bring the message and my working papers. I may need them.'

As instructed, Thomas confined his letter to Margaret to

assurances about his own welfare, and to earnest enquiries about her health and that of the girls. He promised to return home soon. The town, the castle, the message and the abbey would have to wait until he did so. Abraham's murder he might never tell her about. Having finished his letter, he turned to the message. It had not, unfortunately, magically decrypted itself, and there it lay before him, challenging him to reveal its secrets. Forty-five digits — he guessed fifteen numbers of three digits each — four hundred and fifty-six letters, separated by one hundred and thirty-eight spaces, occupying ten lines on one sheet of paper. And possibly hiding something of grave importance to the outcome of the war.

He looked again at his own text:

O N E E Y E I S B R O W N Y E T T H E O T H E R I S B L U E

and its encryption, using THOMAS as the keyword, as

H U S Q Y W B Z P D O O G F S F T Z X V H T E J B Z P X U W

There were the repetitions of BZP, coinciding with ISB in the plain text, and there was the interval of eighteen letters between the start of the first sequence and the start of the second.

He turned back to the encrypted message. The numbers would have to wait. He would gamble on their being codewords, and therefore outside the encryption of the rest of the text. There were the seven repeated three-letter sequences — RFU, WHT, QFV, RVV, IFS, AAD, WWJ — and one four-letter sequence — WZTD, which he had marked by putting a line under them. The letter distances between all repeating sequences were divisible by five, one and themselves, but by no other number. One letter only would have meant a single shift and could be discounted. But there might be more repetitions. Finding them was laborious work, and he could have missed some. If his theory was right, however, and his simple test suggested that it was, the distances between any unnoticed repetitions would also be divisible by five, and would be repeated in the plain text, albeit with different letters. He was almost certain that the keyword had five letters.

That evening, Simon came to collect the letter to Margaret. As usual, he brought food from the abbey's kitchen, which they shared, and grim news from Oxford. New taxes were being levied on the townspeople, and the colleges were being forced to supply new regiments to defend the town. Even the college servants were not exempt.

The mention of college servants reminded Thomas of Silas Merkin. He must try to contact Silas. 'Not actions likely to endear the king and his court to the people.'

'Indeed not. The queen, too, is despondent. Her mood, as ever, reflects that of the king.'

'And Jane? Have you seen her?'

'I have. She is well, and asks after you. An admirer, Thomas, I fancy.'

Thomas felt himself blush. 'Come now, Simon, I hardly think so. We get on well. Nothing more.'

'Well, Jane would like to visit you. I'm reluctant to arrange it because she would learn where you are, which might be dangerous for her and for you. She's probably being watched, and Rush must on no account learn of your whereabouts.'

'It would cheer me greatly to see her, Simon. Can you not think of a safe way for her to come?'

'If you wish it, I'll try. But do not raise your hopes. Rush's men are everywhere.'

'And what of dear Abraham, Simon?'

'The coroner released his body today. He will be buried in two days' time at the Church of St Barnabas, just outside the west wall. He liked the place. The funeral is set for ten.'

Thomas was silent. He felt guilty for not having grieved properly for his old friend, and now he could not attend his funeral. He would have to mourn in private.

'Here's the letter, Simon,' he said, handing it over. 'God willing, it will arrive safely, and there will be a reply.'

The next morning, Simon did not visit and Thomas's breakfast was brought by an elderly monk who could see little and said nothing. When he had eaten, Thomas laid out the encrypted message on the table and studied it again. It was still the same:

URF UBD HE XQB TF KGA OEMD RRFUO TLC WMG LRB WHT R XHGORKZ IO KPW769

WA MQFV BVMF HPL ZFTD RVV57 4SEWMFREJ VGL SVKMGE 852 GTSC WZTD QE

TIJG IVL GJT RA KDOE IK EOJAAQLV GGJR MQU IOIGSI GRQF HBFZG JGY

ALG EE OLWEEA GJR YIFS1 82AEL2 64SGE SC AAD ZVY JP KP WXR JB JTN XBZ77

5XNW WJBS LA LWAK371 EAIH TPA AD RVV BAP TWPVV AGDN WWJ URR VUT

IW EW HTI QCT WY QDT37 11E852 769UMHT RKC CONT WSGV WMG IEN DJEE KW

IHV ZW PNU EAIH371 ZV GJR YIFSS NQ DA BV NGGCVL LD SVMC IRLKW DN

KMJ BS WINDU IITAE KW42177 5OX LCIVK IJM LXMV IFS PCI UT FFZ

SEPI MZTNJQGCOW3 71E ZDWZTD QE SZGJ GYB LD 574SKIFS RVIV N GFL

OX LC QFV WV AZPLCJJX NX IF TNU BG IHZA OP RJWGC

And still it revealed nothing of itself. Having been intercepted nearly two weeks ago, it might, in any case, no longer be useful — a thought he quickly put aside. His job was to decrypt this text, whatever it turned out to be.

Proceeding on the assumption that the keyword consisted of five unrepeated letters, Thomas wrote out each of the letters that would have been encrypted using the first letter of the keyword. Ignoring all numbers and spaces, he began with the first letter, U, followed by the sixth, D, the eleventh, B, and each following fifth letter, until he had listed ninety-two letters. In a text of four hundred and fifty-six letters, the first letter of the keyword would have been used ninety-two times, and the other letters ninety-one times. It was a painstaking task and easy to make a mistake. He worked slowly.

Next he added up the number of times each letter had been used. He found that the frequencies ranged from nine (T) and eight (D, G, I, J) to none at all (F, M, O, Y, Z). He allowed himself a small smile. This distribution looked promising. If T represented E, the alphabetical shift dictated by the first letter of the keyword was fifteen. And when he checked the other frequent letters, T emerged as a near certainty for E. If he was right, the first letter of the plain text was F — a shift of fifteen places from the first letter of the cipher text, U, and, most important of all, revealing that the first letter of the keyword was P. So far so good. Monsieur Vigenère was smiling. He turned to the second letter.

Again he wrote out all the letters in the cipher text which had been encrypted, this time by the second letter of the keyword, counted the frequency of each, and applied the same logic to the result. It made nonsense. If any of the most frequent letters represented E, there would be no Rs, three Qs and two Xs in the second letter sequence. Thomas threw down his quill, splattering ink on his papers, and cursed. Either he had been wrong all along, or he had made a mistake in writing down the letters or in counting them. He checked his counting. It was correct. He cursed again. He would have to work his way laboriously through the text to search for a mistake. He lit the stub of a candle and rewrote the second list of letters, starting and ending with R. When he compared it to the original list that had proved useless, his mistake was obvious. In the seventh line, he had missed the double S and jumped from listing the second letters to listing the third. No wonder the letter distribution had been chaotic. Montaigne spoke sternly. 'If only talking to oneself did not look mad, no day would go by without my being heard growling to myself, "You silly shit."' '*Merci, monsieur*,' replied Thomas.

The first glimmers of light on the morning of Abraham's funeral were appearing through the barred window above his bed. Thomas put his papers under his bed, splashed his face with water, and put on the habit and sandals he had worn in the garden. Taking the elm branch for a walking stick, he slipped quietly out of the door and into the courtyard of the abbey. He could hear voices in the chapel, but saw no one. All at prayer, no doubt. A prayer for Thomas Hill would be welcome, if only the monks knew who he was. The key to the monks' door within the huge abbey gate was in the lock. Thomas let himself out, and turned east towards Oxford.

Within the hour, having passed only a milkmaid and two boys gathering mushrooms, he saw the steeple of the Church of St Barnabas above a small copse of oaks. He was hungry and thirsty. With no money for food, he would have to rely on nature. A narrow stream ran alongside the copse. Lying on his stomach on the bank, he could just reach the water, and, with cupped hands, slake his thirst. He took a small pebble from the stream and put it in the pocket of his habit. In the copse, he found blackberries. Water and berries for breakfast. Not as good as Margaret's bread with cheese and eggs, but it would have to do. He found a comfortable place from which he could watch the church unobserved, and sat down to wait.

The church bell started ringing as the funeral procession approached from the direction of the town. It was a small gathering — just Silas Merkin and three others carrying the coffin, a handful of elderly mourners and Simon de Pointz. Thomas slipped the pebble under his foot, took up the elm branch, and limped around to join the back of the procession as it entered the graveyard. No one appeared to notice him. He kept his hood on and his head down, and, when they reached the grave in which Abraham Fletcher would be laid to rest, stood a little back from the other mourners.

The service was mercifully brief. Some prayers and a few words from the parson before the coffin was lowered into the grave. Sensible, unsentimental Abraham would have approved. Thomas turned to leave. Better to be away before the others. He limped back down the path towards the graveyard gate. Glancing up, he saw two men, both armed, standing just outside it. Rush's men, without a doubt. He could not turn back without drawing attention to himself, so he continued on down the path, hoping that the two men would take no interest in a limping friar.

As he approached, however, one of them called out. 'Good morning, father, a sad day. Was Master Fletcher a friend?' Thomas said nothing. These men would have his description, and to reply he would have to raise his head. The man spoke again. 'I asked if Master Fletcher was a friend. Do you not answer a civil question?' With no idea what else to do, Thomas stayed silent and kept limping towards them. The two men stepped in front of the gate and barred his way.

A hand gripped his shoulder, and a voice behind him said, 'You must forgive Father Peter, gentlemen. He's deaf as well as lame. He and I were old friends of Master Fletcher. I will see Peter safely home.' Rush's men shrugged, and let them pass. Simon kept a firm hand on Thomas's shoulder until they were well out of sight and earshot. Beyond the copse, they stopped and Simon released his grip. Thomas bent to remove the pebble. 'For the love of God, Thomas, what do you think you're doing? Rush himself might have been here.' Simon was furious.

'It was necessary.'

'Necessary? Necessary to be arrested and hanged? Or necessary to be thrown back into that cell?'

'I was released on the orders of the queen.'

'Thomas, you know perfectly well that that won't stop Rush finding a way of silencing you. You acted rashly.'

'Then I apologize. My confinement is irksome. I needed to see the sky and to hear voices.'

'In that case, I will accompany you back to the abbey. You can look at the sky while listening to my voice.'

As they walked, Simon described the mood at court. Following the death of so many loyal friends, the king had returned from Newbury suffering from a deep melancholy, which the murder of Abraham Fletcher had only made worse. His majesty now saw treachery behind every smile, and a spy in every room. Rush had protested about Thomas's release, claiming to have absolute proof of his guilt, while the queen had insisted on her faith in Jane's assurance of his innocence. Rush had demanded to know where Thomas was hiding, and did not believe that the queen had not been told. In his present state of mind, there was no telling what the king might do.

'Did I tell you,' asked Simon as they reached the abbey gate, 'that Rush's father was a gaoler in the Tower? The story goes that he took a bribe to let a wealthy merchant, accused of treason, escape, and used the money for his son's education.'

'How do you know that?'

'We friars have ways of knowing things, Thomas, and we like to gossip. It's our besetting sin.'

'What else do you know about him?'

'Only that, as a young man, he studied at Cambridge and was friendly with Hampden and Pym, both scholars at Oxford. Hampden, of course, is dead, and Pym, they say, hasn't long to go. Let us hope that they are soon joined by their old friend.'

'A trifle unchristian, Simon, don't you think?'

'No, Thomas, I do not think. The man's evil. He should be in hell. And the sooner you decrypt the message and provide proof that he's a traitor, the sooner we'll send him there. Have you made any progress?'

'As a matter of fact, I might have.' Thomas tried not to sound smug. 'I shall know for certain by this evening.'

'Good. I shall call tomorrow morning, when I trust you'll be able to tell me more.'

Back in his room, Thomas started again on the second keyword letter. Two letters stood out in his list — R and E — both with ten appearances. He would assume one of them represented E. He started with R. He soon found, however, that if R represented E, the second letter of the keyword would be N and the distribution of other letters was equally unconvincing. So E represented itself, and the second letter of the keyword was A, and the second letter of the text, R, was itself. He had the first two letters of the keyword, P and A, and the first two letters of the text, F and R.

The third letter of the text, F, turned out to be O. FRO_ had the look of FROM. He moved speedily on to the fourth letter.

This one looked easy. With twelve appearances, I was the most frequent letter, followed by A and Q, with eight each. He tackled I first. It worked. The fourth letter of the plain text was therefore M, and the first word FROM, as he had hoped. Thomas now had four letters of the keyword — PARI.

'I do hope it's PARIS,' he said out loud. 'Monsieur Montaigne would be much amused.'

Assuming it was PARIS, he quickly decrypted the next four letters of the text, BDHE, revealing JOHN. This message had been sent by a man named John.

Thomas was halfway through decrypting the whole message when the old monk brought his dinner. He gobbled it down without noticing what it was, and resumed his work. After another hour, he was able to write out the full text, putting his assumptions about the code numbers in brackets:

FROM JOHN PYM TO COLONEL CROMWELL OUR LATEST APPROACH TO THE
[KING]
HAVING BEEN SPURNED AND [LONDON] DEFENCES NOW SECURE [OXFORD]
PLAN WILL BE CARRIED OUT AS SOON AS POSSIBLE. YOUR VICTORY AT
GAINSBOROUGH
STRENGTHENS OUR HAND. [182?] AND [264?] ARE BUILDING UP THEIR
STRENGTH.
[775?] INFORMS US THAT [QUEEN] WITH CHILD AND MAY LEAVE SOON FOR
FRANCE.
IF WE STRIKE WHILE [QUEEN] IN [OXFORD], [KING] MUST ACKNOWLEDGE
OUR INFLUENCE THERE AND WITH [QUEEN] IN OUR HANDS WILL BE
FORCED TO SEEK TRUCE ON TERMS FAVOURABLE TO [421?]. [775?] WILL
ADVISE TIME
AND PLACE FOR APPREHENSION OF [QUEEN] WHO WILL BE BROUGHT TO
[LONDON]. STAND READY. GOD WILLING WE SHALL BRING AN END TO THIS
WAR SOON.

He guessed from the context the codes for the king and queen, and for London and Oxford. 182, 264 and 421 probably did not matter much. The critical code was 775. If it could be shown who 775 was, the traitor and murderer would be revealed. A pity the letters of his name had not been encrypted with the cipher. He would wager his life that they would spell out RUSH.

Thomas sat and stared at the message. No wonder it had been encrypted with the Vigenère square, complicated further by numerical codes, and hidden in the messenger's hat. Simon was due in the morning, but if the queen was in danger of being abducted to London, should he hurry immediately to Merton? Would he be heard, and would the king believe him? He decided that the queen would be safe in her lodgings at Merton, with the college gates closed and guarded, and her own Lifeguards on watch. Anyone attempting to apprehend her would surely do so when she had left the college.

Sleep was out of the question. He made careful copies of his decryption and of the encrypted message, replicating as best he could the encrypter's hand. It was something he always did when making a copy, just as he always tried to find a way into the encrypter's mind. Then he lay on the bed and waited for dawn.

CHAPTER 12

D awn had only just broken when Simon burst in. 'No time to explain,' he gasped, throwing a Benedictine tunic, scapular and hood on to the bed. 'Put those on, get on your knees and pray. And keep praying until I say you can stop.'

'Simon, what in the name of—'

'Pray, Thomas, and make haste.' And with that, he was gone.

There was an unusual urgency in Simon's voice which made Thomas do as he was told. He slipped the tunic over his head, tied it at the waist with the cord from his Franciscan habit, buckled on the scapular and put the hood over his head. Then, feeling very foolish, he knelt by the bed as if in prayer. It seemed a good moment to ask whoever might be listening to take care of his sister and nieces while he was away, and, because he had never been able to take praying seriously, to request that, having now been both a Franciscan and a Benedictine, he would be spared the dreary black of the Dominicans.

He was trying to think of something else to pray for when

there came the unmistakable sounds of soldiers clattering about on the flagstones in the abbey courtyard, and voices raised in anger and command. So that was it. Unwelcome visitors, probably on the instructions of Tobias Rush, and certainly searching for Thomas Hill. Simon must have got wind of them, and warned him just in time. He adjusted his hood to make sure his face was hidden and turned his head away from the door. The voice outside was harsh and insistent. 'What's in here?'

'This is the room of our brother Peter. He stays here alone. His soul is troubled and his body sick. Please do not disturb him.' It was a voice Thomas did not recognize.

'My orders are to search every room.'

'Then, if you must, I ask you to be gentle. Peter is easily frightened.'

Thinking that whoever Peter was, he was not alone in this, Thomas wriggled deeper into his tunic and hood. The door was thrown open and he heard the men enter. Tempted as he was to sneak a look at them, he managed to keep his head bowed in solemn prayer. 'You there,' demanded the soldier, 'get up and show your face.' Thomas ignored him and kept praying. 'Get up, damn you, or I'll get you up myself.' Still Thomas remained on his knees.

The other voice spoke. 'It would be a grave mistake to touch Brother Peter. His mind is deranged and he is infected by unholy poisons. I have seen this before. The infection can be passed by touch.'

'Is that so? In that case, you get him up.'

'That I cannot do. It might drive his mind still deeper into torment. Peter is sick and harmless. Can you not leave him to his prayers?'

'Get him up and let me see him.'

'I cannot.'

Thomas heard a sword being withdrawn from its scabbard and involuntarily tensed his back. 'As you wish . . .' The sword clattered on to the stone floor, and the man cursed loudly. 'You'll pay for that, you fucking monk.' It was more than he could bear. Thomas looked up from his prayer and saw the back of a soldier of the King's Lifeguards and the face of a tall Benedictine monk, the soldier's sword in his hand. Only he was not a Benedictine monk, he was Simon de Pointz, a Franciscan friar. Quite unperturbed, Simon stared at the soldier, and spoke in the voice Thomas had not recognized.

'I think not. Here we serve only God, and it is God who commands us to take care of this suffering creature. Search where you please. Peter will not be harmed.' The soldier stared back. Then he turned and stormed out of the room. Simon signalled to Thomas to resume his praying, and followed the defeated soldier. He closed the door carefully behind him.

Still on his knees, Thomas wondered again at the extra-ordinary presence of the man. Having arrived unknown and uninvited, he had convinced Thomas to leave his home and family and to travel with him to a foul, dangerous place, where sickness and death were everywhere, and now, without so much as raising his voice, he had faced down a soldier of the king intent upon carrying out his orders. And he had done so at great risk to himself. Fortunate for the king that the wayward Norwich boy had become a Franciscan, not a Parliamentarian.

Quite suddenly, the sounds of the search disappeared and the abbey grew quieter. Daring to hope that the troops had given up and left, Thomas got to his feet and stretched his back. He could guess what had happened. The men at Abraham's funeral had reported back to Rush that two friars had been there, one of them looking after the other. Rush had assumed that Thomas had slipped through his net and sent men to search every monastery and abbey around Oxford. Thanks only to Simon, the fish had escaped the net again.

Or had it? Hearing footsteps approaching his door, Thomas was back on his knees in a trice, head bowed in solemn prayer. He heard the door open and held his breath. 'You can stop now, Thomas, unless you have more upon which to ask for God's guidance. They've gone.' Thomas got up again and faced Simon, now back in his familiar grey habit.

'Rush's men?'

'Yes. By a stroke of fortune, I passed them on my way here and arrived just in time. Otherwise you would be on your way back to Oxford Castle. Happily, the abbot had spare tunics to hand, including a long one, and I was able to dissuade their leader from dealing with you as King Henry's knights dealt with Thomas Becket.'

'Again I owe you my thanks, Simon. Do remember, though, that I am only here because of you, and I may yet have further need of your services.'

'Let us pray not. Now, knowing that you make little sense until you have breakfasted, I have arranged for food to be brought. I am impatient to hear of your progress on the cipher.'

'Good. Simon, why the voice?'

'Ah, an interesting question. I am not entirely sure myself, except that I believe Richard Burbage liked to assume the voice of the character he was playing, even before learning his words. He claimed that it helped him to forget who he really was, and to become the character.'

'As actors do.'

'Actors, yes, and traitors. Good God, I almost forgot.' Simon took a letter from inside his habit and handed it to Thomas. 'This arrived yesterday from Romsey. Good news, I trust.'

Thomas was about to open the letter when a loud knock on the door signalled the arrival of breakfast. It was brought by a slightly built friar who kept his eyes to the floor. 'And we want to know how the work is going. Have you made progress?'

'We?' asked Thomas, looking pointedly at the other friar, who had so far kept his face hidden under his hood.

'Ah. Of course.' Simon nodded to his companion, whose hood came off to reveal a serenely smiling Jane Romilly.

'Good morning, Thomas. We thought to surprise you, although the disguise was necessary to gain access to the abbey. The abbot would not approve of a lady visitor.'

Torn between Jane, the letter and the decrypted message, Thomas blathered. 'Lady Romilly. Jane. An unexpected pleasure. How are you? Well, I trust. And the queen? Is she well?'

Jane raised an eyebrow. 'The queen's spirits are low, but she is well, thank you. As am I.'

'Good, good. Excellent. That is a comfort. You must have been here when the search was on.'

'I was. Disguised as a Benedictine and making an excellent mutton stew in the abbey kitchens. Our friends will have a good dinner tonight.'

'You weren't searched?'

'Thankfully not,' laughed Jane. 'The poor man might have died of shock.'

Or delight, thought Thomas. 'It's well that you've come. I have news. The message is decrypted. Here it is.' Thomas passed his decryption to Simon, who read it twice and handed it to Jane.

'The brackets, Thomas? Guesses?' asked Simon.

'Guesses, yes, from the context. 182 and 264 could be any of their commanders, and 421 may be Parliament. They matter little. It's 775 we need to know.'

'It's Rush, isn't it?'

'We know it is, but this is not proof. Rush would just laugh at it.'

'Are you quite certain of the decryption, Thomas?' asked Simon.

'Quite certain. The idea I mentioned worked.'

'Then, proof or no proof, the queen is in grave danger of being abducted. We're lucky they haven't already tried, if this is their plan. The king must be told at once. Jane and I will leave immediately.'

'Why me?' asked Jane. 'You'll travel faster without me, and I can add nothing to the task. Go alone, Simon, and I will wait here until you return.'

'Leave you here? The abbot would never speak to me again if he found out. A woman alone in the abbey. My soul would be in mortal danger. Yours too, I daresay.'

'Nonsense, Simon. Your soul is quite safe, as mine shall be. Thomas will make sure of it, won't you, Thomas?'

'Certainly I will. Go, Simon, and return as soon as you've warned the king. I'll show Jane how a Vigenère cipher works.'

'Very well,' replied Simon with a nod to Jane. He handed her a key. 'Lock the door after me. And be here when I return.'

'Read your letter, Thomas,' said Jane when Simon had gone, 'and then we'll eat.'

Thomas broke the seal and read the letter. It was short and direct. Margaret thanked him for writing, albeit belatedly, and was glad to learn that he was in good health. She and the girls were also well, but missed him greatly. Lucy asked if he would be home for her birthday at the end of October. The town had been quiet since he left. News of the war arrived daily, occasionally something about the king and queen in Oxford. And, finally, she had received two unsigned letters advising her to take great care of herself and her daughters in these troubled times. The hand was untutored and the grammar poor, and she had dismissed them as the work of some mischief-maker. Still, she hoped they would see Thomas soon. They all sent fondest love.

Uncertain quite what to make of this, Thomas read it out to Jane.

'I'm sure it's no more than a local man with his eye on a handsome widow. While you're away, perhaps he's hoping to persuade Margaret that she should take a husband. Can you think of anyone who might do that?' she asked.

'Several, but I'm not so sure. Margaret wouldn't have mentioned it unless she had some concern.'

Jane rose and took his hands in hers. 'Be calm, Thomas. Margaret and your nieces merely want to see you safely home. We must deliver you to them just as soon as we can. Now let us eat our breakfast.'

'Why are the queen's spirits low, Jane?' asked Thomas, as they ate.

'Her majesty's mood is a mirror of the king's. When he laughs, so does she. When he is despondent, so is she. When he is anxious, his stammer gets worse, and that makes him angry. Then the queen is angry, and the mood at court is black.'

'Was it Newbury that so affected him?'

'Partly, yes. The carnage, they say, was fearful, and he lost many friends. Falkland especially he mourns. And Essex has reached London with most of his army intact. Newbury was a disaster. Three thousand men lost, and for nothing. But there has also been news from the north. The Scots have signed Pym's Solemn League and Covenant. They have promised military support against the king in return for a guarantee of no interference in the Scottish Church, and reforms to the Church of England. Her majesty is particularly vexed, and the king now expects the Scottish Covenanters to march south in the new year. For a Scot, it is doubly hard to bear.'

'And it could alter the course of the war. If the king has to strengthen his defences in the north, his forces will be greatly stretched. Parliament will seek to take advantage. I fear we'll see a good deal more bloodshed next year.'

'If only a peace could be negotiated. Talks have been going on for months, yet that is all they are. Talks. And, by all accounts, ill-tempered talks. Ill-tempered talks, and no listens. Talks without listens achieve very little, Thomas, don't you think?'

'I do. And I think you should be a writer, Lady Romilly. You have a way with words.'

'And what should I write? Plays, essays, philosophy?'

'You should write poetry. Lady Wroth's poems have become quite popular, and I'll wager this war will find more ladies putting quill to paper. Love, war, death, misery — the very stuff of poetry. Why not try your hand?'

'Would you be my tutor, Thomas? I should need guidance.'

'Naturally. That is exactly why I suggested it. Shall we begin at once?'

'We shall.'

Three hours later, tutor and pupil, arms and legs entwined, awoke in the narrow bed. 'You're an excellent pupil, Lady Romilly. Alas, however, I have neither wine nor sweetmeats to offer you. Instead, would you care for instruction in the matter of the Vigenère cipher?'

'I think not, Thomas, thank you. I have enough to remember for one day. And I have something important to tell you.'

'Then perhaps we should clothe ourselves. Simon has seen my naked form before but not, I trust, yours. He might be laid low with guilt.'

'Simon is not alone in bearing the burden of guilt. Sit down beside me, please, Thomas,' replied Jane, clothed again. 'This is not going to be easy, and whatever your reaction to what I am going to tell you, I shall understand. If you wish it, I shall leave and you will never see me again.'

'Good God, Jane, after what we've just shared?'

'Especially after what we've just shared. Had I told you earlier, it might never have happened.'

'I'm listening, Jane.'

Jane reached into her habit and produced a key. She held it up. 'The key to your room, Thomas.'

'Where in the name of God did you get it?'

'Tobias Rush gave it to me.'

Thomas stared at the key, then at Jane. Her face was expressionless. He pushed himself off the bed and went to the far corner of the room. He stood with his back to the wall and looked at her. His voice was icy. 'You had best explain.'

'Very well. As you know, I left my parents in York to accompany the queen to Oxford. My loyalties were divided, but I decided that service to her majesty must come first.' She laughed lightly. 'Now I'm not so sure.' Thomas said nothing; he was watching her eyes. 'Tobias Rush first approached me in the summer. He said that he knew about my parents and would ensure that they were safe as long as I carried out some simple tasks for him.'

'Simple tasks?'

'That was what he said. And remember, the king trusted him, so I had no reason not to. I was to keep him informed of the queen's plans and of anything she said about the king. It seemed a small price to pay for my parents' safety. I told him whenever the queen was planning to leave Oxford and what she said about the king's mood and his intentions. He knows she is expecting a child.'

'So you knew that Rush was a traitor.'

'At first, I persuaded myself that he just gathered information because it increased his power. It was only when he gave me the key and told me to look for a coded message hidden in your room that I could deceive myself no longer.'

Thomas recalled seeing Rush at Merton the day he had walked in the meadow with Jane. 'Yet you still did as you were told.'

'Yes. I was frightened.'

'Why did you leave the room in such a state?'

'He told me to.'

A thought occurred. 'Were you wearing a new perfume that day?'

'I was. The queen gave it to me. Sandalwood.'

Thomas nodded. 'And how did you know that my room would be empty that morning?'

'I didn't. But the gatehouse was deserted when I arrived, so I took a chance. When you didn't answer my knock, I let myself in.'

'And looked for the message.'

'Not very hard, and I didn't find it. I wanted to get away. Luckily, the gatehouse was still deserted when I left. Rush was furious.'

'You told me that you had no knowledge of a particular message, yet you had.'

Jane nodded. 'I lied because I feared losing you.'

'Did you lie about Abraham?'

'Thomas, I swear I did not. I had no idea that Rush intended to murder Master Fletcher, or that that was where you were when I came to Pembroke.'

'And he took the old man's eyes first. Eyes that could not see.'

Jane looked away. 'The man's a monster. When I heard about it, I confronted him. He laughed and told me that in time of war such things are necessary, and worse happens on the battlefield. He told me to keep quiet or it would go badly for me and my family.'

'And did he tell you to befriend me and to keep him informed of anything I said?'

'After he saw us at the masque, yes. You had been watched from the moment you rode into the city with Simon. Rush saw me as a way of getting even closer to you. He told me that you were not to be trusted. It did not take me long to realize that it was he who could not be trusted.'

Thomas thought about it. Tobias Rush had kept a close watch on him, had him knocked over in the street, had stolen his key, had tortured and murdered poor Abraham, and had him thrown into the gaol. Jane Romilly had deceived him, searched his room and played him for a fool. But she had visited him in the gaol and persuaded the queen to authorize his release. Why?

'And what, may I ask, has prompted you to tell me this now?'

'Thomas, please believe me. I was horrified at Abraham's death, and could not bear the thought of your dying in that awful place. I daren't tell the queen about Rush for fear of his influence with the king, but with Simon's help I was able to persuade her of your innocence.'

'Does Simon know everything?'

'He does. He heard my confession and told me to come here and to tell you the truth.'

'And did he tell you to seduce me first?' Thomas's voice was bitter.

'Oh Thomas, of course not.'

'Rush told me he had his suspicions about you. Why would he do that?'

'To divert attention from himself, and perhaps to find out if I had kept anything from him. Deceit and subterfuge are as natural to that man as breathing. He told me to keep your key. He didn't want to be found with it himself, and would cheerfully have sacrificed me if necessary.'

'I don't doubt it.'

There was a knock on the door. Thomas unlocked it and Simon entered. He looked quizzically at Jane, who nodded.

'The king wishes to see Thomas immediately,' he said. 'We must leave at once. There are horses waiting.'

'What does he make of the decryption?' asked Thomas.

'He fears for the queen. Other than that, he said little.'

'What about Rush?'

'I did not see Rush.'

'Shall we tell the king what we know about Rush?'

'No. We still do not have proof. It would be too dangerous.'

Thomas gathered up his papers, carefully rolling up the original message, his copy of it and his copy of the decryption, and tucked them inside his shirt. Within two minutes they had left the abbey and were on their way.

They rode in silence to Merton, where Simon escorted Jane, still in her friar's habit, to her rooms, and returned at once to take Thomas to Christ Church, where the king awaited them. They were shown into a receiving room in the Deanery, where they waited for the king to appear from his private apartments. 'I take it Jane has told you everything, Thomas?' enquired Simon quietly.

'She says that she has.'

'Then she has.'

When the king entered, they bowed their heads. Thomas looked up and flinched. An unmistakable figure, all in black — his face hidden in shadow — stood behind the king.

'So, Master Hill,' his majesty said quietly. Thomas had noticed that the king's voice was never raised. Perhaps it had to do with his stammer. 'And where have you been hiding, since I returned from seeing loyal friends die in a just cause? We have been most exercised by your disappearance, and the good Master Rush has had to make other arrangements for the security of our messages.'

Thomas glanced at Simon. 'I have been at the abbey near Botley, your majesty. Father de Pointz ensured that neither the abbot nor the monks knew who I am or why I was there.'

'And why, pray, did you choose to hide in an abbey?'

Before Thomas could reply, Simon spoke for him. 'If I may, your majesty, Master Hill was near death when he left the gaol, and had to be nursed back to health. The monks have a number of excellent remedies, which proved efficacious. He also needed solitude in order to work on the intercepted message. Happily, in that, too, he was successful.'

'So it seems,' said the king, stretching out his hand to take a paper handed to him by Rush. 'And a most alarming message it is. If true, my dear queen is in grave danger. I have already ordered that her guard be doubled, and that she stay within the walls of Merton at all times. If false, it must have been designed to cover up some devious plot. Be sure that, if that is the case, we shall uncover its nature, and punish the traitors behind it.'

'Your majesty,' said Thomas, 'the message was given to me to decrypt by Master Fletcher. As you are aware, until he was foully murdered, all intercepted messages were passed to him. If it is false, its contents must have been intended to be revealed. Yet it was encrypted by means of a cipher that is seldom used, and which, until now, neither Master Fletcher nor I believed had ever been broken. It was also hidden. Its writer did not want it found or decrypted.'

'It may or may not have been hidden. Master Rush will trace its source. He will find the man who brought it to Oxford, and any others through whose hands it may have passed. I have no doubt that his interrogations will reveal their guilt or innocence in the matter. However, you too, Master Hill, as Master Rush has pointed out, are not above suspicion. We trusted Master Fletcher, but we can all be deceived. He may have been deceived by you. What have you to say to that?'

'Your majesty, Abraham Fletcher was a good man and your loyal servant. As am I. I make no pretence of liking this or any other war, and I wish to see it over. If I can hasten the day when it ends justly, I shall be content. I have no reason, no reason whatever, to act against your majesty's interests.'

'I note that you have not decrypted the numerical codes in this message. Why is that, Master Hill?'

'I can only guess at some of them in the light of the context of the message. I cannot guess at the names of the Parliamentary commanders, nor at the identity of the man to whom the number 775 refers.'

'It is exactly that man, Master Hill, whose identity we need to know. Whoever he is, he is the man behind this cowardly plot to use the queen as if she were a pawn in a game of chess. Or could it be that this whole thing has been fabricated to cast suspicion on one of our loyal servants?'

'There has been no fabrication, your majesty. I have decrypted the message exactly as it was given to me.'

Rush stepped forward. 'With your majesty's permission. Master Hill, the coroner had grounds for suspecting you of the murder of Abraham Fletcher. As you rightly say, a foul murder. When I visited you in gaol, you spurned my offer of help. I wonder why. And when, through the kindness of her majesty, misplaced kindness in my opinion, you were released, you hid. Furthermore, you now ask his majesty to believe that you have broken a cipher which has remained unbroken for nearly a hundred years. A trifle far-fetched, is it not?'

'All ciphers can be broken. This one was no different. It needed but a stroke of fortune to set me on the right road. Would your majesty care for me to show you how?'

The king was growing impatient. 'Not now. The queen is safe under guard at Merton. For the present, that is what matters. Father de Pointz will return to the queen's service, and you, Master Hill, will be confined here in Christ Church. Master Rush does not believe your story; the queen plainly does. We will think presently on what more is to be done. You will not leave the college grounds for any purpose. If you do so, you will be branded a traitor and treated accordingly. Now leave us.'

Thomas and Simon bowed, turned and left the room. Thomas was immediately flanked by two of the king's Lifeguards. 'You know where I am, Simon,' he said. 'His majesty said nothing about visitors.'

'I shall come soon. And send word if you need me urgently.'

The guards led Thomas through an arch into a small court-yard behind the hall. They entered one of the doorways that opened on to the courtyard, and climbed two flights of stairs. There a door was opened with a key produced by one of the guards, and Thomas was ushered in. The guards left without lock-ing the door. Thomas inspected the room. The king must have ordered it prepared for him. It was spacious and comfortable, with a writing table, chairs, bookshelves, a fire laid in the grate and a window which looked out on to the courtyard. A bed stood against the wall furthest from the door. One stinking cell, one abbey and two college rooms. Four places so far to rest his head. He wondered if there would be a fifth.

The papers went under the bed. When he left the room, they would go with him so that no intruder would find them. He had nothing else but the miserable clothes he stood in. The monks had done their best to clean them, but four days in Oxford Castle had taken their toll. His precious copy of Montaigne and the small bag of money were long gone. He would ask Simon for clothes. Until then, he could do little but read, think and walk in the college grounds.

Not that the grounds were at all alluring. The main courtyard had not only been turned into a parade ground but now also housed a cattle pen, and two other yards acted as stables. As well as overblown army officers and obsequious courtiers, he would have humble grooms and cowmen for company. And Rush. He would be here, lurking like a hungry black crow with its eye on a nest of fledglings. *Prenez garde*, Thomas, this crow won't let you fly away again.

And Jane Romilly. Had she told him the truth or was her 'confession' just another deception? Could someone who had behaved as she had ever be trusted? Had Rush really threatened to harm her parents or had she concocted that story? Was there more to his rescue from the gaol and her coming to the abbey? If there was, even Simon de Pointz was not above suspicion. God's wounds, that would be an unholy trinity if ever there was one – a murdering confidant of the king, a traitorous lady-in-waiting to the queen, and a Franciscan friar who professed to dislike religious dogma. Romsey seemed a long way away.

On the other hand, threats to Jane's parents were consistent with the letters to Margaret – both carried the evil mark of Rush. Attack an enemy's weakest spot; that would be his instinct. And Jane did seem genuinely devoted to the queen, as did Simon. If they had told the truth, both might now be in danger themselves. Rush would not tolerate disloyalty.

Jane Romilly. One eye was blue yet the other was brown. A lady to whom he had made love that very day. A lady whom, despite their different stations in life, he had dared to think of marrying. A lady who had admitted deceiving him and betraying the king and queen. Should he see her again or should he not? Head or heart, Thomas? Reason or sentiment?

For an hour and another hour, Thomas sat and thought. Over and over again he replayed their conversations in his mind, trying to remember her exact words. It got him nowhere. Perhaps Jane had told him everything, perhaps not. He'd find out soon enough. For now, however, he would keep his distance. It would hurt, but it was necessary.

Eventually, his thoughts moved on. Margaret must have been much alarmed by the threatening letters even to have mentioned them. An untutored hand, she had said. Untutored hand or not, it reeked of Rush. Threats to two innocent children. Monstrous. And almost certainly just to get rid of Thomas. Yet, with Rush, one could not be sure. The threats might be carried out just for the pleasure of it. This was a man who was plotting to have the queen taken prisoner and used as a bargaining tool in this cruel, needless war. And, worst of all, he had the ear and trust of the king. Without undeniable proof of the man's guilt, Thomas could say nothing. The king would simply assume that he was trying to divert attention from himself, and have him hanged as a traitor. Thomas Hill against Tobias Rush. Not much of a contest.

The king's summons came the next morning. Master Hill was to attend his majesty in the Great Hall at once. Thomas made ready, the papers again inside his shirt, and left immediately. The king sat in his customary place at the far end of the hall, and Thomas approached in the manner in which he had been instructed. The king clearly enjoyed observing his subjects like this, otherwise he would meet them in his apartments. He sat quite still, and waited. As before, he was surrounded by courtiers, including Rush, and, as before, he spoke quietly.

'Master Hill, I am persuaded by Master Rush that it would be wise to demand from you a description of the cipher you claim has never before been broken, and an explanation of the manner in which you broke it.'

Thomas had been half expecting this. 'That I will certainly do, your majesty, if you wish it. However, since I do not believe that there is anyone else in England who has the means to break the cipher, I suggest, with respect, that an understanding of the decryption technique would be best kept to as few as possible. It may yet prove as great an asset as a loyal army.'

The king took a moment to consider this. 'Very well. You will demonstrate the cipher only to Master Rush and to me. We will begin at once.' While servants brought paper and ink, and all the courtiers but Rush left the hall, Thomas took out his papers and laid the square he had written out and the original message on a table beside the king's seat. He began with the square.

'This is a Vigenère square, your majesty. The letters of the alphabet form the top row, and the first column. A message is encrypted by use of a keyword, which dictates the encrypted letter which will replace each letter of the text. The intercepted message I decrypted used the keyword PARIS. Thus, the first letter of the message, F, was replaced by U.' He traced with a quill the column headed by F to where it intersected the row starting with P. 'The second letter of the message, R, was replaced by itself, because the second letter of the keyword is A.' He pointed to the first letter of the final row.

'What is the purpose in encrypting a letter as itself?'

'Unless the receiver of the message knows the keyword, your majesty, it is as good an encryption as any. Without the keyword, he cannot know, or even guess, that the letter A appears in it.'

'And how did you discover that the keyword used in this message was PARIS?' asked Rush.

Thomas explained how he had realized that the square created a number of single alphabetic ciphers rather than one poly-alphabetic one, and that he had found the length of the keyword, and thus the number of ciphers, by analysing the frequency of repeated letter sequences.

The king did not immediately grasp the importance of this. 'And in what way did this lead you to a successful outcome?' he asked suspiciously. Thomas explained the theories of frequency analysis, and how he had applied them, once he had identified the five ciphers in use.

'I was fortunate, your majesty, in that, in a text of this length, there were sufficient letters in each cipher to make analysis by letter frequency viable. Even then, it was not entirely straightforward.'

'Master Rush, do you understand this?' asked the king.

'I do, your majesty. Master Hill's explanation seems to me to be plausible, although one wonders why, if he was able to decrypt the message with comparative ease, the cipher has remained unbroken for so long.'

'Prison walls, Master Rush,' replied Thomas sharply. 'Prison walls led me to the solution. When one has nothing to do but sit on an excrement-covered floor and stare at a stone wall, it helps to concentrate the mind. I recommend it to you.'

Rush ignored the remark. 'This is the original message, is it not? Did you make a copy?'

'I did.'

'Then perhaps we may have it. We should keep both original and copy in a safe place.'

Thomas handed the copy to Rush, who examined it closely, as if looking for differences. With a smile, he placed it on the table beside the original. 'Your majesty will see that both original and copy were written by the same hand.'

The king peered at the papers. 'It would seem so. How do you account for this, Master Hill?'

'When decrypting a message, it is my habit to put myself, as far as I can, in the shoes of the encrypter. Thus, I try to copy his hand.'

'Then you have done it as well as any forger,' said Rush. 'His majesty might find it difficult to believe this claim.'

'By your leave, your majesty,' Thomas replied, 'if Master Rush would write a sentence or two in his own hand, I will reproduce it so that you are unable to tell the two apart.'

'What would you like me to write?' asked Rush.

'Let us try "One eye is brown yet the other is blue". That should be sufficient.'

Rush wrote the sentence and passed the quill to Thomas. With a quick glance at Rush's script, he wrote a copy underneath. It was an exact match.

'This proves only that, in addition to being a traitor and a murderer, this man may be a forger, your majesty.' Rush spat out the words. The king looked thoughtful.

'You are a man of many talents, Master Hill. I would not want you for an enemy, and I would like to be convinced, as the queen is, that you are our friend. Until I am, however, you will remain in Christ Church. Master Rush will conduct further inquiries.'

And how exactly will Master Rush do that? wondered Thomas, on his way back to his rooms. Threats? Torture? An accident? All three?

CHAPTER 13

E ven in time of war, the king and his household did not believe in stinting themselves, and for two days Thomas enjoyed the offerings of the king's own cooks, who laboured day and night to keep his majesty happy. Breakfasts of buttered eggs and lamb cutlets and dinners of roasted venison and beef, washed down with excellent wines purloined from the college cellars, did their best to keep his spirits up. The meals were brought to him in his rooms by a young kitchen boy, who must have been told to say nothing to the gentleman he was serving. Even Thomas's polite enquiry as to the boy's name was met with blank silence. They were a strange two days. Imprisoned in the college, suspected of treason and murder, yet dining on royal food and drinking royal wine, both served by a silent boy. Luckily, his predecessor must have been a scholarly man, with an interest in ancient history. At least he had Plutarch and Tacitus for company.

The king's summons came on the third morning. A guard escorted Thomas to the hall, where the king waited with his courtiers around him, the Master of the Revels and the Court Painter among them. Just what we need, thought Thomas, dancing and portraits. Enough to frighten away any pikeman. To Thomas's surprise, Rush was not there.

'Master Hill, it appears that your skills are needed once more. Another message has been intercepted,' said the king, waving a paper at him. 'It was hidden in a sword case, and captured near Reading. With Master Rush away on important business, it has been delivered to me. Kindly tell me what you make of it.'

Thomas took the paper from the king's outstretched hand. The message was short — only two and a half lines — and written in a hand he did not know. He quickly counted the letters. There were one hundred and thirty-four. No numbers and no spaces. No clues at all. 'Other than that it is short, your majesty,' he replied, 'I can tell you nothing. I shall need time to study it.'

'Time, Master Hill, is one thing we do not have. The queen will soon leave Oxford, and this message must be decoded before she does. She must not be put in any danger. How long will you need?'

'That depends upon the cipher used. If it is the Vigenère square again, I will have to find the keyword. In such a short message, that may be difficult. There may not be any repetitions, and the frequencies of letters are unlikely to be helpful. There are too few of them.'

'And if it is not the square? What then?'

'Then I should be able to break it within a day.'

'In that case, you will attend us here tomorrow morning. We shall expect good progress, Master Hill. Pray remember that you are not a free man, and that of time we have little. If you are not able to advise me of progress when we meet again, we will be forced to consider other options.'

'I shall do my best, your majesty.'

The king leaned forward and spoke softly. 'Yes, Master Hill, I have no doubt that you will.'

Thomas managed a tiny bow, followed by a swift retreat. This quiet little man, with his pointed beard, his limp and his stammer, was more threatening than any hectoring bully.

Simon was waiting for him in his room. He was sitting by the window, reading the *Iliad*, a glass of Thomas's wine beside him. Apart from the habit, he looked for all the world like a contented teacher of classical literature. 'Ah, there you are, Thomas,' he said jovially. 'An excellent claret. I do hope you don't mind my helping myself.'

'The claret I do not mind, Simon. It is your unspeakable cheerfulness at this hour of the day that I find offensive. Especially as I have just come from an uncomfortable meeting with the king.'

'Uncomfortable?'

'Most uncomfortable. I am unable to leave the college for any reason, I am still under suspicion of murdering my old friend Abraham Fletcher and betraying secrets to the enemy, I have been deceived by Jane Romilly, and I am now expected by the king to decrypt another message.'

'A new message? Is it our French friend again?'

'I do hope not. The king wants it done immediately. He's reluctant to let the queen leave Oxford without knowing what it says.'

'Naturally. No wonder your temper is short this morning. And what of Rush?'

'Not present. Away on the king's business. Or pretending to be. That's why the message has come to me.' He paused. 'How is Jane?'

'Tearful. She regrets what she did and believes she has lost you. Has she lost you, Thomas?'

'I don't know, Simon. I trusted her, as I trusted you.'

'Trusted, not trust?'

'Simon, if Jane has lied to me again, so have you.'

'We knew you would realize that. It's exactly why I insisted she tell you the truth. All of it. And she has. Believe me.'

'I am trying to.'

'Good. Now, what about this message? Can I be of any assistance?'

Thomas thought for a moment. Trusted or not, a willing listener was always helpful. 'Perhaps you can. Fill the other glass, and let us examine the problem together.' He took the message from under his shirt and set it on the table.

XZFMGMAYTDSXPMFMMVNLAJCLTSDVWXLPTICVIPSUGZSRSAAKOAWVIOJW
BVEMWBVRPFNUFGSVTEHZWLEAVEVAILMDPIXBFEMWKLTTHOCACAVS
RXKBYOAAINAXLQEIHLZLCIAWES

'As you can see, it's short. Only one hundred and thirty-four letters.'

'And no numbers this time. Does that mean no coded words?'

'Not necessarily, although we shall assume that to begin with.'

'Is there any significance in the lack of spaces?'

'I doubt it. It might signify a different sender to the last one, or it might be the same sender disguising himself. There's no way of telling.'

'So what now?'

Thomas held the paper up to the light of his window. The paper was good quality and the hand an educated one. He could see no distinguishing marks or hidden symbols. It had been concealed in a sword case, which suggested that the decrypted text would be simple and direct. Senders of hidden messages did not expect them to be discovered, and did not usually bother to obscure their meaning, other than with a cipher. With luck, this one had been encrypted by means of a simple alphabetic substitution cipher or a keyword. They would start with those.

'Now we look for clues.'

The word LEAVE, in the middle of the second line, leapt off the page. The letters EAV of LEAVE were also followed by EVA. That too might or might not be significant. And they noted the repetition of WBV and the four instances of double letters, but no other particular instances of letters appearing together. Partially coded messages were not unknown, especially if they were also hidden, and, if this was about the queen, the word LEAVE might very well appear. But there were no other plain words. Why would one word alone appear unencrypted? It might be genuine, a trick, a mistake or a coincidence. Or it might tell the receiver what the keyword was. They tried that first. Ignoring the second E, they tried a cipher alphabet starting LEAV, and continuing B, C, D, F. . . It did not work. LEAVE was not a keyword and was put to one side.

To find another keyword or a simple shift, they would have to analyse the letter frequencies. At first glance, the distribution was encouraging. Without LEAVE, there was a single Q, two each of J, U and Y, eight each of L and M, nine Vs and twelve As. Concentrating on the high numbers, Thomas set about finding the most common letters, E, A and T, while Simon tried the lowest numbers, looking for the least frequent letters, J, Q, X and Z. That too produced nothing, and serious doubts were creeping into Thomas's mind. If the sender of this message had used nulls, misspellings or other trickery, the decryption would take longer, and the king would not be happy with longer.

One bottle of claret became two, food came and went, and still they had made no progress. By mid-afternoon neither of them had come up with the slightest sliver of a clue as to the method of encryption. Simon was the first to call a halt. 'Thomas, I'm not used to this type of work. I've been over and over this damnable message and it has made my head ache. Shall we take a stroll?'

Thomas looked up from his page of numbers and letters. 'Odd, that. Praying used to make my head ache. Come on then, friar. A little air may help.'

With Thomas confined to the college, there was nowhere much to stroll other than round and round the big quadrangle in the middle of which noisy cattle waited to be milked or eaten. 'Are you really a Franciscan, Simon?' asked Thomas suddenly.

'Now that's an odd question. Why would you think otherwise?'

'The words you used about yourself. Pragmatism and humour. Not very friarly words.'

'Monks may be recluses, friars are not. I choose to live in the same world as you. I find both qualities useful.'

'And you don't behave like a man of the church. You travelled to Romsey to fetch me, disguised me as one of your own, protected me from Rush and brought Jane to visit me in the abbey.'

'Were these not Christian actions, Thomas? Except, perhaps, for the last, and that was a simple act of kindness to you both.

Even a Franciscan knows worldly love when he sees it. Rest assured, Thomas, I am what I appear.'

'As you wish.' They made another circuit of the quadrangle. 'Now, this accursed message. We'd better break it or I may not be anything much longer. This is what I think. We've tried everything I know and achieved nothing. I'm afraid it's Vigenère again, this time without codewords.'

'Why would the numbers have been omitted?' asked Simon.

'The strength of codes is that they can be quickly decoded by the intended recipient. In the case of the square, they also make the frequency analysis harder by reducing the number of letters in the text. This is a very short message, which in itself is protection against decryption. If the keyword has, say, five letters, there will be no more than twenty-seven letters in each group. Too few to be much use, although I shall of course try.'

'And do you see Rush behind it?'

'I do. He's no fool. He suggested to the king that I show them how the decryption of the last message worked, and he's realized that, unless the text is short, the length of a keyword can be worked out. And he may have inserted nulls or misspellings, or both, to throw unwelcome hounds off his scent. Why otherwise would the encryption be as it is? If Rush wrote this message, it may well concern the queen, and we must discover its contents.'

'What about the word LEAVE?'

'It must be a coincidence. When it came up, the encrypter left it there to confuse further. Such things happen. I'll leave LEAVE alone.'

'So a long night of counting letters and looking for vowels, is that it, Thomas?'

'It is.'

'I would gladly offer to help, but the queen will expect me for her evening devotions.'

'Of course. I'm used to working alone.' They came to the college gate. 'Now be off with you, and please ask Jane to visit soon.'

'I shall. Goodbye, Thomas. I'll offer a prayer for you.'

The long day did indeed turn into a long night. Every effort to pin down just one letter of the keyword had failed, and Thomas was losing heart. Twelve hours of toil had achieved nothing. By the early hours, he had tried everything he could think of, and had even guessed keywords that might have dictated the alphabetic shift. Nothing had worked. Tomorrow's meeting with the king would not be a pleasant experience, but he had to plead for more time.

The next morning, the king was in no mood for explanations or excuses. 'So, Master Hill, am I to understand that you have made no progress whatever?' he asked, impatiently tapping his stick on the floor. Tobias Rush stood at his shoulder.

'I have made progress by the elimination of simple ciphers, your majesty,' replied Thomas, trying to keep his voice steady. 'This message has been encrypted by a very cautious man indeed. He hid it, encrypted it with some complex method, which I am now sure is the Vigenère cipher, and may also have left false trails.'

'I would be a great deal more pleased if you were able to tell me that you had broken the cipher, as would Master Rush.'

'Indeed I would, your majesty,' agreed Rush, with a smirk that the king could not see. 'As you know, I was unconvinced by Master Hill's explanation of his previous effort and his lack of progress now reinforces my view. I wonder whether your majesty would be well advised to entrust the message to another, more reliable man. I have someone suitable in mind. Master Hill would not then be needed and could be sent home, or, if your majesty wished, held at your pleasure.'

The king raised an eyebrow. 'What have you to say to that, Master Hill?'

Thomas knew he had to take care. Rush would have him thrown back into that cell as quick as you like. 'I am at your majesty's service. I ask you to believe me when I say that I have made progress, and am confident of success. We are dealing with a very complex cipher, with only one hundred and thirty-four letters to work on, and anyone taking over from me would wish to start again using his own techniques. He would not wish, as I would not, to accept the workings of someone else. That would create more delay, which could be fatal to our cause.'

'So what is to be done?'

'I need more time, your majesty. All ciphers can be broken. It just takes time.'

The king hesitated. 'You have already tried my patience, and I am reluctant to delay the queen's departure any longer. If you cannot bring me the decrypted message by tomorrow morning, you will be released from your duties. In that case, Master Rush will advise me on what further course of action to take. Good day, Master Hill.'

A stay of execution, thought Thomas, walking back to his room. Damocles' sword still held by a thread above his head. Twenty-four hours to break the cipher. To work, Thomas, to work.

His room was just as he had left it, except for one thing. His working papers — all but the original message under his shirt — had gone. While he had been with the king, Thomas had had an unwelcome visitor. Another one. A tidy one, but nevertheless unwelcome. And there was only one person who could have arranged it, knowing for certain that Thomas would be otherwise engaged. Not that there was the slightest reason to inform the king, or anyone else. Rush would simply accuse Thomas of destroying the papers himself in order to provide an excuse for failing to decrypt the message. And, on reflection, perhaps it was not such a bad thing. An uncluttered table might help unclutter the mind. He still had the message itself, and could, without much difficulty, resume where he had left off. Rush might even assume that the copy that had been taken was the original, and that Thomas had no other. All the more reason to surprise the repulsive creature.

He started by reworking the distribution arising from a seven-letter keyword. When the first letter threw up impossible combinations, he knew he was wasting his time. Not enough letters, with or without tricks. Unclutter the mind, forget this approach, Thomas, and think of something else.

But what else? How could he break a Vigenère cipher without being able to attack it by frequency analysis? And a Vigenère cipher he was now quite sure it was. Anything else would by now have revealed itself, and it was just what the devious Rush would have done. Find his enemy's strength and render it useless. A short message, the cipher and tricks. Unbreakable.

But break it he must. He would count each letter distribution separately, starting with a four-letter keyword and working his way up to eight. The chances of its being longer were remote. Too complicated and time-consuming to encrypt and decrypt. If he learned nothing from that, he would have to look for nulls, just as he had before, only this time in the context of the square. He'd need Simon's prayers, or the meeting next morning with the king would be his last.

It started badly. The first letter of a hypothetical four-letter keyword yielded four Is, four Ts and six voids, and the other three letters produced similar distributions. Quite useless. Five- and six-letter keywords were no better. Shapeless distributions, offering no clues as to where the most common and uncommon letters hid. After fifteen separate counts, Thomas started making mistakes. He had to rewrite the list of letters produced by the third letter of a seven-letter keyword, and miscounted twice.

Thomas was standing by the window deep in thought when Simon burst in carrying a sack. He was ashen. 'Thomas, Jane has been attacked. She was found this morning in the river, unconscious and having lost much blood.'

'Is she alive?' Please God, he thought, let her be alive.

'She is. Just.'

'Who did this to her?'

'We don't know. She was found by a student walking beside the river. It must have been shortly after the attack or she'd have been dead. He dragged her out and carried her to Magdalen. An officer's wife there recognized her and sent word to Merton. She's there now.'

'Who would do such a thing?'

Simon laid a hand on Thomas's sleeve. 'That, my friend, I cannot say. Thomas, there's something else. I fear Jane was raped, and cruelly so.'

Thomas slumped on to the chair and closed his eyes. One eye is brown yet the other is blue. Present tense. Is, not was. The message would have to wait. 'I must see her.'

'Thomas, if you're caught outside Christ Church, you'll be hanged. And Rush will be watching for you.'

'I must see her.'

Simon sighed. 'I thought you'd say that.' He tipped the contents of the sack on to the floor. 'I've brought you a habit, and I have an idea. It's dangerous, but I can think of nothing else. To try to leave by the main gate would be suicidal.'

While Thomas undressed and put on the habit, Simon explained his plan. 'When the queen arrived in Oxford, the king had gates built into the east wall of Christ Church, the walls of Corpus Christi and the west wall of Merton. They enable him to visit the queen discreetly. They are guarded only when the king is with the queen, and, except when in use, the only keys are kept in the king's and queen's private apartments. I have borrowed the queen's keys.'

'Does the queen know?'

'She does not. Nor, yet, does she know about Jane. I will tell her when the outcome is known.'

'I'm ready. Let us try.'

'Are you quite certain, Thomas? This is extremely dangerous for you and, probably, for me.'

'I wish to see Jane.'

'Very well. Wait by the window. I will go down first and signal to you when it's safe to follow. We'll walk together, as if in conversation. Don't hurry, and keep your head down. If there's anyone about, we'll walk past the gate and go round again. I'll lock it behind us, and we'll walk around the back of Corpus Christi to the Merton gate.'

As soon as Simon had left, Thomas stood by the window, keeping himself from view. The encrypted message was inside his habit. He saw Simon walk towards the middle of the quadrangle, look up briefly, turn and walk on. He made no signal. There must have been someone there. Thomas kept watching until Simon reappeared from the direction of the Great Hall. This time, he stopped under the window and raised his hand. Within a minute, they were heading for the king's gate.

The gate was really a door. Cut into the wall, it was tall and thick, with oak timbers and iron fixings. No intruder was going to force his way through such a door, and, as Simon had predicted, it was unguarded. He produced a batch of heavy iron keys from under his habit and inserted one in the lock. It would not turn. With a quick glance over his shoulder, he tried another. This one turned smoothly and the door swung open. They were through it at once, and Simon immediately locked it from the other side. Seeing no one about, they made for the path along the south wall of Corpus Christi, and turned left towards the gate in the Merton wall. As they approached it Simon again produced the keys, intending to open the gate and enter the college as quickly as possible. Once inside Merton, they would be safer. He had the key in the lock and was about to turn it, when four soldiers in the red uniforms of the king's Lifeguard of Foot appeared from the direction of Merton Street. Simon quickly removed the key from the lock, hid it under his habit, and walked briskly towards the soldiers. Thomas followed him. These Lifeguards had not spent their morning guarding the king's life. They were loud and drunk. Seeing Thomas and Simon approaching, one of them said, 'Well now, gentlemen, a pair of monks to keep us pure and holy. Just what we need. Good day, monks. What about a little prayer for our souls, or has the queen used them all up?'

'God bless you, gentlemen,' replied Simon, as he tried to walk past.

A large Lifeguard blocked their path. 'He might, monk,' he said, a hint of menace in his voice, 'but we'd like you to. And your friend.' He looked at Thomas, who was trying not to show his face. 'A good friend, is he? We all know about monks and their unholy ways.'

'We are Franciscan friars on the queen's business,' said Simon sternly, 'and cannot be delayed further. Kindly let us pass.' The large Lifeguard did not move.

'What business might that be, I wonder?' asked the first one. 'Praying or poking? The queen has lots of pretty ladies to tempt you.'

'That is a vile accusation, and I can see it comes from a vile man. We are men of God. Stand aside and let us be about our business,' snapped Thomas.

'And why would we do that, monk?' asked the large one. 'I don't care for men in skirts who keep out of trouble and leave us to do all the fighting. They might as well be women.'

'And we know what women are for, eh?' A third Lifeguard, emboldened by his colleagues, entered the fray. 'What's under those skirts of yours? I wonder. Perhaps we should take a look.' He reached out and lifted the hem of Thomas's habit. Thomas grabbed his forearm and wrist with both hands, straightened the arm, pushed hard, and watched the soldier fall backwards and land on his backside in the dirt.

'No match for a monk, eh, Step?' The large Lifeguard bellowed with laughter. 'Let me show you how it's done.'

'I don't advise it,' said Simon calmly. 'Just because we're men of God does not mean that we cannot defend ourselves. Furthermore, the queen awaits us. If we're late, she will soon know why.'

Unimpressed, the Lifeguard took a wild swing at his head. Simon moved deftly to one side, avoided the blow and hit the Lifeguard with a short, sharp punch in the throat. With a strangled gurgle of pain, the man collapsed in a heap. Neither of the still-upright soldiers made any effort to help him. Simon and Thomas turned and retraced their steps to the gate. Before the soldiers could stop them, they were through it and into Merton. Simon locked the gate and put a hand on Thomas's shoulder.

'What a war. Even the king's men resent the faith of his queen. What do they think they're fighting for?'

'Themselves, Simon,' replied Thomas, 'themselves.'

Jane had been taken to her rooms near the Warden's lodgings, where the queen had set up her household. When Thomas and Simon entered, they found her on a large bed, cushions under her head, and covered by an embroidered blanket. An elderly lady sat by the bed, a pile of linen cloths beside her. She rose when they entered. 'Has there been any change?' asked Simon.

'None,' replied the lady. 'She's still losing blood, and has not yet spoken.' Thomas noticed a second pile of cloths on the floor, these ones stained with blood. He went to the bed and took Jane's hand in his. She did not stir.

'She's very pale. Can the bleeding not be stopped?'

'I am trying, father, but the wounds are deep.'

'I am not a friar, madam,' Thomas said gently, 'though it's better you don't know my name.'

'He is a friend,' Simon reassured her. 'Do not be concerned.' The lady nodded, but said nothing. 'Would you leave us with Lady Romilly, please? We will call if she wakes.' With a glance at Jane, she quietly left the room.

Thomas sat on the bed, still holding Jane's hand. Simon stood at the end of the bed and said a prayer. When he had finished, Thomas spoke quietly. 'Abraham, now Jane. I wish to God that Abraham had never mentioned me to the king, or that we'd turned you away when you arrived at our door, Simon. Murder, torture, rape. All in the name of a stupid, vicious war.' Before Simon could respond, Jane opened her eyes, saw Thomas and smiled weakly. Thomas put his finger on her lips. 'Don't try to talk. You've lost a lot of blood, but you're safe now.' Another tiny smile, and her eyes closed again.

To Thomas, it seemed like hours before Jane stirred again. He sat silently, holding her hand and willing her to survive. He knew now that she had told him everything. Without warning, her eyes opened, he felt the slightest squeeze of his hand, and she whispered something. Unable to make it out, Thomas leaned forward until his cheek was touching hers. He could just hear the words. 'Rush sent them.'

'Sent who, Jane?'

Her answer was even quieter. 'One was Francis.'

'The others?' But Jane could not reply. Thomas lifted his head and nodded. Rush and Fayne. He should have guessed. 'They'll hang for it. Now rest.' The effort had been too much. Jane's back arched, and she moaned in pain. Simon went to the door and summoned the nurse, who bustled in and lifted the blanket. Jane's legs and stomach were covered in blood. Between her legs, the linen cloths were sodden. When the nurse removed them, blood gushed on to the bed. Her eyes had closed and there was no sign of her breathing. Simon bent to put his hand to her neck, and his ear to her mouth. When he rose, he shook his head and made the sign of the cross. Jane was dead.

*

While Simon prayed for her, Thomas sat motionless, her hand still in his. Then, suddenly, without word or warning, he placed her hand on her breast, got up from the bed and left. While Simon prayed, he ran down the staircase, across the Merton courtyard and through the gate. In Merton Street, he slowed to a fast walk. He passed soldiers, beggars, whores, merchants and scholars, and saw none of them. He trod in mud and excrement, and was cursed when he collided with a fruit-seller, knocking the man's box of apples to the ground. He walked up Magpie Lane and Catte Street, along Broad Street and towards the castle. He saw none of the staring faces, and heard none of the shouted insults. For an hour, and then another hour, he walked the streets, cursing Rush the murderer, cursing the king for his summons, cursing Simon for fetching him, even cursing Abraham. And, above all, cursing himself. For coming to Oxford, for Jane's death, for leaving Margaret and the girls, for his stupidity. By the time Thomas found himself back at Christ Church, his fury had been replaced by cold, hard determination. He strode through the college gates, and past two guards watching everyone leaving the college but showing no interest in anyone arriving. He made his way around the cattle pen to his rooms. He met no challenge. If he had, he would have ignored it. Jane Romilly, whom he had dared to love, was dead. If he was to prove that Rush and Fayne had killed her, he had work to do. He would grieve for her when that work was done.

CHAPTER 14

XZFMGMAYTDSXPMFMMVNLAJCLTSDVWXLPTICVIPSUGZSRSAAKOAWVIOJW
BVEMWBVRPFNUFGSVTEHZWLEAVEVAILMDPIXBFEMWKLTTHOCACAVS
RXKBYOAAINAXLQEIHLZLCIAWES

One hundred and thirty-four letters, which could well prove Rush responsible for the murder of Abraham and the rape of Jane. Not to mention a traitor and a torturer. Thomas was sure they had not been encrypted by simple substitution, or by a Caesar shift. That left Monsieur Vigenère, whom he had already defeated once. But this time the message was short, there was only one repetition of more than two letters, his analysis of letter frequencies had yielded nothing, and the keyword was neither LEAVE, nor PARIS, nor LONDON, nor ROME.

Now what? Try every country and every city he could think of? Try random words that came to mind? Or think of something else, some new way of attacking Vigenère? For a long time, Thomas sat and stared at the text, occasionally scribbling words on a sheet of paper. Spain, England, France, Italy, Abraham, Jane. ONE EYE IS BROWN YET THE OTHER IS BLUE. Jane Romilly. Rush, Fayne, Parliament, Pym, Traitor. Romsey, Thomas Hill, Jane. He had no more than twelve hours to decrypt this message, and he had no idea what to do other than try possible keywords. Hardly scientific, or even artistic. Where was Hill's magic when it was needed?

He wrote out a new square, and started with cities – MADRID, LISBON, ATHENS, VIENNA; then countries – SPAIN, AUSTRIA, ITALY, GREECE. Nothing. He tried a random assortment of words and names – FAIRFAX, MILTON, OXFORD, HONOUR, TRUTH, PIETY, PRAYER. Again, nothing. His head ached.

All through the night, Thomas fought off sleep and kept working on the message. It was futile. By dawn, he was beyond sleep and had nothing left to give. He had failed. The message's secrets, whatever they were, remained secrets. Rush would escape, and his own fate was in the hands of the king. Best to face it with as much courage and dignity as he could manage. He washed, shaved, put on a clean shirt and waited to be summoned. He heard the guards tramping up the staircase, and rose to open the door. There were two of them, both ill-tempered, both complaining loudly. 'Backwards and forwards across the yard and up some damned staircase. That's all we do. We're soldiers, not servants,' grumbled one.

'I'd rather be killing Roundheads,' said the other.

'Good morning, gentlemen,' said Thomas, as they reached the top of the staircase. 'Is the king ready to see me?'

'He is, sir,' replied one, 'and his majesty is in no mood to wait.' With a final look around the room, and armed with the message and his copy of the square, Thomas followed the soldiers back down the staircase. They marched around the cattle pen in the middle of the quadrangle, and towards the Deanery. They were still complaining. 'Up and down, backwards and forwards, forwards and backwards. It's not proper work for the king's guards.'

'It is not. We might as well be messenger boys.'

Backwards and forwards, forwards and backwards. Why had he not thought of that? 'You silly shit,' said Montaigne. Before he could give the idea more thought, he was ushered into the receiving room, where the king sat, tapping his stick on the stone floor. Guards were stationed around the room, members of his household behind him. This time there was no sign of Rush. 'Master Hill. My temper is short. The queen must leave Oxford, and I am tired of hearing that this message has not been decrypted. I trust you bring us better news.'

'Your majesty, my efforts have failed. I have not been able to decrypt the message.'

The king's face darkened. 'In that case, I cannot see that we have any further use for your services, Master Hill. You will be taken to the castle and held there until I have decided what shall be done with you.'

'Your majesty, although I have not yet broken the cipher, there is one idea that I have not yet had the chance to try. May I have your consent to make one final attempt?'

'Surely, Master Hill,' replied the king in a voice that was scarcely more than a whisper, 'you have had sufficient time by now. We have waited patiently for you to bring us the contents of this message, and we have been disappointed. The queen should already have left Oxford. What grounds are there now for believing that you will break the cipher?'

'I may not, your majesty. I may fail again. But is it not worth allowing a few minutes more — ten at the most — just in case I am right?'

'Tell me, pray, how this new idea has suddenly come into your head at the very last minute? Is that not a little strange?'

'It is, your majesty. I cannot account for it, except that providence can play unexpected games.'

The king hesitated, then beckoned to one of his servants. 'Fetch paper and ink. We will watch Master Hill at his final attempt.' The servant scurried off, and soon returned with quills, paper and a pot of ink. Thomas took the message and his square from under his shirt and sat at a small table in the corner. But for the scratching of his quill, the room was silent. Even the king had stopped tapping his stick on the floor. Thomas closed his mind to his audience, and concentrated on the message. Above the first ten letters of the text — XZFMGMAYTD — he wrote out PARIS backwards, twice. Then he referred to the square, and wrote a third line of letters above that. Within a few minutes, he had FROMRUSHTO. *From Rush to.* Surely this was it. The keyword PARIS one way, and SIRAP the other. Simple and clever. Very nearly too clever for Thomas Hill. Resisting the urge to shout Eureka and claim victory, he continued on across the first line. The stick started tapping again. Thomas tried to ignore it.

The eleventh letter of the text was decrypted as A. The recipient's name must begin with A. But the next three letters were PYM. A Pym? Why not John Pym or J Pym, or just Pym? Thomas knew the answer as soon as he decrypted the twenty-second letter. It was B. As he had suspected, there were nulls in this message, and it looked as though they occurred at every eleventh letter. That would be quite enough to eliminate any repetitions, and to render frequency analysis useless.

'I believe we have waited long enough,' said the king. There was a ripple of assent from the audience.

'Your majesty,' replied Thomas, standing up and bowing low, 'I can inform you with confidence that my idea was correct. I have decrypted enough of the message to be sure that I have the key-word. It will take me ten more minutes to complete the decryption.'

The king stared at him. 'You are fortunate that I am a patient man, Master Hill. In the full knowledge of the consequences of failure, you may proceed.'

Thomas worked as fast as he dared. Mistakes in decryption, especially using the square, were all too easy. After eight minutes he had:

FROMRUSHTOAPYMQUEENWIBLLLEAVEWITCHINDAYSFORBDRISTOLENREOU
TEXETERFANDFRANCESGHOULDWEATTHEMPTTOEXECIUTEPLANINBJRISTO
LIAWAKITINSTRUCTLIONS

And after nine:

FROM RUSH TO PYM. QUEEN WILL LEAVE WITHIN DAYS FOR BRISTOL EN
ROUTE EXETER AND FRANCE. SHOULD WE ATTEMPT TO EXECUTE PLAN IN
BRISTOL? I AWAIT INSTRUCTIONS.

That was it. Proof. Rush the traitor, Rush the murderer. 'Your majesty,' said Thomas, 'I ask that you and I are left alone. The contents of this message are so grave that no one but you should know them.'

Another ripple from the courtiers, this time of dissent. The king waved it aside. 'The guards alone will stay.' The courtiers trooped out, and the king looked expectantly at Thomas. 'Well, Master Hill, and what is so grave that I alone should hear it?'

'This message reveals that the queen will travel to Bristol and Exeter, and then to France.'

The king was on his feet. 'That cannot be. The queen's route has been kept a close secret. Almost no one knows it.'

'I fear, sir, that the sender of this message knows it.'

The king held out his hand for the text. He read it twice, and sat down. 'I cannot accept this without further evidence. Tobias Rush is a loyal and trusted servant. To be told now that he is a traitor is beyond comprehension. And you, Master Hill, after your theatrical display, what am I to make of you?'

'I can understand your majesty's dilemma. I wish that the keyword had occurred to me before. That it came to mind only on my way here this morning is indeed strange. I blame myself for not thinking of it sooner.'

'And what is this keyword which eluded you for so long, Master Hill?'

'Your majesty will recall that the keyword to the first intercepted message was PARIS. This one turned out to be the same letters, but backwards. SIRAP. Messages go back and forth. So did the keywords.'

'Could you be mistaken as to the sender's name?'

'No, sir. The sender's name is Rush.'

The king closed his eyes. 'It is beyond belief.'

'If I may, your majesty,' went on Thomas, 'there are other things of which you should be aware. I am quite sure that Erasmus Pole was not murdered in Brasenose Lane, but his body dumped there after he had been killed somewhere else. Why would the murderer do that other than to conceal his motive? The murderer of Abraham Fletcher was looking for something, and tortured him when he could not find it. He could not find it because I had it. It was the first message. My room was also searched but, fortunately, the message was not found. Master Rush arranged for me to be imprisoned in an effort to get rid of me, and to retrieve the message. Again, we were fortunate. It was hidden, and, in your absence, the queen graciously commanded my release. Without her intervention, I would certainly be dead. Your majesty will also have heard that Lady Romilly, lady-in-waiting to the queen, was cruelly raped and murdered. However, she lived long enough to reveal the identity of the man behind this bestial crime. It was Tobias Rush.' There was little point in mentioning Fayne. He would be no more than a name to the king, and Thomas had no proof of his association with Rush or his conduct at Newbury. There was more to be done before Francis Fayne faced justice.

'Merciful God. Tobias Rush, to whom I have entrusted many secrets, and whom I trusted with the queen's life. Is there more?' asked the king.

'Rush knew how I had decrypted the first message. He's a clever man. He used the Vigenère square again, but in a very short message with no repetitions or numbers, and with nulls — that is, extra letters inserted in the text to confuse a decrypter. Without the keyword, the message was impregnable. It was only by chance that I guessed it.'

'Master Rush is one of the very few who knew of our plan for the queen to travel to Exeter from Bristol. He is away now making arrangements.'

'When does he return, sir?'

'Tomorrow.'

'Your majesty, Tobias Rush is ruthless. He must be apprehended before he gets wind of what we know. The queen herself might otherwise be in danger. He would almost certainly have sent a copy of such an important message by more than one carrier.'

'He will be met by my Lifeguards when he arrives at the city wall. They will escort him here to face his king. Only when I have interrogated him myself will I know for certain whether or not he is a traitor. Meanwhile, Master Hill, you will remain in your rooms. A guard will be posted outside the door. Master Rush's rooms will be searched. I will send for you if I wish to speak to you further.'

After little sleep and no breakfast, Thomas was tired and hungry. There was no elation at breaking the cipher and proving Rush's guilt, or relief at his own reprieve. Abraham and Jane were dead. Both had died in agony, both at the hands of Rush. And Jane had been raped by Fayne. The breaking of the message was nothing beside that. He needed to think about them before he could begin to get over his loss. Having scavenged bread and cheese from the college kitchen, he returned to his room, lay on his bed and pictured Jane's eyes.

He was asleep when the guard threw open the door. 'Master Hill, the king wishes to see you at once.' In the bedchamber, Thomas heard nothing. The guard went in and shook him. 'Master Hill, you must arise, sir. The king has summoned you.' Thomas struggled awake. Four hours' sleep felt like four minutes. The guard helped him up. 'Get dressed, sir. I will take you to the king.' Please God, thought Thomas, no more ciphers. I haven't the strength.

On a table beside the king stood a small iron box. It had been forced open. 'This box was found concealed behind a wall in Master Rush's rooms,' the king told him in a quiet voice. 'It contained these two documents.' He handed them to Thomas, who unrolled one. On it had been written a column of letter sequences. The sequences were five or six letters in length. He put it down and unrolled the other one. On this was a column of numbers, which did not correspond to the number codes used in the first message. In both cases, Thomas recognized the hand of Tobias Rush.

'What do you make of them, Master Hill?' asked the king.

'The alphabetical list is probably an encrypted list of key-words, sir, and the numerical list a list of codewords. They are both written in Tobias Rush's hand.'

'Of that I am aware. Can you decrypt them?'

'As we already know some of the number codes being used, and we know PARIS is one keyword, it should not be difficult, your majesty.'

'In that case, start work at once, and bring me the results the moment you have them.'

Taking the two documents, Thomas bowed and left. Ciphers for sleep. A poor trade.

He started with the letters. If he was right about the numbers, they were less important. He looked at the list.

MQQHTT
WKHRSG
NCGVNJ
QCUMX
BVKISY
MKVFTT

O C S P J Y

N K O E S

If they were keywords, one of them would be PARIS. Only two of the sequences had five letters — QCUMX and NKOES — one of which would be it. It did not take Thomas long to find out which. He very quickly established that each letter of the plain word was encrypted by a letter of the alphabet the same number of places after it as its position in the word. So in PARIS, P became Q, A became C, R became U, I became M, and S became X. He soon had the list in plain text.

L O N D O N

V I E N N A

M A D R I D

P A R I S

A T H E N S

L I S D O N

N A P L E S

M I L A N

Keywords to Vigenère squares or alphabetic shifts, which would be used in turn, replies using the same words backwards. After MILAN, the sender would go back to LONDON.

The numbers also submitted without a fight. The man who had devised these ciphers was not the most imaginative encrypter that Thomas had ever faced. He had disguised the numbers in a similar way to the letters, only backwards. He had used the numbers one to nine, and returned to one after nine. There were ten further numbers which Thomas decrypted, but could not, without a context, put names to. And there, for all to see, was 775, now revealed to be Tobias Rush. The senders of messages would have committed to memory the names represented by each number.

On receiving the decrypted lists, the king said only that Thomas would no longer be under guard, that he might leave Christ Church as he wished, and that arrangements would be made to escort him back to Romsey. Until then Thomas must stay in Oxford in case of further developments. He now knew with certainty that one of his most trusted advisers had been sending and receiving encrypted messages on behalf of his enemies, and that he would have had access to all incoming and outgoing messages from the man who had replaced Thomas.

Thomas went first to Merton, where the queen's household was preparing to travel. In Merton Street, horses were being groomed and carriages polished. Inside the college, under the watchful eyes of the queen's ladies, servants bustled about with bags and boxes. Thomas doubted if any of them knew when they were leaving or where they were going, but whenever and wherever it turned out to be, they would be ready.

Simon was in his room, reading his Bible, when Thomas arrived. 'Not preparing for the journey, Simon?' he enquired.

Simon looked up and smiled. 'Thankfully, a Franciscan has little to prepare, other than his soul. He has everything invested in that.'

'Judging by the number of horses and carriages, and the heaps of baggage, you won't be dining on shaggy inkcaps this time.'

'Probably not. I wouldn't mind, but her majesty's household expects something rather more substantial.'

'Does anyone know when you're leaving?'

'I don't think so. Even the queen is vague on the matter. Do you know why?'

'I do,' replied Thomas, taking a seat beside Simon. He told Simon about backwards and forwards, his last-minute decryption, about the contents of the message, and about the lists found in Rush's rooms.

'Is the king now persuaded?' asked Simon.

'Almost. He has sent a troop to intercept Rush on his way into Oxford. He intends to interrogate Rush himself. I have warned him, however, that such a message would certainly have been sent by more than one route and that Pym will know of the plan for you to travel to Bristol before Exeter.'

'Then no doubt the plan will change.'

They talked of the queen, Margaret, Polly and Lucy, Oxford and the war. And, finally, they talked of Jane. 'The queen is distraught at her death. She was very fond of Jane. She insisted that her body be taken to York,' said Simon. 'She would have wanted to be buried near her family.'

'If Rush should hang for nothing else, he should hang for Jane. The rape and murder of a woman he had already tormented with threats against her family.'

'I agree. Rush is beyond my understanding.'

'And Fayne should be hanged, too. We must find proof.'

Thomas knew all was not well the moment he set foot back in Christ Church. A group of Lifeguards stood inside the college gate, shuffling their feet and looking sullen. A second group had congregated at the other end of the cattle pen, near the Great Hall. Both groups seemed to be waiting for something. He asked one of the first group what news they brought.

'News that our captain is giving the king at this very moment,' replied the soldier, 'and I thank God it's him, not me.'

'I am Thomas Hill, adviser to the king. May I know what the news is?'

The soldier exchanged a glance with the man next to him. 'The king will know by now, Master Hill, so I may as well tell you. We were sent to intercept Tobias Rush on his way into Oxford from the west. The king wanted him brought straight here.'

'Is he dead?'

'No, sir, far from it. While we were engaged with his guards, he slipped away. Just turned his horse and galloped off. We hadn't time to stop him.'

'Did you give chase?'

'We did, sir, but he was gone. His majesty will not be happy. The captain told us it was a task we had better not fail in. I hope his majesty will give us another chance.'

'I wish you well, Captain. Tobias Rush must be brought to justice.' Rush, now a proven traitor, still at large. Perhaps Fayne, his murdering accomplice, might lead Thomas to him.

Thomas went from Christ Church to Pembroke, where Silas met him in the courtyard. 'I'm happy to find you looking well, sir,' he said, shaking Thomas's hand. 'There's been all manner of stories going about. We heard you'd been put in the castle gaol, then you'd disappeared, then you'd come back and were under guard in Christ Church.'

'Servants' gossip, Silas.'

'I suppose so, sir. Is it true?'

'Some of it. But I'm free now, and looking forward to going home.'

'When will you be leaving, sir?'

'The king expects me to travel with the queen's party in a few days' time. Before then, I have a task to perform and I should value your help, Silas.'

Silas's eyes narrowed. 'It wouldn't have to do with Tobias Rush, sir, would it? I wouldn't want to stand too close to him.'

'Not Rush, Silas, Francis Fayne. Has he been seen in the college?'

'Oh no, sir. Captain Fayne has left us. He was here one day, gone the next. Never a word of explanation, and no one knows why, or where he went.'

'No idea where he might be?'

'None, sir, and I'm not in a hurry to find out. Loud-mouthed beggar, he was, spent his days gambling and whoring. Never saw him do any soldiering.'

'He's a member of Sir Henry Bard's regiment now. Do you know where they're billeted?'

'I don't think they're in any of the colleges, so they'll be in the town. The almshouses, sir, I daresay. God knows how Fayne got himself a room in Pembroke.'

'Thank you, Silas. I'll start there. Let me know if you do happen to hear anything.'

'I will, sir. Treat him with caution, mind. He didn't take kindly to your last meeting.'

Thomas spent most of the following day knocking on the doors of rows of modest houses in Brewer Street, Littlegate and the narrow streets around them. Every one of them had been commandeered and was occupied by army officers and their families. Most of the wretched townsfolk who had been forced to hand over their homes had left Oxford and were living in neighbouring villages. Some would have found a roof to sleep under, others would be sheltering as best they could in the woods and haystacks.

By the evening he was sick of asking the whereabouts of a Captain Fayne, and sicker still of the blank looks and shakes of the head that he received in reply. Even members of the same regiment could not say where Fayne was, only that he had disappeared. He might be dead, he might have deserted and gone home. No one managed a good word for him, or even much interest. Either Fayne had covered his tracks very well, or he was accorded no more respect by his fellow soldiers than he was by Thomas.

If the army neither knew nor cared about Captain Fayne, perhaps the whores and drunks of the city did. That evening, Thomas set off from Christ Church, walked up St Aldate's and Cornmarket and turned into Market Street. The last time he had walked in this part of the town had been after watching Jane die. Then he had seen nothing. Now he saw everything. Even at that hour, Market Street was busy. Traders were trying to sell off what remained of their wares while thrifty housewives tried to shave another farthing or two off their prices, and ragged boys moved in and out of the crowd, looking for an easy pocket to pick or purse to snatch. Failing those, an apple or a bun from an unguarded stall would be slipped into a bag and taken home for dinner. And, if it were possible, the open drain which ran down the middle of the street was overflowing with even more muck and shit than it had been before. Thomas held a handkerchief to his face and picked his way carefully towards the Crown.

The inn was as busy as ever. Thomas wormed his way in, nudging and inching between drinkers and getting cursed and elbowed in return, until he reached the hatch from which the land-lord dispensed his wares. From there, with his back to the wall, he looked around the room in the hope of spotting a head of long fair hair. It was a vain hope. Francis Fayne, by his height and his appearance, would stand out in any crowd, and he was not stand-ing out in this one. Nor was he at the table at the back where they had played hazard. Not that Thomas had really expected to see him. A man who has been party to rape and is known to have con-sorted with a traitor does not disappear only to reappear at one of his old haunts. But, his fellow soldiers having been no help at all, Thomas had to start somewhere, and the Crown was as good a place as any.

Taking a wooden tankard of ale from the landlord, he edged back into the middle of the room where he joined a circle of drinkers, none of whom he recognized. 'Good evening, gentle-men,' he offered, raising his tankard. 'Permit me to introduce myself. Thomas Hill, newly arrived in Oxford, and in need of advice from wiser heads.'

'Master Hill,' replied one of them, 'welcome to an overcrowd-ed Oxford. What brings you here?'

Thomas was ready for this, and used the answer that he had agreed with Abraham. 'I came to visit an old friend.'

Another soldier eyed him suspiciously. 'An odd time to choose to make a visit.'

'Indeed. But time waits for no man and I fear there will not be another chance. It was now or never.'

'We are but humble soldiers of the king,' said the first man. 'What advice is it you seek?'

Thomas did his best to look embarrassed. 'Being away from home, I have in mind to take the opportunity to, er, sample new pleasures. I wondered if you gentlemen might be able to recommend a suitable establishment for a man such as I.'

The second man guffawed. 'He wants a whorehouse. God's wounds, man, Oxford is full of them. Take your pick. Take precautions, though, or you'll get more than you bargained for. There's plenty of pox about.'

Thomas smiled nervously. 'Yes, yes, I daresay. It's just that one seldom has an opportunity for a little, er, variety, and I am inexperienced in such matters. Could you possibly recommend somewhere?'

A third man joined in. 'You'll find several excellent establishments in Magpie Lane. Try your luck there.'

Thomas inclined his head to the man. 'I'm obliged, sir. Magpie Lane. And where would that be?' He knew perfectly well where it was. He had walked down it on his first day in Oxford.

'It joins High Street and Merton Street. You'll know it by the whores lining the road. The ones who are too old and too ugly to work with roofs over their heads.'

'Thank you, sir. Again, I'm obliged. May I refresh your tankards, gentlemen?'

Having made good his offer, Thomas returned to the group. 'I almost forgot, sirs, there is another matter upon which you might be able to help me. I believe my cousin's regiment is at present stationed in Oxford. Colonel Pinchbeck's. Would you happen to know if it is?'

'It was, sir. After Newbury, what was left of it joined with Sir Henry Bard's. And what is the name of your cousin, if I may ask? If he's a stout soldier and a drinking man, we might know him.'

'Francis Fayne. Captain Fayne.'

There was an awkward silence. Then the first man spoke.

'Fayne. Not a name to endear you to us, Master Hill. Or to anyone in Oxford, I daresay.'

'Oh, and why is that?' asked Thomas.

'The man's a gambler, and a poor one at that. He owes money all over the town.'

'I'm distressed to hear it, most distressed. However, I promised my wife that I would seek him out if I could. Do you know where I might find him?'

'In a brothel, in a tavern, in his grave? Who cares?'

'I gather feelings for Captain Fayne run high. Most unfortunate. I shall have to keep this from dear Prudence. And you cannot suggest where he might be?'

'He disappeared not long ago. Probably ran off to escape his creditors. There's a good few who'd like to find him.'

'I am not a military man, but is it not odd for a captain simply to disappear? Will his regiment not look for him?'

'Ordinarily, they would. But these are not ordinary times. Men go missing and there's no one to look for them. We're all needed to fight the war.'

'What would happen if he were found?'

'He'd be hanged. The king doesn't much like men who run away.'

'No, indeed. Well, I shall just have to tell Prudence that he was off fighting somewhere.'

'Off whoring somewhere, more like.'

'Quite. Now I must take a stroll to Magpie Lane. Good day, gentlemen, and thank you for your advice.'

Thomas left the men to their drinking and made his way back to the door. Neither drinkers nor soldiers knew or cared where Fayne was. The man was a gambler and a libertine, he had no friends, and there was no sign of him in Oxford. Even in a dung heap there is one creature more repulsive than the rest.

Even in Thomas's student days, Magpie Lane had been notorious. It was where many a young scholar had woken up with a head throbbing from drink and an unfamiliar face beside him. Brothels lined both sides of the narrow lane, and, as the soldier had said, whores long past their best plied their trade wherever they could for a few pennies, serving what a merchant might have called the less discerning end of the market.

He knocked on the door of the first house. It was opened at once by a young housemaid, and he stepped inside. Without a word she escorted him to a room at the back, where men and women in various states of undress lolled about, drinking, eating and fondling each other. Some of the men were managing to drink, fondle and smoke a long-stemmed clay pipe all at the same time. A large lady, her face powdered and her head adorned with a wig luxuriant enough to rival any lady at court, emerged from another room. She beamed at Thomas. 'Good evening, sir. Welcome to our little establishment. Shall you take a glass of wine while you consider how best we may serve you?'

Might as well, thought Thomas. I shan't be taking anything else. 'Thank you, madam.'

A glass of wine was brought, Thomas was shown to a chair, and, before he could protest, three women, not one of them older than eighteen, had arranged themselves around him. Despite himself, he looked at them. Neither ugly nor pretty, neither slim nor fat, they might have been chosen for their ordinariness.

'Are you new in Oxford, sir?' asked the brothel-owner. 'I don't recall seeing you before.'

'I am,' replied Thomas, taking a sip of wine. 'Your house was recommended to me by a friend. Francis Fayne, of Sir Henry Bard's regiment.'

'Francis Fayne? Name don't ring a bell, does it, girls?' The girls shook their heads. 'What's he look like, this Fayne?'

'Tall, fair hair, a handsome fellow.'

'We'd remember him, then, wouldn't we, girls?' This time the girls nodded. Thomas wondered idly if they were ever allowed to speak. 'No, sir, can't say as we know Master Fayne. Never mind, you're here now, so what's it to be? We're offering one for half a guinea, two for fifteen shillings.'

'Two what?'

The woman laughed. 'Two girls, sir, of course, what did you think I meant? Choose any two of these lovelies and they're yours for fifteen shillings the night.'

Thomas looked thoughtful. 'A most attractive offer, to be sure, and one to take advantage of. Yet I find myself at this moment not entirely ready to make the most of it. Allow me to pay you for the wine, and I will return when circumstances are more, ah, pressing.'

The woman was taken aback. She was unused to gentlemen changing their minds once they were there, and her current offer had proved most popular. 'Well, sir,' she replied, 'you won't find better girls in Oxford, though I do say it myself. But if you're not up to the task, I'll take a shilling for the wine and bid you good evening. We've plenty more customers to come.'

Deciding not to protest at the price of a small glass of in-different claret, Thomas handed over a shilling and made his escape. His first visit to a brothel had not been a success. Back in Magpie Lane, he mopped his brow, took a deep breath and pre-pared himself for another try. Good God, what wouldn't any of those girls have given for the looks of Jane Romilly. Raped and murdered on the orders of Rush, and with the help of Fayne. Find him, Thomas, and find him fast.

Six more brothels and six more glasses of wine later, Thomas had no more idea of where Fayne might be than he had had that morning. The closest he had come was a girl at the fourth house, who claimed to have entertained a gentleman matching Fayne's description some weeks before. She had not seen him since. There had been no other hint of the man.

Having knocked on doors all morning, played the part of an erring husband with the soldiers in the Crown and visited seven brothels, Thomas was tired and miserable. Head and legs aching, mind numb, no further forward. It was time to return to Christ Church.

By that time, Magpie Lane was alive with the whores who preferred to work in the dark. A drunken soldier might be more inclined to part with his money if he could not see a face pitted by pox or ravaged by leprosy. Thomas had taken no more than a few steps when the first one accosted him. 'What's your 'urry, sir?' she growled, taking out a fat breast to show him, 'I got another one just as good.' Thomas hastened on without looking. Then two more jumped out of the shadows. 'You look a strong sort,' hissed one. 'Fancy a pair o' lovely ladies? Only a shilling, and you'll go 'ome an 'appy man.' The other grabbed his sleeve and tried to pull him against the wall. Thomas jerked himself free and ran for it. Things must be bad if even the whores were offering special rates.

He kept running until he reached Christ Church. Half fearing that an order to present himself to the king might await him, he was relieved to find no guards outside his room, no orders and no visitors.

*

When Simon knocked on his door the next morning, Thomas struggled off his bed and groped his way to the door, cursing the oaf who called upon a gentleman at such an ungodly hour. 'Good morning, Simon,' croaked Thomas, 'why so early?'

'You look unwell, Thomas,' replied the friar, inspecting him. 'Do you need help?'

'What I need is sleep. Failing that, breakfast. Have you brought any?'

'Alas, no.'

'Then go and find some while I dress,' ordered Thomas, closing the door.

Simon was back within ten minutes, bearing bread and cheese, and a jug of ale. 'There you are, Thomas,' he said cheerfully, 'eat that while we talk.' Thomas took the tray and sat at his table. 'I came to tell you that the queen has had no word from the king, despite making it clear that she is anxious to leave Oxford. She is determined to have the child in France, and is understandably nervous about crossing the Channel late in the year. Her last crossing was unpleasant.'

'So you've told me.'

'His majesty is reluctant to let her go while Rush is free, although how he thinks Rush will be caught now, I do not know. The man could be anywhere.'

Thomas swallowed the last piece of bread, and took a gulp of ale. 'I spent yesterday looking for Fayne. He's disappeared. There's no sign of him.'

Simon looked grave. 'Thomas, you have performed a great service for the king. Abraham and Jane are dead. You will soon be going home. Rush and Fayne will pay for their sins in this life or the next. Should we not leave it at that?'

'No, Simon, we should not. Fayne was involved in Jane's rape and murder, and I want to see him hanged for it. What's more, he's a coward. He avoided Newbury by pretending to be delayed on the way there. I'm sure of it. And he's left gambling debts all over Oxford.'

'So he's a gambler. What does he play?'

'Hazard. For high stakes and not very well.'

Simon laughed. 'There are many like him. The queen's guards spend their days at cards and dice, winning and losing small fortunes. The prospect of imminent death on the battlefield can make a man reckless. Not that Fayne's corpse will ever be found on a battlefield, by the sound of it.'

'A gibbet would suit him better. I'd put him on one myself if I could.'

'Thomas, that's not like you. I thought you abhorred violence.'

'I abhor injustice more. A murderer should be hanged.'

'Are you sure of his guilt?'

'I am. It rings true. Find a man who might lure her to her death, exploit his weakness and bribe or threaten him to do it. It reeks of Rush.'

'It does. One might almost feel sympathy for Fayne.'

'For the love of God, Simon, not an ounce of sympathy for Fayne, please. Remember what he has done.'

'We are taught to distinguish between the sinner and the sin.'

'That isn't what you said about Rush.'

'In his case, I make an exception. Anyone who can do what he did to Abraham, and would have done to you if he'd had the chance, is evil itself. Also, I have never met Fayne. That makes it harder to condemn him.'

'De Pointz's pragmatism again, Simon?' Simon smiled broadly, showing his gravestone teeth. 'Well, pragmatically, if we find Fayne, he might tell us where Rush is. We must find them.'

'Have you considered, Thomas, that it was not many days ago that your only wish was to go home? Now you wish to stay. Strange, is it not?'

'It is. My old friend Montaigne said that there is no conversation more boring than the one in which everyone agrees. He might as well have said there is no man more boring than the one who never changes his mind.'

For some minutes they sat in silence, neither knowing in which direction to take the discussion. Then there was a knock on the door. Expecting a messenger from the king, Thomas opened it. It was Silas. 'Silas, come in. Father de Pointz is here. What brings you to Christ Church?'

'Good morning, gentlemen,' said Silas with a hint of a bow. 'I've come to tell you that two men have been asking for Master Hill. They didn't say why, but I thought you should know.'

'Who are they, Silas?' asked Thomas.

'Gave their names as Philip Smithson and Hugh Tomkins, both captains.'

Smithson and Tomkins. Thomas recognized the names at once. Fayne's dice-playing companions. 'Did they give no clue as to why they're looking for me?'

'None, sir.'

'And what did you tell them?'

'Only that I would try to get a message to you. I didn't tell them where you are.'

'Good. Come and sit down, Silas. This needs thought.'

Silas found a chair, and sat nervously on the edge of it.

Lording it over young Pembroke scholars was one thing, calling on Master Hill and Father de Pointz in Christ Church, now the home of the king, quite another.

'What do you make of it, Simon?' said Thomas. 'Friends or foes?'

'I couldn't say. Who are they?'

Thomas told them about the dice game and how he knew them. 'In that case, I would treat them with caution. Your enemy's friend is also your enemy, or something like that,' said Simon.

'Something like that. Yet I'm not so sure. I had the impression that Fayne's company was forced upon them.'

'How so?'

'Their manner when he lost his money and stormed out. An eyebrow raised, a hand on my shoulder. Small things in themselves, but perhaps adding up to something more.'

'Thomas, we should be cautious. Why would they contact you unless Fayne had told them to?'

'There's only one way to find out. I must meet them. With suitable precautions, of course. Any suggestions, Silas?'

'Two, sir. Don't meet them alone and meet them where you are safe from surprise.'

'Such as?'

'The Pembroke library, as you may remember, has a gallery. I could easily hide there and keep an eye on you. I have a pistol.'

'And I will accompany you,' said Simon. 'Two of them, two of us.'

'Having seen what you are capable of, Simon, I couldn't possibly refuse your offer. How will we tell them, Silas?'

'They told me how to get a message to them, sir.'

'Good. Then tell them we will be in the library at four o'clock this afternoon.'

'I will, sir. And, sir, do take care. I haven't fired a pistol for twenty years.'

'Then let us hope you don't fire it today. Four o'clock, Silas. Tell them.'

'Four o'clock, sir. Goodbye, gentlemen.' Silas rose and, with another hint of a bow, left to deliver the message.

By fifteen minutes before four o'clock, when Thomas and Simon were seated at a reading table in the middle of the library of Pembroke College, there had still been no news of Rush either from the queen or directly from the king. There were several such tables in the library. When Thomas had last been there, each had been occupied by scholars reading and writing, and from time to time rising to take a book from the shelves that covered all four walls of the room. The library had smelt of leather bindings, ink and scholarship, and he remembered it fondly as a place of quiet learning and shared fellowship. Today it was cold and deserted. The shelves and books were in need of dusting, the floor needed sweeping and every candle had burned down to a flat stump. Thomas could smell only damp and decay. He closed his eyes and waited.

When the door opened, he looked up sharply. Silas came quietly in, the two captains behind him. They were as Thomas remembered — dark, bearded, leather jerkins and breeches, feathered caps, tall boots. In a city of such men, quite un-remarkable, and both appeared unarmed. No swords, no pistols. Silas led them to where Thomas and Simon sat. Both men removed their hats and bowed. The taller one spoke first. 'Master

Hill, I am Philip Smithson and this is my fellow captain, Hugh Tomkins. We thank you for agreeing to meet us.'

'I recall both of you and I'm intrigued to know why you wish to meet me. This is my friend Simon de Pointz.'

Neither man seemed put out by the presence of a Franciscan friar. 'Father de Pointz,' said Tomkins, 'an honour.'

'Thank you,' replied Simon. 'Do sit down. Merkin will see that we are not disturbed.'

'I will, sirs,' said Silas, making for the door. Outside, he would climb the narrow twisting staircase which led up to the gallery, from where he would be able to watch and listen.

When the two men had sat, Thomas took charge. 'Now, gentlemen, you have asked for this meeting. Tell us what it is you wish to discuss.'

'Before I do, Master Hill,' replied Smithson, 'be assured that we are unarmed and mean you no harm.' Thomas nodded. 'We asked to meet you because we heard that you have been looking for Francis Fayne.'

'And where did you hear that?'

'You visited the Crown and, er, certain other places. News gets around.'

'Very well, I have been searching for Fayne. What of it?'

'We too would like to find him, and we had in mind a joining of forces.'

'Why do you wish to find him?'

This time, Tomkins answered. 'Fayne owes us money.'

'Money? Is that all?' asked Simon.

'No. The man is a coward. He persuaded Colonel Pinchbeck that he should take his troop on a scouting mission on the way to Newbury, on the pretext of making sure the enemy had not set any traps. They arrived after the battle had ended, claiming to have been delayed by a skirmish but in truth having spent the day at rest.'

'That is a most serious accusation,' said Simon. 'If proved, he would hang.'

'He would, and he would deserve to. When good men are giving their lives for what they believe in, cowardice cannot be condoned.'

'I was at Newbury and saw Fayne arrive in the town. He did not look as if he had been in a skirmish, let alone a battle.'

'I am ashamed to admit that I know the man,' said Smithson.

'Is this why he has disappeared?'

'We think not. He cannot know that one of his men has let slip the truth. We think there must be more to it.'

'What?'

'We wondered, as you have been looking for him, if you might know the answer to that question.'

Thomas and Simon exchanged glances. Simon nodded, and Thomas said, 'We know that he was involved in the rape and murder of Lady Romilly, a lady-in-waiting to the queen.'

Both captains looked shocked. 'We heard about this murder, but we had no idea that Fayne was involved,' said Tomkins.

'He was acting on the orders of Tobias Rush, one of his majesty's closest advisers, now to be arrested for treason.'

'Then he's a traitor and a murderer as well as a coward. When he learned that Tobias Rush was to be arrested, he would have feared being exposed. That's why he's in hiding.'

'Might he have left Oxford and gone home?'

'I doubt it,' replied Smithson, thoughtfully. 'Would he make the journey to Yorkshire alone, and how would he explain himself when he got there? His family are well known in the county. They would not tolerate a hint of scandal.'

'He might have gone elsewhere.'

'He might, but I sense he is not far away.'

'And there is little point in looking for him unless we assume you're right,' said Simon. 'The question is, how are we going to find him in time?'

'In time for what?'

'Thomas and I must leave Oxford soon.' Simon covered his mistake smoothly. It would not have done to mention the queen's departure, however well known it might be.

'I learned nothing at the Crown or in Magpie Lane,' pointed out Thomas. 'Have you gentlemen any ideas?' Smithson shrugged and Tomkins shook his head. 'Then allow me to suggest a plan. Fayne is an inveterate gambler. Let us use his weakness to lure him out of hiding.'

'It would take a big bait to tempt him out of hiding if he's in fear of being hanged,' said Tomkins.

'What do you have in mind?' asked Smithson.

'I have in mind a game of hazard for very high stakes and against a very bad opponent.'

'For that we shall need money and a player we can trust. Not you, Master Hill, as Fayne knows you, or either of us.'

'No. We shall have to find someone else.'

Simon coughed delicately. 'Fayne does not know me. May I offer my services?'

'You, Simon? What do you know about hazard?' asked Thomas.

'In the inns and taverns of Norwich, a young man may learn many things.'

'I don't believe you.'

'Why on earth not? Am I too stupid?'

'No, no, it's just that . . .'

'Try me. Ask me a question.'

'What is a nick?'

'A winning throw by the caster.'

'Main of seven, chance of nine, how much does the caster win if he wins the hand?'

'One and a half times the stake.'

'With a main of five, what are the odds on the caster winning?'

'Just under one in two.'

Thomas sat back in his chair and put his hands behind his head. 'Father de Pointz, you never cease to astonish me. Praying, fighting and now gambling.'

'Fighting and gambling only when necessary. Praying I do every day, as should everyone.'

'What do you think, gentlemen?' Thomas asked the captains.

'I think we have the perfect man for the task,' replied Tomkins, 'but how are we to entice Fayne into the trap? I doubt he'd show his face in Oxford, even for a thousand guineas.'

There was a voice from the gallery. 'One moment, sirs,' called out Silas, standing up so that he could be seen. 'I shall come down.'

Thomas and Simon had forgotten Silas hiding up there. Neither of the captains showed any surprise. They must have assumed that they would be watched. Silas came into the library and stood at the table. 'If you'll pardon me, sirs, I don't think you'll require any further protection, and I have a suggestion.'

'Excellent, Silas,' said Thomas. 'Are you another expert player of hazard?'

'No, sir, nothing at all like that, although many of my young scholars have enjoyed the game over the years. Indeed, I recall you yourself playing the occasional hand, Master Hill. The thing is, since the court has been in Oxford, one or two houses have turned themselves into agreeable places for dice- and card-players. They offer good food and wine and a bit more comfort. They charge for it, of course, but the winners are happy enough to pay. There is one such place — very popular with merchants and the like — which might be suitable. Very discreet, no signs, no prying eyes or wagging tongues. It's a house just inside the west gate.'

'Have you been there, Silas?' asked Simon.

'No, sir, but I have heard it's frequented by well-to-do gentle-men who like to play for high stakes. No weapons are allowed in the house.'

'Sounds perfect.'

'I agree,' said Thomas. 'We have the bait and we have a place to set our trap. Now how do we persuade Fayne to take the bait?'

This time it was Tomkins's turn. 'Word of new players gets around like the pox. If Father de Pointz goes there this evening dressed as a travelling merchant, and is seen to lose plenty of money, I'll wager Fayne will soon hear about it. If he's in the county, that is.'

'If he's not, we're wasting our time. But we won't know unless we try. So, Simon will lose heavily at this house tonight, let it be known that he is in Oxford for a day or two and will be playing there again tomorrow evening. Have you got plenty of money to lose, Simon?'

'The money will not present a problem. Losing it will be more difficult.'

'Well, make sure you do. A winning merchant is not what we need.'

'And you, what will you be doing, Thomas?'

'I shall be nearby.'

'And us?' asked Smithson. 'What would you have us do?'

'You won't be needed tonight. Tomorrow you'd best not show your faces. Hide somewhere outside, somewhere you can watch the door. If he arrives, guard the door. If he tries to run, stop him.'

'Why don't we shoot him?'

'Fayne may be a traitor and a coward, he may be a rapist, but he must face the king's justice, not ours. We'll take him alive if we can. Six o'clock tomorrow evening, gentlemen. Silas will show you where. Let's hope the bait smells tasty enough to bring the creature out of his lair.'

A little before seven that evening, Silas led Thomas and Simon to the house. As he had said, it was close to the west gate — close enough for a man who did not want to be seen in the town to slip in and out safely. It was two storeys high, with leaded windows and a tiled roof. A substantial house, brick-built in the Dutch style, restrained in design and displaying no sign of what went on inside. Thomas guessed that it belonged to a town official or a lawyer. It was not extravagant enough for a merchant.

From somewhere, Simon had acquired a long black coat edged in fur, a plain white shirt and black woollen breeches. His sandals had been replaced by soft leather boots. As they approached the house, he jangled the coins in his pocket. 'I hope you're as rich as you sound, Simon,' said Thomas, 'and penniless when you leave.'

'Don't worry, I shall lose everything but my faith, and the clothes I stand up in,' replied Simon in a strange voice.

'Why are you speaking like that?' asked Thomas.

'Don't tell me you've forgotten my acting skills. This is my merchant's voice.'

'Of course it is. Foolish of me. In you go, merchant, and lose convincingly. Remember you're our bait and we need Fayne.'

Simon knocked boldly on the door and was admitted at once. When he did not immediately reappear, they assumed that he had been accepted as a genuine gambler looking for an evening's entertainment.

'You go back to the college, Silas,' said Thomas. 'I shall stay here and keep an eye on things.'

'As you wish, sir, but take care.'

'Thank you, Silas. I will.'

When Silas had gone, Thomas walked around the house. The windows were small and there was no door at the back. Visitors could come and go only through the door at the front. He peered through a window, but the glass was too thick to see through. The walls must have been thick, too; he could hear nothing from inside. A very private house indeed.

It was no more than fifty paces to the west gate, and in the fading evening light. Thomas could just make out the guards stationed there. He thought he could see six of them. How secure really is Oxford? he wondered. A few more Newburys and it would be very weakly defended, and vulnerable to attack. He hated to think what Parliamentary artillery might do to the town. Christ Church in ruins, Pembroke a heap of rubble? God forbid. Then what would the king do? Sue for peace or take his court somewhere else? No doubt the former was too much to hope for. His majesty was not going to back down now. The plot to take prisoner the queen and her unborn child showed that Pym and his colleagues would negotiate a peace, but only on terms that the king would not accept. Stalemate.

He was jolted from his thoughts by the crack of nailed boots on the cobbles. The guard was about to be changed. The ancient gates were guarded even though the town had long ago spread outside them. It wouldn't do to be seen loitering in this quiet part of the town, so he strode purposefully towards the arriving troop. When he had passed them, he turned and repeated the exercise with the troop that was being replaced, ending up back where he started. What in the name of the king and all his men do you think you're doing, he thought, walking backwards and forwards along this dark street like a thief in the night? If Margaret could see you now, she would think your brain was addled. And perhaps it is. Being arrested for behaving suspiciously is more likely than catching Fayne. With Simon inside the house, however, it was too late to change his mind. Simon might need help, and Thomas dare not desert his post until he came out. He would just have to suffer silently.

Two silent hours later, Thomas was cold and bored. Wishing he had thought to wear a thicker coat, he wrapped his arms around himself and jumped up and down in a futile attempt to keep warm. He had watched as gamblers had come and gone — not one of them remotely mistakable for Francis Fayne — some alone and miserable, others laughing and boasting about their skill with the dice or the cards. Thomas, hidden in the shadows, heard everything and smiled. Gamblers were the same wherever you went. When they won it was skill, when they lost, ill luck. Still there was no sign of Simon. Either he was enjoying himself so much that he was in no hurry to go home, or he was having trouble losing his money. Thomas was just beginning to wonder if he could stand waiting there any longer, when the street began to fill with women. They came in ones and twos and took up positions near the house. When one of them saw him, she pointed at him. 'Look at that, girls,' she squawked, 'we got competition tonight. Must be some funny ones playing. What's your name, dear? Got a friend in there, 'ave you?' Thomas, not knowing whether to answer or not, pretended not to hear. 'Lost your tongue, 'ave you? Shame, you might need it later.' The women in the street cackled. Thomas turned his head away and willed Simon to appear.

At ten o'clock, the door opened and the remaining gamblers emerged into the night. Ten o'clock, early though it was, was evidently when the house closed for the day. Perhaps the owner liked to get rid of his visitors before he retired. They were immediately surrounded by women loudly describing their charms, promising excellent service, and not being easily put off. Some followed a chosen target down the street, others hung on to an arm or a waist until they were accepted or thrown off.

Simon was one of the last to emerge. He called a cheerful good night to his new friends, fended off a persistent woman who clearly knew money when she saw it, and strode away towards Christ Church. Thomas ran to catch up with him. When Simon heard him coming, he turned and waited. 'Ah, Thomas, there you are. I do hope the waiting wasn't too tedious.'

'It was. How did the evening go?'

'It wasn't an easy part to play, but I believe I carried it off rather well.'

'And?'

'I had to be at my best to lose to those clods. Or do I mean worst?'

After three cold, solitary hours, Thomas's temper was short.

'For God's sake, Simon, I know you have a high opinion of your theatrical talent, but this is not a play. Abraham and Jane are dead, Rush is still at large, and we are trying to find Fayne. Did you lose your money?'

'Of course. My apologies. I must have been carried away by the moment. Eventually, I did. And I made it obvious that there is plenty more where that came from and that I would be back tomorrow. I even asked if there were any young men in town who might like to play for higher stakes.'

'And are there?'

'It seems that there might be. Word of a visiting merchant with deep pockets and a knack of laying foolish wagers will be passed on. There's a decent chance Fayne will hear of it and come tomorrow.'

'Was there any mention of Fayne?'

'No. Nor of Francis. Christian names are preferred.'

'A pity. I had hoped he would be known there. Anything else?'

'Only that they are expecting me tomorrow evening at seven.' They had reached Merton, where Simon bade Thomas good night and went to change his clothes before evening prayers with the queen.

Back at Christ Church, Thomas wondered again what foolishness he had embarked upon. A devout Franciscan acting the part of a gambling merchant, and a homesick bookseller lurking in the street for three hours — all in the vain hope of luring their prey into a trap. And planning to do it all over again tomorrow. What would Montaigne have said?

After an interminably long and wearisome day, Simon the merchant and Thomas the watcher set off again the following evening for the house by the west gate. They found Tomkins and Smithson already there and anxious for news. At least this time Thomas would have company. When Simon had left them to be about his business, he told them what he knew. 'We must hope that Fayne does not owe money here,' he said.

'It's unlikely because it's the rougher places he prefers, where he can drown his disappointments and take his revenge on helpless women,' replied Tomkins.

'Helpless women' immediately brought to Thomas's mind a hideous picture of Jane lying on a bed bleeding to death. Had other women suffered as she had? If so, all the more reason to find Fayne. One eye is brown yet the other is blue. The eyes that had shown him the way to break the cipher. Beautiful eyes, a beautiful lady. Rush might have escaped, but if there was a grain of justice in the world Fayne would show his face tonight.

The three men stood together in the shadow of a broken wall almost opposite the house, very near to where Thomas had kept his vigil the previous evening. Thomas Hill, Hugh Tomkins and Philip Smithson — each of them for their own reasons determined to find Francis Fayne. Looking at the others, Thomas could see precious little difference between them. Both were medium height, about Thomas's age, dressed in black coats, hats, breeches and boots, and armed with swords and knives. They looked exactly what they were — officers of his majesty's army. Simon, Silas and he had agreed that the two men were genuine in their loathing of Fayne, and desperate to bring him to justice.

To pass the time, Thomas asked, 'Are you gentlemen in the same regiment as Fayne?'

'No, sir,' replied Tomkins. 'Fayne was in Colonel Pinchbeck's

Regiment, now joined with Sir Henry Bard's. We are with Colonel Bagot.'

Thomas knew of the regiment. 'Ah, yes. Richard Bagot — one of the first regiments formed to fight for the king. Were you at Newbury?'

'We were, sir, and by God's will, lived to tell of it. Many friends died there.'

'And you're sure Fayne avoided the battle by subterfuge?'

'Quite sure, sir,' replied Smithson. 'He claimed to have been in a skirmish, but he was lying. One of his men admitted as much.'

'Yet you play dice with him.'

'We did. Not any longer. You saw yourself what the man's like. An evil temper and quick with his fists. When we heard about Newbury, we had no more to do with him.'

'Do you think he'll come tonight?'

'Who knows, sir? We can only wait and pray.'

'Indeed. Although I'll leave the praying to you. I've never been much of a hand at it.'

'Not a church-goer, sir?'

'Family occasions only. Now, if Fayne arrives, we'd better have a plan.'

'What do you suggest, sir?' asked Tomkins.

'Well, I have inspected the house. There are no other doors, or windows wide enough for a man to squeeze through. It would be a mistake to charge in after him. Others might take his part. We could find ourselves trapped and outnumbered. We'll wait until he comes out. Simon will be behind him, and we will be in front. He won't escape.'

Smithson and Tomkins exchanged a look. 'That sounds sensible, sir,' said Smithson. 'We'll wait on your order to take him.'

'Good. Now I shall wait here. You two go to either end of the street. Between us, we'll see him if he comes.'

With three pairs of eyes watching, they would surely not miss Fayne if he came. The question was — would he come?

For an hour and then another, they saw the comings and goings of visitors to the gambling house, the guards changing and a woman noisily vomiting against the wall. They heard dogs barking, cats wailing, and a man and his wife arguing angrily in a nearby cottage. They did not see or hear Fayne. Each man kept steadfastly to his appointed position, not wanting to be the first to weaken. As the evening grew colder, a man peering out from the house opposite would have seen three men, apparently unconnected, stamping their feet and blowing on their hands, and wondered why they did not go and find fires to sit in front of. Thomas was very close to giving up and leaving Simon to lose his money alone, when all three of them saw a solitary figure enter the street from the direction of the gate and walk towards the house. Each of them shrank back into the shadows and watched.

Although the man walked with shoulders hunched and head down, they could tell that he was tall. As he approached the house, he turned and looked furtively around, as if afraid of being seen. His face was in shadow and his head covered by a broad black hat. He reached the door of the house and knocked. The door was quickly opened, and the man took off his hat before entering. Even in the dark, his long fair hair was clearly visible. It was Fayne.

The moment he entered the house, Smithson from one end of the street and Tomkins from the other ran towards Thomas in the middle. No more than a pace or two from him, both turned sharply towards the house. Smithson knocked, the door was opened and they disappeared inside. Thomas, too astonished to react, stood and stared blankly at the closed door. As his wits returned, the realization dawned that he had misjudged them: they had planned to ignore Thomas's instructions to take Fayne alive. Simon might be in danger. He too ran to the door and knocked loudly.

As always, the door was opened at once. Instead of being ushered in, however, Thomas was knocked to the ground by a figure hurtling out. From inside came confused shouts of alarm and instruction, followed by Tomkins and Smithson, swords drawn, pursuing the fleeing figure. Thomas struggled to his feet and gave chase. As a student, he had been a noted runner, seldom defeated over any distance less than a mile, and often the toast of those wise enough to put their money on him. A little out of practice but unencumbered by a sword, he quickly closed on the two men, and overtook them just as they reached the end of the street. For some reason, the fleeing Fayne had run off in the direction of the town, not the gate, from which he might have been able to make his escape. Thomas raced past Tomkins and Smithson, just in time to see Fayne disappearing round a corner. He paused to throw off his heavy coat, then he was off again and picking up speed. As long as he kept Fayne in view, the bigger, heavier man would not throw him off.

It did not take long. Within a minute, Thomas had caught Fayne. He launched himself at the man's back, bringing him down with a crack of bone. Fayne was on his face, screaming. Thomas, up on his feet again and puffing from the race, saw that the man's leg was twisted at an awkward angle. Fayne rolled over, held his knee, saw Thomas and cursed. He had come unarmed. If he had carried either sword or pistol, he would not have been admitted to the gambling house. And with a broken leg, he would not be running anywhere. Thomas stood over him and wondered what he was going to do when the other two reached them.

By the time they came clattering up, Thomas had recovered his breath and was standing in front of Fayne.

'What the devil are you two up to?' he shouted. 'We agreed not to act until he came out.'

They were both puffing and blowing. Tomkins recovered first. 'We want justice, sir. He's a coward and a traitor, and he should die.'

'And so he will. We agreed. But on the end of a rope, not at our hands. Why did you do it?'

This time, Smithson answered. 'Master Hill, you are a brave man and a good one, but you are not a soldier. To a soldier, cowardice is worse than murder, and should be punished by instant death. We feared that you would be less certain in your opinion.'

Thomas's voice was icy. 'Captain, this man also raped and murdered an innocent lady, who was my dear friend. He will hang for it. Your stupidity could have exploded like an over-primed cannon and blown up in our faces.'

There was a croak from behind Thomas. 'I did not rape her.'

Thomas turned to face Fayne. 'That we shall ascertain.' Then he spoke to Tomkins. 'Go and find Father de Pointz. Smithson will stay with me while I ask this man a few questions.'

When Tomkins had gone, he spoke to Smithson again. 'When I have finished, you will take him to your colonel. You will not dispense your own justice. Is that clear? Listen carefully and remember what he says.' Smithson, though unaccustomed to being given orders by a bookseller, nevertheless nodded dumbly, and stood beside Thomas in front of a groaning Fayne. If his face was anything to go by, the man was in a great deal of pain. Thomas would have to be quick or Fayne might pass out.

'Now, Fayne, you will answer my questions. If you do not, or if I think you are lying, Smithson will kick your knee. Hard. Do you understand?' Fayne managed a weak nod. 'Good. Did you take money from Tobias Rush?'

'Yes.'

'Why?'

'To walk by the river with Jane.'

'Did you rape her?'

'No.'

'Kick him, Smithson.' Smithson kicked the knee and Fayne screamed. 'I will ask again. Did you rape her?'

'No.'

'Who did?'

'Two others.'

'How do you know?'

'I saw them.'

'Who were they?'

'I don't know. Rush's men.' Fayne was fading fast and Thomas had no time to waste.

'Why did you arrive late at Newbury?'

'Delayed.'

'Another kick, if you please.'

But before Smithson could deliver the kick, Fayne shrieked. 'No. Waited outside the town.'

'Until it was over?' Fayne nodded. 'Until it was over, Fayne?'

'Yes.'

'Why have you been in hiding?'

'Rush.'

'Rush?'

'Both men found with throats cut.'

'And you feared having yours cut too?'

'Yes.'

'Where is Rush?'

'I don't know. Long gone.'

That was it. Fayne passed out in pain and his head slumped to the ground. 'Did you hear all that?' Thomas asked Smithson.

'I did.'

'So you are witness to Fayne's confession to being a traitor and a coward, and to assisting in the rape of Jane Romilly.'

'Yes, sir.'

'Good. Your colonel will be interested in your report. If he does not get it, and Fayne, I will deliver it myself.'

'Yes, sir.'

There was the sound of running boots and Tomkins appeared with Simon. Thomas spoke first to Tomkins. 'Fayne has confessed to three crimes, any one of which would hang him. You and Smithson take him to your colonel and give him a full report. You'll have to help him. His leg is broken.' Between them, they hoisted Fayne to his feet and half carried, half dragged him off. 'One more thing,' called Thomas after them, 'my thanks for your help.'

'Do you think Fayne will last the night, Thomas?' asked Simon.

'I doubt it. He'll die of his wounds before they can hand him over.'

'Is he wounded?'

'Not yet.'

'Did he know where Rush is?'

'No. Long gone, he said. I daresay he's right.'

'Alas, I fear so. Now let us get back to Merton where I can get out of this foul coat, you can tell me everything and we can see if there is any news from the king.'

Sitting in Simon's room, with Simon back in his habit and Thomas sipping a glass of his wine, Thomas told him everything that had happened and what Fayne had admitted. 'I'm sorry they charged in,' he concluded. 'I had no idea what they were planning.'

'I assumed not,' replied Simon with a grin. 'It took me quite by surprise. One moment Fayne walks in, the next those two come thundering in behind him. It was just as well he was too quick for them, or it might have been chaos. He was out of the door before they could reach him. I followed as quickly as I could, but several alarmed gamblers had to be gently moved out of the way first. He was only just in time.'

'Who was?'

'Fayne. I had only two guineas left. Another minute or two and he'd have been too late.'

'Bad dice, Simon?'

'Very. If I say so myself, I am a most accomplished player of hazard, but even I could not stem the losses tonight.'

'Have the Franciscan coffers been seriously depleted?'

'In money, somewhat. In the pursuit of justice, not at all. Money well spent.'

'Most pragmatic, Simon.'

'If only Rush had not escaped. Catching the dog is one thing, its owner quite another.'

'At least he can do the king no more harm. Is there any message from the queen?'

'None. Perhaps tomorrow.'

CHAPTER 15

There was no news the next day, or the day after that. Thomas waited for a message, but none came. The king was saying nothing, and the queen's temper was sorely tried. Simon reported that she had taken to shouting at her ladies-in-waiting and ignoring her servants. Even Master Hudson, of whom she was very fond, had come in for abuse, and had stomped around complaining that he did not care to be called a tiresome little toad.

At Christ Church, the king's mood had descended like the blackest of clouds. Voices were hushed, the college was quiet, there was little of the old activity. Men and women spoke and moved as if wary of incurring the royal anger and being despatched at once to the scaffold. Only the noisy cattle in their pen were oblivious. Thomas sat in his room, reading a little but mostly thinking about his sister and his nieces. He wondered if the king would remember his promise to provide an escort home, and, if so, how long he would have to wait. For all the service he had given, Thomas Hill, cryptographer and bookseller, would not be high on the royal list of priorities. New codes would have to be devised and distributed for all messages to and from the king's commanders, an assessment of the damage done by Rush would have to be made, and new plans put in place. Thomas might be forgotten altogether.

And, all the while, the news filtering in of the war was not good. Oliver Cromwell's cavalry, supported by the Earl of Manchester and Sir Thomas Fairfax, had sent a Royalist army running for their lives through the Lincolnshire countryside, and, in Scotland, the Earl of Leven was gathering his forces for an advance towards Newcastle. Nottingham and Manchester were in Parliament's hands, and Chester was under threat. In the south and the west, bands of clubmen had become serious obstacles to the occupation of towns and villages, with the result that the king's soldiers were going hungry. It would not be long before they started deserting in droves — just what the clubmen wanted.

Thomas heard nothing of Romsey, still in Royalist-held territory, but the forces of Parliament now held both Southampton and Portsmouth. If Romsey's merchants were unable to send their cloth to the ports, trade would dry up and everyone in the town would suffer. Simon had brought plenty of money for Margaret, and they had a decent amount under the stairs, so Thomas had no fears on that score; even in times of scarcity, food could always be bought by anyone with the price for it. For her safety, however, and that of the girls, he feared greatly. He had experienced soldiers from both sides in the town, and he knew what they could do. They could drink, fight, steal, rape and kill. He wondered, too, if there had been any more threatening letters. The chances were that they were nothing, albeit a frightening nothing. And if they were something, especially something devised by Tobias Rush, God alone knew what might have happened.

On the third day, Thomas awoke desperate to escape the confinement of his room and the oppression of the king's mood. He walked round Christ Church Meadow, heaving again with artillery pieces, mortars and stores of small arms, up St Aldate's and Cornmarket, and back towards Merton by Broad Street and Catte Street. In Broad Street, John Porter's bookshop was closed, having run out of either books or customers. Everywhere there were even more beggars and whores, and more filth and decay, than when he had first arrived in Oxford. Refugees from villages burned down to prevent their falling into enemy hands had poured into the town, as had the maimed and wounded from each new engagement, while the reinforcements the king had demanded from the Shires were arriving in their hundreds. Barely a house or a college room remained unoccupied by soldiers or members of the royal households. All around, Thomas saw disease, poverty and degradation. Oxford had long since ceased to be a university town; it was a military encampment.

A military encampment with a difference. In Catte Street, a line of revellers, the men in the red uniforms of the king's Lifeguards, their masked ladies in flowing gowns, danced down the street to the music of flutes and pipes. They were led by a young man in blue whom Thomas recognized as Prince Rupert, a lady on either arm, singing lustily and trying vainly to keep time with the tune. Thomas stepped aside to let them pass. The dancers took no notice of the limbless beggars lining either side of the street, or of the abuse shouted at them by watching townspeople. A woman in an old straw bonnet and a torn dress, who tried to join the dance, was shoved roughly aside. It was a spectacle that Thomas had not before encountered. Starving beggars and dancing soldiers. What a war.

Before Merton, he went to the Physic Garden, where Jane had shown him daisy fleabane and they had walked together between stands of lavender and beds of violets. The violets were over, but the lavender still flowered. He twisted a head from its stem and rolled it between his fingers. Its scent was the scent of Jane. He had never had the chance to learn about flowers and to impress her with his knowledge, to invite her to Romsey, to woo her properly. Now there never would be a chance.

At Merton, he found Simon sitting on a bench in the little quadrangle behind the chapel, a quiet spot away from the comings and goings in the front quadrangle. Thomas sat down beside him. 'Has there been any news?' he asked yet again.

'None that I know of. The second message changed every-thing and the queen still awaits instructions from the king as to her day of departure, and her destination. Her mood, as ever, reflects his – black, sullen and ominous. And she still grieves for Jane.'

'As do I.'

'Have you heard from the king?'

'Nothing. I still hope for an escort home, but his majesty will have other and more pressing affairs to attend to.'

'Among them, the capture of Tobias Rush, I hope.'

'I doubt he'll be caught now. He could be in Manchester or London or Cambridge. Somewhere he can't be reached.'

For an hour they sat together, sometimes talking, sometimes sitting in silence. When Thomas rose to go, he had made up his mind to seek an audience with the king and to ask for permission to go home. Surely his majesty would not refuse such a request. He would ask him at once.

That evening, however, his request for an audience was refused. The king was too busy to see him. Frustrated and furious,

Thomas stormed out of Christ Church, hoping to cool his temper by the river. He had come here under sufferance, he had done what was asked of him and he wanted to go home. Perhaps, rather than waiting for the king to provide an escort, he would take his chances and go anyway. Tomorrow morning, he would just walk out of Oxford, find a horse and make his way to Romsey. If he had to, he would hide in woods and live on toadstools. He had lost a dear old friend and a lady he loved. He missed his sister and his nieces. He had been away far too long.

Much cheered by his decision, Thomas returned to Christ Church, going over in his mind the practicalities of the journey. He had enough money, he could buy a horse, he knew the route. Once he had gone, the king would forget him. He'd be quite safe in Romsey. Three days on the road and he would be home. At last.

The blow that knocked him cold came from behind the door as he entered his rooms. He saw and heard nothing. It was a blow from a heavy object, delivered by someone who knew what he was about. A blow to render his victim unconscious, not to kill him. When Thomas came to, he was on his back, ankles bound together and wrists tied to the frame of the bed. His movements were restricted to raising his throbbing head and wriggling his backside. Through eyes that refused to focus, he thought he saw a black-clad, crow-like figure approach the bed. The figure stooped to examine its prey. In its hand it held a cane with a silver top. It spoke.

'Master Hill, we meet again.'

CHAPTER 16

Rush pulled up a chair and sat by the bed. He pushed one strip
of shirt into Thomas's mouth and secured it with a second,
tied around his head. Then he held up the silver-topped cane
where Thomas could see it, and drew out of it a very thin blade.

'The finest Spanish steel, Thomas, made especially for me by
the best swordsmith in Toledo. Its point is as sharp as one of your
sister's sewing needles. As you can see.' Holding the sword by its
silver handle, his eyes never leaving Thomas's, he touched
Thomas's arm with the point. A trickle of blood appeared. 'The
secret is in the mix of metals. That and the exact heat of the forge
and the length of time the sword is in it. The smiths measure the
time by reciting prayers. Then the blade is cooled with oil. A fine
Toledo sword is every bit as much a masterpiece as a Michelangelo
sculpture.'

A slow smile crept across the narrow face. 'I can see that
you're surprised to find me here, Thomas. I quite understand. I
could have been in London by now, yet somehow the idea of our

meeting again proved irresistible. I am unaccustomed to defeat — a poor loser, you might say — and unwilling to concede victory, especially to so unworthy an adversary. Tobias Rush bested by a Romsey bookseller? I think not. With a little help from some friends, it was not difficult to return unnoticed to Oxford, or to enter Christ Church and wait for your return. You'd be surprised just how many of us there are in the town, and we are more each week. Disenchantment with the king grows with his every extravagance, and those of the queen, and it does not take a military eye to see which way the war is going. I believe I may claim, in all modesty, to have been instrumental in recruiting a good many to our cause.

'And I had expected to go on doing so. Until, Thomas, you stumbled upon a means of decrypting our messages. You look surprised. Of course I know about the second message, revealing the queen's destination. Not only did it arrive by only one of its two routes, but certain friends here alerted me to its interception. So you discovered our plan. An excellent plan, too, if I may say so, devised by myself. Imagine it. The queen and her unborn infant in our hands, her devoted husband unable to do anything to recover her but to accede to our demands. The war would have been over within days.' Rush bent his head to Thomas's ear and whispered, 'Now, Thomas, I am going to allow you to speak. But if you so much as raise your voice, you will immediately lose your right eye. Do I make myself clear?' Thomas nodded, and Rush removed the shirt from his mouth.

'There, now we can talk man to man. How is your head?' Thomas said nothing. 'Very well. I recall from my visit to the prison that you are prone to spells of sullen silence. I shall continue. Assuming that my rooms have been searched, we will no

longer be using the codes and keywords that may have been found
there. Monsieur Vigenère has served us well for over a year, but he
too will now have to go. How clever you were, Thomas, and how
fortunate, to discover his secrets, and ours.'

'Why did you kill Erasmus Pole?'

'Ah. He speaks. A question, though not a very interesting one.
Pole had become a liability. After the affair at Alton, we had to
decide whether to keep him. We decided not to. He was an old
man and had outlived his usefulness.'

'Why did you take a blind man's eyes?'

'Now that is more interesting. They were no use to Master
Fletcher, of course, but that is not quite all. I find a certain satis-
faction in the neat removal of an eye. I imagine a surgeon feels the
same way when he cleanly removes a musket ball. A neat incision
and out it pops. A good job, performed by an expert. Does that
answer your question?'

'Did you order the murder of Jane Romilly?'

'I thought we would come to that. Lady Romilly disobeyed
me. She persuaded the queen to authorize your release from gaol.
That could not be tolerated.'

'Why was she raped?'

'That I put down to the exuberance of youth. They doubtless
allowed themselves to be carried away by the moment.'

'Fayne was one. Who were the others?'

'How do you know about Fayne?' Rush's eyes narrowed and
his voice was suspicious.

'He told me before he was executed.'

'Fayne's dead? Excellent. That saves me the trouble.'

'Who were the others?'

'They were the same men who inconvenienced you on the

way back from Newbury. I had hoped that they would find what I was looking for.'

'They killed both coachmen.'

'Yes. Necessary casualties. They would have killed you, too, had I not instructed them most clearly not to.'

'Why?'

'Is that not obvious, Thomas? If you were dead, I would not have known what you had done with the message or whether you had decrypted it. Our plan would have had to be abandoned. As, I fear, it has been.'

'Jane bled to death.'

'Such a pity. A lovely lady. But she betrayed me.'

'Did you instruct Fayne to search my room?'

'Fayne? Good God, no. I would never entrust a stupid soldier with any task requiring discretion or intelligence. His clumsy efforts earlier, however, gave me the idea of instructing Lady Romilly to do so. You naturally suspected Fayne again. And I must thank you for alerting me to his liking for dice. It gave me a most useful argument when I did have need of him.'

'Round Hill was your doing, wasn't it?'

'It was, and I'm proud of it. Essex's men should never have gained the high ground. If the king had held it, Newbury might have turned out very differently. A brilliant deception.'

'You'll burn in hell, Rush.'

'Very probably. And you'll be able to tell them to expect me.'

'You're a vicious murderer, a traitor and a coward.'

A shadow passed over Rush's face. 'A coward? No, Master Hill. I have no time for soldiers or soldiering, but a coward I am not.' He shoved the shirt back into Thomas's mouth and secured it. 'Now we shall see who's a coward.' He ripped Thomas's shirt down the front, and dragged the point of the blade diagonally across his chest. Thomas's back arched against the pain, and blood from the wound dripped down his stomach. Again the blade sliced his flesh, its line forming a cross with the first cut. Rush rose and fetched a pail of water from the washstand. He threw it over Thomas's chest. 'There. We don't want you bleeding to death quite yet, do we? The water will help to keep you going.' Thomas closed his eyes and bit down on the shirt in his mouth. The cuts had been finely judged. Deep enough to cause pain, not so deep as to kill.

Rush sat back on the chair and admired his work. 'Not a bad start, although the smaller cuts are more difficult to make precisely. How fortunate that we have all night. A man's pleasures should always be taken slowly. Speaking of which, I found an excellent bottle in your cupboard. Are you thirsty? No? Well, I am.' The bottle produced, Rush poured himself a glass and sipped it appreciatively. 'The college cellars are one of the few good things about this city. I daresay that's why the king chose to come here. This is a splendid claret. Are you sure you wouldn't care for a glass?' Unable to speak, Thomas forced himself to keep his eyes open, willing Rush to see the contempt in them. At the same time, he wished he could close his nostrils. The stench of the man was overpowering. If witches carried the smell of evil, Rush reeked of the devil himself. Thomas gagged on the shirt in his mouth, and swallowed the bile in his throat.

'Your sister, I'm told, is a handsome woman,' went on Rush, 'and your nieces very pretty little things. I have not yet had the pleasure of meeting them myself, although I hope that will not be long delayed. Ah, you're wondering how I know. I have friends in Hampshire. One of them has been keeping a close eye on your sister and her daughters.' The threatening letters. Rush's doing. 'We did think you might hurry home when you heard news of them. Alas, you chose to stay in Oxford. Most unwise.'

Rush poured himself more wine and took his glass to the window. 'A lovely city, Oxford, as is Cambridge, which I know better. I was there myself, you know. I studied law at Peterhouse. Nothing like as grand as Christ Church, of course, but a charming college. Do you know the most unusual thing about both places? People listen. They learn by listening. Everywhere else, I find people do not listen, they merely wait for their turn to speak. Sometimes, they don't even do that. They interrupt. I learned to listen at Peterhouse, and the habit has never left me. In gathering information, I find it an invaluable skill.' Taking up the sword, Rush pressed the point under Thomas's ear and drew it down his neck and across his throat. Thomas felt a trickle of blood.

'I do hope you're listening, Thomas. You would be foolish not to. I'm going to give you another chance to speak, but do remember what I said. A shout or a scream will cost you an eye.' The shirt was removed, and Thomas swallowed hard, the taste of bile still in his mouth. Rush continued his monologue. 'The best thing about this war is that it has brought with it opportunities for a man clever and daring enough to take them. Opportunities to become rich, opportunities to become powerful. Military men are so splendidly stupid. They hack each other to death while others are quietly seizing these opportunities. When they realize what has happened, it will be too late.'

'Hell will be too good for you, Rush.' Thomas's voice rasped in his throat.

'So you have made clear,' laughed Rush. 'Fortunately, I don't believe in hell. Or heaven, for that matter. Believing in either makes life so much more difficult. Nor do I care much whether the country is ruled by king or commoner, Catholic or Puritan. Charles Stuart, John Pym, Oliver Cromwell, the Vicar of Rome, it's all the same to me. There will be rich and poor, clever and stupid. Happily, there will always be more poor and stupid.' He took another sip of wine. 'Which are you, Thomas? I wonder. Clever or stupid?'

Thomas turned his head and spat out a mouthful of bile.

'If that is an answer, I fear I do not understand it,' continued Rush. 'Let me put the question another way. There is a place on my staff for a man as skilled as you. In view of recent developments, I shall be returning to London, where John Pym, as you will know, is dying. There I shall take up a new position under his successor, working to spread fear and discontent among the soldiers of the king. I shall need clever men around me, and I shall need one who can ensure that our communications go undetected by the enemy. A chief cryptographer. For the right man, the rewards will be great.' Deceit, treachery, subversion – Rush's weapons, and every bit as lethal as his blade. 'Have you nothing to say to my generous offer?' Thomas remained silent. 'In that case, I will try a little persuasion.' Holding Thomas's head still, Rush drew a neat circle of blood around his right eye with the point of the blade. 'There, just right if I should happen to need a target. And if you persist in this stubborn silence, I shall indeed need one.'

With his chest, neck and face cut and bloody, and unable to see much out of his right eye, Thomas considered risking a scream. But Rush would not hesitate to plunge that blade into his eye, and, in any case, a scream might not be heard. Rush sat on the left side of the bed, so he concentrated on wriggling his right hand. There was a slight give in the rope that held him to the bed frame. With a lot of work, he might be able to loosen it enough to slip his hand through. The question was, would he have time to do it? The blade appeared again. This time, it sliced through his breeches and down his leg to the knee. Then it travelled up the other leg, stopping just short of his groin. Blood dripped on to the bed. Rush threw another pail of water over him.

'So important in discussions of this sort to know when to pause,' he whispered in Thomas's ear. 'One wants one's listener to be able to give one his full attention and to encourage him to make a sensible decision. I have made my offer, Thomas. The matter is now in your hands.'

'I would require a guarantee of absolute safety for my family,' whispered Thomas, trying to ignore the pain.

'And naturally you shall have it. They will join you in London, where you will be found an excellent house, with appointments and servants appropriate to your position.'

'How will this be arranged?'

'That need not concern you, Thomas. I shall personally supervise the arrangements for their safe passage from Romsey. And I shall escort you to London myself.'

'How do I know I can trust you?'

'Trust? What has trust to do with it? Be realistic, Thomas. Why would I lie? You have something of value to me. I'm offering you the choice of saving your life and your family's lives, or a painful death, ignorant of what lies in store for them. Which shall it be?'

'I need time to consider.'

'Don't be absurd. Time to consider what? Which eye I shall take first? Whether you will bleed to death? The issue is clear. Decide.'

'I need time. You said I have something of value to you. Allow me an hour to consider your offer.'

'Very well. An hour. Not a minute longer, or be sure that you have seen your last dawn.'

Thomas closed his eyes. Perversely, Homer, of all people, came to mind. When his beloved 'rosy-fingered dawn, child of the morn' arrived, would Thomas be able to see it? Rush was expert with his Spanish blade. A twist of the hand, and his eye would be gone. At least the bleeding from his neck and chest had stopped. He tried to think clearly. The rope around his wrist had moved very little despite his efforts to work it loose, his ankles were tied together and Rush was sitting no more than a few feet away. Go with him or die here. Scylla and Charybdis — more Homer. With no idea of what to do if he did manage to free his hand, he clenched his teeth and kept working on the rope, which had already rubbed his wrist raw. Rush had twisted it twice around his wrist, then looped it around the wooden frame of the bed and knotted it tightly. To release his hand he would have to loosen the knot enough to pull it through. The indestructible Odysseus might do it; Thomas Hill probably not.

After no more than a few minutes, Rush, who had been sitting very still, stirred. 'Did I say an hour, Thomas? How foolish of me. I find that my patience has already run out. What is your decision?' Thomas needed more time. The rope was definitely looser, and, by squeezing his fingers together, he could pull his hand through the loop as far as the ball of his thumb. Ten minutes might be enough.

'How will we get out of the college undetected?'

Rush smiled and pulled from his pocket an iron key. 'The king's private gate should serve us. I took the precaution of having a key made for myself when it was built.'

Thomas feigned ignorance. 'The king's private gate? Is there such a thing?'

'There is. Now tell me your decision.'

But Thomas did not have to answer. There was a loud hammering on the door, and an urgent voice outside. 'Thomas. Wake up. We're leaving within the hour and you're to come with us.' It was Simon.

Rush was on his feet at once, his sword at Thomas's throat. 'Not a sound, Hill, or it will be your last.'

Simon hammered on the door and called out again, this time louder. 'Thomas. Wake up. We must hurry.'

Thomas felt the point of Rush's sword prick his throat. Rush would have locked the door after knocking him out, and Simon would not have a key, although Rush could not know that. He had to alert Simon without being immediately skewered. He made his hand as small as he could and wrenched it hard. It very nearly slipped through the rope. One more try and it would come. He had to make Rush look away. Risking the point of the sword, he turned his head towards Rush, looked past him, widened his eyes and raised his eyebrows as if in astonishment. Rush caught the look and turned. Thomas jerked his hand free and grabbed Rush's wrist, twisting it as hard as he could. The sword dropped from his hand and rattled on to the floor. He shouted as loudly as his dry throat would permit. 'Simon, kick the door down.'

Rush snarled, pulled his wrist free and bent to retrieve the sword. As he did so, the door, with a crack like a musket, broke free of its lock and opened into the room. Rush picked up the sword and moved towards the door, where Simon stood watching him.

'Well, priest, not a good time to call.'

The words were hissed. Rush took two quick steps and thrust

the sword at Simon's groin. For a big man, Simon could move very quickly, as Thomas had seen before. He stepped to his left, and chopped down on Rush's arm with the edge of his hand. Rush cursed, but did not drop the sword. Now he knew what his opponent could do, he would take more care. Simon still stood at the door, not giving Rush the chance to get past him. Even unarmed, he would be a difficult obstacle to move. Rush circled cautiously around him, the sword pointing at his face. A false move and this man might disarm him. To test his speed, he jabbed at his eyes and stomach, his own eyes never leaving Simon's. Simon deftly avoided the jabs, until Rush subtly changed his angle of attack, and drew blood from his cheek. Simon barely flinched. Again, Rush drew blood and again Simon ignored it. Given a chance, he would break Rush's arm, and Rush knew it.

While they watched each other, Thomas struggled with the knot that tied his left hand to the bed frame. He got it free and reached down to tackle the rope around his legs. Rush must have seen the movement from the corner of his eye. He backed away from Simon towards the bed. A quick thrust into Thomas's unprotected throat, and he would turn back to Simon. Thomas could not free his legs in time. He sat up and waited for the strike, hoping somehow to parry it. It never came. The moment Rush turned his head towards Thomas for the thrust, Simon launched himself at his back. Both men crashed on to the bed, pinning Thomas underneath them. Simon grabbed Rush's arm in both hands and bent it backwards. Rush screamed and the sword fell from his hand. Winded and unable to move his body, Thomas managed to free a hand and jab his fingers into Rush's throat. At the same time, Simon grabbed him by his hair and jerked his head back. Rush screamed again and flailed wildly with his arms. It did no good. Simon de Pointz was a strong man. He held Rush easily, pulled him off the bed and dumped him on his face on the floor.

'The ropes, Thomas, if you can,' he said. 'We'd better tie this thing up before it can slither away.'

Thomas freed his legs and used the ropes to tie Rush's arms and legs securely, while Simon sat on his back and held him down by the neck. Unarmed, Rush was no match for his tall opponent.

'You're an unusual friar. I thought Franciscans were peaceful souls,' said Thomas, standing up to examine his handiwork.

'In the backstreets and alleyways of Norwich, a boy learned to defend himself. St Francis would not disapprove of self-defence.' Holding him by his hair, Simon hoisted Rush to his feet. 'And if he had known this creature, he might even have advocated striking first.'

For the first time since Simon had broken down the door, Rush spoke. 'Curse your eyes, monk.'

Simon shook him by the hair. 'Save your breath, Rush. You'll need it for the king. And I am not a monk, as you well know.'

Rush spat on the floor. 'Pathetic little man.'

'You can tell him that yourself. Clean yourself up, Thomas, and then let us escort Master Rush to his majesty.'

With his swordstick, Rush was an expert. Only drops of blood were seeping from Thomas's wounds and he was able to stop the worst of it by pressing a damp cloth over them. The dried blood he washed off. A simple salve would heal the wounds; he'd have to speak to Simon later. Having made himself as respectable as he could, Thomas took one arm, Simon the other, and together they marched Rush off to meet his king.

*

In the early hours of an October morning, his majesty was not best pleased to be roused from sleep to be told that Master Hill and Father de Pointz were outside and must see him at once. His first thought was that something untoward had happened to prevent the queen leaving the city quietly. They had said their farewells the previous evening, swearing undying love and reassuring each other that they would meet again soon. Arrangements for her journey had been hastily revised and she would now travel to Salisbury on the way to Exeter. Both Hill and De Pointz were supposed to be going with her. What were they doing here?

He soon found out. A long fur robe over his nightgown, he stormed into the receiving room, where Thomas and Simon held Rush between them. Six Lifeguards stood around the walls. It took the king a moment to take in the scene. Tobias Rush, the traitor who had escaped capture, back in Oxford and held by these men. How? 'I once observed that my birds had flown,' he said, regaining his wits. 'Now I observe that one has returned. Guards, take this man in charge.' Two guards jumped to it, taking Rush from Thomas and Simon. 'Now, gentlemen, perhaps you would explain yourselves.'

When they had done so, the king turned to Rush. 'I once trusted you. Now I know you to be a traitor and a murderer, and of the foulest kind. Before you are executed, you will reveal everything you know about our enemies. Take him to the castle.'

'Your majesty, if I may explain . . .'

'Take him.' With a protesting Rush between them, the two guards marched out of the room. 'Betrayed by his own vanity and greed. How foolish.'

Indeed, thought Thomas, but he isn't the first and he won't be the last.

'Is the queen safe?' the king asked Simon.

'She is, your majesty.'

'Then we shall delay her departure until Master Rush has told us what he knows. I will send word to her. Master Hill, you will be summoned when there is news.'

Outside the Deanery, Thomas asked, 'A word of thanks would not have been out of place, Simon, don't you think?'

Simon shrugged. 'His majesty takes the loyalty and suffering of his subjects for granted. He expects no less.'

'Royal vanity. Doubtless an altogether finer quality than the common variety. For his sake, I do hope so. Now, Simon, as the door to my room has been kicked in by an intruder, I would rather lay my head elsewhere. Have you any suggestions?'

'Merton always welcomes you, Thomas. My bed is your bed. I must attend the queen.'

Having told Simon everything Rush had said, Thomas returned that evening to his room at Christ Church, to find that royal vanity had allowed a gesture of royal kindness and the lock on his door had been repaired. The only thing I know is that I know nothing, he thought. Socrates, or possibly Plato. They're easily confused. Very few men survived more than a taste of the type of examination conducted at the castle, and he guessed that the royal summons would come within a day or two.

A day or two with little to do but read, think of home and wait impatiently for news. That made for a long day or two, and Thomas's temper was not improved by the steady autumn rain that discouraged walking in the meadows or the Physic Garden.

On the first afternoon he paid another visit to John Porter, and on the second he called on Simon.

Simon too had heard nothing. 'The queen's temper is as short as yours, Thomas. She is desperate to reach France in time for the birth, and she does not like ships that are blown about by autumn gales.'

'Let us hope Rush speaks soon. I may die of frustration if he doesn't.'

'Be patient, Thomas. I promise you will soon see your family again. It's simply that the king will not hear of the queen leaving the safety of the town until Rush has disclosed everything he knows about the plot to capture her.'

'He might die before doing so.'

'He might. The king thinks not. He has faith in his interrogator.'

Despite himself, Thomas shuddered. 'How much longer can he survive before talking?'

'A day or two. Then the queen will leave, and we shall accompany her. The king will double the strength of her guard and we will take a different route to Exeter.'

'Why not just let her go?'

'The king would much prefer to have broken Rush before she leaves, and to know exactly what his enemies have planned.'

'Rush claimed that Oxford is brimming with spies. If so, the king's enemies will know by now of his arrest, and have changed or abandoned their plans.'

'Nevertheless, the king's mind is made up.'

Simon was right. No man could survive more than two or three days if that was what the king had ordered. He would speak or die. The summons came that evening. Thomas was escorted to the Deanery and shown straight into the king's receiving room.

'Master Hill,' said the king without preamble, 'an hour ago I received word that Tobias Rush had died from his wounds under examination, having told us nothing. I went at once to the castle to see the body for myself. I am not sorry to say that he had suffered as a traitor should suffer. His limbs were broken and his face a bloody mess of flesh and bone. Had I not been informed, I would not have known him. I have ordered his remains burned. I shall pray for his soul, evil and treacherous though it was.'

'I too cannot say that I'm sorry. He was a traitor, a torturer and a murderer.'

'He was, and a clever and devious man. How he hid his treachery from me for so long, I do not know. He has done our cause much harm, and only time will tell if it can be repaired. Thank God he is dead and can do no more. Now, the queen and her party will be leaving Oxford immediately. As we learned nothing from Rush, her guard has been doubled. You will travel with them to Salisbury. From there, you must make your own way home.'

'Thank you, your majesty.'

'Good. Then it's settled. Farewell, Master Hill. God be with you.'

CHAPTER 17

To Thomas's relief, the queen's considerable party of carriages, courtiers, servants and guards arrived in Salisbury without mishap, two days later. They had met no Parliamentary cavalry, no clubmen or highwaymen, and no serious impediments to their progress. Riding in a carriage at the back of the procession, Thomas had not set eyes on the queen, never mind spoken to her. The Generalissima had kept to her own carriage at the front, flanked by her Lifeguards and a troop of Prince Rupert's Bluecoats. As he was in the mood for neither polite conversation nor loyal deference, the arrangement had suited Thomas well enough.

At Salisbury, they halted to rest the horses before continuing on towards Exeter. Thomas was expecting to leave the party there and make his own way to Romsey. As he was saddling a horse, however, Simon strode up, leading another. 'Her majesty has consented to my escorting you home, Thomas. I advised her that it would be wise for me to do so.'

'Wise, Simon? Wise for whom?' replied Thomas, pretending not to be pleased. He had not been looking forward to finishing the journey alone.

'For you and your family. When travelling unaccompanied, you have a habit of getting into difficulties. Her majesty wishes you to get home safely.'

'Very well. No doubt Margaret will be delighted to see you again.'

'Not, my friend, as delighted as she will be to see you. However, I will not be able to stay. As soon as I have safely delivered you, I must rejoin the queen.'

They covered the fifteen miles to Romsey in less than three hours, arriving in mid-afternoon. On the outskirts of the town, they dismounted and led their horses over the river, past neat rows of cottages and into Market Square. The town was quiet and none of the few people about took any notice of them. Outside the Romsey Arms there were no drinkers, although Thomas could hear voices inside. Looking around, he could see nothing much changed in the weeks he had been away. Romsey, it seemed, had so far avoided the fate of so many towns up and down England which had been devastated by the ravages of war. They walked up Love Lane, past the baker's shop, to the bookshop.

Thomas knocked loudly on the door. It was a new door, made of very stout oak, with a formidable lock and fixed with three large iron hinges. It was not a door that a thieving soldier could easily kick in. The windows were also new, with thick shutters and sturdy frames. There was no answer. He knocked again, and shouted out. 'Margaret, the owner of this bookshop is outside, and he would like to come in.' There was no reply. He tried again.

'Margaret, it's Thomas. Open the door.' Still no answer. He rattled the door handle and gave the door a push. It did not move. He tried the windows. Peering between the shutters, he could see that they were all barred. The bars, too, were new. Margaret really had taken precautions.

'They've probably gone for a walk in the meadow,' he said, more to reassure himself than anything else. 'We often go there.'

Simon heard the concern in Thomas's voice. 'Or to visit a friend, or to church, or to buy bread. They could be anywhere, Thomas. There's no cause for alarm. It's not as if they knew we were coming.'

'No, of course you're right. It's just that I'm so looking forward to seeing them.'

'And you soon will. However, if I'm to rejoin the queen before nightfall, I must be on my way. I promised her that I would not dally.'

Thomas held out his hand. 'Farewell then, Simon. Thank you for your company. Thank you also for getting me out of that hellhole of a gaol, and for preventing Tobias Rush from removing my eyes.'

Simon's smile was sad. 'I grieve that Abraham and Jane are dead, but you, thank God, are alive. You're a clever man, Thomas Hill, and a brave one.'

'I hardly think so.' Thomas released Simon's hand. 'Now go, Father de Pointz. Go safely, and do not call upon me again. I wish to spend the rest of my days peacefully with my family.'

'I pray that God and the war will permit you to do so. Farewell, Thomas. God bless you.'

Thomas watched Simon lead his horse back down Love Lane. Simon did not look back. What an extraordinary man, thought

Thomas. Deep devotion and unshakable loyalty married to world-ly knowledge and a shrewd mind. A man whose principles are very much his own. I wonder what life has in store for him.

And now what? It would not be easy to break into the shop with Margaret's new defences in place and he had no idea where she and the girls might be. Deciding that there was no point in guessing, Thomas walked back to Market Square and into the Romsey Arms. There were a few drinkers there, most of whom he knew at least by sight. One of them saw him and held up a hand in greeting. 'Good day, Thomas. We haven't seen you for weeks. Have you been unwell or did you go and join the king's army?'

'Neither, thankfully. I've been visiting an old friend. The bookshop is locked up. Do you happen to know where Margaret is?'

The man shook his head. 'I'm afraid not.' He raised his voice so that everyone could hear. 'Thomas Hill has lost his sister. Does anyone know where she is?' There were a few ribald comments about her being carried off by lusty young men, but no one knew where she was. Neither she nor her daughters had been seen in the town for some days. Two years ago that might have been cause for alarm, but, in time of war, people came and went constantly.

'Have we had any more military visitors?' asked Thomas.

'Not since those cavalrymen in August. It's been quiet.'

That was something to be grateful for. But it was the letters that really worried Thomas. Could the girls have been abducted? That was well within Rush's evil reach. Thomas would have agreed to almost anything if they had been in danger, and Rush had known it. What's more, with Rush dead, his henchmen would now be waiting in vain for further orders. God alone knew what they might do when they tired of waiting or learned of his death.

Not wanting to be drawn into further discussion, Thomas left the inn and wandered slowly back up Love Lane. The shop was still locked up and deserted. He knocked on their neighbours' doors. None of them knew where Margaret was, or when she had left. She had left no messages and no instructions. They knew only that Thomas had been away and were happy to see him returned safely.

By the time it was getting dark, Thomas had learned nothing. The only thing for it was to find somewhere to sleep, and to start again the next morning. It was early autumn and the nights were cold, too cold for a haystack, so back he went to Market Square. The door to the old abbey was unlocked, as it always was. Thomas let himself in, found a hymnbook, found a pew at the back, and lay down with the book as his pillow. It was neither comfortable nor warm, but it was dry. He closed his eyes, folded his hands across his chest and tried to empty his mind.

Four hours later, he gave up all thoughts of sleep and, pulling his coat around his shoulders, ventured out into the night. Better to pass the time wandering around the town than lying on a hard wooden pew. His back was already stiff. Four more hours and he might never have got up. He walked around the square, where even the Romsey Arms was quiet. Shutters were open, but no light shone through the windows. No voices disturbed the silence. It was an unfamiliar Romsey, a Romsey he barely knew. The town was asleep, even if Thomas Hill was not.

Thomas turned into Love Lane, and walked to the shop. He stood outside it, gazing, unseeing, at the new oak door. Polly, Lucy, Margaret — where were they? Had they come to harm? Abraham and Jane murdered, Oxford gaol, Rush, Fayne, surely not all just to find his family dead too. Yet that was the war —

thousands of individual tragedies adding up to one collective disaster. More than six thousand individuals had died at Newbury alone. How many more Newburys would there be?

A black cat ran across the street and brushed against Thomas's leg. He shuddered at its touch. If the war had affected the mind of a man as lacking in superstition as he, would the shadows and shapes of Oxford stay with him for ever? Unthinkingly, he made his way to the river, and strolled downstream until he came to the place from where he used to fish. There the bank was low, a line of willows growing along it, and the river running faster as it narrowed. It was his favourite spot for catching the fat brown trout that lurked under the overhang of the bank. Ripples on the water glinted in the darkness, and he could almost see the fish waiting to be caught. With his rod and line and a few flies, he would have had his breakfast in no time. A pair of juicy trout sizzling in the pan and eaten with slices of new bread and Margaret's butter. A king's breakfast.

The first glimmerings of dawn were in the sky. Thomas retraced his steps to Love Lane. Still the bookshop was locked up. What else did he expect? The letters had frightened Margaret and she had taken the girls somewhere safer. If she had been in Romsey, someone would have known where. But where had she gone? Their friends were all Romsey people, and they had no family elsewhere. She would not have taken the children to an inn, and after their experience on the day Simon had arrived, she would not have taken them anywhere held by soldiers of Parliament.

Then it occurred to him. Andrew Taylor's sister lived in Winchester. She and Margaret had kept in touch for a while after Andrew's death. Winchester — Royalist-held, a decent road and no more than twelve miles away. There was every chance that she had gone to Winchester, and he had better get there as quickly as he could. In any event, it would be better than wandering around Romsey, unable to open his own door or sleep in his own bed. He should have thought of it yesterday.

Despite the hour, he woke the landlord of the Romsey Arms and persuaded him to arrange for a horse to be saddled and ready. The prospect of doing something positive lifted Thomas's spirits, and he was soon on the road to Winchester. It was a cool, dry morning, and he would be there well before noon. He remembered Emily's house in the middle of the town. It would be an excellent place for Margaret and the girls to stay — spacious and comfortable — and, if he was not mistaken, very near a fine inn. He would find them there, stay the night and return with them to Romsey the following day.

He was less than halfway to Winchester when the horse threw a shoe. Thomas dismounted at once, inspected the hoof, cursed his ill luck, took up the reins and led the horse on. They would have to walk to the next inn or farrier, which would probably be in the village of Hursley, three or four miles on. The road was too stony to take risks, so progress would be slow.

Slow it was, and Thomas became increasingly impatient. Any thought of arriving by midday was abandoned, and by the time they reached Hursley he was beginning to wonder if they would even make Winchester before dark.

A coach stood outside the Shepherd and Flock in Hursley. Had it been going to Winchester, it would have passed Thomas on the road. So unless he could persuade its passengers to turn round and go back where they had come from, it would be no use to him. He led the horse to the smithy behind the inn, asked for it to be re-shod as quickly as possible and went in search of refreshment.

The coach party were sitting at a table in the inn — two men facing the door, and two ladies with their backs to it. The coachmen, both armed, sat at a separate table. 'A tankard of ale, please,' said Thomas to a man wiping down tables, 'and some bread and cheese.' From the corner of his eye, he saw the men in the coach party look up at the sound of his voice, and one of the ladies turn to inspect the new arrival. For a second or two, she stared at him, then rose suddenly from her seat and launched herself across the room. She threw her arms around his neck and held on as if her life depended upon it. Eventually he was able gently to ease her off. He put his hands on her shoulders and held her at arm's length. Tears were pouring down her cheeks. He was weeping and laughing at the same time. 'Good Lord, Margaret,' he managed, 'this is not quite where I had expected to find you.' Unable to speak, Margaret nodded and smiled. 'Where are you going?'

'To Romsey,' she whispered, wiping away a tear.

'And where are the girls?'

'At Emily's house.'

'I thought they might be. I was on my way there. Are they well?'

'Quite well. And you, Thomas, are you well?'

'Well enough, thank you. And relieved to be home. Or almost home.'

In reply, Margaret started sobbing again. 'I'm sorry, Thomas,' she said, 'it's just such a relief to see you.' She studied him. 'You look well. A little thinner, perhaps, and the beard will have to go, but otherwise well.'

Margaret's travelling companions had been watching with interest, wondering if this could be a prodigal husband. 'Does this mean you will be travelling on with us, madam,' asked one of the men, 'or returning to Winchester?'

'My apologies,' she replied. 'This is my brother, Thomas Hill, whom I haven't seen for some weeks.' Thomas bowed politely. 'Well, brother,' she went on, 'Winchester or Romsey? Which shall it be?'

After some discussion, it was agreed that Thomas would follow behind the coach to Romsey, and Margaret would set off again to Winchester the next day. That would give them the chance to talk before the girls demanded all Thomas's attention, and enable Margaret to prepare them for their uncle's return.

While his horse was being shod, Thomas sat beside Margaret and ate his bread and cheese. When she asked about the cuts on his neck and around his eye, he said merely that he would tell her everything later. She explained that they had been living with Emily for a month, and that she was making her second trip to ensure that the shop was secure and all was in order.

'It's certainly secure,' he said. 'Even the owner can't get in.'

The bookshop was indeed in order. Thomas's quills, ink and papers stood on his writing table, the shelves were tidy and the floor swept. Margaret told him to sit while she fetched something from her bedroom. She returned with a handful of letters. 'There are six of them. The last one arrived two weeks ago. They were all pushed under the door at night, for me to find in the morning. Read them, please.'

It did not take Thomas long. They were short letters, and very much to the point, each one more threatening than the one before. Their message was the same. In time of war, a young widow and her daughters were not safe alone, and should take particular care. Who knew what awful things might otherwise happen to them? Who knew what vile ideas might enter the heads of drunken soldiers? The letters were all in the same hand, and unsigned. Thomas looked up. 'Are these why you took the girls away?'

'Yes. I thought they'd be safer.'

'You were probably wise. However, I know why these letters were written, and I know who was behind them. The writer himself is actually of no account. It was the man who composed them who was dangerous.'

'Was?'

'Happily, yes.' It took Thomas over an hour to relate the story. He told Margaret about Tobias Rush, and about Abraham's death. He missed out the worst of the gaol, and left a certain amount unsaid about Jane Romilly. Otherwise, his account was full and accurate. 'So,' he ended, 'there is nothing now to be frightened of. The girls can come home, and we can reopen the shop. Tobias Rush is dead. The king himself saw his body.'

The next morning, Margaret set off in the coach back to Winchester to collect the girls. After a busy time pottering about in the shop, Thomas wandered down to the Romsey Arms to see what news there was, and for a little refreshment. At the junction of Love Lane and Market Street, he stopped to admire the view. The autumn leaves were turning red and orange, the fields a deep green. He could hear voices coming from Market Square, and guessed that the inn was busy.

There were no drinkers outside, but inside it was noisy and crowded. A troop of the king's dragoons, in their multicoloured coats and feathered hats, had arrived and were keeping the serving girls busy.

When she saw Thomas, Sarah shrieked a greeting. 'Master 'ill, 'aven't see you for ages. Where 'ave you been?'

'Nowhere much, Sarah. How's Rose?'

'Much too big to work, silly cow. Baby'll drop any day.'

'You're busy today.'

'Soldiers on their way to Oxford. Same lot as was 'ere a few weeks ago.'

Thomas looked around. Sure enough, there was the fat dragoon who had sat on him, and there was Captain Brooke. He took his ale and found a seat in the corner, from where he could watch and listen. He was not in the mood for argument or banter. Or for being sat upon. He heard the dragoons recounting their experiences in Lord Goring's army, which had consisted mostly of monumental bouts of drinking and whoring, his lordship setting an excellent example to his men in both pursuits, and he watched them spending a good many shillings on ale, shillings they had doubtless removed, without consent, from their owners. He was about to leave when the captain noticed him in the corner.

'Well, well. If it isn't our friend the bookseller. Hill, isn't it? We met when we last visited Romsey.'

Thomas rose. 'Thomas Hill, sir. Your memory does you credit. I gather you and your men have been serving with Lord Goring.'

'That we have, the drunken old goat. Now we're on our way to Oxford. The king has demanded reinforcements. Do you know Oxford?'

'I was a student there many years ago. It's a beautiful town.'

'Then let's hope we don't have to defend it from rampaging

Puritans. And what have you been doing since last we met, Master Hill?'

'Oh, business as usual, captain.'

'The quiet life, eh? I envy you. And what about that French fellow of yours? Mountain.'

'Montaigne, captain. Michel de Montaigne.'

'What was it he said? I couldn't make head nor tail of it.'

'*To learn that we have said or done a stupid thing is nothing; we must learn a more ample and important lesson: that we are all blockheads.*'

'That was it. Damned odd.'

Thomas grinned. 'Not so odd, captain, when you think about it. Now I must escape before one of your men knocks me down and sits on me. Goodbye, captain.'

'Goodbye, Master Hill.'

Author's Note

Hazard

By the seventeenth century, the game of Hazard had become popular at all levels of society. Francis Fayne and his companions played a version in which the 'caster' or thrower of the dice chooses the 'main'; in other versions the caster may throw the dice to establish the main.

The rules of the game are such that a sensible caster always chooses a main of seven; Francis Fayne did not always choose seven because the odds against the caster winning with a main of five, six, eight, or nine are slightly longer and thus yield a better return if he is successful.

An explanation of the game can be found in the Britannica Online Encyclopedia.

Coroners

In cases of unnatural death the ancient office of Coroner combined the duties of policeman, detective, forensic scientist and magistrate. The Coroner summoned a jury to consider such cases, which might then be referred to a higher court. It was the duty of anyone finding a dead body to report it to the Coroner, although during the Civil War this of course did not always happen.

Having been tipped off by Tobias Rush, Henry Pearson

ordered Thomas's detention until a jury could be summoned. Deaths among prisoners in Oxford gaol awaiting trial were very common, thus saving the courts time and money.

Abbeys

Although Thomas Cromwell, on the orders of Henry VIII, master-minded the dissolution of all the religious houses in England, a number of abbey buildings, especially near large towns, did survive. Some, like Romsey, were purchased by the local people and used as their church; others were bought by wealthy landowners seeking to expand their estates.

I have taken the liberty of assuming that the abbey house near Norwich which sheltered a young Simon de Pointz, and the abbey near Botley at which Thomas was hidden, were among those that survived, and that, a hundred years later, friars and monks had quietly returned to them. They would certainly have had the blessing of the devout Queen Henrietta Maria.

The Vigenère Square

The Vigenère square, which gave Thomas so much trouble, was perfected by Blaise de Vigenère, a French cryptographer, in the middle of the sixteenth century. Other than Thomas, no one found a way of breaking the cipher until the nineteenth century, when the remarkable and eccentric Charles Babbage did so, using much the same technique, just to prove that he could.

In fact, the cipher was never used very much, partly because it is laborious to encrypt and decrypt, and partly because other, equally secure ciphers were developed.

Thomas was fortunate in three respects. In the first message he found as many as eight repeated letter sequences, and the key letters E, A and T were easily found. Having identified these, he was able to find the displacement and thus the keyword, PARIS. It might not have been so.

He was also fortunate in missing a ninth repetition — EKW — which, by chance, was an anomaly. It is possible for different sequences of plain-text letters to be encrypted with the same cipher-text letters, and in this case the letter distance between the two appearances of EKW was sixty-four, which is not divisible by five, and might therefore have delayed Thomas further or even thrown him off the scent entirely. Of such small things history is sometimes made.

The second, much shorter message he could not decrypt by analysis, and managed it only with an inspired guess.

REFERENCES

Among the many books and other sources I consulted, I should mention:

Charles Carlton, *Charles I: The Personal Monarch*
Ivan Roots, *The Great Rebellion 1642–1660*
Diane Purkiss, *The English Civil War: A People's History*
Michael Braddick, *God's Fury, England's Fire*
Iris Brooke, *English Costume of the Seventeenth Century*
Simon Singh, *The Code Book*
Stephen Pincock, *Codebreaker: The History of Codes and Ciphers*
David Lindley (ed.), *Court Masques: Jacobean and Caroline Entertainments, 1605–40*

ACKNOWLEDGEMENTS

In writing *The King's Spy*, I am grateful, first and foremost, to my wife Susan for her patient support. My daughter Laura and son Tom were also very helpful with suggestions and observations, as was my brother Michael.

Without exception, those to whom I turned for information or advice went out of their way to help, including the Romsey Library, Pembroke, Christ Church and Merton Colleges, Oxford, the Coroners' Society of England and Wales and the Sealed Knot Society, and I thank them. The book might never have seen the light of day without the support of Fraser Jansen of Waterstones, to whom I owe a very special thank-you.

I am immensely fortunate to have Emma Buckley as my editor. It has been a pleasure working with her and her colleagues at Transworld.

After reading Law at Cambridge University, **Andrew Swanston** held various positions in the book trade, including being a director of Waterstone & Co., and chairman of Methven's plc, before turning to full-time writing. Inspired by a lifelong interest in seventeenth-century history, his Thomas Hill novels are set during the English Civil Wars and the early period of the Restoration. He lives with his wife in Surrey.

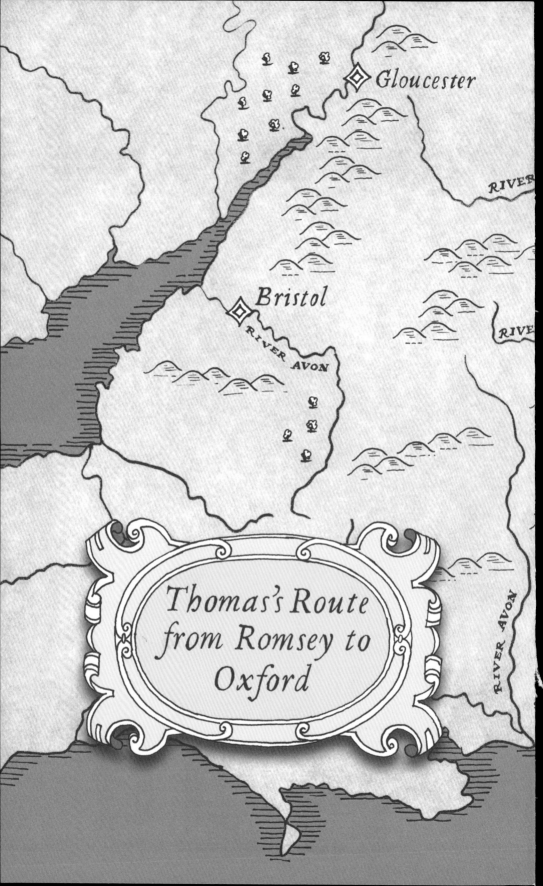